I0819923

MYSTICAL MAYHEM

MYSTICAL MAYHEM

A New Breed

CORA RICHARDSON

Cora Richardson

Contents

First Printing, 2022

Preface

In the beginning, there was one dimension. All magical creatures lived together, there were many wars and many deaths. Once the first vampire was created, it was clear that they would be the dominant species if something wasn't done to stop them. The witches divided into thirteen covens. The high priestess of all the witches appointed a high priest or priestess for each of the covens. The original high priestess along with all of the newly appointed leaders of each of the covens, came up with a plan, they would divide the earth into thirteen dimensions. It would take so much magic to do this that every witch performing the spell would die. They all made the sacrifice so that their heirs could live in peace. The vampires were placed on dimension one, where they would be forced to remain for all time as long as they were provided with food, which would come from the only dimension with no magic at all, 13. In exchange for a supply of their blood, which contained wonderful healing properties.

After the spell was cast and the leaders were all dead, the covens had to appoint new leaders. They could not all agree on new rules for the new world(s) so they refused to appoint a high leader of all covens. They scattered about, but they stayed in dimension 12, for the most part, a few stragglers decided to leave their covens and live alone on other dimensions. Witches were the only magic left on dimension 12, and all they had to worry about were other witches, some didn't think the separation was a good idea, so wars between the witches continued. There would be an occasional death in the never ending war, but they did try to avoid killing each other for the most part.

Two moons were visible in dimensions 1 through 7, they were always in the same phase, and they made the nights much brighter. The Phoenix could not go beyond dimension 8, if they even existed anymore, they had either gone into hiding or somehow vanished because they haven't been seen for a couple of centuries. Gremlins couldn't be seen past dimension 9, they were just terrible little creatures anyway. Mermaids couldn't be seen past dimension 10, though they seemed to all be in dimension 2. And last of all, Demons couldn't go beyond dimension 11.

The first vampire was created from the offspring of a demon and a witch, when he became mortally wounded, his mother tried to heal him, the spell ended up turning him into a deadly creature of the night. After this happened, it was made law by all magical creatures that mixed breeds would be illegal. Half-breeds were not allowed to exist, the chance could not be taken that another monster would be created. A lot of the magical community hated this law, after all, you can't help who you fall in love with. So this caused more dividation, especially between the witches.

Anytime someone broke the law, the witches would hunt down the offspring and destroy it before it ever had a chance to live, until a witch was magical and smart enough to keep her offspring hidden. At least until she becomes of age, if a witch isn't given their powers at birth, they will automatically come into them at the age of twenty-one. So, two thousand years later a new war begins, a war for the freedom to love who you choose to love and to create new breeds of magical creatures without repercussions...

One

An Introduction

My name is Gabriela. I live in a small town in Tennessee about an hour from Nashville. I'm just a normal 20 year old, well I guess, my birthday is November 11th which is next Friday. Yep I'm going to be 21 I'm so excited! A little bit about me. I've got the whole Snow White look going on you know, the pale skin, dark hair, dark eyes. I'm about 5'9 I go to the gym a lot so I'm pretty built, but not like a bodybuilder, more like tone. I grew up in a really small town. I never knew my mom and my dad. I grew up as an orphan from house to house, from abuse to abuse. But somehow despite all that I feel like I am emotionally stable. I manage a small restaurant, the owner is never here. Mr. Parkins and his wife had a dream of a small restaurant. Right after opening it, his wife got sick, six months later she passed away. After that he couldn't stand to come in so he hired me and I manage it for him with the help of my assistant manager, Dan. Dan is an older black man close to retiring but the restaurant gives him something to do, keeps him from getting bored. Other than the two of us we only employ five other people Betty, Carl,

Mona, Andy and Monica (everyone thinks Andy and Monica have something going on).

I only have about four really close friends. Rachael, she's ten years older than me, but we're into the same kind of music and really hit it off. Michael is about 15 years older than me but he's into the same kind of music and we really hit it off. Then there's Anna, we hit it off because we like the same kind of shows but she's really clingy and really starting to get on my nerves. And how do I describe Jason? I met him in the Foster system growing up and he also started going to the same gym I go to. He's so handsome, he's about 6 ft tall short blonde curly hair, and muscles for days. okay so I may have had a crush on him in the past but we've actually gotten too close so he'll just forever be one of my best friends.

I live in a small studio apartment that I share with my two cats, Stitch and Rayne. I kind of think I'm destined to be the old cat lady. I'm not home a lot, I'm either at work, out with my friends or at the gym. I don't like being alone. I used to read a lot but I haven't in years. It's almost like I'm scared I slip away into another world. So I just try to keep my days filled with work and friends. Staying busy helps keep me from feeling lonely. So, at the end of a long day I just go home, and go to bed.

I have a love-hate relationship with sleep. Sometimes I have the most vivid dreams, sometimes they're good and sometimes, they scare the crap out of me. I would say most of the time my sleep is dreamless. But those rare times when it's not, like a dream I had when I was 7 years old and I can still remember it. It was like I closed my eyes here and woke up in another world, a world that had two moons. My seven-year-old mind was so freaked out all I kept doing was walking around saying "there's two moons, there's two moons". Or this repetitive dream that I used to have, either I was surrounded by wolves or snakes or ghosts and I couldn't get away. I would always wake up as they had me surrounded and I was either standing on a table or something other than that above them with nowhere to go. I'm sure it's just my brain's way of handling all the abuse that I had to endure my whole childhood. Other than these minor details I think I turned out pretty good despite everything that's happened.

Going to bed tonight I'm only thinking about good things about how Rachel, Michael, Jason, Anna and myself are going out next Friday to celebrate my 21st birthday. Yes I'm still very excited about it. I know it's kind of lame, but hey I get to have a drink in a bar legally.

So, of course, I dreamed. I dreamed that Monica and Andy we're getting married. I was walking on the street toward the church. I felt uneasy because I've never felt comfortable in a church, I don't believe in the Christian religion. I went to church with several different families as a child and I just never felt comfortable nor believed anything that they said. And in my dream as I was walking towards the church, a psychic had a tent setup to give readings, she jumped up towards me. She grabbed me by the arm and started saying "it's coming and I can't protect you" over and over until I woke up. I woke up sweating and panting, there was something so familiar about the woman but I don't think I've ever seen her before.

The uneasy feeling was hard to shake. At work, Dan came around a corner and said "Good Morning!" and it made me jump. "Sorry, didn't mean to scare you, why are you so jumpy? Got anything to do with that bruise on your arm?" Dan said. I just looked at him, then looked at my arm. He was right there was a bruise and it was right where the woman in my dream had grabbed me, the bruise looked like a handprint. "I had a bad dream last night, I must have done it in my sleep" I said and walked away. Now I was even more freaked out. I can't remember ever having a bruise from a dream. Maybe I did grab it while I was asleep, anything is possible, except a figment of my imagination giving me a bruise...

The rest of the day continued uneventfully except for a few jumps here and there, I just couldn't shake the uneasiness. Even one of our regular customers, David, seemed to notice. He always came in for lunch and sat in the same booth. David is a very tall man, at least 6'8, not a bad looking guy probably in his mid 30s. I asked him where he works once and he looked at me and said he's with the secret service and winked at me. I laughed, and told him he could have just said it was none of my business. He usually got a salad, but occasionally got a plain, well done burger to go with it. Today, he asked me about the bruise, I told him I got it while fighting ninjas and winked at him. He didn't laugh, he looked really concerned and asked if I was in any kind of trouble. "I was just kidding, it's kinda dumb and embarrassing, I guess I did it to myself while I was asleep" I told him. "You sure you're okay?" David asked. I said "Yeah" and walked away because he was starting to weird me out.

I went to the back of the restaurant because I was done with customers for the moment, and by that, I don't mean there aren't anymore, I meant that I couldn't deal with them anymore so I started doing some extra cleaning. I tried to think about my birthday coming up to get my mind off all the weird stuff. Today is Tuesday, I started texting my friends on a group message to see what they had planned for Friday.

I'm down for whatever, it's your birthday! - Racheal. *I say we go to Nashville and hit Broadway.* - Micheal. *Yes! I love Broadway!* - Anna. *I don't really care, do you care if I bring a date?* - Jason. *I'm sure Broadway will be fun, and why would I care if you bring a date Jason?* - Me. Although I did care, it was like a punch in the gut, guess I wasn't completely over that crush. *Is she anyone I know Jason?* - Me. *And who is going to be the designated driver?* - Me. *I will, I don't really like drinking a lot anyway!* - Anna. *I don't think so, her name is Carly* - Jason. *okay, I'll see you guys on Friday, can't wait* - Me.

Racheal, knowing about my crush immediately sent me a one on one message. *Wow, I can't believe he's gonna bring a date to your birthday celebration!* - Racheal. *Yeah, well, who am I to tell him he can't?* - Me. *You could have said that you just wanted it to be people that you know.* - Racheal. *It is what it is, I would rather have him there with another woman than to get mad at me and not come, I'll be fine.* - Me. *One of my regular customers is acting strange today, so I decided to stay in the back and clean for now.* - Me. *Acting weird how? Like maybe he wants to ask you out? That would be great, that's what we need to do is get you a date for your birthday!* - Racheal. *No, that's not what I meant and I don't think so, I'm good, I promise.* - Me. Then I started hearing the sounds of "it's getting busy" so I told Racheal that I had to go help with customers.

I went up and saw that indeed they were getting busy. I started to bus tables but I noticed that David was *still* sitting at his table. So I asked someone else to do that and I went to the kitchen to help Dan. "Why is David still here? He doesn't usually stay this long does he?" I asked. "He pulled out a laptop and asked for the Wi-Fi password, I guess he just decided to work from here today." Dan said. "Table 12 is asking to speak to the manager!" Betty yelled. I looked up, table 12 was next to David, but not him. I pulled Betty to the side and asked if she had any idea what it was about and she told me that it took a while to get to them so they were probably going to complain about that. I said okay, and went out to try to make the customer happy.

I walked up to the table, it was a short older woman with another younger woman. "Hi, I'm Gabriela, I'm the manager, how can I help you?" I said with a smile. "My niece and I stopped in for lunch and it took TWO HOURS, why would it take TWO HOURS?" The woman said, raising her voice. " I apologize for that ma'am that's not normally how we handle things here" I said, trying to calm her down so that she didn't disturb the other customers. "I will pay for your meal and get you a coupon for the next time you come in," I told her. "If you will excuse me for a moment, I'll go get the coupon" I said. I walked back to the office and filled out the coupon, I was probably only gone a total of three minutes, but when I came back they had left. David was also gone and both tables had already been cleaned. I asked Dan if maybe they had gone to the restroom or something, but he acted like he didn't even know what I was talking about.

After the rush was over and everything was clean and re-stocked, I told the crew that I was going home. I needed a break from today's weirdness. There is a little old graveyard on the way to my apartment that I sometimes like to stop and walk through. It's so peaceful and it relaxes me. So, I stopped there today. There was a chill to the air and a slight breeze blowing leaves around, it made the whole thing seem magical. Tennessee weather is so crazy, like each of the seasons refuse to end to let the next one begin, so today in early November the high is 79 degrees and sunny. I don't usually look at a forecast because, like I said, Tennessee weather doesn't care about a forecast. I suddenly felt like I was being watched. I looked around and didn't see anyone else. I heard cars driving down the road in the distance but it was hard to make out what they were because I was so far from the road.

I still couldn't shake the feeling of being watched, so I started heading back to my car. While I was walking back a rabbit jumped out of a bush and I screamed because it scared me. It jumped because of my scream then sat there paralyzed with fear, I felt so bad for the poor little guy. I walked away from him so that he knew I didn't plan on eating him. After I was about five feet away, I looked back and he was gone. As I got closer to the road I saw another car parked, it looked empty, the graveyard wasn't very big, if someone else was here, I would see them. "Hello" I yelled. Nothing. No leaves rustling or fallen sticks cracking, silence, even the wind had stopped and the silence was very eerie. I started walking faster toward my car. I reached my car, unlocked it and jumped in. I didn't realize it, but I must have been holding my breath. I locked the car doors and let it out, all the emotions started coming with it and I just sat in my car and cried for at least ten minutes.

When I was finished crying, I looked around, the car that had been parked fairly close was gone now. I didn't notice when it left. How could I have not seen whoever was driving it? Today was just not my day, I just needed to go home, take a hot, relaxing bath and snuggle with my kitties in my pajamas and watch a good movie. I started my car and drove to my apartment. When I walked in the kitties greeted me with meows of excitement like they always do. I made sure they had food and water in their bowls then went to run my bath water. I was lucky that I had a bathtub, most studio apartments just have a shower stall. Rayne, my fluffy black cat started meowing at the window. Stitch a gray/black tiger striped fat boy followed her.

I pulled the shades apart to look out, and I saw the same car that I had seen at the graveyard. I quickly shut the shades back. It didn't look like anyone was in the car again. I started shaking, I was so scared, I knew that something wasn't right. Someone was watching me, but why? I didn't want to call the police, because what if I was crazy, maybe it's someone that lives nearby. I didn't want to be alone though. *Hey, would anyone wanna come over and keep me company? We can watch a movie or something.* -Me, on the group text. No reply after ten minutes. I looked out again, the car was gone. I started feeling a little easier. I told myself that it must be someone that lives nearby or visiting someone nearby. I never heard back from any of my friends, so I just continued my night as I had planned. Took a nice bath, watched a happy movie and snuggled with my kitties and fell asleep. My sleep was dreamless that night.

I woke up feeling a little better. Checked my phone, still no replies, I found that odd. I looked out the window, I didn't see the car. I started getting ready to go to work. My phone started going crazy as soon as I left my apartment. It was like, something had been blocking my signal and everything was coming through all at once. That was weird, never had that happened before. I messaged everyone and told them I was fine, I don't know what happened and that I must have lost signal and didn't realize it. I pulled into work and saw the car sitting there. The one that I had seen twice yesterday was now parked at my job. I went in the back door and immediately looked around. There were several customers, about seven tables already and a couple walking in. The only customer I recognized was David. I started asking the employees if they drove the car and they all said 'no.' I looked around and I didn't feel like anyone looked suspicious, or that they were there to stalk me.

I walked out to say hello to David, I mean, he's only been here everyday for at least a year. Kinda felt like I knew him a little, not gonna lie, he has made me feel uneasy at times, but not like he would harm me. "Hey there, how are you today Mr. Secret Service?" I said to David. He leaned in, and kind of whispered, "If you tell everyone, it's not a secret." "Isn't your birthday coming up?" he asked. I just looked at him for a stunned moment, how did he know? I couldn't recall having a conversation about my birthday with him. "Sorry, I heard Mona say something about it, I was just making conversation" he said after seeing the look on my face. Mona was one of the waitresses. "Oh, it's okay, I've just been a little 'jumpy' lately" I replied. "So, got any big plans?" he asked. "I'm just going out with some friends, oh I think Dan needs me in the kitchen, I'll see ya later" I said, trying to get away from him.

"Wow, he sure has become talkative in the past few days" I said to Dan as I walked into the kitchen. He looked at me and said "Mmmhmm" "What?" I asked. "You know he's flirting with you,"

Dan said. "No, I don't think so, that's not the vibe I'm getting, I just feel like he's being nosey and I can't figure out why" I said. "Yeah, Yeah" Dan said as he walked away. I felt my phone vibrate and looked down. *Sorry I haven't messaged you in a few days, I got supper swamped at work. How have you been, still excited about your birthday? -* Micheal. *I'm good, of course I'm still excited, I'm gonna be 21!* - Me. *Well, good, I'm looking forward to celebrating with you.* -Micheal. *Okay, lunch rush is starting, I'll talk to you later, and you can message me anytime, bye.* -Me.

After making it through the lunch rush, I looked around the dining room. David had actually left, I had expected to look up and see him sitting at his table. After I helped get the kitchen and dishes cleaned up I told Dan that I was headed out. Dan worked Monday through Thursday and Monica was the new weekend manager, I came in everyday for a little while and helped through rushes, did orders and scheduling. I walked out and got into my car. I looked around and didn't notice the car that I had seen yesterday and this morning. Maybe I was just paranoid, it is a small town and it is possible that someone else would be in the same place as me three times I suppose. I didn't stop at the graveyard because it now made me feel uneasy. I had to stop at the store for cat food and snacks then went straight home.

I had another dreamless sleep that night and I woke feeling refreshed on Wednesday morning. I went to the gym as soon as I got up. As soon as I pulled into the gym, I noticed Jason's truck in the parking lot. I saw him as soon as I walked in, I waved at him but I didn't walk over to him, I didn't want to disturb his workout. His tan skin was wet from sweat and his muscles were bulging. Man, I wish he liked me, he was so amazing, body and soul. But, of course he doesn't. That's life right? I've only ever had one boyfriend and he cheated on me, so of course I have major trust issues. Jason saw me wave and nodded his head as if to say 'hello'. So I went to the restroom to do my stretches and get ready to start my routine. While I was lying down, lifting, Jason came over and straddled me, all I could think was, damn dude you just like messing with my head. But apparently he thought of me more as a sister, he was telling me how much I would like Carly, his new girlfriend. "Yeah, I'm sure I will," I told him, and I was going to try not to dislike her just because of my feelings for him, that's what I told myself.

After the gym I went home to take a shower before work. I don't like taking showers in public places. My apartment was part of an old house that had been converted into six apartments, mine was on the main floor on the left side. I noticed something laying at my door as I was walking up. I hadn't ordered anything, maybe it was something that belonged to a neighbor, left at my door by mistake. When I reached my door, I realized it was a bouquet of flowers. I looked at the card to see what name was on it so I could try to get it to its rightful owner. It said Gabriela, and that's all it said. I looked around, I noticed the car from yesterday was parked about a block away, but it didn't look like anyone was inside again. They must live nearby I told myself, as I went to unlock the door, I noticed I was shaking. I took a picture of the flowers and posted it on all my social media accounts and asked who sent them. I got lots of 'hearts' and 'those are so pretty' but no one admitted to sending them.

I put the flowers in a vase with water and got in the shower. After my shower, I got dressed quickly and went to work. The car was there. I was starting to get angry, I didn't even feel scared anymore, I felt violated. So, I pulled out a piece of paper and wrote 'please introduce yourself to me, I don't like feeling like I'm being stalked - Gabriela' and put it on the windshield. Yes, I knew it could be a dangerous move, but I was done with this nonsense. I walked inside, David was there, I said hi to him as I walked by then headed to the back to put my stuff in the office. I asked Dan about the car again, he still didn't know who it belonged to. He told me that

David's food was ready and asked if I wanted to take it out, I told him, sure. I grabbed the tray and took it out to David's table. "Salad with steak today," I said as I put the food down on his table. "How are you today?" he asked. "I'm good, got a good workout before I came in," I said. "Where do you workout?" he asked. "At the gym," I said, walking away.

He seemed to be interested in what I do outside of work. I didn't like sharing that kind of thing with people, I guess that's why I didn't really have a lot of friends, but I just have a general feeling of untrust with the human race in general. I didn't feel like David was trying to ask me out, but I did feel like he wanted to be a friend. I didn't know why he wanted to be my friend, my untrust for the human race made me a hard person to get to know. After the lunch rush I noticed that he was still here, so I walked back out to his table. "Was everything okay?" I asked. "Yes, it's always delicious, that's why I'm always here" he replied. He had his laptop out again, "What are you working on?" I asked. "Just some top secret stuff," he replied. I stood there for a second looking at him and he smiled at me. "Well, I have to go back and help get everything cleaned up," I said. "Okay, see you later," he said,

I sent a message on the group text, *would anyone like to go for a walk with me this evening in the graveyard?* - Me. *Why the graveyard?* - Micheal. *Because I like it, it's peaceful and relaxing to me.* -Me. *I can, what time?* -Anna. *Great, meet me there at six* -Me. After everything was cleaned up, I went to check the dining room one more time. David had left. I told everyone that I was leaving and headed out, the stalking car was gone, I hope they got my note.

I drove to the graveyard. Anna's car was there, so I pulled up next to her and got out. She got out when she saw me and we hugged each other. "It's good to see you," I said. "Yeah, you too, it's been a few weeks," she replied. "Yeah, 'adulting' gets in the way sometimes," I told her. The last time we hung out, we went to a haunted house together, it was really fun. We walked through the graveyard, catching up a bit. I told her about the car I've been seeing everywhere I go, she said that I should call the police the next time I see it. "I don't know, what am I going to say?" I asked. "Tell them you keep seeing the same care everywhere you go and you are scared" she replied. "I don't know, I feel like I am over reacting" I said. "Well, how about this? Take a picture of the car the next time you see it and show it to everyone. That way if you do come up missing at least we have a clue." Anna said. "You know what? Even though I feel like you are being sarcastic, I think I will do that." I said. "I need to get home, get a little cleaning done and get some sleep. Just one more day until Friday." I said with a little squeal. "Alright, I will pick you up at 5 o'clock Friday evening, I'm excited too." Anna said with a smile. I gave her a hug and we told each other to be careful before I got in my car and headed to my apartment.

That night my dreams were like what I imagine a serious drug trip would be like. In my dream, I was in a house that had a hiding space, like a whole little apartment in the middle of the house and the house was round. I don't know what I was hiding from, but I was being hunted by someone, or something. I kept getting lost inside the house and one room that had been closed off was haunted. I somehow broke into the closed off room and ghosts started chasing me then, I woke up, my heart racing, sweating, trying to calm myself. I got up to get a drink of water. That wasn't the first time I had dreamed of that house. Maybe I had been to a place like that as a baby and my subconscious remembered. The times I wasn't in group homes growing up, I was with horrible people. I don't understand how they even became foster parents.

I looked at the clock and it was 3:33 a.m. I peeked out my window shade, the stalking car wasn't anywhere in sight. I checked to make sure my door was locked and I lay back down. I managed to drift back to sleep, this time a dreamless peaceful sleep. I woke up feeling like I hadn't slept at all. Despite that, I got ready to go to the gym. I didn't see Jason at the gym today. I didn't see anyone I knew. I just put my headphones in and blasted my rock/metal playlist to get the adrenaline flowing.

After my workout, I went home and got a shower then went to work. The stalking car wasn't there. I guess my note worked, who knows, maybe it was all a coincidence that they were at the same place as me the last few days and maybe my note scared them as much as they scared me. I walked in, David wasn't there today. I asked Dan if he had come earlier and he said that he hadn't seen him. Lunch rush started picking up, I saw David walk in about thirty minutes into the rush. I guess he was just running late today. Dan looked at me and said "there's your boyfriend." "He's not my boyfriend," I replied. I walked out to get his order, "I'm just going to have a salad today" said David. "Okay, no problem, I'll get that right out," I said. He ate his salad and left before I could get back out today.

After the rush I talked to Monica, making sure she understood that I wouldn't be here tomorrow (Friday) or Saturday. Dan had said if they needed anything that they could call him. I didn't want to worry about work while I was trying to celebrate and enjoy my twenty-first birthday. The whole crew was going to be here with her too so I didn't feel too bad about not being here. I stayed over and made sure that they had plenty of stock to make it through the weekend and got some extra cleaning and stocking and sorting done just in case the owner decided to stop by. I wanted to make sure there wouldn't be anything for him to complain about.

Before leaving the restaurant, I sat down in the dining room and started texting my friends, finalizing plans for tomorrow night. *Hey guys, is everyone still going tomorrow?* -Me. *Yes, I told you yesterday, I'll pick you up at your place at 5!* -Anna. *Yeah, me and Carly will be there, which bar are we meeting at?* -Jason. *Is Honky Tonk Central good?*

-Racheal. *Yeah, I'll be there, and Honky Tonk sounds good, we can always bar hop from there.* -Micheal. *Okay, sounds great, I'm excited! I'll see you all tomorrow night!* -Me.

I went home, since I didn't have to get up early, I decided to watch a movie. I watched a romantic comedy because I didn't want to be scared by horror or depressed by drama. After I watched the movie I pampered myself a bit, took a bath, did a face mask and gave myself a pedicure. I bought a super cute outfit a few months ago for tomorrow. A black dress that came down to about two inches from my knees, straps across the top with a cleavage window. Some really cute black sandals and I had an appointment to get my hair done at one o'clock. I was totally prepared to act like a Nashville tourist even though I lived an hour away. I planned on getting wasted of course, that's why I took Saturday off from work too. I trusted my friends would keep me out of trouble. After all my pampering, I felt super tired, I looked at the clock at twelve thirty a.m. I layed down in my bed and fell asleep quite fast. I had a nice dreamless sleep that night. I woke up feeling refreshed and twenty-one.

I got up and started getting ready to go to the gym, yes I was still going on my birthday. Going to the gym wasn't a chore for me, I loved going so it was more like fun. I guess it was my outlet, a way to get out energy that builds up inside me, that way I don't explode or do something stupid. Jason wasn't there today, it makes my workout better without distraction anyway. Plus I was going to see him and meet his new girlfriend tonight, obviously I wasn't looking forward to that. I just need to get over my crush. Maybe I should be open to dating.

After my workout, I went home to get ready for my hair appointment. As I pulled into my apartment I noticed the stalker car was parked in the same place I had seen it before. I went into my apartment quickly. I followed Anna's advice once I got inside and got a picture of the car. It wasn't a very good picture because it was a little ways up the street and I was taking it through my window while trying not to be seen. I sent the picture to Anna. *Why are you sending me a picture of a row of cars?* - Anna. *The tan one, is the one I told you about, the one that I've been seeing everywhere.* - Me. *Well, I can't even really tell what kind of car it is, you can't get a better picture?* - Anna. *No, not really, sorry. Maybe when they kidnap me and are loading me into the trunk I can get a better picture.* - Me *HaHa, not funny.* - Anna. *What are you doing now?* - Anna. *I'm getting ready to go get my hair done.* - Me. *Okay, I'll see you afterwhile, and Happy Birthday!* - Anna. *Okay, and thanks!* - Me.

After I got a shower, I put on my dress, because I didn't want to get my hair done, then mess it up by changing clothes. I got in my car, the stalker car was gone. I drove to my hairdresser, which was twenty minutes away. I've been going to the same lady for five years now. Tammy always did my hair the way I wanted it. Her studio was built onto the side of her house now. She used to rent a space in town, but her boyfriend built the add-on for her so she didn't have to travel. And she's good enough that her clients will come to her so she's quite happy with the way everything has turned out. As I pulled in something caught my eye, two houses away there was a car parked in the driveway that looked like the stalker car! Surly it wasn't, this was twenty minutes away! I got out of my car and took out my phone, and used the zoom function this time to get a little better of a picture, it was still fuzzy looking and not clear.

I walked into the salon, "Hi Tammy, how are you doing?" I asked. "I'm great," she replied as she snipped some hair off an older lady's head. "Just give me a few minutes, I'm almost done here" she said. "No problem, I'll just have a seat" I said. "So you said today is your birthday?" Tammy asked. "Yes, I'm going to Broadway with some of my friends to celebrate, I need you to make me look pretty," I said. "Well, you are already gorgeous, so it won't be hard" she said as she was now cleaning up the chair and sweeping up the hair. "I remember when I was twenty-one, times were a lot different," the older lady said. I looked at her for a second, I didn't know this woman, and I didn't say that I was twenty-one, something inside me told me to lie and I have no idea why. "Oh yeah, me too, I'm twenty-five now" I said, laughing nervously. The woman and Tammy both laughed with me and I felt less tense. The woman paid and left and I sat down in the chair.

"Are you really twenty-five?" Tammy asked. "No, I was just making a joke, it worked, you both laughed" I replied. "I thought you were younger," she said, still laughing. "So, what do you want?" she asked. "I'm not sure, maybe some big loose curls, but do you think that will last all night?" I said. "Yes, I have a spray that will hold up for a week if you don't wash it out" she said. "Awesome" I replied. So she started working on the curls, after she had been working on my hair for about thirty minutes, I heard the door open and looked over. "David!" I said, surprised to see him there. "Oh wow, this is kinda awkward, I just came to get a haircut" he said. Tammy told him it would be about fifteen more minutes and he could have a seat and wait. He sat down, his knees still high in the air because he was so tall, I giggled a little under my breath at the way it made him look. "How do you guys know each other?" Tammy asked to break the silence. We both started speaking at the same time then both stopped and an awkward silence followed. I decided to break the silence, "David is a regular customer at my restaurant" I said. "Oh, okay" she replied. "It has the best atmosphere and best customer service around," he said. "Aww, thanks" I replied. "Those curls look really good on you," he said. "Thank you," I replied. "You're welcome, oh, and happy birthday" he said. "I almost forgot, then I figured you were getting ready to go out," he added. "Yeah, she's going to Broadway to get waisted" Tammy said laughing. I had managed to keep him from finding out what I was doing until now. I just sat there in awkward silence and Tammy realized she shouldn't have said anything and mouthed 'I'm sorry" in the mirror to me. I shrugged my shoulders and kept silent. David had picked up a magazine to look like he was distracted.

After she was finished with my hair, I paid her and said 'thank you' and whispered 'don't worry about it' to her so she didn't feel bad about it. David looked up, having not noticed my dress earlier because I was covered by the apron thing that hairdressers put over you to keep from messing up your clothes or getting hair on you. His eyes widened, "You look really beautiful, your date tonight is a really lucky guy" he said. I blushed, "Thank you, I don't have a date though, I'm just going out with friends" I replied in a tone that let him know that I didn't want a date. "Oh, well, I hope you have fun and be careful," he said. "Thanks, I will," I said. "I'll see you later" I added as I was walking out the door. As I walked out I looked where the stalker car had been parked. It was gone.

Driving home, I felt hungry and realized that I hadn't really eaten, so I decided to go through a drive through to save some time. I hardly ever ate fast food, It was delicious. I pulled into my apartment and looked up and down the street for the stalker car, it wasn't there. My phone rang and I jumped out of my skin. It was Anna telling me she would be here to get me in an hour. I told her that's fine, I just needed to finish my makeup. So, I went inside to do just that. As soon as I walked in, I noticed a bad smell, it smelled like death. I called for my cats, they both came, I hadn't been gone that long. Maybe it was something outside. But then I walked by the flowers that had mysteriously showed up and they were dead, the smell was coming from the flowers! It smelled like rotting flesh. I grabbed a trash bag and threw them away, vase and all. I have never had flowers that smelled like that when they died. After I took them out to the trash, I finished getting my makeup on.

Anna pulled up right as I was finishing. I made sure the cats had food and water, made sure I had my ID, phone, keys, and some cash and I locked the door on my way out. "Hey" I said. "Happy birthday! You look amazing!" Anna said. "Thank you so much! You do too!" I said. "You know those flowers that someone sent me the other day?" I said. "Yes, I'm so jealous, I never get flowers," she said. "Yeah, well, when I got back from getting my hair done today, they were dead, but they smelled like a dead animal" I told her. "What? I've never heard of that" she replied. "I know, it freaked me out a bit, I have no idea why they would smell like that, I've never heard of anything like that before" I said. "I don't know, but how about we stop and get some iced lattes before we head to Broadway" Anna suggested. "Sure," I said. She paid for my coffee and said 'happy birthday' again, I told her thank you again. And we headed to Broadway.

Friday night traffic was bad. So I got on the group text. *We are stuck in traffic on 40.* -Me. No worries, *I'm still about fifteen minutes out.* -Racheal. *Me and Carly are pulling into a parking garage now, no worries though we will still be here when you get here.* -Jason. *I'm in an uber on the way, probably about ten minutes out.* -Micheal. *Why did you take an uber? You could have rode with us.* -Me. *I didn't want to bother anyone, it's no big deal, I'll see y'all there.* -Micheal. *Okay, I am so happy that you all are coming out with me to celebrate my birthday! Best friends in the world!* -Me. About twenty minutes passed before we got into town, then we drove around for another ten minutes trying to find parking. The evening air was still warm, I was hoping it wouldn't get too cold that night since I wanted to show a lot of skin.

It was about 6 o'clock when Anna and I walked into the bar. Jason walked up to me immediately, "Wow, you look amazing!" he said. "Thanks!" I replied. "This is Carly," he said, pointing at the girl by his side. She was pretty, blonde hair, blue eyes, short, probably about 5'2 and petite. "Hi Carly, I've heard a lot about you, I'm Gabriela," I said. "It's nice to finally meet you Gabriela, I've heard a lot about you too" she replied. "Good things, I hope" I said while giving Jason a teasing look. "Mostly" she said laughing. Micheal walked in and I went up to him and gave him a hug. He looked worried or stressed about something. "Is everything okay?" I asked him. "Yeah, just a weird uber driver," he replied. Then Racheal walked in, so I went up to her and gave her a hug. "You look so pretty!" I told her. "Thank you, You look amazing!" she replied. We asked for a table and decided to eat a little bit before we got too drunk. I ordered a salad since I had the fast food burger earlier. Racheal got a pretzel with cheese dip, Micheal ordered a burger and a beer, Anna ordered a pasta dish. Jason and Carly got an appetizer sampler and shared it.

After we were finished eating, we decided to play a game. We were going to go into each bar on Broadway and have one drink at each, whoever survived the night without throwing up or bailing on us would be the winner. The first bar we went in, I had a Jack n Coke. The rest had beer. "You aren't gonna make it long drinking like that" Anna said. She was drinking soda since she was my designated driver. "Oh well, IT'S MY BIRTHDAY!" I yelled. The singer of the band must have heard me because he gave me a shout out before he started the next song. I held up my cup to 'cheers' him. At the second bar, I decided to 'calm it down a bit' and just ordered a beer. I wasn't feeling anything yet. At the third bar, I ordered a shot of Fireball. I was starting to feel good. A tourist in a cowboy hat asked me to dance, I looked at my friends and shrugged my shoulders, and said, why not? He started twirling me around the dance floor, I felt good, I felt free. When the song ended I went back to my friends and they all laughed at me. "I'm having fun!" I told them. At the fourth bar, I ordered another Jack n Coke. I really like the band that was playing here, they were doing classic rock covers. The drummer had a style like Tommy Lee, one of the singers and guitar players was very tall, at least 6'8, the other singer and keys player was a little older and the bass player was a woman that hit all those AC/DC high notes. Carly asked me to go dance with her, so I did. "I got you another drink too, it's call sex on the beach, I think you will like it" she said as she handed me a reddish looking drink. "Thanks!" I replied. I took a drink to taste, it was really good. "I do like it," I told her.

Carly started dancing close to me, I got the feeling that she was either trying to turn Jason on or make him jealous. We started twirling around the dance floor faster, I could have sworn I saw a familiar face in the crowd. "I'm not feeling well," I said and ran toward the restroom. I don't really remember much after that, I don't remember getting to the restroom, just blank darkness. There was a split second of consciousness, I was being carried by someone tall.

I woke up in a dark room that I didn't recognize. Had I been kidnapped? I was in a bed, it looked like a bedroom, but not one that I recognized. It was dark outside. I started feeling around for my phone, it wasn't on me, I checked the bedside table, nothing of mine there. I put my feet on the floor, I walked to the window and looked up in the sky because the moon seemed to be very bright. Two moons! There were two moons, what the *hell* was going on?

Two

The Ascension

Why was I in a world that I had dreamed of? Was this a dream? "I think she's awake" I heard someone from another room say. I started to feel panic, was I about to be murdered? I heard footsteps coming closer, I looked around and didn't see a closet. I checked the window, at first it wouldn't budge, but then it opened for me. Where was I gonna go though? I have no idea where I could possibly be, but I jumped out of the window anyway. I started running, there was only a field that seemed never-ending, I didn't see any other buildings besides the house that I just left. "She got out!" I heard someone say from the house. It wasn't long until I heard and felt someone coming up behind me. I was almost in a wooded area, I could hide there! "Gabby! Please stop, I'm not trying to hurt you!" I heard a familiar voice say.

I stopped and turned around, it was David. I hit the ground and started crying, he was there by me now. "Why would you do this to me? Where am I?" I said, while sobbing. "I promise, I am *not* going to hurt you, I am trying to save you, this was the only thing I knew to do because they found you. Please come back to the house with me," he pleaded. I shook my head 'no' while still crying, he had kidnapped me! I was in shock. He sat down on the ground in front of me, "please? I want you to meet my wife and let me explain to you what is going on inside, please?" he begged. I looked up at him, sitting down he was still taller than I was. "You're married?! Why are there two moons?!" I said, starting to calm down. "Will you come back to the house with me if I answer those two questions now?" he asked. I looked at him for a minute then agreed by nodding my head quietly. "Yes, and you are in a different dimension" he said with a serious face.

I didn't know what else to do besides follow him back to the house, so I got up, not believing the different dimension line, but followed him back to the house anyway. When we walked inside there was a woman, she was probably about an inch taller than David. "This is Sarah, my wife," he said. "Okay, now tell me why you have kidnapped me!" I yelled. "Please calm yourself down, no one is going to hurt you, we are trying to help you" Sarah said. "You keep saying that, but not telling me how you are *helping* me" I said. "Well, you jumped out of a window and ran away for one" Sarah said. "*You kidnapped me!*" I said, starting to get angry. "To be fair, David is the one that did that, not me," Sarah said. "Hey, don't say that," he replied. I rolled my eyes, "seriously, please tell me why you yanked me from my birthday party and brought me to your home, in a 'different dimension'" I demanded. "Okay, let's sit at the table and have a coffee and talk like civilized people," David suggested. I agreed, because what else am I going to do?

We sat at a medium sized dining table and Sarah brought out coffee and sugar and cream and sat down with us. I fixed myself some coffee and looked at them. "I'm not sure where to start since she knows nothing," David said, looking at Sarah. "What are you trying to tell me?" I asked. "You are not human," Sarah said. "Okay, we start with that," David said. "Excuse me?" I said. "You were born to a witch, the other witches heard about you and didn't think you should exist, so they set out to destroy the abomination they believed you are" Sarah said. "Your mother put several spells on you to 'hide' you from them and then left you at an orphanage" David said. My head was spinning, "you knew my mother?" I asked. "No, I never knew her," David said. I have been kidnapped by crazy people and they are going to kill me, that's what was going through my head.

"I knew someone that *did* know your mother, and it was someone that I cared about, that person made me promise to protect you before they passed away" David said. "Is my mother still alive?" I asked. "No, the witches got to her, they tortured her trying to find you until she died" he said. I started to cry again "so she's dead because of me" I said. "More of a reason not to let her death have been in vain" Sarah said. "What do you mean?" I asked. "Once you hit the age of twenty-one the spells she cast upon you wore off, they were already getting weaker over this past week. The stronger witches were able to find you. The complaining woman at the restaurant was one. She was going to kill you, so I stopped her." David said. "What do you mean, you stopped her?" I asked. "I did what I had to do, Gabby," David said.

I sat back in my chair, *was this real?* I am sitting in a different dimension, drinking coffee with my regular customer from my restaurant and he's telling me that I am a witch that my mother died to protect me and he 'took care' of someone that wanted to kill me like three days ago. "Tell me about the dimension, thing, how did we get here" I said. "Okay, that one is a little hard to explain, but I will try" David said. "There are thirteen planes of existence, we just call them Earth 1 through 13, you live on 12, this is 2. Through each plane more magic is filtered out. So on Earth 13 there is no magic at all, it's the most mundane place of them all. Earth 1 is the most violent and is the only place that the most vile creature in the universe lives because they have been trapped there by very powerful magic. Or else they would escape and take over all 13 worlds." David explained to me. "So, how do we get to the different worlds?" I asked. I still wasn't fully convinced that any of this was real. "Dimensions" He corrected. "A spell that opens a portal" he continued. "Who can do the spell?" I asked. I was wondering if whoever was after me could just come here. "Yes, witches on 12 can cast the spell to open the portal to come here." He answered, as if reading my mind. "But, time works differently in each layer, time gets slower, two weeks here, is one night on 12. So I figure we have about two weeks to train you in magic and physical defense before they realize you aren't there. Or your human friends start to panic and think you are dead. I used your phone and sent them a message saying you were going home in a cab because you weren't feeling well so they wouldn't worry." David said. "True kidnap fashion" I said.

"So what exactly happened, I remember not feeling well and trying to get to the restroom" I said. "Your friend's date is a witch, she put sleeping powder in your drink. She is still out there, I needed to get you out fast so I didn't have time to take care of her." David said. "Why do they want me dead?" I asked. "You are special, as I mentioned before, there are other things, creatures, that a lot of people fear, a mix of those creatures and people are really scared because they don't understand your power. They are afraid you will kill them, so they set out to kill you before you can," he said. Sarah had gone back to bed several hours ago. But I had so many questions there was no way I could sleep without some of them being answered. "So, what am I?" I asked. "Do you know any myths? Or legends? Or religion?" he asked. "No, not really," I answered.

"A long time ago, in the beginning, all of the dimensions were one. Beings of all kinds started forming, believe what you will on how they come to be. Some believe in an almighty creator and some believe they came from different worlds. But at some point, they came into being. Angels were here, and some mated with humans forming a new race, the Nephilim, or giants." "Giants?" I said, interrupting him. "Yes, giants, no human grows over 6'5, if someone is over 6'5 they are half or at least part giant." Looking at him, obviously over 6'5, "So you are a giant?" I asked. "Half, yes. And so are you." He said. "*What?*" I said. "I'm not even that tall! I'm average, I'm 5'8!" I argued. "Your mother, put several spells on you to protect you, stunting your growth was one of the spells" he said. "Are you serious? Witches can just use spells to do *anything*?" I asked. "Not all, but your mother was very powerful, she was already a threat because the witches were scared of her power, then when she fell in love with a giant and you were born, well you are the first witch that is what you are, born of an extremely powerful witch and a giant. You are feared because they don't know what you could do to them" he said.

"Even if I have the power to destroy someone, what makes them think I would?" I asked. "I'm not a cold blooded killer, I don't want to go around killing people" I added. "Your humanity, I believe is also a spell from your mother. Maybe she thinks you are the key to peace among all of our kind and every kind for that matter. You were treated horribly as a child by many of your guardians and yet you don't hate them." He said, but it seemed like it was a realization for himself. "Ugh, it seems like she messed with my free will," I said. "You probably would have killed them with no remorse and ended up being locked away in a prison or executed if she hadn't," he said. "Oh, well, thanks mom" I said, still not sure if I was grateful or pissed off about it.

"So, what kind of training are we doing?" I asked. "There is still a lot that you don't know about Gabby," he said. "Why do you call me that? I demanded. "I've been watching you for a while, so I gave you a nickname, why not?" He said. "It sounds so childish," I said. "Deal with it," he said. "Are we related?" I asked. "No, but your brother was my best friend. He is the one that I made the promise to, to protect you. He was a good man." David said. "What happened to him?" I asked "He was your half brother to be exact, he was only half giant so from your dad's side. But the witches didn't want him standing in their way when it came to destroying you, so they disposed of him" he said with a tear coming to his eye. "Is my dad still alive?" I asked. "I don't know. I'm not even sure who he is, I never met him." He said. "But for now, we need to get some rest," he said, yawning. "One more question?" I said. "Tomorrow," he replied. "Fine, am I sleeping in the cell that I was in earlier?" I asked. He rolled his eyes and smiled at me. "I guess so," I said.

I lay in the bed with my mind racing, how was I supposed to *sleep*? I'm literally living in a nightmare where I am being hunted by something that I don't understand. I don't even understand what I am. Why was my mother so much more powerful than others of her kind? Was my dad still out there somewhere? Might I have other half siblings that I don't know about? What kind of magic could I do? Why are there two moons? Then I started thinking about how many half giants I have seen in my world. Did they know what they were? Then I started thinking about my friends and wondering if they bought the message that David had sent. I started worrying that my enemies would go after them to try to get to me. I needed to get back to my world as soon as possible, but I also needed more answers. At some point, I finally drifted to sleep from pure exhaustion.

"Time to get up!" I heard coming from the hall, I felt like I had just fallen asleep, but I was eager to find out more about who I was and to start learning how to do magic, so I stumbled out of bed. "Morning" I said, as I stumbled into the hallway. "Is there coffee? Or are we just gonna jump right into it?" I asked. David smiled at me, "Of course there's coffee, what a silly question" he said. We sat down at the table like we had the night before and had coffee. "Did you sleep well?" Sarah asked me. "Not really, too much on my mind and I'm in a different dimension, so I found it hard to fall asleep" I said honestly. "Well, I guess that would be the normal response to all of this," she said. David just looked at me like he was confused.

"I had a dream about this place when I was seven," I said. "It wasn't a dream, your brother, Samuel, brought you here, you started freaking out so he decided you weren't ready so he sent you back" David told me. "Wow, that's crazy," I said. "Everything is going to be crazy to you right now, it would be 'crazy' to anyone" Sarah said. "We have a witch that is a friend that is going to help you with tapping into your powers" David said. "I thought you said all the other witches want me dead?" I said. "Not *all*, just most," David said. "There are thirteen original covens, at least two of them are allies, five are known enemies, the other six, we will just have to figure out in time" David said. "Wow, okay, so I have some witches I can trust, some that want to kill me and some that I don't know if they want to kill me or be my friend, got it" I said, rolling my eyes. "You do that eye roll thing a lot," David said. "Sorry" I said, rolling my eyes again.

"On today's agenda, Sarah is going to teach you dimension history for a couple hours, I will work with you in defense training for a couple of hours, then Arturo should be here this afternoon to start your magic training. We will continue this process everyday for the next two weeks, here. And hopefully by the end, you will be able to go face your world. I am sending my brother back with you. Sarah and I are expecting our first child and she really wants me to stay here with her. My brother, James, will be here towards the end of your stay and will return with you when you go" David explained to me. "So, am I always going to have a bodyguard?" I asked. "And congratulations on the baby," I added. "Until I am certain that you *don't* need a bodyguard, yes, you will have someone if things get 'out of hand'" David said. "Great," I said, rolling my eyes.

Three

Training

"Alright, let's get started then" Sarah said. "Do you have any specific questions before we get started?" she asked. "About the dimensions? I don't think so, I don't know enough to ask anything yet" I replied. "Okay, so there are thirteen dimensions of Earth, I think we already told you that you live on 12 and we are currently on 2." She said, I nodded to show that I understood that part. "So, on 1, there is a certain creature that stories reach all the way to thirteen, but they have been magically trapped on 1 because they are far too dangerous to every creature in existence. That creature is known as the vampire." she said. "Vampires?" I said. "Vampires are real?" I added. I mean, I guess I shouldn't be surprised about that since I am a half witch half giant, right? "Yes, vampires are real and they are relentless, they will kill anyone and anything just to feed. When they were trapped there, there was an agreement made, because their blood does have healing properties, it was agreed to keep them alive. Humans and animals are taken twice a year from thirteen and put into 1 so they can survive" she told me. "That is horrible! You take people and animals to feed monsters?" I said, almost crying. "I don't personally, but yes and when the delivery is made, they supply blood for healing, it's still very hard to come by, so try not to get mortally wounded." she said.

I was finding it hard to process that people and animals were being sacrificed to get a little bit of a 'magic healing potion'. "Can't witches come up with something so that I can be completely closed off? And we wouldn't have to 'feed' them?" I asked. "Witches have some amazing gifts and have been able to heal their own, but vampire blood works to heal *all* creatures" she said. "On 1, time moves a little faster than here, it gets slower in each dimension. But when the vampires were trapped there, a spell was also done to make sunlight only last for five hours, because sunlight does kill vampires" she said. "How do vampires exist? Do they reproduce?" I asked. "Vampires exist because of a spell gone wrong, no they don't reproduce, if someone dies with vampire blood in their system they will become one. Anytime the blood is used to heal someone, they are put on lock down for forty-eight hours to prevent that from happening," she explained.

"Do you have a good understanding of 1 now?" she asked me. "Yes," I told her. "Good, on to 2 now. Every magical creature under the sun and two moons can be found here, in their true form" she said. "What do you mean by true form?" I asked. "Well, most of them can live on 12, but they appear different. Your fireflies are fairies, dragons, are reptiles, shape shifters can't change, they are always in their animal forms." she explained. "Fairies?" I asked. "Yes, anything you have ever heard of is real and a lot of things you haven't heard of as well" she said. "Can we see these creatures?" I asked. "You will see the harmless ones for sure before you go," she told me. Wow, I was going to see a fairy, I got a little excited about that. "Some things can't exist beyond certain dimensions. They can only exist so far, but if something exists in 2, it will or can exist in 1. Does that make sense to you?" she asked. "Yes, I think so," I said.

After a couple hours with Sarah and eating some lunch, I headed out to a field where David had told me to meet him. The grass or wheat or whatever was growing was up to my waist. It was around 2 o'clock and one of the two moons was starting to come up on the horizon already. "David!" I yelled. I didn't see him anywhere. I heard a rustling sound coming from behind me, I turned around as a huge black cat was jumping toward me. I screamed 'STOP!' and put my arm up. The cat froze in mid air, and I froze at the sight of the frozen cat. I heard clapping and David laughing. "Great instincts" he said coming from behind a shed. "It's okay, you can put her down now, this is Margo, she volunteered to help a little with training" he said. "How do I put her down?" I asked shakily. He came over and grabbed my upper arm and started lowering it, the cat went down with it. "Now, relax, and pull the magic back into you" he told me. "How?" I asked again. "Just relax and imagine that it is coming back into your arm" he told me. His voice was relaxed so that helped me to relax. "It worked!" I said, as the cat gently hit the ground. It was a black panther. Moments after she hit the ground she became a beautiful black (naked) woman, David threw a blanket at her that I hadn't even noticed he was carrying.

"You scared me for a moment" Margo told me. "Back at ya" I said. "It's nice to meet you, I don't think I've ever met a shape shifter before" I told her. "Oh, I'm sure you have" she said winking at me, "It's wonderful to meet you" she continued. "When David told us you were here, I told him that I would love to meet you, daughter of Valery and Jess" she said. "Did you know my parents?" I asked. "Enough small talk, Margo, you can come to dinner tonight and get to know Gabriela if you like, but we have training to do and a limited time to do it in" David said, while throwing me a big stick.

"okay, I will see you tonight" she said and walked away. David immediately started coming at me with another stick, I blocked the first few times he did it, then he kicked my feet out from under me and showed me that he could have gotten a death blow to my abdomen. "Well that wasn't fair" I said. "Oh, you think your enemies are going to *fight fair*?" he said sarcastically. "Fine" I said. We continued for about fifteen minutes. "I need a break" I said. "Again, do you think your enemies are going to give you breaks to catch your breath?" he said. "Can't I just use magic?" I asked. "Most of your enemies will also have magic to use, and those that don't could still be protected by it" he said. "You have to learn to fight, to defend yourself. You are already strong, I think your mother gave you a love for the gym spell too, but you need to learn to defend when you are being attacked, it needs to be an instinct." he told me. "A love for the gym spell? Is that a real thing?" I asked. "I don't know, maybe?" he replied. So, I got up and we continued to fight with the sticks for what seemed like forever. Then I noticed someone walking up to the house and David stopped. "Arturo is here, for your magic training" he said. "Can I get a little rest and a snack in first?" I asked. "Sure, take fifteen minutes to gather yourself" he said.

I plopped to the ground and sat there for a few minutes. David had gone back to the house. The air felt nice here, wasn't humid like it was in Tennessee on 12, it was weird calling my planet a number or several numbers. One of the moons was completely up in the sky now and the other was starting to come up. It was beautiful here. After sitting and enjoying the view for a moment, I got up and walked toward the house. I went inside and there was a bowl of fruit on the table, I grabbed an apple. "There you are," Sarah said. "David and Arturo are waiting for you in the basement" she told me as she showed me the doorway to the basement.

"Hello Gabriela," Arturo said as I walked down the stairs. "Hi," I said. Arturo was dark skinned with straight, short black hair. He was about six foot tall so a little taller than myself but standing next to David he looked short. "I am going to start with teaching you simple spells, ingredients, and incantations before we go into using your inner powers, which David tells me you used today," Arturo said. "We have a lot to go over, and very little time. There's no way to cover it all, I am having my apprentice put together a book to send back with you so you can reference once you are gone" he continued. "First we will start with some plants, their uses, and alternate names" said Arturo. "Well, I don't need to be here for this, have fun" David said, patting my shoulder as he walked up the steps to leave. Arturo started pulling plants out of a bag and telling me the names and magical properties of each one and alternate names of the ones that had them. It was a long two hours but I made it through. I began to smell dinner coming from upstairs and my belly growled on que. "If you don't have any questions for me, I believe it's time to eat," Arturo said. I just smiled at him and shook my head to let him know I didn't have any questions. I was wondering how my magical training could possibly be the most boring, more so than the history training, but I didn't want to ask him that aloud.

We both walked up the steps. Margo was here, I walked over to her and gave her a hug. "Please stay for dinner, Arturo, " David said. Arturo nodded his head in agreement. We all sat down to eat, the food looked absolutely amazing and tasted amazing too. "You were going to tell me how you knew my parents?" I said to Margo. "Your mother saved my life once, I had wandered into lion territory while playing as a child. They had me cornered, I was a goner for sure. Then Valery showed up and used her magic and scared them away. It was late so she took me home with her until the next day when she took me back to my home. I met your dad, Jess that night too, but I didn't stay in contact with him. Valery continued to come visit me, she brought me gifts, as I became older, she became a valued friend. She told me of her daughter and of the great things she would be and do and how we all had to come together and teach and protect her when the time came. And it seems that the time has come. You look a lot like her, she was beautiful too." Margo explained. I blushed, "Thank you" I said.

I was happy to hear stories of my birth mother and father. But it was bittersweet knowing that I would never meet her and I didn't know if I would ever get a chance to meet my dad. After the dinner guests had left, I was getting ready for bed when David came to my door. "Can I come in for a minute?" he asked. "Sure," I said. "How are you feeling about your training today?" he asked. "Starting to feel a little sore from your training, Sarah was very informative, Arturo was boring" I said, honestly. "There is a lot to learn in every aspect and it's not always going to be 'exciting'" David said. "You get your strength from your dad," he continued. "So because I'm physically stronger, I am a big threat to the witches?" I asked. I still didn't understand why I was such a big threat that they wanted to kill me. "Sarah told you about the vampires right?" he asked. I nodded. "They were created by accident, a hybrid that had never existed before, a demon/witch became mortally wounded. His mom, a witch, tried to heal him, he died anyway, when he woke twenty-four hours later, he killed everyone in sight, including her. He was caught and studied, found that his blood had healing properties, and could also create more. They were uncontrollable and didn't have any humanity in them. So they were locked away on 1. I tell you this because you are a hybrid that has never existed and this is the reason you are feared and the reason that some want you destroyed." he said. I yawned. "I will let you get some sleep now, see you tomorrow for more training!" he said. "You sound way too excited about that," I said, narrowing my eyes.

That night I dreamed, I dreamed that Jason was in danger and I needed to get to him to protect him. I saw Carly in my dream, she told me that he was hers now and she'll do what she pleases with him. I wanted to tear her face off. I punched her and told her to never threaten my friend again. "Time to get up!" I heard a voice coming from the hallway say. I made some kind of audible moan. "Okay" I said. I stumbled out of bed and headed for the kitchen. "Coffee" I said, like a zombie. I sat down with my coffee. I sat there quietly, thinking about my dream. "Can witches send messages in dreams?" I asked. "What did you dream about?" Sarah asked. "I dreamed that Carly was holding Jason hostage" I said, looking at David since he knew who I was talking about. "It's possible, I can send someone to check on him if it will make you feel better," he said. I nodded. "Okay, are you ready to get started on learning your dimensions?" Sarah asked. "Sure," I said.

"Okay, today, I will teach you about 3 through 7," she said. David got up, "I will go prepare today's lesson too" he said as he walked out. "3 through 7 are the easiest, they are pretty much the same, with the same creatures, the second moon gets less visible, with 7 being the last place you can see it at all. It's very faded on 7, but it can be seen. Humans become more populated on each one too. There are a few humans on 3, and a few million on 7. Any questions?" Sarah said. "With more humans, are there less magical creatures?" I asked. "Not yet, once we get to 8, you will see less magical creatures and less magic altogether" she replied. "Do the humans know? About magic?" I asked. "Some do, some don't," she told me. "Okay" I said. "If you don't have any more questions, you can take a break before time to train with David," Sarah said. I nodded.

I went to 'my' room and sat on the bed. I was worried about Jason and my other friends. I was worried the witches would hurt them to hurt me. I lay down on the bed just thinking, and I guess I drifted to sleep. I didn't dream. The next thing I knew, Sarah was shaking me saying that I was going to be late for my training. I sat up, "I'm sorry, I must have fallen asleep" I said. I got up and went outside to meet David.

He was standing out in the open today. "You did well yesterday, I think we should move on to something else" he said. "Have you ever studied karate or any other fighting style?" he asked. "No," I said, shaking my head. "Not even boxing at the gym?" he said surprised. "No, I just do strength and cardio at the gym," I replied. "Okay, we will work on boxing today" he said as he picked up some boxing gloves from the ground that I hadn't seen because the grass was so high. "Why do we train in such high grass?" I asked. "Witches can use spells to 'hide' so I figure any disadvantage or anything you aren't comfortable with will give you a better understanding of what a battle with a witch will be like" he said. "Okay, so you have thought of everything" I said with a little giggle. "Joking aside, I'm serious," he said, throwing the gloves at me. So we spent the next couple hours hitting each other. We both had black eyes and bruises when it was over. "I wanted this to happen" David said pointing to his eye. "I want Arturo to show you some healing spells today" he added, winking at me. "That sounds more exciting than learning about rocks," I said.

When Arturo walked up, David met him and told him to add the healing spell teaching in today so I could heal his eye. Arturo agreed that he would, after he taught me the different properties of different crystals and stones. I rolled my eyes and followed them inside. We ate a snack then headed to the basement. After an hour and a half of learning about stones Arturo looked at me and said, "Now, tell me which plant and which stone or stones you would use in a healing spell." Arturo said. "Ginger or Sandalwood and quartz or amethyst will work" I said. "Correct, now go pick them out," Arturo said, pointing at a table where many herbs and stones lay. I didn't have any problems picking them out, it was like I was a natural. "Very good, and I thought you weren't paying attention," Arturo said. "I wasn't really" I said, winking at him. "So, I am going to let you do the rest on your own, see how much of a 'natural' you really are" Arturo said. "Okay" I replied. I had the herb in one hand and the stone in the other. I sat down on the floor, Indian style and imagined the pain was gone, imagined that it never existed. I heard a gasp and looked at Arturo, he looked amazed, he also looked clear, not blurry. "What?" I asked. "I have never seen someone heal themselves like that" He stated, looking astonished. "So, it worked?" I asked. He laughed while saying "Yes, but why did you choose to heal yourself before David?" "It's not life threatening injuries and I figured I could heal him better if I was healed first" I replied. "You are absolutely correct" He said then turned to David and simply said "natural". I healed David the same way that I had healed myself and we headed upstairs for dinner.

Sarah had prepared a wonderful meal once again. Arturo didn't stay, he said that he needed to get home, so it was just David, Sarah and myself. "Arturo is *very* impressed with Gabby's magical abilities," David said, talking to Sarah. "I think she is learning everything very quickly," Sarah said. "Thanks," I said, blushing. "I'm just doing what I'm told, to be honest, everything is still really weird for me. I was taken from my world into a different world and I have magical powers because I'm a witch and I'm extra strong because I'm half giant. I'm still not sure that I'm not dreaming" I said laughing. "When we do send you back, it's important that you don't tell any of your friends what happened. I know that will be hard, but it's for their own good. If they know, they will become targets as well," David said. "How do we know that my enemies haven't already assumed that I *have* told them? Wouldn't that make them a target anyway? Just by association. And wouldn't they *need* to know if their lives may be in danger?" I asked. "You make a good point, but no, you are powerful enough that you can put protection spells on them, hide them from other witches," David said.

I was thinking about what David had said as I lay in bed that night and tried to sleep. I guess he was right, why drag innocent people into a battle that isn't theirs? I also knew that I wouldn't have to face it alone, then I started thinking about Jason and how Carly had used him to get to me, she could have killed him if she wanted. My heart broke at the thought of losing him or any of my friends. I started imagining that I was throwing protection over all of them, kind of like a blanket. Witches couldn't find them or hurt them, I drifted to sleep while I was still thinking about it.

I woke up to David shaking me, "What's wrong?" I asked after seeing worry in his face. "I yelled and you didn't wake up so I came in, and saw you like *this*!" He said, still worried. "What?" I said. I got up and walked to the mirror, my nose had apparently bled a *lot*. My face had a lot of dried blood on it. I had no idea why this had happened. "Have you ever had this happen before?" David asked, still looking concerned. I just shook my head silently, still looking at my reflection. "How do you feel?" David asked. "I'm just shocked," I answered. I looked back at the bed and there was a *lot* of blood on it. "Oh my *goodness*!" I said. "I am so sorry, I messed up your bed" I said, blushing from embarrassment even though you couldn't tell it because of all the dried blood still on my face. "Don't worry about that!" David said. Sarah finally heard all the commotion and came in to check on us. "Oh my! What happened?!" she said. "Not sure," David said, still showing concern. "She didn't wake up when I called out in the hall, so I came in and saw her covered in blood, she finally woke up after I started shaking her." he told Sarah. "I think I'm okay, I'm really sorry about the mess, I'm going to go clean up" I told them. They both looked at me and nodded silently.

After a shower and cleaning up, I joined them at the dining room table. They both looked up at me. "You look better, still feeling okay?" David asked. I nodded, but didn't say anything. I did feel tired, drained. But I wasn't sure I should say anything. "Do you think it was an attack?" I asked. "No, you are safe here. We have a lot of protection spells from several different witches on the place. The only ones that know that you are here are Arturo and Margo and I know they wouldn't tell anyone" David said. "Okay" I said. Not sure what else to say. "I asked Arturo to come earlier today, maybe he can figure out what is going on," David said. I nodded again, I started feeling dizzy so I sat down. "Are you sure you feel okay? You look a little paler than usual and you aren't speaking as much as you usually do" Sarah said. "I feel a little tired and slightly dizzy, but other than that, I feel fine," I said. David and Sarah looked at each other with concerned faces. "You did lose a lot of blood, maybe we should call a healer" Sarah suggested. Healing, I could do that myself, I had done it yesterday, so I excused myself and went downstairs to get the herb and crystal to do what I had done to heal my black eyes the day before. I did just as I had done the day before, with the herb in one hand and the stone in the other and sat down Indian style on the floor. I wasn't sure what I was healing, so I just imagined that I wasn't tired, or dizzy, and that's the last thing I remembered before I woke up back in the bed.

I opened my eyes, Arturo was there, sitting in a chair. He was reading a book and hadn't noticed that I was awake. I tried to raise up, but I didn't have the strength. "Hi" I said to get his attention. "Hello" he replied. I tried to raise my head again. "No, just rest" he said. "What's wrong with me?" I asked. "You have magic sickness" he said. "What does that mean?" I asked. "When a witch uses too much magic, it drains them, all you can do is recharge," he told me. "But, I don't understand *why* you have it. I am certain that's what it is though. All the symptoms you have are what happens, except normally, we just rest and recharge and get back to normal" he said. "It's like your magic is being used before it can recharge, like you are working an ongoing spell" he continued. "You have been out for two days," he said. "*What*?" I said, not believing him. "Yes, two days, and you appear to still be incredibly weak" he said. "Yeah, I feel like I can't even get up," I admitted. "And you tried to magically heal your magic, that made things worse obviously" he said. "I didn't know," I said. "That's right, you didn't, there is a *lot* that you still don't understand, and you shouldn't just go off and perform magic until you do" he scolded. "I'm sorry" I said. "You had to have done other magic besides what you did with my supervision to be in this shape, what did you do?" he demanded. "I didn't do any magic," I said.

I felt very weak and like I was getting weaker by the minute, and according to what I heard Arturo tell David I was right. "Magic is constantly and strongly running out of her, she *will* die if we can't stop it." "Is someone pulling it out of her?" David asked. "I don't think so, I think she has done some kind of magic and she's not telling us, until she does tell us, there is nothing I can do" Arturo said. Arturo came back into the room and saw that I was awake. "You heard what I said?" he asked me. I nodded my head. "I know you are weak, but please let me help you, tell me what you did" he said. I shrugged my shoulders, because I honestly didn't know. "What were you thinking about before you went to sleep, before you were sick?" he asked. It took me a few minutes to remember, "Protecting my friends" I managed to get out. "Of course! That's it! You cast a protection spell on people in a different dimension. That would *kill* a normal witch instantly, it's just taking more time on you. You have to call that magic back to you, I promise we have witches on 12 to watch after them, trusted allies and you will be back to help watch them in no time. So just imagine the magic you sent them coming back to you" Arturo said. I did, I imagined taking back what I said, what I had imagined, pulling the blanket back over myself until I passed out again.

I woke up feeling a lot better, it must have worked. I walked to the dining room but I didn't see anyone. I looked out the window, it looked like it was probably late afternoon/early evening. "David? Sarah?" I called out. Sarah came out of their bedroom. "Gabriela! You're up! How are you feeling?" She asked. "I feel a lot better," I said. "Arturo said that he was sure he found the problem and you would get well, we just waited, you slept for two more days, you must be starving" Sarah said. I nodded, I hadn't really noticed until she said something, but I guess I haven't eaten for four or five days, so it makes sense that I would be starving. "I'll start cooking, eat some fruit for now and I will get you some water also, have a seat" she said pointing to the table. David walked in from outside. "Wow, you're up!" he said to me. "Yeah, I said as I took a bite from an apple.

"Do you know how bad you scared us? Do you understand that you could have died? And if you weren't half giant, you would have *died*!" he scolded. "I do now, but I didn't cast the spell on purpose, I was just thinking about how vulnerable my friends are and I wanted to protect them" I said. "Don't think about it anymore, they are protected, I promise" David reassured me. "Okay" I said, now eating a banana. "I'm feeling better, a lot better, good enough to go kick your butt" I told him. "We'll see about that tomorrow. I want to give you at least a half of a day and night to recover fully. I might feel bad if I hurt you so soon after you being sick" he teased. "My enemies wouldn't care," I said. "No, they wouldn't, but I do, I will kick your butt tomorrow" he said. I shrugged my shoulders and kept eating.

Arturo came for dinner that night so he could observe how I was doing. "You have *got to be more careful* with your magic, anytime you think with intent or 'imagine' something, you are casting magic!" he scolded. "I'm sorry, I didn't know, I do now though" I told him. "Don't be too hard on her Arturo, I've already given her hell for it" David said. "I really didn't know," I said. "I know, and that's the problem. There is so much that you don't know and I only have a small amount of time to teach you a lifetime of knowledge" Arturo said. "Well, now I know what it feels like when I overuse my magic. How long did it take you to learn that?" I asked Arturo. "I've only seen it in others, I have never done it myself" he told me. "I feel like

I should have told you about the fact that you can't cast magic to other dimensions," he said. "Don't blame yourself," Sarah said. "We don't blame you, and I'm sure Gabby doesn't blame you," David told him. I shook my head, "of course not." After eating for an hour straight, I actually felt tired again. "Let's go for a walk before you go to bed again" David said. "It's not good for the body to have so little movement for so long," Sarah said. So David, Sarah and I went for a walk, Arturo went home seeming satisfied that I was going to be fine.

Walking around the property at dusk was beautiful. Both moons were high in the sky already. A tiny creature flew up to me and landed on my arm, it was a fairy! "Oh my gosh! It's a fairy!" I said to David and Sarah. They laughed at me. "Yeah, they're pretty cute," David said as one landed on the back of his hand. "Tell me about them!" I said. "What you see is what you get, sometimes they get in the house and that upsets them so they will take your stuff and hide it" Sarah told me. "Hmmm" I said. "That sounds like they are a little mean," I said. "Not mean, they don't like to be trapped inside anywhere, so hiding your stuff is their way of letting you know that they want to be let out" Sarah said. "Do they grant wishes?" I asked. "No, not that I know of," David said. "I think you are thinking of a djinn, and I'm sure if you have heard of them that you also know they are nothing to mess with, the 'wishes' they grant always come with a greater price" Sarah said. "Oh, yeah, I know," I said. The fairy flew away. "So fairies on 12 are fireflies?" I asked "Yes, because of the limited magic on 12, but some still want to live there, they appear as fireflies" Sarah said. "This was supposed to be a relaxing walk, not a lesson," David said. "We should go inside and get ready for bed, be prepared to jump back into teaching and learning tomorrow" Sarah suggested. David and I both nodded in agreement.

I didn't let my mind wander once I laid down. I didn't want to accidentally cast another spell and make myself sick again. I drifted to sleep fairly quickly, I started dreaming. I dreamed that I was back outside and the fairy came back to me. This time she spoke to me. "Hello" said the fairy. "Wow, you can talk?" I asked. "Only here," she said. I didn't understand what she meant by that but I nodded my head at her anyway. "Are you the very powerful witch that everyone is talking about?" she asked me. "Who is everyone?" I asked. "Everyone," she repeated. She made a motion with her arm as if there were an audience in front of us. "The whole world, the fairies, the shapeshifters, the mermaids, everyone" she explained. "Possibly" I said. "I have been told that I am more powerful than most, but I don't really feel like I am" I told her. "You are the daughter of Valery?" she asked. "Yes, Valery was my mother," I said. The fairy looked scared for a minute. "You will do good things with your power?" she asked. "I hope so, I don't want to do bad things," I said. She bent down and kissed my hand, looked satisfied with my answer and flew away.

I woke up to the familiar sound of David yelling through the hallway. I mumbled so he knew I was alive and awake. I put my feet on the floor and stretched, I noticed a pink dot on my hand, it was where the fairy had been in my dream. Looking closer I could see it was a tiny heart. I went to the dining room and showed Sarah and David. "They have not only given you their approval, but also their protection" Sarah said. "What does that mean?" I asked. "Fairy magic is hard to explain, personally, I've never seen it so I really don't know what to tell you" Sarah said. David shook his head to let me know that he didn't have an answer for me either, "ask Arturo this evening," he said.

"While we are on the subject of dreams and marks from them, remember at the dinner when you asked about the bruise on my arm?" I said to David. "Yes, are you saying it was from a *dream?*" he asked. I nodded my head and told him about the dream and the woman that grabbed me. "I wonder" he said mostly to himself.

"Wonder *what?*" I asked. "You seem to somehow have a connection to a ghost dimension, the dream realm or whatever you want to call it. It's like you exist there in the flesh where the rest of us only go in our astral forms" David said. "What?" I asked, still confused. "Again I'll have to refer you to Arturo on this one, I don't know how to give you answers when I don't understand it myself" David said. "Not to change the subject, but my brother, James will be here tomorrow. He can help with the physical training and you will have a week to get to know him before you both go to 12" David said. "A week?" I asked, confused. "Yes, you were out of it for four days, remember?" David said. "Oh, it's strange, I just lost those days I guess" I said. "Well, we need to not waste anymore time and get to work," Sarah said.

"We can jump right into today's lesson. You remember everything so far?" Sarah said. I nodded, not understanding how I would know if I forgot. "We are in realm/dimension 8. On 8 the magic is still the same but starting to get weaker. 8 is the last dimension you will see a phoenix" Sarah explained. "A phoenix? Like in Arizona?" I asked, confused. "You've never heard of a phoenix?" she asked, surprised. I shrugged my shoulders to let her know that I had not heard of whatever she was talking about. "A phoenix is a birdlike creature, human sized, walks upright like a human. There are only a handful of them, they do not reproduce, but they cannot be exterminated." She told me. I gave her a confused look, "so it can't die? Is it considered good or bad?" I asked. "It can die, when it dies, it bursts into flames and then rises from its ashes. And good or bad, I guess it depends on who you ask and which one you meet, just like humans or any other conscious being" Sarah said. "Do you know a phoenix?" I asked. "No, I'm not sure anyone can 'know' a phoenix," she said. "Oh" I said, nodding that I understood. "And we aren't sure what has happened to them, they haven't been seen in a long time," she added.

David did not take it 'easy' on me in physical training, he wanted to 'make up for lost time.' He was teaching different fighting styles, kicks, punches, slides and jumps. "How do you know all this?" I asked while dodging a swing kick. "I learned as a child, with the lesson that all of the realms are cruel in some way and you need to know how to defend yourself" he said as he barely dodged a punch from me, he smiled at how close I came. "Tomorrow, we will start incorporating magic into your fighting," he said. "Might be a good idea, since I will be defending myself against people using it" I agreed as I landed a kick to his midsection. He let out a small moan of pain. "Are you okay?!" I said as I went closer to check on him, he kicked my feet from under me. "Never show mercy, it's a weakness when in battle" he stated. "Noted" I said as I tried to suck the air back into me that was knocked out by the fall. He helped me up and pointed, I looked where he pointed, it was Arturo walking up. "That time already?" I asked. "Time flies when you're having fun," David said, shrugging his shoulders.

I met Arturo in the basement, seeing how magic almost killed me. I was a little nervous and I think he could tell. "The more you understand magic, the less it can hurt you," Arturo said. I nodded in agreement with him. He taught me how to 'hover' in midair, he taught me to freeze things in time. I practiced that with a pet mouse he had brought. He also taught me to disintegrate plants. "I have some questions about some things that have happened that I think are magical," I said. "Okay," he said, sitting down. I told him about the dreams where I carry marks with me from them. "It is rare indeed, so rare that I have never known anyone that could do it, I *have* heard of it though" he explained. "The woman could have possibly been your mother," he added. Then I told him about the flowers that smelled of rotting flesh when they died. "Someone sent you a corpse flower, it was a threat" he told me. "Oh" I said surprised. "It was a few days before my birthday, so I thought it was a gift," I said with a giggle. "Now that you know a little more, how are you feeling about magic?" he asked. "I don't know how to 'feel' about it, I mean, it's turned my life upside down, it's forcing me to learn to defend myself against my would be killers. How would you feel if you were me?" I asked him. "I'm not sure, because I don't understand how it is. I grew up learning magic and 'knowing' that it is real" he said. I nodded at him. "And I don't know what that is like," I said.

Dinner was relatively quiet tonight. I think everyone was tired. Sarah had found a book about different creatures and the different dimensions that she gave to me. "You can study it now if you like, but take it home with you when you go," she said. "Thank you," I said. "Will I be able to come back and visit? Meet your baby?" I asked. "Yes, you will learn the spell to travel dimensions" David said. I smiled, I was becoming quite attached to them. They were a real, loving family, something that I had always craved.

Four

Training with James

After dinner, I went to my room and looked through the book that Sarah had given me. A few things I noticed in the book that we hadn't talked about yet were mermaids and unicorns. According to the book, unicorns were almost extinct and expected to be so within the next twenty years. I looked at the book's publish date, it was twenty-five years ago. I wonder if they were all gone now? And mermaids were not beautiful friendly creatures, they were horrid monsters that dragged people down to the depths of the ocean to their deaths. I drifted to a dreamless sleep.

I woke the next morning the same way, with David yelling down the hall that it was time to get up. I walked to the dining room, breakfast was waiting, as usual. "Good morning," I said. "Good morning" David and Sarah both replied. "So, what's on the agenda today?" I asked. "Same as everyday," Sarah replied. "James should be here this afternoon," David said. I looked at him and nodded in acknowledgement. "So, how are we gonna do that? Am I gonna have two super big, tall guys attacking me? Because that doesn't seem fair at all." I said jokingly. "You do need to know how to react in an ambush," David said. "I handled it pretty well the very first day, didn't I?" I said, referring to when he had Margo attack me. "What are you teaching today?" David asked Sarah. "9 and Gremlins" she answered. David and I exchanged a look and then started laughing. It felt nice to laugh, I couldn't remember the last time that I had a good laugh.

"Okay, let's get started then" Sarah said, with a little giggle in her voice as well. "Okay, so on 9, the magic diminishes a little more, as you know it does in each dimension" she began. "9 is the last place you will see gremlins," she continued. "Like Gizmo?" I asked. "I don't know a Gizmo, and I doubt that you know any gremlins," she said, rolling her eyes. "Did you just roll your eyes at *me*?" I said sarcastically. We both giggled about it. "What is a gremlin then?" I asked. "A gremlin is a small creature, some would describe them as an evil cousin of a fairy" she explained. "Gremlins will mess with your electrical devices and wreak havoc on your life, they are straight up pests" She continued. "Then what is the reason for keeping them around?" I asked. "They were being exterminated. However, we also noticed a decline in the fairy population along with theirs, so the theory is that each of their lives is connected to a fairy counterpart. So we were forced to stop killing them." She said. "That's horrible," I said. Then we heard a commotion outside, she looked at me and said, "James must be here."

We went outside, sure enough, David was 'play fighting' like a child with another man. They stopped when they realized they had an audience. They started walking toward us. James was probably 6'7, his skin was darker, they must be half siblings and James' mother must have been a darker skinned woman. His body was sculpted perfectly, his black, curly hair was long, down to his mid back. He had a beard on his chin that met with his mustache. His eyes were very dark brown, almost black, he looked my age, maybe a year or two older. And I thought he was very handsome. "Gabriela, this is my brother, James" David said, "James, this is Gabriela" he continued. I nodded my head, I could feel my face turning red. "I thought she was half giant?" James said to David. "Her mom did a spell to stunt her growth to help hide her," David said. "Okay, let's get started with the training," James said.

We went out to the field where we always trained. "I'll let you two have a go at it, so you can see what I've taught her" David said. James dropped and did a round kick and swept my feet from under me. He just looked at David, and then at me and said "well that was easy." I put my arms behind me and sprung up, he may be cute, but his cockiness was starting to make me mad. I used magic to jump high, hover for a second, then kicked him so hard in the chest that he lost his breath. I landed back on the ground and did my own drop down sweep kick and knocked him to the ground. I heard David laugh behind us. James lay on the ground for a few seconds, "okay" he said, then rolled over and jumped back up. We went back and forth until it was time for my magic lesson with Arturo.

The magical lesson today was fun, I learned to make objects float or call them to me. Arturo also taught me a spell to hear others' thoughts, but advised me not to use it unless I was unsure if someone was friend or foe. David and James stepped into the basement when we were about halfway done. I showed them that I could 'pick up' a pencil from across the room and make it come to me. We continued the lesson with them observing quietly in the back. I learned more healing components and a spell to astral project. "Astral projection can be used to get a quick message to someone in a different dimension without physically going to them," Arturo said. "Okay" I said. "That's about all for today, just keep practicing everything that you have learned so far," Arturo said. "Okay" I said.

Dinner was interesting, it was basically Sarah and I sitting quietly, listening while David and James caught up. "I went to 11, where

I helped seal a demon in a cave, he kept trying to find a way to get into 12" James said. "Wow, who sealed him away?" David asked. "Witches from the RavenStar coven" James said. "Do they know why he was trying to get into 12?" David asked. "Not a hundred percent sure, but we think to get to.." James said, pointing to me. "What?" I asked. "Demons can't exist after 11, so the fact that he was trying to get to 12 and possibly vanquish himself in the process, we believe that he was offered something of great value or importance to bring you back" James said. I was starting to get the feeling that James was not very fond of me. "So, what would happen if demons did manage to get to 12 and not die?" I asked. "It would be a constant battle, trying to protect innocent humans and yourself," James told me. I nodded that I understood. "You mentioned a coven, what coven am I from?" I asked. "You are from the Stone coven, and Stone is the last name you were born with. Your mother couldn't let you use it because then it would be too obvious as to who you were" David said. "Yeah, I've always thought my last name was Mason," I said, looking down. It was a small thing I suppose, but just now learning my real last name after twenty one years was a little depressing.

I was thinking about my name, saying it out loud, Gabriela Stone, I did like the sound of it better than Gabriela Mason. "There aren't too many left in the Stone coven, in fact if there are any besides you, they are hiding" David Said. "Raven Star and Earth covens are the only ones we know for sure are our allies, they have proven themselves to us time and time again" James said. "Known enemies of ours are Serenity, Moon, Circle, Star and Forest Moonrise Covens" Sarah said. "And other covens that we don't know where they stand are Hearthstone, Polaris, Evergreen, Sun, and Desert Moonrise" David said. "That's a lot of covens to try to remember, not to mention remembering who is friend and who is enemy and who is somewhere in between" I said. "It is a lot, but I have no doubt in my mind that you will know by the time you leave" David said. "Speaking of that, we moved you out of your apartment, your cats and everything that you need has been moved to a country house twenty minutes away. Someone knew where you lived, Arturo told me about the flowers. The house is a big country house that belongs to the Stone coven, there has been no one in it for at least five years. I found the deed, it is in your name now. Gabriela Stone, and there are fifteen bedrooms so it will be plenty of space so the two of you can have your personal space" David said.

"*The two of us?*" I asked. "I told you that James is going back with you, how can he protect you or help you if he isn't with you?" David said. "I didn't realize I would have to *live* with him," I said. James was standing there through the conversation, he was looking at me like it was the last thing he wanted to do. "Margo is also asking to go, she won't be able to be in her human form and even though the house is in the country and surrounded by woods, I'm still worried that she will be seen. A black panther being seen in those woods would alert humans, they would hunt her down, and that is something that neither of us could live with" Sarah told me. "I could do a shielding spell, keep her hidden, if she really wants to go, right?" I asked. "Possibly, but are you willing to bet her life on it?" David asked. "No, you're right," I said.

"I'm tired, I think I will go to bed, I'll see everyone tomorrow," I said. "Good night" Sarah and David both said, James ignored me. Laying in bed, I thought about how *hot* James was and also how much he disliked me and I wondered why, because he didn't even know me. Before I was about to fall asleep, I felt like I needed to use the restroom, I guess I drank too much water. I opened my door to go and I heard David and James speaking to each other in low voices, I crept up the hall quietly to get closer so I could hear what they were saying. "I'm happy that you have a family now," James said. "I know it's a lot to ask of you, and you don't know how happy it makes me that you are willing to help" David said. "Yeah, just call me the brat sitter," James said. I crept back down the hall after that, and went to the restroom and back to bed where I cried myself to sleep.

The next morning, David yelled down the hallway just like he did every morning. I stumbled out of bed to go to the dining room, I passed James in the hall, he bumped into me. "Ouch" I said. "That didn't hurt," he said. "Why do you hate me so much? You don't even know me" I said. "He's just upset that you kicked his butt yesterday," David said. I gave James the evil eye and looked at David and smiled and said, "I look forward to doing it again today too." David smiled back at me. Everyone was quiet at the table today. I didn't feel very hungry, so I just nibbled on a biscuit and gravy. "Well, you could cut the tension in this room with a knife," Sarah said. I just looked at her and half smiled. "Okay then, we might as well get started," she said.

"After we are finished with dimensions, David wants me to work with you on the Covens" Sarah said. "Okay" I agreed. "Today, we will talk about 10. 10 is the last place you can find mermaids. Did you read the book I gave you? Or at least look through it?" she asked. I nodded, "I did read about the mermaids, they seem like lovely creatures" I said grinning sarcastically. "Well, as horrid as they are, they do serve a purpose, witches can 'borrow' their power so they can breathe underwater" Sarah said. "That's interesting, but why would I need to do that?" I asked. "Underwater is a great hiding place, if need be," she said. "You can cast protection, and cloaking spells all day long, but remember the ones that you are up against can cast spells as well" she said. I hadn't thought about that, she was right, no matter how 'good' I am, they can use magic against me too. "I really hadn't thought about that," I admitted. "I know, and that's partly our fault for not making you think about it" Sarah said apologetically. "It's okay, I should have a little common sense," I said, smiling at her. "It's time to go meet the guys outside," she said. I rolled my eyes and said "yay" sarcastically.

I walked outside prepared for an ambush. I was right, David lunged at me from the left and I froze him in midair with my left hand while James came at me from the right and I froze him with my right hand. I let David down slowly while I continued to hold James up. "It doesn't feel pleasant," David said. "Good," I replied. "Please let him down," he said. "Fine" I said and let him drop to the ground. "Ouch," James said. "That hurt, I think she's getting too cocky," he said to David. "I think you may be right," David said back. They said they wouldn't ambush me anymore if I promised not to use magic, just regular fight techniques. I agreed to play fair as long as they did. I still managed to black James' eye, it made me feel good. "You look like you enjoy that too much, it's gonna be hard for me to send my brother with you if you want to hurt him all the time" David said. "I'll heal him," I said with a smirk.

Arturo walked up, he was ready to do magical training. "I have to heal the jerk," I said. "Oh, okay then" Arturo said with his eyes open wide in surprise. "I thought you two would get along," Arturo said. "Nah, he decided to not like me for no reason, so I act accordingly" I said. James rolled his eyes, he knew it was true. "You may want to start playing nice, I don't think you want her for an enemy" David said to James. I rolled my eyes, to let them know I could hear them and I didn't care. After I healed James' eye, they left Arturo and I in the basement alone. "Sarah told me that witches can 'borrow' magic from mermaids. Can we do that with other creatures?" I asked. "We can, but we have to be careful, other creatures' magic is not meant for us, it's meant for them. It can either be too much for us, or not enough" Arturo explained. "So, if I wanted to be small and fly, could I borrow a fairy's magic?" I asked. "Good example, it would kill the fairy and you would only have the power for a very small amount of time" he said. "Oh, I don't want to kill anyone," I said. "I know you don't, that's why I'm glad you asked before you experimented on your own" he said. "What if I have questions when I am back on 12? Can I contact you?" I asked. "It's best that we keep our contact to a minimum, the spell for interdimensional travel is very complex" he explained. "Okay, but what if I really need to know something?" I asked. "When you have a question, write it down so you don't forget, you can come see me occasionally" he said. I smiled at him. I smelled dinner and my stomach rumbled because I hadn't eaten much today.

I walked up the stairs to the dining room, Sarah, David, and James were sitting at the table. I asked Arturo if he was staying for dinner, he said, no, that he had to get home. "Good evening everyone," I said. "Good evening. You seem to be in a good mood" David said. "I am not really sure why though," I replied. "Maybe the calming spell that I told Arturo to put on you is working," David said. "Why would you do that?" I asked. "On both of you" he said looking at James and then to me. "So we could have a peaceful dinner," he continued laughing. "You don't need to put a spell on me, you can just talk to me if you feel that my behavior is out of hand" I said. He could tell that I would be upset when the spell rubbed off, so he just cleared his throat and changed the subject. I noticed that James wasn't saying anything at all, his spell must have been stronger, or he couldn't take magic as well as I could. "I'm going to head to bed, I think," I said. "Good idea, we only have four more days of training," Sarah said. "I thought we had five?" I said, confused. "We are just going to use the last day for saying goodbye, maybe showing you around some more," David said. I smiled and nodded my head "okay."

Lying in bed I was thinking of how different my life would be when I went back. I had a secret that I couldn't tell my friends. I'm going to have this incredibly sexy guy by my side all the time, but he's not my boyfriend, this is going to be very complicated. I drifted off to sleep. James and I were in a room, the room seemed empty and dark, we were wearing ballroom clothes. He pulled me close to him, music started playing and he started swaying with me. We were dancing. I was aware that this wasn't real, but I was having a good time anyway. When the song ended, he kissed me and said, "you are mine now." "I don't belong to anyone," I told him. I heard people cheering in the background, I looked back at James, there was now an altar behind us, I looked down, I was wearing a wedding dress! "No!" I screamed, then I woke up.

I lay in bed for a few minutes terrified. It wasn't long before I heard David calling down the hall that it was time to wake up. I walked to the dining room like a zombie. "Rough night?" I heard from behind me. It was James, I felt my face turning red. He was shirtless, his body was so perfect and beautiful. If only he weren't such a jerk, he would be absolutely perfect. "I had a nightmare" I told him as I continued to the dining room. "Good morning," Sarah said in a chipper voice. "Morning" I mumbled. "Someone wake up on the wrong side of the bed?" David asked. I shook my head, "just a bad dream" I said. "What kind of bad dream? Do you have any marks or bruises?" He asked. I shook my head, "no, just a 'normal' nightmare." James walked in, "well, I had a wonderful dream last night, I am in a great mood today" he said. I looked at him and he actually smiled at me. *Could he have had the same dream?* I felt my face get hot again. "Well, time to get the day started," Sarah said.

"Dimension 11 is the last place you will find a demon," Sarah said. "What exactly is a demon?" I asked. "Whether or not you believe in the Christian religion, their bible is the closest explanation of angels and demons. You and I, and David and James all are part angels." Sarah said. "Demons want to make everything evil, like themselves. They can haunt, and possess people and areas." She explained. "I'm not sure if Hell exists, but demons believe that they are superior species and that they should be worshiped. Once a demon fell in love with a witch and had a child with that witch, that child later became the first vampire. And this is why interspecies mating is illegal and why they want you dead" she told me. "Seems unfair that I am being hunted just because of who my parents are, I wouldn't hurt anyone" I said. "Seth would never have either, that is his name, Seth.

He was a normal child, although he was allergic to the sun. On his fortieth birthday, he was shot, his mother who was very old now, was watching him bleed out in front of her. She called out for Sammael, his father, even though she hadn't seen him in thirty years. He appeared, looking the same as he had thirty years ago. Wanda, the mother, 'borrowed' power from him to do a spell to heal Seth. The spell turned him into a vampire." Sarah told me. "Soon, he killed everyone around him. After he was caught, he was studied. His blood had healing properties not only for him, but anyone who drank it could heal, even from a mortal wound. Then by accident, someone that had used the blood to heal, died. A few hours later they woke up, the same as him. He helped Seth escape and together, they made more, hundreds before they were caught. They made a deal to supply blood for healing in exchange for their own dimension. So now, as you know, all the vampires are on 1." Sarah said.

"Wow, that's a crazy story," I said. "Crazy, but true," Sarah said. "Are demons immortal?" I asked. "Yes, as are angels," she answered. "I don't understand why people fear what I would become, I am not a demon, I am an angel" I said. "Either way, it is unknown what you could become, people fear what they do not understand, plus, it is against the magical laws for you to exist," she explained. "I think I should head out to kick the guy's butts now" I said smiling. She nodded, "what was your dream about by the way?" she asked. "I don't want to talk about it, I don't think it was magical, just a regular nightmare" I said.

I walked outside, the guys were standing in plain view, I guess they were tired of trying to catch me by surprise and getting their butts kicked. We just worked on normal fighting without magic. I still managed to put them both on the ground several times, I ended up on the ground a couple times myself. After a couple hours of this we called it quits and saw Arturo walking up to the house. "Have fun in your magic lessons today," James said. I looked at him and turned to walk away. "Hey, look, can I talk to you for a minute?" He asked. I stopped and turned around, David kept walking toward the house. I didn't want to be alone with him, even though I knew we would be living together soon. "What?" I asked him. "I'm sorry I have been so rude to you, it's just that, I had a simple life that I enjoyed, and then David calls me up one day and says basically that he needs me to go babysit some girl on 12 that I don't even know. And then when I saw you, and you were *you*, I didn't know how to act, I'm really sorry for the way I have been treating you" James said. "What do you mean by I was *me*?" I asked, feeling my face get hot. He gave me a smile that let me know that he wasn't going to answer my question and I would have to figure it out on my own. I wasn't sure if I liked this version of him. I wasn't sure it was genuine and I don't like fake people. We walked toward the house together in silence.

My lesson with Arturo was simple, thankfully, we just practiced what I had already learned and it came natural to me. I was thankful that it was simple because I wasn't sure I would be able to concentrate on learning new things. All I could think about was James being *nice* to me. How dare he act the way he has, then start being nice all of a sudden. And why did he have to look so damn perfect? I was starting to really dislike him for his mind games. I was getting angry, I accidentally shattered a jar that was on the shelf. "What are you doing?!" Arturo yelled at me. "I'm sorry! I'm just having a hard time concentrating today" I said. "Let's call it a day then" he said. I nodded in agreement, "I can try if you want me to" I said in a pouty voice. "No, we don't need you blowing up the house," he said. I nodded again and made a pouty face. I could smell dinner cooking, but I wasn't sure I wanted to eat.

I went to the dining room just so David and Sarah wouldn't worry about me. I really didn't feel like eating. I grabbed a roll and said, "do you guys mind if I just take this and go for a walk? I feel like being alone right now." "Are you okay?" Sarah asked. James, who had also been sitting there when I walked in, just looked at me. "Oh yeah, I'm fine, I'm just not very hungry and I would really enjoy a walk and being alone at the moment" I assured her. David nodded his head at me. "Okay, be careful, our property is cloaked but you never know what's out there, and be sure not to venture off the property" Sarah said. "Okay, thank you" I said, holding up the roll.

I walked out of the door, I had butterflies in my stomach, this was the first time I had been alone while I was here. I also had the feeling that I would be followed, so I hid behind a nearby bush and waited. Sure enough, David and James came to the front door. "This is your practice," David said to James. James nodded at him then left the house to look for me. Once he was out of sight, I came out from behind the bush, I cast a spell to enhance my hearing so I could hear him if he got close, so I could hide again. It felt like I was playing a game of hide and seek. I walked until I came to a body of water, it was a lake. I hadn't known it was here, the air felt warm so I took my shoes off and stepped into the water, it felt cool on my feet and ankles. I decided to go further in, up to my knees. I felt something brush against my leg and looked down. The water was murky, but I could see that it was some sort of fish. I tried to catch it, but couldn't. I could have used magic to catch it, but I felt like that would not have been fair. "Gabriela!" I heard James yelling from the wooded area nearby. I still did not want to see him, so I got out of the water and put my shoes on and headed back toward the house.

David and Sarah were waiting when I entered the house. "Did you happen to see James out there? He went for a walk shortly after you did" David said. I shook my head, "no, I didn't see him" I said. David looked at me sideways like he thought I was lying. "I didn't see him on purpose," I added with a smile. Shortly after James walked in, he seemed surprised to see me there, "I'm going to bed, I'll see everyone tomorrow" I said. I went to my room and got comfortable in bed. I could see both moons through my window, there were times when I still wondered if all this was a dream. I lay in bed thinking about the day, trying not to think about James. I drifted into a dreamless sleep.

I woke the next morning to David yelling that it was time to get up, just like always. I stumbled out of bed and went toward the dining room. James stopped me in the hallway, "I can't protect you, if you won't let me. David told me that you avoided me on purpose last night" he said. I nodded my head at him in agreement, "I don't always need someone, sometimes I just want to be alone" I said. "I understand that, but if anything happens to you, I would never be able to forgive myself" he said. "If I ever need you, I'm sure you will be there" I said to him, to get him out of my way, I was actually hungry this morning since I didn't really eat much last night. My stomach made a loud rumble to let him know this also and he moved out of my way so I could go to the dining room.

"Where did you go on your walk last night?" Sarah asked. "I walked to the lake, I waded through the water for a little while," I said. "You *what*?! David yelled. "I taught you about the mermaids! How could you be so careless?" Sarah asked, sounding disappointed. "I'm sorry, I just put my feet in the water, I didn't hear or see anything besides a small fish" I said. I saw James roll his eyes from across the table. "Gabby! Mermaids are heartless, the fish was probably a pet of theirs, a tool for them to get you to come out further" David said. "I am fine, I never felt like I was in any danger, besides, I could hear James nearby, so if I would have needed help, I'm sure he would have been there in no time at all" I said. "Please don't forget what you have learned, where you are, there are dangerous creatures here that don't exist where you live" Sarah said. I nodded my head in agreement, "I'm sorry" I said again. "We'll see you outside in a little while" David said, as him and James got up and walked out, I'm sure to talk about me and how dumb I am and how James is *really* going to have to stick to me like glue to keep me safe.

"I still can't believe you got in the water by yourself," Sarah said. "I said I'm sorry, what else do you want from me?" I asked. "I want you to realize the danger you were in, I want you to understand that it would absolutely devastated David and myself if something bad were to happen to you" she said. I nodded, "I feel horrible, I am really sorry" I said. She nodded at me and hugged me. "Okay, I guess we should get started on today's lesson," she said. "Since you are from 12, you know how it works for the most part, and now you understand that there are witches with magical powers there. That is the only magic in that dimension. Magic will work a little differently on different dimensions as well, you will have to practice once you are back there to get the right feel for it." She explained. I nodded my head to let her know that I understood her. "And on 13, there is no magic at all, if you go there, you won't be able to use magic. We have to be sure to leave a portal open to return when we go because we will not be able to open a portal from there." She explained. "And we take people and animals from there to feed the vampires," I said in disgust. "It is a necessary evil," Sarah said in a sad voice.

After my lesson with Sarah, I went outside to fight with the boys for a while, instead, Arturo was there. He said I needed to learn to fight someone with magic, since that's mostly what would be attacking me. He attacked me with spells that hurt when they hit, so I learned his pattern quickly and used defense spells. David and

James watched from the sidelines, I got hit in the head with a spell that put me flat on my back. James was standing over me in no time, "are you okay? Your head is bleeding!" "She's fine, if you can't stay on the sidelines, then please go inside." Arturo said. "We should be training together, that's how it will be, us fighting together" James said. He helped me up. "No, she will not always be with you, and this is why she is learning to fight," Arturo argued. "James, come on, just let him teach" David said, waving James back over. Arturo then began blasting me with spells again, it took me a minute, but I figured out his pattern again and quickly started blocking the spells. "Blocking me isn't going to stop me, you have to fire an offense with your defense," Arturo said. It took me another minute, but I figured out how to do that as well. Arturo seemed happy with the lesson today. "I'll meet you in the basement for some healing," he said.

I walked toward the house, when I looked back, Arturo was talking to James and David. When Arturo got to the basement, we healed each other's wounds. "I was told about your trip to the lake" Arturo said. "I want you to do something, it's complicated magic, but I'm sure you will do it with ease" he continued. "What?" I asked. "You said that a fish rubbed up against your leg?" he asked. I nodded, "yes." "I want you to visualize that you are that fish" he said. I nodded, closed my eyes and imagined I was the fish in the lake. "Are you doing it?" Arturo asked. I nodded my head. "What do you see?" he asked. "I see feet and legs, mine, I assume" I said. "I swam to them, they smell good, I want to take a bite, I touched them as I swam by. The legs left the water" I said. "Stay there, stay with the fish. What are you doing now?" Arturo asked. "I'm swimming back out into the deep, it's getting darker, I'm going down further, there seems to be a light down there. It's a merperson, it's green, but it has a humanoid top with a fishlike tail." I said. "Stay with the fish" Arturo said. "The merperson just grabbed me, it smelled me and its eyes got big" I said. "Can you read its thoughts?" Arturo asked. I nodded, “it smelled me, now it wants me” I said, leaving the spell. I was scared, “I’ve really messed up, haven’t I?” I said. “That mermaid can’t go to other bodies of water, thank goodness, but, if I were you, I wouldn’t go into that water again” Arturo said. I smelled dinner and my stomach growled. I nodded at Arturo, “I won’t.”

I went upstairs to the dining room, Arturo left, I sat down at the furthest chair from James. I smiled at David and Sarah and started eating. “A girl could get fat here” I said, smiling at Sarah. “So could a guy,” David said, laughing. “What did you learn today?” David asked. I really didn’t want to tell him, I didn’t want to get yelled at again, but I figured that if I didn’t tell him that Arturo would, then he would be more mad at me for withholding information. “Oh not too much, just that the merpeople got my scent and now they want me” I said casually. “*What?!*” James said, “How did you learn *that*?” he continued. “A spell, I guess I got into the fish’s head and the merperson's head” I tried to explain. Sarah and David just sat there, looking somewhere in between astonished and terrified. “What? They can’t get to me if I don’t go into the water, right?” I asked. “They have been known to lure people in their sleep, by getting into their dreams.” Sarah said. “You will need to do a dream protection spell before you go to sleep, and we will also put alarms up, just in case you go sleep walking. I will also call Margo and see if she wants to help keep watch” David said. “I don’t think you need to bother her, " I said. “I’m not going to force her to do anything, she’s a night cat anyway” David said, winking at me. I nodded, I may as well accept help if people want to give it to me.

That night, while laying in bed I did a spell, to keep others out of my dreams. Then I lay there in bed for a while, I heard bells, guessing that it was the alarms they were setting up in case I went sleepwalking to my death. How did my life get to this? I have a merperson that wants to eat me, who has ever said that before? I felt like my life wasn’t my own anymore, I didn’t like feeling out of control. Then I started thinking about James. I really wanted to ask him what his deal was, first he was mean and rude to me, now he was acting nice, but like he owned me or something. He confused me so much, I couldn't help the fact that I was extremely physically attracted to him.

At some point I drifted to sleep. I started dreaming of being out in the field under the two moon's light. I turned around and James was there. "I'm not supposed to have feelings for you," he said. "Why?" I asked. "I am supposed to protect you, watch you, but not become personally involved" he said. "The first time I saw you, you were so beautiful, I knew it would be hard, so I was mean to you, I figured if you hated me, you wouldn't want me anyway" he said. I heard a voice coming from the lake, "do you hear that?" I asked. "Hear what?" he replied. I got up to walk closer, so I could hear better. It was a ghostly voice "I just need to talk to you, it's important" it said. "I don't think you should listen to it," James said. I didn't like him this way, he seemed weak and vulnerable. I woke up to the sound of David yelling down the hallway.

I put my feet on the floor, then I realized they were covered in mud and I started screaming. David and James ran into my room, "What is it?! What's wrong?!" they said. "I had a dream that I was out in the field, and the merperson was calling to me and when I woke up, my feet were covered in mud" I said, trying to stay calm, but it clearly wasn't working. "The alarms didn't go off, Margo didn't see you leave your room, I don't understand how this could have happened" David said. "I don't know either, that's why I'm scared right now" I said. "Get cleaned up, and come to breakfast, I'll call Arturo and see if he has any ideas on what happened" David said. James stood there looking at me. "What?" I asked. "Nothing," he answered.

I did what David said, I cleaned up then went to the dining room. Margo was there. "David told me what happened, it's not possible, I was in the field all night" She said. "Did you take a nap at all?" I asked. "No, and even if I did, the slightest sound would have woken me," she said. David came into the room and sat down. "Arturo has suggested restraints or a cage, some way to know for sure that you don't get out" he said. "I'm telling you, she was not outside last night," Margo said. "How do you explain it then?" David asked her. "I can't, the same as you can't, but I know that she was not outside" Margo said. "We could take shifts tonight, watching her to make sure she doesn't sleepwalk," James said. "That's not creepy at all," I said sarcastically. "We are all just trying to keep you safe," Sarah said. "I realize that. I am super freaked out by all this, and don't forget that I am still new to *all* of this" I said.

After breakfast, we decided to continue the day as planned since today and tomorrow would be my last days to learn, and I hadn't learned much about the covens. "You know that the Stone coven is your coven, you may or may not be the last, River is the name of the last known high priestess, it is unknown if she is still alive, if she is dead, you would then be the high priestess of the coven." Sarah said. "What does that mean?" I asked. "To be high priestess of the coven? It means that you are the leader of your people, you make the important decisions for the coven. But if you are the only one, it doesn't really mean much" She said. I nodded in agreement. "Forest Moonrise coven is a known enemy, their high priest's name is Parker. Parker decided to make enemies, not friends with almost every other coven and creature, no one is sure of his motives" Sarah said. "And I will tell Arturo to help with learning the covens as well, we have run out of time, the guys are waiting" Sarah said.

I looked out the window and she was right, they were waiting. I went out to join them. They didn't attack straight away, they told me they had been looking for my footprints in the field, but found nothing. "It's a mystery we may never solve" I said, half jokingly, half serious. We started with the training, it felt like James was holding back a lot, I didn't hold back with him. David wasn't holding back, he enjoyed the training, I could tell, his child would grow up to be a great warrior. I couldn't figure James out, I couldn't tell if he hated me or if he liked me and that was very frustrating. At least I could beat him up to help get rid of some of the frustration. I hadn't realized how hard I hit him, his nose shattered, blood started pouring out. "Oh!" I yelled. "I'm sorry, I didn't mean to do that! Come on, I'll fix it!" I said, grabbing his arm and pulling him toward the house. David followed, not saying anything. I guess he had trust in me to fix it. When we got to the house, I pulled James to the basement, Arturo wasn't there yet. I picked up the items I needed to pull energy from to heal him. It didn't take very long. After I healed him, I grabbed a clean towel and put witch hazel on it to clean the dried blood off his face. As I was cleaning him, I noticed how beautiful he was again, he looked innocent, he grabbed the hand I was using to clean him gently and pulled it back. He just looked at me for a minute, "thank you" he said. Then he got up and went upstairs, I sat down on the floor.

Arturo started coming down the stairs after a few minutes. "Sarah told me you need to learn covens today and tomorrow because we are out of time," he said. I nodded. "Are you okay?" he asked. "Yeah" I said, not really sure if I was. "Okay, let's get started then" he said. "Desert Moonrise coven, it is unknown where they stand, because they don't usually get involved with the rest of the magical community. Leticia is their high priestess" he said. I nodded. "Star coven is however, a known enemy, Vance is their high priest. And Earth coven is a friend, Hale is their high priest, he is only about an hour away from where you will be staying when you go back, so he is someone you could also go to if you have immediate questions" Arturo said. "Okay" I said. I smelled dinner and right on que, my stomach growled.

We went up the stairs together. Arturo said goodbye and that he couldn't stay, before he left. James, David and Sarah were at the table. "Good evening, I am starving," I said. "Good evening," David said. "It's not uncommon to be really hungry after performing magic, not to mention the physical activity" David said, with a little laugh. I rolled my eyes at him. "I'm going to miss that," he said. "I am going to miss having you here, I'm going to cry when you leave, " Sarah said, looking like she was about to cry. "I still have a couple more days, don't cry now please, you will make me cry" I said. James, looking upset, got up from the table and went outside. "What's wrong with him?" I asked. "I'm not sure, I'll go talk to him" David said, as he got up to follow him. I looked at Sarah and shrugged my shoulders, she just looked down and started eating again. The guys weren't coming back inside, so I went out to find them, to see if they had a special plan for my 'sleepwalking' tonight.

I could hear them talking, so I quietly got closer so I could hear what they were saying. "I don't know if I can do this," James said. "I know how much I'm asking, but she needs you, and you know what? I think you need her too" David said. "I have not spent that much time on 12, I don't understand why she *has* to go back?" James said. "Her mother wanted her to be there for a reason, we will respect her wishes, because she was a very smart woman that *knew* things" David said. "I love you brother, but you don't understand what you're asking of me," James said. "I do understand, trust me, I do, and I will owe you my life after this" David said. They sat there silently for a few minutes, I made a rustling sound so they would hear me. "There you guys are," I said, stepping out of the bushes. "I need to know if there is a plan for my sleepwalking tonight" I said. They looked at each other, before David turned to me and said "just go to bed, we will be watching."

I went to my room, and lay in bed, I was trying to understand why it was so terrible for James to come with me. I really couldn't tell if he hated me or not. It was starting to drive me a little crazy, although he seemed to have more of an issue with going to 12 than he did with me, right? I guess I could let it drive me crazy or just stop thinking about it. I did a spell, to protect my body and my mind before falling asleep. I didn't dream, the next thing I knew, I was waking up to the sound of David yelling down the hallway. I stumbled out of bed, clean feet today, and went to the dining room. I was really hungry again and excited to eat. "How did you sleep?" Sarah asked. "Great," I answered. David walked in and James was right behind him. "Could have fooled me, with all that screaming" James said. "What?" I asked. "You started screaming in the middle of the night. David was watching your door, it woke everyone up, we looked in on you, and you stopped." James said. "That's crazy, I don't remember dreaming or screaming," I said. I looked at David, he nodded his head to agree with James. "Wow, that's really weird, I'm sorry that I disturbed everyone's sleep," I said. "Don't worry about that sweety" Sarah said. I smiled at her, she was going to make the best mom, I envied her baby.

"Let's get started, last day to learn and still several things to go over," Sarah said. I nodded, the guys got up and walked outside. "The Circle coven is an enemy, Misty is their high priestess. They are probably your most powerful enemy, their mark is an unseparated yin yang, if you see anyone with a tattoo of it, run" she told me. She drew a picture so I could see exactly what it looked like. "They will also put the tattoo in places where we wouldn't normally see it, so you have to be really careful. The Sun coven is a friendly coven, glad to help out, their high priestess is Pearl. And then the Moon coven, enemy, Xander is their high priest" she said. I nodded, "I don't think I will ever remember all the coven names, symbols and leaders" I said. "We can also write it down for you, so you can take it with you," she said. I nodded.

I walked outside to meet the guys, and they informed me that today's lesson would be 'classroom' training, meaning we would just discuss fighting techniques and only demonstrate if I didn't understand. I rolled my eyes, "okay, I get it, I would be tired of getting my butt kicked every day too" I told them. They both laughed at me. It was bittersweet knowing that I was leaving, not sure when I would see David and Sarah again and having to *live* with James. Someone that I wasn't sure how I should feel about. One day he would be nice, the next he would be evil. I was starting to believe my dream, that he was in love with me, but didn't want to be for whatever reason, so he pushed me away. "I can give myself extra strength with a spell, can't I?" I asked. "Yes, but remember, using too much magic can also hurt you," David reminded me. "Speaking of magic," James said while pointing to Arturo, who was walking up. He waved to get me to 'come on'.

I met Arturo in the basement. "Sorry if I cut into your outside playtime, but we still have several covens to discuss" he said. I just looked at him and smirked. "The Evergreen coven, we aren't sure which side they are on, their high priestess is Harmony. The Polaris coven is also unknown to which side they are on, their high priest is Finn" Arturo said. "Should I find the leaders of the covens that we aren't sure which side they are on and figure it out?" I asked. "We will discuss things that you should do, and things that you shouldn't do tomorrow," Arturo said, while giving me a look for interrupting him. "Another coven that we aren't sure which side they are on is Hearthstone coven, their high priest is Damian. One that we know is an enemy is the Serenity coven, their high priestess is Darcy. And the last coven, we know that they are friends, the Raven Star coven, their high priest is Conan. These covens are scattered all over the world, but your enemies will find you, it is probably a good idea for you to find your ally covens, I would let the others show themselves." Arturo said. I looked at him, I wasn't going to argue with him about it, I would do what I felt was right. I smelled dinner and my stomach growled. "I will see you tomorrow for your farewell party," Arturo said. "I didn't know we were having a party," I said. "Just a chance for everyone to wish you luck and say goodbye" he said, with a smile.

I walked to the dining room. Sarah, David and James were all there. "I think having two meals a day prepared for me is what I am going to miss the most about this place" I said with a smile. "And it's always delicious," I added. Sarah smiled, "thank you dear." "Did you finish your coven study?" David asked. "It was a crash course, I am still going to need them written down" I said, looking at Sarah, she nodded in agreement. "So, we are going to party tomorrow?" I asked. "It's a small get together," David said. "Okay" I said, shrugging my shoulders. James was quiet tonight, I wondered what he was thinking, then I started hearing mumbling. "What is that?" I asked, looking around. "What is what?" David said. "That mumbling sound?" I said. "I don't hear anything, and I hope you aren't trying to read anyone's thoughts, we have ours protected by magic" David said. "Oh gosh! I wasn't really trying to, I'm sorry!" I said. We all laughed, I really needed to learn that everything I think can be magic. "It's okay, accidents happen, that's why we have protection on ourselves for certain things" Sarah said. "And you know, you could always ask if you want to know what someone is thinking" David said. "That's okay, I didn't really want to know," I said, laughing. "I think I'm going to go to bed, are we doing anything for sleepwalking tonight?" I asked. "We will watch you, like we have been," David said. "Okay, goodnight," I said. Everyone said 'good night' to me and I went to 'my' room.

I looked out the window from my room, the moons were high and bright. Tonight was bittersweet, I had grown fond of David, and Sarah, and Arturo and Margo. Fond of the field, fond of the two bright moons. I was going to miss everyone and everything I had done and seen in the past two weeks. I lay down in bed, and I started crying. I was going to miss everything a *lot*. If I had the choice of staying here, I probably would. For the first time in my life I felt like I belonged somewhere, for the first time, I had a family. A real, loving family. Maybe I could mention staying with them tomorrow? I heard my door creak open and looked up, sniffling. It was James. "Are you okay? It sounds like you are crying," he said. "Yeah, just a little sad about leaving," I said, through the tears. He nodded his head, "do you want to talk about it?" he asked. "Sure," I said, patting my bed to invite him over. "Are you sad about leaving too? I know you are mad, but are you sad?" I asked him. "Who said I was mad?" he said, rolling his eyes. I giggled. He smiled, "I was upset at first, but I love adventure. And that's how I'm looking at it, this is an adventure" he said. "This is the first time I have felt like part of a family, and this place is beautiful," I said. "I wish I could stay," I added. "That's not an option right now, but we never know what the future may hold," he said. I nodded and started falling asleep, he sat there on the foot of my bed until he thought I was asleep, when he got up, it actually woke me all the way back up. I watched him walk out of my room and close the door. I heard someone say "shh" in the hallway. Then I drifted to 'real' sleep. I didn't dream again that night.

I woke up naturally the next morning, no one yelling that it was time to get going. The sun looked pretty high, I stumbled out of bed, no dirty feet. I walked into the dining room, the food had been cleared, but there was a plate sitting where I normally sit, covered with a towel. Sarah walked in, "I saved you some food" she said, nodding toward the plate. "Thank you," I said. "Sorry if it's cold," she said. "Don't worry about it, I'm sure it will still be delicious," I said. "Where is everyone?" I asked. "They are preparing for our guests, *your* guests. We let you sleep as long as you wanted, so you would be well rested and ready to go home" she said. "I wish I could just stay here, I love this place, and I love you guys" I said. "Oh, sweety, we love you too, and we are going to miss you so much, but there are things that have to be done. Sometimes our lives aren't what we want them to be, but we just have to do it, and try to enjoy it the best we can" she said. I nodded, with a pouty face, but then I smiled at her. "I'm going to go see if I can help with anything while you finish your breakfast," she said. "Okay" I said, taking a bite of a biscuit.

After I finished eating, I went outside to see what everyone was up to. They were putting paper lanterns out. "This is pretty, it looks like you are setting up for a wedding" I teased. They laughed at me, "sorry if it's a bit much, we don't have a lot of gatherings" David said. I smiled. "I get it, I don't think I have ever had one," I said. "I just have a few friends and we normally just go out somewhere" I added. "Yes, I know," David said. "Oh, I almost forgot, stalker," I teased him. He laughed. "Are there people coming that I haven't met?" I asked. "Yes, the party is for me too, since I am leaving with you, so some of my friends are coming to say goodbye" James said. I nodded, "I'm sorry, I hate that you are giving up your life here to come babysit me" I said, sincerely. He just looked at me and nodded. People began to show up, so I decided to go inside and get changed and get everything ready to go.

Sarah was inside, getting food ready for the party. "Do you need any help?" I asked. "Oh no sweetie, I'm fine, go enjoy yourself" she replied. "I was just going to get changed and start getting my stuff ready to go," I told her. "Okay, I put the list of covens on the nightstand in your room," she said. "Thank you," I said. I walked into the room, even though I missed my friends and my cats, I had grown so fond of this place. I was really going to miss it, the spell to go to different dimensions was complicated for a lot of reasons, so it wasn't like I could just pop in and out whenever I wanted to. But I will come back eventually. I sat down on the bed and had a good cry, until I felt like I should get up and clean my face and try to look presentable.

I went back outside after getting cleaned up, Margo and Arturo were here now, along with about five other people that I didn't recognize. Sarah had joined everyone outside as well. Fairies started gathering around me and landing on my arms and shoulders. I stopped, "hello, little ones" I said to them. One on each side of me buzzed up to my face and kissed my cheeks. "Aww, thank you" I told them. One of them looked really sad. "Don't be sad, I will come back to visit, this isn't 'goodbye' it's a 'see ya later.' I can ask if it is possible, if any of you would like to come with me." I said to them. The sad one perked up, she flew up to my face, I'm pretty sure she was the one that I had met already, she was nodding her head. "I'll tell you what, go tell your friends that you will see them later and meet me back here, and I will ask if it is possible" I told her. "Are you going to hang out with the fairies all night? Or are you going to come hang out with your other friends too?" David yelled sarcastically.

I joined the others, they had a beautiful bonfire going. I hugged Margo then I hugged Arturo, "thank you both for everything you have done for me" I said, smiling. "Of course, your success will also be our success," Arturo said, smiling back. James was off in his own group. I sat down close to Sarah, "I would be lying if I said that I wasn't scared or that I wouldn't miss this place or all of you" I said. "You will be fine, and I will be going with you," Margo said. I looked at David with wide eyes, he nodded in agreement. "It's her life, plus, I'm trusting that you will also protect her" he said. I nodded and got up and hugged her. "Please don't eat my pet cats" I whispered in her ear with a laugh. She giggled. "Speaking of coming with me, there is a fairy that wants to come as well, I told her I would ask if it was possible" I said to David. He nodded, we will have to get you all straight to the farm house. It would look a little strange to see you and James driving a vehicle down the road with a black panther in tow" he said with a laugh.

James walked over, "My friends would like to meet you" he said to me as he put out a hand to help me up. I nodded and took his hand for help. We walked over to where they were standing. I could tell that three of them were half giant because of their height, the other two I wasn't sure what they were. One of the half giants stepped up to me, "Hi , I'm Theo, it's nice to meet you" he said. I nodded. The next one that stepped up was a female that was a little shorter than myself, "I'm Emma, it's a pleasure to meet you" she said. "What do you do?" I asked. They all started laughing at me and my face turned red. James looked at me and rolled his eyes. "I'm sorry, I guess I shouldn't have asked that," I said. "It's okay," she replied. "I'm a wolf," she added, winking at me. "A werewolf?" I asked. "There's no such thing, I'm a shapeshifter that turns into a wolf" she said, sounding a bit offended. "Oh, I'm sorry, I knew that" I said, smacking my face with the palm of my hand.

The next person, a half giant, walked up "I'm Alice" she said, putting her hand out to shake mine. I shook her hand, "nice to meet you" I said. The next person, a big guy, but not more than 6'2 came up to me, "I'm Philip, and I will be going with you guys" he said. "Oh, okay, well, it's nice to meet you, what will you be on 12?" I asked, trying to reword how I asked what they were. "I'm a horse," he said. "*A horse?*" I asked, astonished. "Yes, and I'm very fast too," he said. "You know that we have a panther coming with us right?" I asked him. "Yes, we will be able to recognize each other for what we are," he told me. I nodded. The next guy who was clearly a half giant walked up, he was handsome, he had straight blonde hair, blue eyes, and muscular with a nice tan that glowed in the fire light, "I'm Levi, and the pleasure is all mine" he said, as he pulled my hand to his mouth and kissed the top. "That's enough Romeo," James said, with a smirk.

"Everyone come get some food!" Sarah yelled to us. We all started walking over. The food was delicious, music started playing and people started dancing, everyone was laughing and having fun.

The air felt perfect as well, overall, everything felt perfect. I felt as though I was surrounded by family and friends, and everyone was happy. Levi asked me to dance, I nodded and he started twirling me around. I saw James out of the corner of my eye, was that his jealous look? Who knew? I was having fun. The music changed to a slower beat and Levi pulled me close, "too bad I didn't get to meet you before now, you are gorgeous" he said. "Thank you," I said, blushing. James walked over and cut in, "watch out for that one" he said, nodding his head toward Levi, "he just likes to put notches in his belt" he said. I looked at him confused, "he wants to make you another 'number'" he said. "Oh" I said, nodding. "We should introduce Margo and Philip to each other," I said to James. He nodded in agreement. After we went and introduced them, David said that it was getting late and we needed to wrap it up and get going. The fairy came back, she landed on my arm. "Do you still want to go?" I asked her, and she nodded. I found a jar for her and poked holes in the lid so she wouldn't run out of air, and I put her in my backpack.

Five

Going Home

After gathering everything that we needed to open the portal, David gave us clear instructions that we had to be touching each other so that we would all go to the same place and not four corners of the Earth. We all nodded in agreement. "And remember, when you get back, it will be the day after your birthday, no one will have noticed that you were gone. You will have to prepare a story for why you no longer live in the apartment and you may have to disguise James to look like me for a little while, since they are used to seeing me and not him." David said. "Wow, okay" I said. Someone was walking up behind us, it was Levi, "I'm going too" he said. "No, you're not," James said. "What's your problem, why would it hurt to have someone else there to fight on your side?" Levi asked. "He has a point," David said. "No," James argued. "It's already going to be hard enough to explain how I have a new house with a horse and one guy," I said. Arturo told us to close our eyes, I peeked just a little and could see a swirl of blue and purple lights come up from the ground, like a tornado without wind. My body went completely numb, not even a sense of 'heavy' it felt as though my body didn't exist, only my consciousness. Levi said, "I'm going" and grabbed my shoulder.

The next thing I knew, I was standing in an unfamiliar field with James, Levi, a beautiful brown horse with a black mane and a black panther. James punched Levi square in the face. "OH!" I screamed. They were fighting and yelling at each other, Margo and Philip got between me and them and pushed me toward the house, as if to tell me to let them fight. So, I went inside, the house was old, but beautiful. I had left the door open and could still hear the guys beating each other. So I went and closed the door. I needed to check out the house and get used to my surroundings. The cats heard me and came running. "Hey, babies, how are you doing?" I said to them, they meowed and purred. I found a bedroom that must be the master, it had an attached, upgraded bathroom with a huge bathtub and separate shower stall, "mine" I said to myself as I put my bag on the bed. This room was as big as my old apartment. I suddenly didn't feel so bad about having a roommate, well two now, I guess.

I continued to explore the house, it had a beautiful, fully stocked kitchen, too bad I wasn't Sarah and I didn't cook. I went upstairs, where I found four basic rooms and two basic bathrooms. I would make the guys stay up here, I thought to myself.

I finally heard the front door open, "Gabriela!" I heard James call out. I looked down the stairs, he was carrying Levi. "Did you *kill* him?" I asked. "Almost, can you heal him?" he asked me as he lay him down on the couch. "Let me find my stuff!" I said, as I went into the room where I had put my bag. "Hurry," James said, sounding defeated. I found what I needed quickly, and went to Levi's side and began the spell. It worked, he appeared to be healed, but he wasn't waking up. "Why isn't he waking up?" James asked. I felt for a pulse and found one, "I don't know, he's alive, if he doesn't wake by morning, we can take him to a hospital" I said. James nodded his head. "What were you thinking? Why would you do this to someone?" I asked him. "I was so angry at him and in the back of my mind, I was thinking, Gabriela can fix whatever I do, so let him know how seriously pissed off you are," James said. "I'll never forgive myself if he dies" he mumbled as he walked into another room. I felt Levi's head to see if he was running a fever, he felt normal.

I went outside to check on Philip, there was a nice large barn that he had found and he looked quite happy with it. The air felt cold and crisp, it had an old familiar feel to it. The air felt slightly different here than it did on 2. Philip pushed me with his head, I giggled, "what?" I asked him. He turned his head to his back, "you want me to ride?" I asked him. He nodded his head and neighed. I looked around, I didn't know anything about riding a horse and I didn't see a saddle anywhere. "I don't know how," I told him. He lowered down his body and pointed at his back again for me to get on. So, I did, no saddle, he was very tall when he got up, I tightened my legs around him the best I could and hugged his neck, I was practically laying down on him. He trotted around the farm, I saw Margo watching us from a tree, I giggled. Philip took that as a sign that I was having fun, so he started running. It felt amazing, the cool air hitting my face, blowing through my hair, it was a rush that I had never felt before. We rode close to the house, where James was standing on the porch, "can you stop" I said to Philip. He got close to the house and stopped, he lowered himself so I could get down. I pet his nose and told him good night.

"Is he still out?" I asked as I walked up to James, he nodded silently. "I think he will be fine, worrying yourself isn't going to help anything" I told him. "I'm going to go to my room and get ready for bed," I said. "Lock your bedroom door, spell it too" James said. "Isn't the whole property spelled?" I asked. "Yes, from people and things that aren't already on it" he said. "You think that someone that came with us wants to hurt me?" I asked. "Maybe, I don't know, I don't understand why he jumped with us at the last minute, after me telling him no" he said motioning his head toward Levi. "Okay, I will spell my room and lock the door" I said, to make him feel better.

I went to my room and I locked the door behind me and did a spell on the door and window for extra protection. I started running a bath while I was taking my things out, I found the jar, "Oh no, I almost forgot about you!" I said. When I looked into the jar, sure enough there was a firefly. I didn't know what to do with it, winter was coming on, I didn't know what happened to them in the winter, did they die? Did they hibernate? I would have to study that, in the meantime, I set the jar on the dresser. I went into my bathroom and closed the door, it felt so amazing to step into the bath water. I sat down in the tub and lay my head back and relaxed. I almost fell asleep, I didn't realize how tired I was. I got out and put on some pajamas and got into bed. I fell asleep fast, it was a dreamless peaceful sleep.

The next morning I woke to the sound of arguing, it was James and Levi, I was relieved that Levi was awake. I couldn't really tell what they were arguing about, so I went out to the living room. They stopped arguing and looked at me, "sorry if we woke you" Levi said. James looked at him and stormed out the front door. I followed him outside, he was on the porch, which was a nice big area, I walked up behind him. He heard me coming, "he thinks that I almost killed him because I don't want any competition" he said, not turning around to look at me. "I didn't realize there was anything to compete for," I said. James let out a sarcastic laugh and walked away. "Okay" I said out loud. I walked back inside, Levi met me at the door, with a cup of coffee, "I wasn't sure how you take your coffee, but I tried" he said. I smiled, "thanks" I said to him. "I need to find my phone, everyone is going to be worried about me, have you seen it?" I asked him. He pointed to the kitchen, "thanks" I said again.

What happened -Racheal. *Where are you?* -Micheal. *Please answer us and let us know that you are okay!* -Anna. *I need to talk to you.* -Jason *Oh my god, I'm at her apartment, she's not here, I don't even see her cats in there! I just picked her up here yesterday!* -Anna. *Guys! I'm so sorry that I worried you, I am okay. Yes, I am staying somewhere else, but I am fine, maybe I can meet up with you guys later this evening or tomorrow.* -Me. *Wow, do you know how worried we were? I was about to call the police to file a missing person report.* -Racheal. *I said, I'm sorry, I really didn't mean to worry you and I can't really explain everything right now, but I promise I am okay and I really am sorry, I can't talk right now though, I have to get settled in where I am.* -Me. No one responded, I could tell they were really mad at me and I felt horrible about it.

I heard the front door open, I went to check it out, Levi was sitting on the couch, sipping his coffee and Jason was standing just inside, staring at him, the tension was very high. "Anyone know how to cook? I'm hungry" I said, breaking the silence. James looked at me, still looking angry "no" he said. "Great, I guess we are going to starve then" I said sarcastically. I could cook a little, I guess it was time to YouTube some recipes.

James went upstairs and Levi joined me in the kitchen. We started looking through the cabinets for ideas on what to try to cook. He found some flour and said, "let's make biscuits." "Okay" I agreed, half seriously and half sarcastically. "So, why did you do what you did? And why is James so mad about it?" I asked. "After meeting you, I thought you were gorgeous, and I didn't want to miss an opportunity to get to know you better. Plus, I have nothing back there, I needed a new adventure," he said. I blushed and smiled at him. "I know I shouldn't have waited until the last minute, the way I did, honestly, I had no intention of coming with you until you were about to go, then I realized that it would be a long time before I would see you again. And as for James being mad enough to kill me,

I think that he has feelings for you and he didn't want me to get in the way" he said. I felt my face turn red, and I started shaking my head, "no, I'm sure that's not why he's mad" I said.

"I'm mad because now I have two imbeciles to babysit. How long have you two been in here? The whole kitchen is covered in flour, I won't live like this, clean it up" James said, walking into the kitchen. "I am *not* an imbecile, we planned on cleaning it up, and you are sure as hell not my dad, so don't *ever* talk to me like that again!" I responded. Levi just put his hands up and said, "yeah, what she said." It made me laugh. James rolled his eyes and walked out the front door. I was still upset with him, who did he think he was? I followed him to try to get some answers as to why he was acting this way. I caught up to him at the barn. I watched him go inside and I followed, being sneaky so he wouldn't see me. He was talking to Philip. "She looked happy last night when you took her for a ride," James told him. Philip neighed, and nodded his head. They both became silent, so I walked in. "James?" I called, as though I didn't know he was in there.

"Yeah" he answered. "You seem really different, you want to tell me what's going on with you?" I asked him. "Levi used to be one of my very close friends, now I feel like he's an enemy," he said. "Why?" I asked. "He knows that what he did was wrong, maybe you should just try to talk to him" I continued. James shook his head, "he knew how I felt, I told him no before he did it, and he did it anyway." "I understand, you feel betrayed, but, his intention wasn't to hurt you" I said. "I see he has already won you over" he said to me. "Excuse me? What is that supposed to mean?" I asked. "You are standing here, trying to convince me that he's not the bad guy here, so I guess that makes *me* the bad guy, right?" he said. "I never said that! Everyone makes mistakes, does that mean that they have to pay for them forever?" I asked. "Your idea of forever is a *day*?" he asked, sarcastically. I rolled my eyes "no, I just think the sooner you two make up, the sooner we can all sit down together and make a plan" I said. "I am an adult, I can sit down with people that I don't like and figure out a way to work with them," he said.

He went to the barn door, "come on, let's go sit down like adults and discuss what needs to be done" he said. I followed him, and we walked back to the house silently together. When we got inside, I noticed a lemon smell mixed with the smell of biscuits. Levi had found some lemon cleaner, and completely cleaned the kitchen, and the biscuits were on the table, they actually looked good. I grabbed one and me and James sat down at the table. "Levi, will you join us so we can discuss a plan?" I called out to him. "Sure, does anyone want any coffee?" he asked. We both shook our heads that we didn't want coffee.

"I told my friends that I would meet with them either this evening or tomorrow. I don't go back to work until Monday" I said. "I don't think it's a good idea to meet with your friends" James said. I rolled my eyes, "I'm not just going to stay here in the house with the two of you all the time" I said. "I'm pretty sure the witch that attacked you, your friend's date, is part of the Circle coven, they are your most powerful enemy. Why would you give them easy access to you?" James said. "Well, I don't want to live in fear and run my whole life, so I want to find a way to end it," I said. "You want to kill every witch?" James asked. "No!" I said, surprised, "I don't want to kill anyone!" "They want you dead," he replied. "Not all of them, how about we find the ones that we know are on our side, I can work with them on a solution and you two can just be bodyguards." I suggested. "That's actually not a bad idea she has there," Levi said. "Let witches handle witch business, and we just standby until we are needed" he continued. James just sat there looking at the two of us for a few minutes. "Okay, we can try it, if you can get the leaders of the covens to come here and meet with you, we will see what you all can come up with together. I nodded at him, "thank you" I said.

"There must be a way that I can meet with my friends safely," I said. "I can go with you," Levi said. "And who am I supposed to say you are? I just hung out with them last night, in their time" I said. "Tell them that I'm your boyfriend, we met and it was love at first sight, I mean, you did just meet me last night" he said laughing. "I'm not going to lie to my friends," I said, rolling my eyes. A smirk went across James' face. Levi looked a little disappointed, but not devastated. I looked at my phone just to check messages. *I really need to talk to you, please, can you call me?* -Jason. I looked at James and Levi, "I need to make a phone call" I said to them, and I stepped out of the dining room and into my bedroom. *Yes, is now a good time?* -Me. My phone rang just a second after I sent the message, it was Jason.

"Hey, what's going on?" I asked. "Carly did something to me" he said. I felt my heart sink. "Are you okay? What did she do?" I said, starting to panic. "She drugged me or something and I woke up and I have a tattoo on my chest, she told me to go home and deal with it, I don't even know what that means," he said. "A tattoo?" I said, confused, but feeling a little easier. "Yes, it's a circle with markings inside it, I think it's a different language, I don't know what it says" he said. "Can you text me a picture of it?" I asked him. "Yeah, I can" he replied. "Done" he added. I looked at my phone, the picture came through, it looked like something magical, but I wasn't sure what it could be. I hoped that it wasn't a curse. "How are you feeling?" I asked him. "Hungover" he answered. "Hey, you don't plan on seeing her again do you? I asked him. "No, she drugged me and put a tattoo on my chest, I don't plan on seeing her again" he said sarcastically. "Just making sure, I think she may have put something in my drink too, " I told him. "What? Why do you say that?" he asked. "I had a black out moment too, a friend helped me get home, " I said. "I'm going to see what I can find out about this tattoo for you, I'll text you if I find anything" I said. "Okay, talk to you later," he said.

I showed the picture to James and Levi. "Do either of you know what this is?" I asked them. "Yes," James answered. "Okay, what is it?" I asked him. "It's a spell, to turn a human into a creature" he said calmly. "*What?!*" I yelled, starting to shake and cry. "What's going on? Who is the mark on? James asked. "Carly put it on Jason" I said, barely able to keep myself from breaking down. "Calm down," James said. "I'm not sure which markings these are, so I don't know what she's trying to turn him into. The thing is, most humans can't survive this curse, their bodies weren't built for magic and it kills them." James said. "That is not helping me to calm down," I said. "You need to go get him and bring him here, so we can watch after him and see if there is anything we can do for him," James said. I nodded my head, "how are we going to do this without telling him everything?" I asked. "We will have to tell him, either he will become one of us or die, so there's that" James said. "Stop saying that he's going to die please," I said. "I will go with you to go get him, I'm sure this witch that put the mark on him is watching and waiting for you to come help him" Levi said. "I hope so, I'm going to kick her ass!" I said. James and Levi both smiled. "I'm serious! Why would she bring an innocent human into this?" I said. "They will do what they have to do, I would say the witch that kills you would get greatly rewarded for doing so" Levi said.

The property where we were living was completely shielded by magic, we could not be found by magical creatures or by humans. They only saw it as a wooded area, which we were surrounded by woods. We had to walk about a half of a mile to the main road where we had a pickup truck and my car parked in a pull-over spot. Levi and I took my car and started heading to Jason's apartment. I called him on the way. "Hello?" he answered. "Hey, so me and a friend of mine are coming to get you, I found out some things about the tattoo" I told him. "Why are you coming to get me? I don't feel good, I just want to lay in bed" he replied. "I know, but this is very important, you trust me don't you?" I asked him. "You know I do, but this is crazy," he said. "Oh, I know, but you haven't seen the crazy part yet, please just trust me, get ready, we will be there in twenty minutes" I said. "What do you mean, I haven't seen crazy yet?" he said. "Please, I will explain on the way, just get ready" I said. "Okay" he finally agreed. "Okay, see you in a few" I said before hanging up the phone.

We circled his apartment a couple of times, looking for anything unusual, we didn't see anything so we pulled in. We walked up to his door, his apartment was like my old one in the sense that it was a part of a house that had been divided up. I knocked on the door, and he answered right away. He didn't have a shirt on, the mark looked very red. "I told you to be ready," I said. He was holding a shirt in his hand, "can I just bring it with me? It hurts to put it on" he said, pointing at the mark. "Sure" I said, just to get him going before we were attacked. "You're tall," Jason said as he walked past Levi. As we were walking to the car I felt a change in the atmosphere. "Do you feel that?" I said. Levi looked at me, worried, Jason said, "feel what?" "Get him to the car!" I yelled at Levi. Levi didn't argue and hurried Jason to the car. I looked around, I still didn't see anything, but I felt it, I knew magic was being used nearby.

It hit me suddenly, it felt like someone punched me right in the gut. I doubled over and let out a "oh" then I felt a blow to my back, that one knocked the wind out of me, and I fell to my knees. "Show yourself you bitch!" I yelled, when I was able to draw breath again. Carly stepped out of the bushes, I saw Levi start to get out of the car so I locked the doors to trap him and Jason inside. I didn't care to talk to her, she was clearly out for blood, so I went into defense mode. I dropped quickly and did a round kick, she jumped to avoid it. I went in quick for an elbow to her back, then kicked her knees from the back, she fell. She started using magic to push me away from her, I used a spell to counteract hers, we went back and forth for a minute, but I was stronger. I put a paralyzing spell on her. She lay there on the ground, "if you want to save him, you better not kill me" she said. I didn't know what to do, I couldn't let her go, I couldn't trust her, but killing her... how could I *kill* her? Levi had somehow managed to get out of the car, I guess my spell had worn off when I started using my magic to fight. "Go to the car now!" he yelled at me angrily. I nodded and did just that. "What the hell is going on?!" Jason yelled at me. "I will explain later, I promise!" I said. I looked up at Levi, he was carrying Carly to the bushes, to hide her body.

He came back to the car and didn't say anything, he looked angry. I mouthed, 'is she dead?' To him. He nodded his head slightly to let me know that she was indeed dead. On the car ride home, everyone was silent. I could only imagine what was going through Jason's head, and I was sure that Levi was going to let me have it for locking him in the car. I somehow fell asleep before we got back to the house, I guess I needed a small recharge after using magic the way I did. I was woken up by "we're here" from Levi. "What do you mean, there's nothing here?" Jason said. I opened the door, "come on, it's just inside the woods, I told him. He looked so scared and helpless, for a moment, I saw him as the little boy I had met in a foster home. Once we were close enough and inside the shield he could see the house and field. Philip was in the field, and James was standing on the porch waiting for us. "Who's that? And for that matter who is he?" Jason said, pointing to Levi. "I'm sorry, we didn't really have time for an introduction, this is Levi, and that is James. I will explain who they are later" I said. "Why did Carly attack you? Did he kill her?" Jason asked me, loud enough for Levi to hear him. "Let's just get inside, I'll explain," I said.

When we got to the door, James could see that Levi was angry. "What happened?" he asked, looking back and forth at both of us. Neither of us said anything. "I'm sorry, I didn't want you to get hurt," I said softly. He didn't respond and kept on walking. I got

Jason inside and led him to the couch. I tried a healing spell immediately, some of the redness seemed to go away, but that was all, the mark was still there. "I could have told you that wouldn't work," James said. "What did you just do?" Jason asked. "Magic" I said. He looked at me like I was crazy. "Carly was a witch," I said to him. "Was?" James asked. I looked at him over my shoulder. "We can talk about that later. Will you look at the mark and see if you can figure it out?" I asked him. He came closer to Jason, "it's a witch's mark, if he lives, he will be a witch" he said. "What?!" Jason yelled. "And he will belong to the one that turned him, or at least that coven" James said. "I don't *belong* to anyone. And what do you mean if I *live* I will be a *witch*?" Jason said. "This mark is to turn humans into witches, most humans can't survive because they are not genetically made for magic" I explained. "But I'm here, and I will do everything I can to help you!" I said, as I started crying. "Hey, don't cry, I'm gonna be okay" he said to me as he reached out and brought me into him for a hug. I tried to avoid touching the mark because I didn't want to hurt him. I stood up and nodded, "do you want some coffee or anything?" I asked him. "No, I think I just need to sit here for a minute and think about everything," he said. I nodded and looked at James and motioned for him to follow me to the kitchen.

"So, what happened out there?" he asked as soon as we were in the kitchen. "She was waiting for us, and as soon as I realized it, I told Levi to get Jason to the car, then I locked them both inside the car with magic while I fought her." I said. "Why would you do that?" he asked. "I didn't want anyone to get hurt," I said. "We are here to protect *you*, so *you* don't get hurt," James said, scolding me. "I know, the magic wore off after I had her beat to the ground, Levi is the one that took care of her," I said, looking down. "Wow, I can understand why he is so mad, I still can't believe you locked him in a car" James said, still sounding angry. "I'm sorry, I just felt like I needed to protect them," I said, defeated.

Levi walked into the kitchen, still looking angry. "I'm sorry, please don't be angry with me, it was a reflex, to protect you" I said. He gave me a confused look. "Protect *me*?" he said, sarcastically, then walked back out of the kitchen. "He's gonna need some time to cool down," James said. I nodded and walked back to the living room where Jason was still sitting on the couch, staring out of the window to his side. "How are you doing?" I asked him. "Seriously?" he said, sarcastically. "I know, it's a lot, I was the same way, except I had been taken into another dimension" I told him. He just looked at me like I was crazy. "I know trust me, waking up in a strange place, seeing *two* moons in the sky" I continued. "Okay, now you're making stuff up," he said to me. "No, I swear, *and* it all happened in just one night to you, but it was two weeks for me. I said. "So, what? You're telling me that you were taken last night into another dimension and you spent two weeks there, last night?" he asked, sounding very confused. "I know this is a lot to take in at one time, I really do, so I'm going to try not to tell you anything else, but I will answer any questions you have, if I can" I told him. He just sat there, staring at me.

"I am going to contact Conan, of the Raven Star coven" I told James. "Yeah, it won't hurt, contact as many of the witches as you can" James agreed. I looked out of the kitchen window, Levi was riding Philip around the field. I went to my room and pulled out the crystal ball that Arturo had given me. He gave me instructions on how to use it to contact other witches. I started concentrating and working it, the ball started swirling inside, and a man appeared inside the ball. "Are you Conan?" I asked, "Who's asking?" he replied. "I'm Gabriela," I said. "Oh, your reputation precedes you," he said. I gave him a confused look. "I need help, a witch from the Circle coven placed a curse on a human friend, one that will turn him into a witch or kill him trying" I explained. "Is there a cure? Can we do anything to help him?" I asked. "I don't know of a way to remove the curse, but, I do have a spell that can make his body more accepting of the magic, so he has a better chance of survival. But if he does survive, he will belong to the coven of the witch that turned him." he said. "I know," I said, nodding. "Can you come to us?" I asked him. He nodded, "I'll be there in an hour or so," he said, looking at his watch.

I got out the piece of paper that had all the covens written on it. I needed to contact as many as I could, maybe someone, or the combination of all of us, would be able to cure Jason. The only other coven that we were sure wasn't an enemy was the Earth coven. So, I dove into the crystal ball and found Hale, the high priest of the Earth coven. I told him about Jason's curse and he also agreed to come to try to help him. I decided to contact one more, one that we weren't sure on which side they stood on. I chose to contact Damian of the Hearthstone Coven. Once contact was established and I could see him clearly, I realized that he was quite a bit younger than the other two men. He couldn't be much older than myself, he had dark skin with wavy black hair and brown eyes with thick eyebrows. He was quite handsome. "Are you Damian?" I asked. "I am," he replied. "What can I do for you?" he asked. "I'm Gabriela," I said. He knew the name, I could tell. "Why are you contacting me?" he asked. "I have a friend who has been cursed, I'm looking for help" I said. "What kind of curse?" he asked. "One that will kill him or turn him into a witch" I said. "There is no cure for that," Damian said. "I know, I just really need to help him," I said. "Do you know which coven the witch was from that cast the spell?" he asked. I nodded that I did know, but I wasn't sure if I wanted to share that information with him. "I will come see what I can do, maybe make him more comfortable, if you would like?" he said.

Something in me told me I could trust him, as long as he didn't know that it was the Circle coven that placed the curse, but would he know when he saw the mark? "I'm sorry, we can't have any visitors at the moment, but if there is something you can tell me how to do, that would be helpful" I said. "You contacted me, yet you don't trust me" he said, curiously. "What do you mean?" I asked, acting like I didn't know what he was talking about. "Don't play dumb with me, what did you really expect when you called me?" he asked. "I don't have hidden agendas," I said. "But you do, and I am losing respect for you, every time you open your mouth and lie to me," he said. "I have no problem meeting you another time," I said, firmly. "It will have to be under different circumstances, and I need to help my friend now" I said to him. I didn't want to lose a potential ally, but something told me I could not let him near Jason. "Okay, after your friend is either a witch or dead, you contact me, we will schedule a meeting" Damian said. I nodded in agreement before breaking the connection on the crystal ball.

I decided not to take any more chances on unknown loyalties and went to find James and Levi to let them know that Conan and Hale would be here. I could tell that Levi was still mad at me. I got him cornered and alone, "please forgive me, I didn't plan to do what I did" I said. "That's the biggest problem, you just did it, without planning, without thinking," he said. "I was thinking, I was thinking that I needed Jason to be safe and he needed at least one of us to keep him safe. I was thinking that I could defeat her, because I have magic and you don't. The only thing I didn't think was that I would have to kill her, I've never thought about killing anyone" I said. He nodded, "I came here because, yes, I did have a crush on you, but also to *protect* you" he said. "You think too much of others before yourself, and that is going to get *you* killed," he said. "Maybe you're right, I can't see myself letting anyone die for me" I said. "And that is your problem. Your life, unfortunately, is tied to a whole lot of other people's lives, it isn't your own to give," he said. I looked at him, very confused. "What do you mean my life isn't my own?" I asked. "Your life or your death affects so many things, it affects the future, the present and the past all at once. If you were to die now, the enemy would win." he said.

"I still don't clearly understand what it is we are fighting for" I said. "For love, for family" Levi said. "They want you dead because they don't understand you, because a long time ago a creature similar to you, became something so great and terrible that they had to lock it away in a dimension of its own." he said, with all the passion he could conjure. "I am not like him! He was half demon! I have angel blood in me! I am the opposite of him!" I said, almost laughing. "Even so, you could potentially become a very powerful being, hell, you are already more powerful than most witches, if not all. My point is, they do not understand, so they want you dead!" he said. "And not only that, it is law that two different creatures cannot reproduce. Your parents loved each other at one point, why is it so bad for them to want a family?" he continued, more calmly. Jason heard us arguing and came in. "This is all still nuts to me, you know that right?" Jason said, looking at me. I just nodded my head and walked out to sit on the porch.

Levi followed me outside, "do you have any idea why I was so upset about you locking me in the car?" he asked. I nodded my head. "I don't really think you do, you have never killed anyone and I don't think you can. What was your plan? Did you think if you kicked her ass one time that she would just leave you alone forever?" he asked. "I didn't really have a plan for that, it didn't even cross my mind, but maybe we could have convinced her to come to our side" I said. He shook his head, "she just would have kept coming for you until she won by killing you," he said, in a low voice. James came out of the barn, where I assumed he had been talking with Philip. I saw Margo at the edge of the forest, she wasn't easy to spot in the shadows. "The other witches should be here soon, I need to go meet them by the road" I said. James heard me as he walked up, "I'll go with you" he said. I nodded, “will you please stay with Jason and watch him?” I said to Levi, he nodded.

“Are you and Philip pretty close?” I asked James as we walked to the road. “He’s never done anything to betray me,” he replied. “You’re still mad at Levi?” I asked. “I don’t trust him anymore, it's hard to have any kind of relationship without trust,” he said. I nodded, “have you known people that have been cursed with the same curse that Jason has?” I asked. “No, but, I’ve known people that have known people," he answered. “Have you heard of anyone surviving?” I asked. “Only one, and they weren’t the same as they were before,” he said. “What about vampire blood?” I asked. “No, it’s too much of a risk, if he died anyway, he would become a vampire, you would have to send him to 1 and still never see him again” he said. I let out a sigh and nodded as we approached the road. Conan was waiting and Hale drove up as we were walking up.

“Thank you both so much for coming” I said to them. “I am happy to assist you, your mother was a dear friend” Conan said. “I am eager to see how you will change our world,” Hale said. I gave him a sideways look, “change our world?” I asked, with a half smile on my face. “Yes, you will be the one that brings all of us together, I can feel it,” he said. I liked this guy, we walked them onto the property. “This place is beautiful, and there is a lot of natural magic here, I can feel it,” Conan said. They were both older, probably in their fifties. Conan was taller than me, probably around six feet, he had dark brown hair with gray coming in. Hale had blonde hair, was about the same height as me and from his body language, I would say that he preferred male lovers. “This place is gorgeous,” Hale said. “Have either of you ever dealt with this curse before?” I asked them. “I have, a long time ago, she didn’t make it” Conan said, his head hanging down. “I have not, I’ve heard of it, and I have heard of survivors,” Hale said.

"Do you think it's possible to remove the curse completely? No turning, no dying?" I asked them. "I don't think so," Conan said. "Do you have a spell in mind for us to try?" Hale asked. James who had been quiet the whole time said, "don't get your hopes up, I think the best case would be that he survives and becomes your enemy." I gave him an evil look, I didn't like that response. "Maybe you should let witches handle witch business" I said. He just nodded and didn't say anything. "First, I want us to all do a healing spell on him at the same time and see what happens," I said, to Conan and Hale. "Yeah, we can try that, but I don't think you are going to have any better of a response than if it were just you or just one of us doing the spell" Conan said. I nodded, "I understand, but I still want to try," I said. They both nodded at me.

When we reached the house, we were greeted by Levi, "I think the curse is getting worse, he snapped at me and asked me why I killed his girlfriend" he said. I looked at him with an obvious worried face as we walked by to go inside where Jason was sitting. Levi grabbed my shoulder, "his loyalty to the enemy is dangerous" he said. I looked at him, "you will *not* hurt Jason! I will defend him as he is stabbing me in the heart if I have to" I said to him firmly. He looked at James and said, "she's going to get us all killed with her human attachments" he said to him. James just shrugged his shoulders, "maybe you should have realized what you were getting into before you literally jumped into it" James said to him. I walked inside with Conan and Hale.

Jason looked at me, "who are these clowns?" he said, sarcastically. "These *clowns* are here to try to help you," I said. "Like you helped Carly?" he said, with more attitude. "Jason, she hurt you, she hurt me, she wanted to *kill* me." I said. "You didn't even know her," he said, still defending. "Neither did you" I said, in defense. "We were in love, we were going to get married and have a family, but your friend *killed* her," he said, pointing out of the window at Levi.

"Would you listen to yourself? You met her a *week* ago" I said. "Love doesn't know time" is what it sounded like he said as he fell asleep, from a sleep spell that Hale put on him. "Sorry, I just think arguing is pointless at this time," he said. I nodded, feeling ashamed that I was even trying to talk some sense into him.

Conan, Hale and myself started the healing spell together. The mark actually faded just a bit, but it was still there. "We may have slowed it down a little, but it's still there," Conan said. "I think the only way this plan would work is if all the leaders from each of the thirteen covens came together and did it," Hale said. "That's impossible, when I know at least five of them want me dead" I said. "Yes, I know," Hale said, with a sadness in his voice. James stepped into the house. "Why don't you go study and see if you can come up with a spell that can help" he said to me. I nodded. "If you guys can, see if you can give him a better chance of surviving the curse" he said to Conan and Hale, they both nodded in agreement.

I went to my room to have peace and quiet so I could concentrate. I couldn't bear the thought of Jason dying just because he knew me. I didn't want him for an enemy, but that was something that could be fixed in the future, as long as there was a future. I looked at the firefly in the jar, I had studied about them and found out they hibernated in the winter, so I got her everything she needed, added dirt, she seemed to be adapting just fine in there. I had an *idea*! I busted out of my room, speaking louder than I should have been because I was excited. "What if we put a very heavy sleeping spell on him? Like a coma? To give us more time to remove the curse?!" I yelled. Conan and Hale looked at each other, "It may work" Conan said. James, who was standing close enough to Jason that he could stop him if he suddenly woke and tried to attack anyone, smiled, like he was proud.

"I think if all three of us do the spell together, it will be strong enough to hold until we release it ourselves" I said. "And I could take him to a hospital far away, and say that I found him like this, they will keep him as a 'John Doe' and take care of him!" I said. "It's a very good idea," Hale said. "I think we should do it now," I said. They both nodded in agreement and we began performing the spell together. It worked, Jason fell into such a sleep that we couldn't wake him. "Thank you both so much for coming here and for helping me" I said to Conan and Hale. Hale hugged me, "anytime, dear" he said. I felt a little bit of relief come over me, but I knew we weren't out of the woods yet.

Conan and Hale both agreed to stay for dinner. Yes, I invited people to dinner and I can't cook, so I ordered takeout. After I went and got the food and came back, we all sat down at the table, I almost felt like I was back at David's house. I looked over at James, he smiled at me and I smiled back. "So, what is your plan?" Conan asked. "I know you don't plan to hide here forever," he continued. "No, I don't plan to hide forever, and I don't really have a plan yet, just playing it by ear" I said. "You will eventually have to have a plan," Conan said to me. I just nodded at him, I didn't want to share too much with anyone, so whatever I had in mind, I was going to keep it there.

After dinner, Conan and Hale left. James and I put Jason in the car and got on the road. I wanted to take him far enough away so that if our friends went looking for him, they wouldn't find him. I started heading south, we drove for what seemed like hours, even though it was probably only thirty minutes, in silence. I sneezed and James jumped because he wasn't expecting it, I laughed at him, he just smiled back. "Are you mad at me?" I asked him. "No, I'm just worried," he answered. "Worried about what?" I asked. "Just everything in general, having to constantly watch our backs, about Philip and Margo" he said. "What about Philip and Margo?" I asked. "They can only stay in animal form for so long, usually about two years, before they lose their human side completely" he said. "We are far from two years, we've only been here a couple of *days*" I said. "I know, and it seems so long for me, I am not used to the time shift here" he said. I nodded, assuming he meant that time moves slower here.

After driving for a couple of hours, "you want me to drive for a while?" James asked. "No, I'm fine, unless you just really want to drive," I answered. "You can have it a little while longer then, where are we going anyway?" he asked. I shook my head, "not sure yet, but we have to get far enough away that he won't be easily found" I said. James nodded his head. "You seem different here than you did at David's" I said to him. "The atmosphere is different here," he replied. "Are you glad that Levi came yet? I think it's a good thing that he's here, think of how exhausted you would be if you had to babysit me all on your own," I said, jokingly. He just looked at me for a minute, "you're right, I am glad that I have his help," he said. "Why didn't you want him to come with us?" I asked. "Because, I saw the way he looked at you, he's a player, he wanted, and maybe still does, to add you to his collection of broken hearts," he said. "Oh, well then, he can't break what he doesn't have," I said. I saw him smile from the corner of my eye.

"And what is it that *you* want me for?" I asked, boldly. He let out a nervous giggle that almost made me laugh, but I was staying serious. "Okay, from the moment I first saw you, I thought you were gorgeous," he admitted. "Yeah, yeah" I said to get him to keep talking. "David told me not to pursue my crush, he said it would complicate things too much, make our mission harder. And I could see that you liked me too, so I started being a jerk to you, to make you hate me. Then I realized that you hating me wouldn't make our mission any easier either, so I stopped, I just tried to bury my feelings for you, I guess that didn't work, huh?" he said. "No, not really, and were you really in my dream? The one with the mermaid?" I asked. He looked confused and shook his head 'no'. "I am attracted to you, but I can also control my feelings. I was attracted to Levi when we first met, but now, I feel a more sibling-like feeling for him" I said. "I'm sure he will be thrilled to hear that" James said, sarcastically.

"We need gas, look for an exit with a gas station" I said. He nodded, after a couple of minutes he pointed to a sign that said 'exit in two miles, gas, food, lodging' I nodded, "good, I need to stretch my legs too" I said. Jason was lying in the back seat covered with a blanket, if anyone noticed him, our plan was to say that it was his birthday and he drank too much, so we were taking him home. It was dark out, so I wasn't really worried about anyone seeing him. I pulled off at the exit and pulled into a truck stop. They had a full service restaurant. "I'm going to go use the restroom, will you watch Jason?" I said to James. "Yeah, I'll pump the gas too," he said. "Okay, do you want anything?" I asked him. "Water," he said. I nodded, "no problem" I said. I went inside the store, it was busy with truck drivers and travelers, I found the restroom in a hall in between the cash registers and cases with little crystal figurines.

After using the restroom, I went to the sink to wash my hands, and I felt it, the same thing I felt before Carly attacked me, someone was using magic. I looked around, nothing looked out of the ordinary, but then everyone left the restroom and I was alone. I could still feel the magic in the air. An African-American woman walked in, she was looking at me, I soon realized she was the one using magic. She slammed my head into the mirror above the sink before I could do anything. I used magic to throw her against the wall, I held her there quite easily. "What is your problem?!" I screamed at her. "You!" she screamed back and then she spat at me, which caused a slight distraction and a weakness in my spell, so she was able to counteract it and get out of it. She came at me again, but I stopped her this time. I grabbed her hair and pulled her head back. "I don't know who you think you are, but you fucked with the wrong person!" I yelled at her.

"You killed my best friend, my sister," she said. "*I* didn't kill anyone!" I said. "I have never killed anyone, and I don't want to have to" I said. "If you are talking about Carly, yes she is dead because she attacked me, but I didn't kill her!" I continued. "It doesn't matter, she's dead, because of you, and I will avenge her death!" she screamed as she broke free from me. She managed to knock my legs from under me, I hit the floor hard with my head, a sharp pain shot through my body and I let out a scream. I felt dizzy, I knew I couldn't let myself pass out, I did a super quick healing, just enough so I could get back up and fight. It was just me and her here now, I knew James wouldn't come to help, he didn't know, I would have to end this, I would have to kill her. I pinned her against the wall again. Before I could think about it anymore, I snapped her neck, she fell to the floor and I watched the light go from her eyes. I stood there looking at her for a moment, then I heard footsteps. The spell she cast to keep people from coming in was broken now that she was dead, I quickly did a spell to make me invisible and walked out as women started walking in. I heard them scream at the sight of a dead woman on the floor. I went straight outside, I didn't see anyone around, so I ended my invisibility spell.

I ran to the car and got in the passenger side, "Let's go!" I yelled. James had been walking around outside of the car to stretch his legs. "What the hell happened?!" he yelled. Besides my sense of urgency, I also had blood on my face from it being slammed into the mirror. "One of Carly's friends followed us somehow" I said as I started crying. "I killed her," I whispered through my tears.

Six

Life after murder

James pulled the car over and held me while I cried. "I'm so sorry I wasn't there," he said. I shook my head, still crying, "it's not your fault" I said. He held me silently a little longer. "We need to get Jason to a hospital, I will do a spell to keep anyone else from following us" I said. James nodded, "did you ever decide where we are going?" he asked, as he pulled back onto the road. "New Orleans isn't too much further, probably a couple of hours, that will work" I said. He nodded, "are you sure you want him so far away? It will be hard for you to check on him" he said. "I don't need to anyway, I can't take any more chances of being followed" I said. I lay my head against the window and closed my eyes. I saw her dead eyes staring at me, so I opened my eyes and just stared at the road silently.

"I'm sorry, " James said after about thirty minutes of silence. I jumped a little at the sudden sound. "I don't really want to talk about it," I said. "You need to think, you need to get it out, I'm here, I'm listening, talk to me" he said. "Have you killed anyone before?" I asked him. "Yes, I have, sometimes it's necessary, kill or be killed" he said. "I keep seeing her eyes, the way the light just left" I said, quietly. "You just have to tell yourself that it was necessary, it was, necessary wasn't it? She would have killed you and then came after Jason," he said. "You would have stopped her from getting Jason," I said. "But you would have been gone," he said. "I don't think I could live with myself if you..." he said, without finishing. "Two days, we have been here, two people are dead now, how am I supposed to live with the guilt?" I asked. "Maybe there is a spell that can help, or maybe, you can just listen to me, you did what had to be done" he said.

I noticed that we were getting close to New Orleans. "I'm going to do a glamor spell on us, so that we won't be recognized by cameras. Then we can take him to the door, say we found him lying on the side of the road" I said. James nodded his head, "sounds good" he said. We were about fifteen minutes from the city and I noticed an exit with a hospital sign on it. "There, the next exit," I said. James nodded in agreement. He pulled off the exit and we followed the signs that directed us to the hospital. I did the glamor spell to disguise us. He pulled up to the emergency door and we got out, I started yelling for help, I was trying to act the part that I looked. I looked like a preppy blonde cheerleader. "Please help!" I yelled again. James, who looked much shorter in his disguise, was pulling Jason from the back seat. A stocky short older man came out of the entrance, "what's going on?" he asked. "We found this guy laying on the side of the road! He has a pulse, but we can't wake him up!" I said, frantically. James was still pulling him from the car. "Okay, stop!" the man said to James. "I will get help, we don't want to hurt him by moving him," the man said. James nodded at him and put Jason down slowly. The man came back out with help as he had said, they got Jason onto a gurney and wheeled him inside.

After they were out of sight, we jumped into the car and left, before they could come back and ask us any more questions. I removed the glamor spells because we looked ridiculous. I looked in the mirror, I still looked more ridiculous as myself, I still had dried blood on my face. Once we were out of view of the hospital, James pulled over. "Why don't we get a hotel room?" he suggested. I looked at him for a minute. I didn't want to get a room with him, but I was tired, and we were about seven hours from home. I reluctantly agreed by nodding my head in defeat.

We found a cheap motel, that wasn't too bad. After we checked in, I went to the bathroom and cleaned the blood off of my face. I didn't bring any extra clothes to change into, but I did feel just a little better. The room only had one bed, of course. "It's okay, I can crash out on the floor, I don't mind at all," James said. I nodded, this was his idea anyway and I wasn't going to sleep on the floor. I tried to close my eyes and I saw *her eyes* again. My eyes popped back open. "I don't know if I will be able to sleep," I said. James popped his head up, "how can I help?" he asked. "I don't think you can, you can't turn back time and you can't bring her back from the dead" I said, sarcastically. "No, I can't do either of those. I can come sit with you, I promise I won't do anything to you" he said with a nervous laugh. I nodded and moved over to give him room to come sit on the bed.

He sat down with his back on the headboard. I moved in closer to him, I put my head on his chest and I started crying again. He rubbed my head, "I know, and for what it's worth, if I could take it from you and have it myself, I would" he said. "Why are you being so nice to me now?" I asked, through the tears. "I told you already, there's no point in being any other way, especially now. You are hurting and I'm just trying to be here for you" he said, defensively. "Okay" I said. I lay there on his chest until exhaustion eventually took me over and I fell asleep. Of course she was there in dreamland, just waiting for me to join her. We fought over and over again all night, with the outcome always the same, her cold dead eyes looking up at me.

James woke me up right before it was about to happen again, I was glad that I was spared from at least one. "How do you feel?" he asked. "I watched her die in my sleep on repeat all night" I responded. "I'm sorry, there has to be something we can do," he said. I looked at him and shrugged my shoulders, I really had no idea, but if we could find something, I would be grateful. "Why don't you call Conan and Hale? Maybe one of them will know what you can do" he said. I nodded, "it won't hurt to try" I said. "Are you ready to get home?" he asked. "Yes" I said, nodding my head. I wanted to get changed into some clean clothes and actually take a shower, or a nice long bath.

We left the hotel and got back on the road. The car ride was mostly quiet. I did call Conan and Hale, they both agreed to meet us back at the house to try and ease my crazy mind. When we were almost back, I told James, "thank you." "For what?" he asked. "For being here, for helping me, for helping me fall asleep last night, I could go on and on" I said. He actually blushed! "Wow! Did you really just turn *red*?" I asked, teasingly. "No," he said, turning his head to try and hide it. "Human emotion is okay, you know," I said. "I don't have time for emotions," he said. "Okay" I said, sarcastically.

Conan and Hale were waiting at the road, as promised when we pulled up. "I am still amazed at the glamor on this place, no matter how hard I try to see through it, I can't," Hale said. "You killed someone?" Conan asked, looking at me sideways. "It was necessary, kill or be killed situation" James said, in my defense. "Well, in the life that we live, I will tell you that it is impossible to make it through *without* killing someone else," Hale said. I nodded at him, "but it doesn't change the feeling of guilt" I said, as I lowered my head. We led them to the house, Levi was waiting on the porch, we hadn't contacted him or let him know anything, he was going to be pissed.

James asked Levi to join him in the barn, so he could tell him what had happened. Conan, Hale, and myself went inside the house to try and fix me. "I can feel a spell on you, that is old, your mother must have put it on you to keep you from accidentally hurting anyone as a child. It's kind of like it gives you more humanity that most humans have, is the best way I can describe it. Maybe if we can remove that spell, it will help you" Conan said. "Us remove a spell that Valery did? Yeah right." Hale said. "I believe that the three of us could do it," I said. "Why was my mom so powerful?" I asked. "No one knows, magic just loved her and she used it gracefully" Hale said.

We all began working on removing the spell that she had placed, first they had to show me how to find it. I found several spells placed on me, it's like my entire life has not been my own. I could feel the spell start to unravel and I almost lost concentration because of it. After about a solid thirty minutes, I felt it release, I felt different, I felt free, I felt like I could make a decision if I wanted to, and I felt like killing someone who came after me was just an evil necessity. "I think it worked," I said. "You think? Or do you actually feel different?" Conan asked. "I feel it, I feel free," I said. Hale and Conan both nodded at me. I must have fainted after that, because that's all I remember before hitting dreamland.

I was on the streets, walking somewhere, but I didn't know where. I passed by a tent, and a woman came out, it was the same woman as before, the psychic that had grabbed my arm, the one that David said could have been Valery. "Mom?" I asked. "I did all that I did to protect you!" she scolded. "What are you talking about?" I asked. "Don't undo what I have done again if you want to have any chance at all of making it through this!" she said. "I'm sorry" I said, and she walked away. I kept walking through the street trying to find her, but there were a lot of people and more and more just kept flooding in, until I couldn't really see anything.

When I woke, everyone was surrounding me, and they had placed a cold wet towel on my head. "Ugh" I groaned, "does this really do anything to help?" I asked, pulling the towel off and holding it up. "What happened?" James asked, "is it the same thing that happened before? Using too much magic at once?" he continued asking questions. "Probably, but it could have just been Valery, she's not happy about me removing one of her *protection* spells from myself," I said. Hale let out a gasp, "you saw *Valery*?" He asked. "Yes" I said, nodding my head, "this is the second time I've seen her" I continued. Conan just looked at me with a worried look on his face. "What?" I asked him. "It's impossible," he said. "The living cannot interact with the dead, no matter how much magic is used, it is simply impossible" he continued. "I don't know why or how it happened, but it did, I even had a bruise from her grabbing my arm the first time" I told him.

I saw Levi walk out of the room from the corner of my eye. I sat up on the couch and told James to come sit next to me, looking at him and patting the seat next to me. Conan and Hale both stepped outside on the porch for fresh air. "How did Levi react when you told him everything?" I asked James. "He wants to leave, he says he is not part of this mission and he realizes that he should have never come" James said, bluntly. "I should talk to him, it's really not a good idea for him to leave now" I said. James knew that I was right, I had a feeling deep inside of me that Levi would prove to be useful in the future. "I want to ask Conan and Hale if they can stay here with us, the house is huge, plenty of room" I said. "I don't have a problem with that," James said. "Good! I'll ask them, but first, I do want to talk to Levi" I said. James nodded his head in agreement.

I walked upstairs to find Levi, he was in his room, I knocked on his door, which was open, but I didn't want to be rude and just walk in. "Yeah" he said, looking up at me. "Can I come in, can we talk?" I asked. "Sure," he said. "I'm sorry that what happened while we were gone happened, I'm sorry that we didn't contact you and tell you" I said to him. He just looked at me for a moment, "you guys don't need me here, I'm just a body here, in the way" he said. "That's not true and you know it" I said. "You love him, don't you?" he asked. "My feeling for anyone is none of your business, and it has nothing to do with our mission" I said, defensively. He nodded his head, "I know, but I thought it would be easier for me to stay if I had a chance," he said. He was making me angry now, "if that is the only reason why you came here, then I really don't care if you stay or not" I said, as I got up and left the room.

I guess the spell removal was already working, because I didn't feel bad for saying it, it felt justified in my head. He couldn't just go out into this world and try to make it on his own, and I knew that. He also couldn't go back to 2 just yet because of the amount of magic and the strain it puts on your body, it can only be done after everything has fully recovered from the last time, which takes about two months, most wait at least three months just to make sure. I found James standing in the kitchen, "how did your talk go?" he asked. The spell took away my willingness to hide my affections anymore, so without answering his question, I walked up to him, put my arms around his neck and up into his hair and pulled his face toward mine and kissed him, I kissed him like I have never kissed anyone else before. He kissed me back, his lips moving with mine and put a hand on each side of my head to control my movement. For a moment, the world and everything in it, besides us, disappeared.

After we stopped kissing, I looked at him and smiled, then I walked outside without saying a word. He stood there, silently for a while. I found Conan and Hale on the porch. "Hey guys, I wanted to talk to you about something" I said to them both. "You have definitely helped me a lot, in the short amount of time I have been back, and I thought it would be very helpful if you were both here. Before you say anything, hear me out, I realize that you have your own lives, what I want to do, is to get every coven on the same side, put an end to this stupid war and killing. If you decide to stay, the house is huge, you can definitely have your own space, your own room, and you know how good the glamor is on the place, you would be safe here" I said. "How long do you think it will take?" Conan asked, "because the covens have been divided for a very long time" he continued. "I wish I could give you an amount of time, but I have no idea" I admitted. "Well, I am single and alone and having company would actually be nice for me," Hale said. I smiled at him, "so you're in?" I asked. "I'm in!" he said with excitement. "Can you give me some time to think about it?" Conan asked. "Sure, in the meantime, if we get attacked again, I'll just have to call you to come back, which, you know, will probably be tomorrow anyway" I said sarcastically. He rolled his eyes at me. "I'm not sure I even like the new you" he said, also sarcastically.

Hale needed to go get some of his things, so I asked Levi to go with him, and protect him. Levi was happy to go, happy to have a purpose in the mission again. Conan told me he would be in contact soon when he left, I nodded and told him he had better and not to take too long. When everyone was gone, I went looking for James, I knew I would find him in the barn talking to Philip and sure enough that's where he was, he wasn't talking anymore when I walked in, he was quietly brushing Philip's mane. "You better be careful, If I didn't know any better, I would think you two were a couple" I said, teasing. He stopped brushing and looked at me. I turned and started walking out of the barn, knowing he would follow me, and sure enough he did.

He caught up to me, midway to the house. "What was that, in the kitchen earlier?" he asked, seriously. "I don't know what you mean, was Levi trying to cook again?" I said, teasing. He rolled his eyes at me. "You know what I mean," he said. "Not really" I said, with a smirk. "So are we forgetting that it happened?" he asked. "As if you could" I said, as I started skipping like a child to get ahead of him, I did just a little, so I sat down on the porch. "Where is everyone?" he asked. "Conan went home, Hale went home to get his things to come back, so I sent Levi with him to look after him and help him." I answered. "Conan isn't coming back?" he asked. "He said, he will have to *think* about it" I said. James just looked at me and nodded his head, then his eyes got wide, as I think it finally hit him that we were here alone.

I stood up and walked over to him, looked him in the eyes and kissed him again. He put his hands on either side of my face as he kissed me back. After a few intense moments, I broke the kiss, I looked at him and smiled. I wanted him, and for whatever reason, I guess that was selfish, but I know longer cared that it was selfish. He smiled back at me. He brought his head down and rested it on mine, with our foreheads touching. "David didn't want us to be together," he whispered. "Excuse me? What does it matter to him?" I asked. "He said there were so many reasons why it's a bad idea," he told me. "Well, I think it's clear how I feel about you, you should think about how you feel, not how anyone else feels," I said. Apparently he liked that comment. He smiled at me as he scooped me up and carried me inside.

He took me to my bedroom where he set me on my bed and pulled his shirt off. I pulled him down to me and kissed him, he moved his kisses from my mouth to my neck and started to kiss harder, I let out a moan and he pulled my shirt off. I slid my hands down his torso, to his pants and found the button, I worked it undone and started pushing them down with my feet. He moaned with excitement as he continued kissing me, my neck, my breasts, down to my stomach. I let out another moan, and his head came back to my mouth. "Are you sure?" he whispered. I let out a "Yes!" with a moan. I looked into his beautiful eyes as he entered, he felt so good, I moaned and my eyes rolled back into my head.

After we both orgasmed, he rolled over to my side, we both lay there, catching our breath. After a few minutes, I rolled over and put my head on his chest, I could hear his heart beating. He started playing with my hair and for all the magic I had learned recently, this felt more magical than anything else to me, just lying here with him, hearing his heartbeat in my ear. And at some point, I drifted to sleep. Valery was waiting, scolding. "What do you think you are doing?" she demanded. "What do you mean? Are you watching *everything*?" I asked. "I don't have to watch, to know," she replied. "You are making things as complicated as possible, just stick to your plan with no more distractions please" she said. She took a pen and wrote something on my hand. I nodded at her, not sure why, I started not feeling in control of myself, like I was in a real dream. I heard the mermaids sing and then I woke up with a start.

James was still here, I didn't wake him as I got up and went to the kitchen and made me a cup of coffee. I looked at my hand, sure enough, although it looked like I had washed my hands at least two times since she had written it, but still, my hand said, 'call Damian again.' Suddenly, there were arms wrapping around me, I jumped and almost threw him to the floor before I realized it was James. "Sorry, why are you so jumpy?" he asked. I showed him the writing on my hand, he squinted his eyes. "I can barely see it, who does it say to call?" he asked. "Damian," I said. "Did you write that in your sleep?" he asked. I shook my head 'no,' "Valery did" I said, simply.

"What do you mean? She was in your dream again? And she wrote on you? In your dream?" James asked. I just nodded, the answer to all his questions was 'yes'. "This is getting out of hand, can we do anything to block her?" he asked. I shrugged my shoulders and said, "I don't know, apparently it's 'impossible' anyway, so I really don't know if there is anything that we can do. I will talk with Hale about it when he gets back" I told him. "She's not happy about us," I said. "What do you mean? Was she *watching*?" he asked. "I said the same thing, she said she didn't have to watch to know" I told him. His shirt was still off, I turned around and put my arms around him, he put his hand under my chin and pushed it up toward him and kissed me. I pulled away from his kiss to ask him "should we keep this a secret from the others?" "Why?" he asked. "Well for one, to keep them from bitching at us, and for two, to keep jealousy out of everything" I said, talking about Levi. Sure Levi was handsome, but he didn't hold a candle to James, at least not through my eyes. "We can keep it to ourselves for as long as possible," he agreed.

"Okay, I'm going to go get a shower" I said. He nodded, "I should go do that as well," he said. After my shower, I came out of my room and found that Hale and Levi had returned. "Great you guys are back, did you have any issues?" I asked, sincerely. "No issues, everything went smoothly," Levi said. "How did you sleep?" Levi asked. And I got the feeling that he could sense what had happened and was waiting for a confession. "Funny you should ask that!" I said, as I turned toward Hale, "Valery was in my dream again, she wrote this on my hand." I held up my hand which was even more faded now that I had taken a shower, you could barely see it. "I can't read it, it's too light," he said. "It says to call Damian again," I told him.

"Do you know if there is a way we can block her from getting to me?" I asked Hale. "She has bruised my arm and now written on me, I think she could do anything she wants to do and that really freaks me out" I told him. "She's your mother, do you really think she would ever do anything to hurt you?" he asked. I saw James coming down the stairs and Levi looked relieved. "Good morning everyone, what is going on?" he asked as he got to the bottom step. "I was just asking Hale if we can block Valery" I said. "I wouldn't know where to start with a spell like that, honestly, I have never heard of the dead interacting with the living," Hale told me. I nodded my head, but I wasn't going to just drop it. Something inside me told me that I needed to block her, maybe she wasn't even Valery, I hadn't seen a picture of her, so I really had no idea that it was really her.

"Did you meet her?" I asked Hale. "No, unfortunately," he answered. "Do you know anyone who might have a picture of her?

What if it's not even her that has been attacking me in my dreams?" I suggested. I saw a look of worry go across James' face. "What do you mean?" James asked. "Why would my own mother leave a bruise on my arm or scare me?" I asked. "I mean, I didn't know her, I've never seen a picture of her, the only reason we thought it was her was from my description of her " I said. "I really think you guys should figure out a way to block this person, whether it's your mom or not," James said to me. "That's exactly how I feel," I said, as I looked at Hale. "I'll start looking in my books" he said, as he walked away, sounding defeated. "So, what did you two do last night?" Levi suddenly asked. I mumbled "I had a crazy dream, haven't you been listening?" as I walked away into my room. I didn't hear James say anything, and I wondered to myself if it was a good idea to hide things from our friends. I guess it was a case of what they don't know, can't hurt them.

I looked through my books as well, trying to find something, anything. There was no protection from dreams or from the dead that I could find. Then I had an idea, I went to find Hale, so I could go over it with him. I finally found the room he chose, I think it was the last room I checked. I knocked on the door frame because the door was open. "You found me," he said, laughing. "So you picked the last room in the hall on purpose then?" I asked him. "Of course!" he said. "Okay. So, I had a thought, what if we cast a protection spell as if it is someone living?" I asked. "What do you mean? I don't see how that could possibly work" he said. "Well, the person in my dream can physically touch me, so why not?" I asked. He shrugged his shoulders, "if you think it might possibly work, I don't see a reason to not try it" he said. We cast the protection spell together and I crossed my fingers that it worked.

Levi came out of his room as I was walking down the hallway. "Oh hey, can I talk to you?" he asked. "About what?" I replied. "I just wanted to say, that I know how I felt about you was a crush, if you are in love with James, and I do believe you are, from the way you look at him, don't hold back to spare my feelings. I'm a big boy, I'll be okay. And I don't plan on leaving," he said to me. I just nodded my head at him and continued down the hall. Did he expect me to say 'thank you' for staying, or for giving me his 'blessing' to be with James? "I didn't mean to offend you either!" he yelled, as I was exiting the hallway.

I walked outside to the porch to just sit and relax and breathe in the cool crisp fall air. I wasn't alone long, James walked out of the front door and spotted me. He smiled and walked over, he sat in the chair closest to me, "have you made up your mind, did you want to make contact with Damian again?" he asked. "Not sure, Hale and myself did do a protection spell, only time will tell if it worked" I said. He nodded, "yeah, it doesn't hurt to try, I guess" he said. "So, Levi gave me permission to be with you" I said, sarcastically. He spit his coffee out everywhere, "*What?*" he said. "Yes you heard correctly, he stopped me earlier and said he wasn't going to leave and he said he didn't care if we were together" I told him. "Well, then" James said, simply while rocking in the rocking chair he was sitting in.

We sat there for what seemed like the longest time, in silence. Finally I said, "my goal is to unite the covens, to end the war, it's not going to happen if I don't get to work on it. I may as well contact Damian again, make sure he is on my side" I said. James nodded while giving me a serious look, "promise me that you will be careful about this, you already know that at least five of the covens want you dead" he said. I gave him a nod of agreement.

I went back inside and went to my bedroom and called Damian again. He answered promptly. "What kind of trouble are you in now, miss?" He asked. I shook my head, "no trouble, at least not immediately" I said. "So you just called to chit chat?" he asked. "No, not that either" I said. "Well then, why don't you tell me why you are calling?" he said. "I'm calling because I want to share with you what I plan to do here," I said. "Why would you share information with me? You barely know me." he said. "I think you will want to join me, and help me once you hear what I plan to do," I said. "Oh, please, do tell," he said, sarcastically. "Before I tell you, I do want to let you know that I already have a couple of high priests on my side, I am not alone" I said. "Okay, I'm listening," he replied. "My goal is unite *all* of the covens, have everyone see eye to eye, no more killing, no more hating, no more banning interspecies reproduction" I said. He started laughing, "so you're telling me that you plan to end a two thousand year old war?" he said, still laughing. "Laugh all you like, there will unfortunately be casualties along the way, so when it's your turn to fight, I hope you are going to battle with the winning side" I said.

After a long pause, he said, "So what would you want from me?" "I want you to prove your loyalty, the time to do that will present itself. So, you need to make a decision" I said to him. "If you want some time to think, I can call you back in the morning" I continued. He nodded, "Yeah, give me a call in the morning," he agreed. I ended the call and went to find James to tell him about the conversation. I found him in the barn with Philip. "So, what are you going to make him do? How will he prove his loyalty?" he asked me. "I'm not sure yet," I admitted. Philip motioned for me to get on his back, like he had done before. James smiled at me, "I'll help you up" he said to me, holding his hand down in a cusp for me to step in. I shrugged my shoulders, "Why not?" I said.

After riding around the field for about thirty minutes, I told Philip to let me down, near the house. I went inside and went to my bathroom to take a shower. After a quick shower, my stomach rumbled, I tried to think when was the last time I ate, I couldn't remember. After getting dressed, I headed to the kitchen. I found stuff to make myself a sandwich. After having a shower, and eating, I felt like a new person. I started trying to think of a way to have

Damian prove his loyalty. I decided on a plan, no one was going to like it, so I didn't share it with anyone. I told everyone that I needed to run to town. All of them refused to let me go without taking at *least* one of them with me, Hale seemed like he would understand the plan before James or Levi would, they simply *would not* let me go through with it.

"Okay, I want Hale to come with me, it will give us a chance to get to know each other better anyway" I said. "I'll come too," James said. "No, you stay here, try to learn how to cook something for dinner" I said, looking at him teasingly. I didn't want him to be suspicious, so I added, "I need some girl talk time anyway" while winking at Hale. Hale looked at James and back at me and smiled. "I'm just going to run by the restaurant, talk to everyone and let them know that I can't come back right now" I said, looking down. "So, you decided not to go back to work?" James asked. "I don't want to endanger them by being there." I said. He nodded. "Plus, we are pretty powerful together," I said, pointing to Hale and myself. They finally agreed to let me go with just Hale.

Once we got to the car, I started telling Hale my plan. "I want to drive somewhere else, so she can't track me and I am going to call Misty," I said. His face turned white. "*Why?*" he asked. "She is our most powerful enemy. I will talk to her, try to get a feel for how she feels, but mainly, I want to know what she looks like, so I can glamor myself to look like her," I explained. "James is going to kill me if anything happens to you. Why do you insist on putting yourself and others that are trying to help you, in danger?" he asked. "That's why I'm leaving the house, there will be no danger" I explained. "Why do you want to look like her? What is your plan?" he asked. "That's how I will test the other's loyalty" I said. "This is a horrible idea," Hale said, as I sped away from the house. I did drive by the restaurant to talk with them, like I had said I would do, I didn't want to be a total liar.

I bought Hale something to eat while we were at the restaurant. Dan made me promise to come back and visit, and that if I changed my mind, they would always welcome me back. I hugged him and told him thank you. When we were finished, I drove to the graveyard that I used to like to visit. "This is a good place, I've always liked this graveyard," I told Hale. "There is heavy protection here," he said. "Maybe when David was watching me before, he had a witch put protection on it, because I liked to come here a lot?" I said with a shrug. "Why don't you get out, go walk around while I make the call, she doesn't need to see or hear you and know that you are with me" I suggested. He nodded, "I won't go out of eyesight," he said. I nodded in agreement.

When he got out, I made the call. Misty seemed to recognize me right away. She had pale skin, with dark curly hair, brown eyes and a thin pointed nose. "I'm impressed that you have the nerve to call me," she said. "I want to know what it would take for a truce?" I said. She laughed, "from the person that has already killed two of my witches?" she said. "I had no choice, they came after me!" I said. "I know you think that I shouldn't exist, and that I need to be exterminated, but I promise you, I am not like Seth, and I never wanted anyone to die" I continued. She seemed to be listening, or making me think she was, as a distraction. "But yet, as I already said, two of my witches are dead," she said. "I just want to unite the covens, abolish outdated laws, can you imagine how powerful we would all be united?" I asked, she seemed like the type that was power hungry, so I tried to feed that part of her. "I am already powerful, why would I want to give my enemies power?" She asked. "They don't have to be your enemies." I said. "I'll tell you what, if you hand over Jason, I will consider it," she said. I just looked at her in shock. "I can't do that," I said. "So, now you understand how it feels to be asked to do something that you cannot do," she said. "I do believe this conversation is over" she added, as she hung up on me.

I put the glamor on myself immediately, before I forgot what she looked like. I honked the horn to let Hale know that I was finished and ready to go. He got in the car before actually looking at me. Once he noticed me, he let out an "Oh" and grabbed his chest. "It's me," I said with a giggle. "I know, I just wasn't expecting this as soon as I got in the car," he said. "I wanted to do it, before I forgot what she looked like," I explained. I also pulled out my phone and took a bunch of selfies, just in case I needed this disguise again. Hale did a spell to figure out where Damian was and we started driving. "Maybe you should just call him and pretend to be her," Hale suggested. I shook my head no, "it would be too easy for him to trace the call" I said. Hale nodded, "what if he sees through the glamor?" He asked. "He won't," I said, confidently.

We got to the house where Hale's spell said Damian was. It was a huge mansion with a gate, "I think if we pull up, he will let us in, but first, I'm going to make you look like someone else" I told Hale. I glamoured him to look like a henchman basically, big muscular guy with a suit and sunglasses. "Oh, I'm kind of cute," he said, as he looked in the mirror admiring his reflection. "Okay, stop that," I said with a giggle. I pulled up to the gate and called inside from the callbox. I was quite nervous, but I didn't let it show. "Misty! What a surprise!" I heard Damian say from the callbox. "Well, don't make me sit out here all day," I said into the box. The gate opened, too late to turn back now.

I pulled into a circular drive, there was a fountain in the middle of the circle, I stopped my car between two sets of stairs that led to the porch. I looked at Haled, and said, "fancy." We got out of the car and walked up one set of the stairs. Damian greeted us at the door, I walked inside with all the confidence I could muster, like I owned the place. Hale followed closely behind me. "I'm shocked to see you," Damian said. I just glared at him, "surely not, I would think you would have been expecting me, with all that is going on" I said. He nodded, and looked at Hale. "This is Ben, he is a dear friend of mine" I said. "My coven does not wish to be involved in this war" Damian said. "Unfortunately, you don't have a choice, it's not an individual war, it's a witch war, and you are a witch" I told him.

"Yes, I am, but this is *not* my fight," he said. "Are you challenging *me*?" I asked. "I am not, I am only challenging what you are saying" he replied. "Have you spoken with the enemy?" I asked. "I have not spoken with anyone," he lied. This was a good sign, I felt like I should make him hate Misty now, force him further into *my* corner. "I do hope you have strong protection for your witches, they will need it," I said. "Is that a threat?" he asked. I smiled at him, "during a war, there are a lot of casualties, even if they choose not to get involved," I said. "The enemy is powerful, maybe even more so than myself, but together we could defeat her," I said to him as one last test. He shook his head, "please leave, I do not wish to get involved in this" he said. I stood up, "fine, have it your way, and have fun at all the funerals," I said sarcastically. I walked to the door and Hale followed.

As soon as we got out of the gate, I took the glamor off. "I think we have got him on our side, or at least, I think we can" I told Hale. Hale nodded, "I agree," he said. I began to drive toward home. That thought was a bit weird to me, I hadn't been in that house for very long, but it felt like home already, like it was exactly where I needed to be. And the people in the house, they felt like family. For once in my life, I had a real home and a real family. Suddenly, a pickup truck ran a red light as I was going through a green light. I barely saw it from the corner of my eye before it struck on my side at a very high speed.

Seven

The war has begun

I woke up in my room, very confused. Was it a dream? What had happened? "Hale!?" I yelled. James came into my room, "he's fine!" he said quickly to calm me down. "What happened?" I asked James. "An attack happened, fortunately, this time, your car was the only casualty" he said. "How did I get back here?" I asked. "Hale, used a lot of magic to warp you both back here and heal you, he's asleep, he used a *lot* of magic" he said. "He has magic sickness?" I asked, just to confirm my suspicion. James nodded, "what did you guys do?" he asked. He would be so angry with me if I told him the truth, but he would also be angry with me if I lied, I was in trouble either way. I told him the truth.

He stood there looking at me in disbelief for a moment. "Why would you do this? You could have been killed, you could have gotten Hale killed!" he started yelling at me. "We are in a war! I am trying to gain allies!" I yelled, in my defense. "That's right! We are in a war, yet you keep going on private missions! You should have told me!" he yelled. Levi heard us yelling and walked in. "You would have stopped me! You think that somehow this war will be won by sitting here and doing nothing because it's safe!" I yelled. "Oh, she's betrayed you now too?" Levi said, sarcastically.

"This has nothing to do with you!" I yelled at Levi. "Yes it does!" James yelled. "We are *all* a team! So whatever one of us does, affects *all* of us!" James yelled. "You are not here to fight this war alone! But if you don't stop trying, you will be!" James said, as he stormed out of my room. Levi stood there and looked at me. I just sat there. I knew deep down inside, he was right. If I didn't start including them, I would end up dead or alone. I walked past Levi without saying anything to go find James.

He was on the porch this time, instead of in the barn like usual. "You're right, I'm sorry" I said, as I sat in the chair next to him. "I'm just scared to tell you things, afraid that you will try to stop me, because of your feelings for me" I admitted. He sat there, looking at me. "This is one of the many reasons David gave me that we should not be together" he said, as he got up and started walking toward the barn. "So, you're just going to walk away? How does that help?" I yelled after him. I just sat there, I didn't go after him, even though I wanted to, I wanted to run to him, kiss him, make him feel better, make me feel better, but I just sat there.

After sitting on the porch for about thirty minutes, I felt a very cool breeze coming. Levi stepped outside, "cold front moving through tonight" he said. I got up and walked inside, I wanted to check on Hale. He was still asleep, it took a lot of magic to do what he did, I can only imagine if one more person had been with us, someone would be dead. I sat there with him for a while, then I decided to call Conan. "What's wrong?" he answered. "Wow, am I really that predictable?" I asked. "Well, you've never called to chit chat," he said. I nodded, "we were attacked, Hale and myself, Hale used a lot of magic to save us, now he has magic sickness" I said. "I'm sure that he will be fine, have him drink some of the tea that I left there when he wakes up" he said. I nodded, "okay, is there anything else I can do to help him?" I asked. Conan shook his head, "no, just have to let his magic rebuild" he said. "Okay, I'll keep you updated, or have him call you when he's feeling better" I said. "Thank you," Conan replied.

After speaking with Conan, I went to my room and lay down on my bed. I must have been more tired than I thought, so I fell straight to sleep. I was in a strange house, I looked out of the window, I didn't recognize anything. But then, I looked into the sky, two moons, was I back on 2? But one of the moons was quite faded, so I could be on 7, or anywhere in between 2 and 7. I heard footsteps coming toward the door of the room I was in. The door opened, the same woman who has been haunting my dreams stepped inside. That's when I realized that I was dreaming. "Who *are* you?" I demanded. "It doesn't matter who I am, what does matter is that you listen to me" she said. "Are you Valery?" I asked her. "You did something very dangerous today," she said, ignoring my question. "What are you going to do when one of your friends dies because of a bad decision you make?" she asked. I held my head down, she was right, I wouldn't be able to live with myself if that happened. "I just want you to listen, to pay attention to what I say. You still need to contact Damian, he will be on your side and he will help you to get others on your side" she told me. "Your friends need you. Go," she said.

I woke to the sound of people running through the house and I was shivering. It was so cold. I put my bath robe on for a little warmth and followed the sound of the footsteps. Levi and James were running around, trying to figure out how to work the heat, it was quite comical actually. If I hadn't been so cold, I would have laughed at them. "Nice of you to join us" James said sarcastically, as he tried to light a pilot light. I lit it with a spell and a nice warm blaze came from the furnace. "I'm going to go into the other room, try to get the wood fireplace working as well," Levi said. "Are Philip and Margo okay?" I asked. "They will be fine, I got a small heater in the barn going, it warmed it by twenty degrees at least in there" James said. I nodded, "Has anyone checked on Hale?" I asked. "No, we've been busy, trying not to freeze to death," James said. I nodded at him as I walked away to go check on Hale.

I opened the door to his room, he hadn't moved since the last time I had been in there, he looked the same. I remembered when I was sick, the sickness wouldn't get better until I let go of the spell that I didn't even know I was casting. And I wondered if he was holding onto a spell? If so, what could it be? Did he know we were safe now, back at the farm house? I sat down on his bed next to him, "Hale" I said, in a low but clear voice. He didn't move. I ran my hand from his forehead, up his hairline, and brushed his hair from his face. He didn't feel warm or cold, and he didn't budge. I suddenly felt like he wasn't here, like his body was here, yes, and he wasn't dead, but his soul was somewhere else. Maybe he astral projected and got lost? Was that possible? How could I find him if that was the case?

I went to find James, to tell him my idea. "It's dangerous to go looking for him," he said. "So what are we supposed to do?" I asked. "I need another witch here! I am not smart enough about magic to do all this on my own" I said. "I understand that, but what if someone has his soul trapped and they are waiting for you to come along so they can trap you as well?" James said. "We have got to be smarter than the enemy, *You* have got to be smarter," he said. "Oh so I'm dumb now?" I asked, feeling hurt. "You have obviously not made the best decisions since we've started this," he said. I looked at him and nodded, a tear fell down my cheek, he was right, I have continuously put them in danger and now, poor Hale may be lost. "Don't do that, don't start crying to make me feel bad," he said. "I'm crying because *I* feel bad," I said, as I stormed to my room.

I called Conan back. I told him my thoughts about Hale and everything that James had said. "It is possible that you are right," Conan said. "James is also right," he added. "The astral world is nothing to mess with, and if someone has his soul trapped, he will die," Conan told me. "So, what do I do?" I asked, desperately. "I will come out, we will try to recall his soul together, get everything we need ready," he said. I smiled and nodded. I started gathering herbs and crystals, and I also got the tea ready for Hale to drink, if we were able to recall his soul. I told James and Levi that Conan was coming to help. "Well, it's too cold out for you to go meet him, I'll go," Levi said. "I can go, I can ride Philip, so it will be a bit quicker" James said. "It really doesn't matter who goes," I said, to try to keep them from arguing. James ended up going, and riding Philip like he said. He put on a lot of extra layers of clothing. "It's so cold, that I would say it's magic, this kind of cold, in November, in Tennessee? I mean, yeah, the weather here has always been crazy, but, this is more than crazy" I said, as I walked James to the door. "Please be careful" I said. He looked me in the eyes for a moment, before going out.

I went back into Hale's room, to sit with him as a distraction from worrying about James. Levi followed me, "don't worry about James, he'll be fine" he assured me. I nodded, even though I knew I couldn't just stop worrying. "Sometimes I still wish that I would wake up, and this would have all been a dream," I said. Levi gave me a smirk, as he quoted Shakespeare to me "'Life is but a dream, within a dream.'" I just sat there, no more emotion to show, I was too worried about Hale, and now, until they returned, about James, Conan and even Philip.

Finally after what seemed like hours, but was only about thirty minutes, the front door opened. I ran to greet them, James pulled Conan inside and they went straight to the fire that Levi had managed to get going. Levi added another log. "Don't sit too close, you need to warm up slowly" I said. "It's like the damn arctic out there!" James said, with a shiver. "Is Philip okay?" I asked him. He nodded, still shivering uncontrollably. I nodded, you two just sit here for a bit, I'll get you some hot coffee to help" I said.

After sitting by the fire and warming up for at least fifteen minutes, Conan said, "This weather is crazy, I almost think someone is using magic to effect it." "Is that possible?" I asked. "It would take a *lot* of magic, and a large group to do it, but, yes" Conan said. "What would be the point of doing it though?" I asked. "That, I don't know," he replied. James stood up, "are you okay?" I asked him. He nodded, but gave me a worried look. I gave him a look, in return and nodded my head toward my room, to suggest I would meet him there. He walked away first, then I looked at Conan and said "excuse me for just a moment."

I walked into my room where James was waiting. "This has to be another attack, or at least part of it" he said, with worry. "We are fine, for now at least, we just need to get Hale back," I assured him. He bent down and kissed me, it took me by surprise, but I enjoyed it nonetheless. When he stopped kissing me, he held his head right above mine and said, "sorry, I just needed to do that." "Don't be sorry" I said, with a smile. He smiled back at me and lay his forehead on mine. "Let's go try to get Hale back" I said. "Okay" he agreed, and took my hand as we walked back out to the living room.

Levi was there with Conan, he saw that James and I were holding hands and turned his head the other way. I guess even though he had given me his 'blessings' he was still a bit jealous. I suppose that was his problem and not mine, as long as he didn't cause any issues, I didn't really care. "Do you think you are ready to go see Hale now?" I asked Conan. "Yes," he said with a nod. Conan and I walked into Hale's room together, I asked James to wait outside, and that if we needed anything, we would call him in. Conan walked over to him, he put his hand on his forehead, "he's really cold" he said, then began to feel for a pulse. I think my heart stopped for a minute, until Conan said, "he has a pulse, it's really weak though."

"I think you are right, I think his astral self is somewhere else, and it will completely drain him, if we can't bring him back," Conan said. "How do we even find him?" I asked, starting to feel hopeless. "Sit here" he said, pointing to the left side of the bed, and "I'll sit here" he said, patting the right side of the bed. "Both of us touching his physical body and meditating, I think will lead us to his astral body," Conan told me. I nodded, to let him know that I understood as I sat down on the bed, like he told me to. He sat on the other side like he said, and he walked me into meditation. "Breathe slowly, regularly, concentrate on your breathing, until you can't hear or feel anything else" he told me.

I did just as he said, and suddenly, I felt like I was floating, I had astral projected! I was floating very quickly through the forest, above the trees, I couldn't feel the extreme cold or the wind blowing through my hair, all I could feel was something pulling me, I was hoping it was my spell, pulling me to Hale. After a few minutes, I was pulled to the edge of a graveyard. I was being pulled and pushed at the same time, it was like, I was supposed to enter, but I wasn't allowed to enter at the same time. I looked at the cemetery gates to get the name, Howard Cemetery, then I released the spell I was casting. I wanted to return to my body quickly, and it seemed like no time at all and I was there. Conan looked like he was still trying, I nudged his shoulder, "I can't concentrate with you pushing on me" he said. "I think I know where he is!" I said, with excitement.

"You seriously already astral projected and found him?" He asked. I nodded, "yes" I said. "I was pulled to a cemetery," I said. "Astrals can't enter cemeteries," Conan said. "I was pulled to it, not into it, but my spell to find Hale wanted me to go into it, I was being pulled and pushed at the same time, until I released the spell and came back" I explained. "Okay, but how would Hale's astral get in there?" Conan asked. "I'm not sure, I'm guessing someone pulled him in, and trapped him. We have to find a way to release him!" I said. "We will have to physically go, I got the name, it was Howard Cemetery" I said. "*What?*" Conan said, with shock. "What?" I asked, confused. "Howard Cemetery is in a small town three hours from here, it's in the town that I grew up in," he explained. "Do you think he has three hours?" I asked, looking at Hale. "I'm not sure, but we need to go right away," he said.

I was explaining to James as I was grabbing herbs and crystals and a couple of spell books, since I didn't know how to release his astral body when I got there, but I had three hours to figure it out. "It's a trap, they will be waiting for you" he said, shaking his head. "I'm not leaving him, he will die!" I said. "I am coming with you," he said. "I don't think that is a good idea" I said, feeling that he would be more of a distraction than help. "I don't care," he replied. I gave him a hurt look, "you don't care?" I said. "I don't have time to argue with you, Hale could die before we even get there as it is now, we have to go" I said, with force. "Will you let Levi go?" he asked, sounding defeated. "No, Conan and I can handle this! Let witches handle witch business" I said.

So that we wouldn't freeze and to save a little time, I warped us to the pickup truck. That was the first time I had done that, it *did* take a *lot* of magic. The windows were frosted, Conan used magic to clear them. "You shouldn't have done the warp spell, I have a feeling we are going to need all the magic we have once we get to the cemetery," Conan said. I nodded in agreement, "what's done is done, I can't take it back now," I said. I called James, "I'm sorry, but I need you there, and I don't need any distractions, call me if Hale wakes up," I said. "Fine," he agreed, sounding a little angry. Conan drove while I looked through the books to try and figure out what had happened to Hale. How did he get trapped in a place where he wasn't allowed to go in the first place?

"I think I found something!" I said with excitement. "What is it?" Conan asked. "Outside spirits cannot enter consecrated grounds, as inside spirits cannot leave" I explained. "Yes, I know that," he said. "There is a spell to release the hold, someone released the hold, got him inside somehow, and then trapped him. We have to do the spell to release the hold" I said. "Is that the only way?" Conan said, sounding worried. "It's the only thing I can find, do you have any other ideas?" I asked him. He shook his head, "No, I'm just worried about what else we could possibly release" he said. "I will text the guys, it shouldn't take Hale long to get back to his body, I will have them contact us as soon as he wakes up and then we can close the hold back. It should be a minimal amount of time," I said. "It may work," he said.

"And if it is an ambush, what is the plan?" He asked. We both knew that we would more than likely have someone waiting for us. "How far away can we perform the spell?" I asked. "I'm not sure, especially since you used so much magic to warp us to the truck," he replied. I called James back. "Yeah" he answered. "As soon as Hale wakes up, let me know, we have to do a dangerous spell, we can end the spell as soon as we know he is safe" I explained. "Please don't get hurt" James said, in a voice I hadn't heard from him before, he almost sounded like a child. "I don't plan on it" I said to try and reassure him.

"We will try to start the spell when we are five minutes away" I said to Conan. "Okay, but I really don't know if that will work," he said. We were about thirty minutes away, "I'm going to close my eyes and rest, try to recharge before we get there," I said. He nodded. I didn't want to lose Hale, or anyone for that matter, I would do anything to help my friends, my family. Before I knew it, Conan said, "we are about six minutes away." I opened my eyes. "Are you ready to begin?" I asked him. "James actually would have come in handy right about now, so I could concentrate more on the spell instead of driving," he said. "Well, it's too late for that now," I said. He held out his hand and I put mine into it.

We started working the spell, he was right, it wouldn't reach quite yet. He pulled his hand away, "no sense in wasting our energy, we'll wait a couple more minutes," he said. I nodded. I could sense magic nearby, so I started looking around. "What are you doing?" he asked me. "You don't feel that?" I asked. "Feel what?" he replied. "I can feel magic," I said. He gave me a confused look. "Really? I just assumed that was something all witches could do," I said. "It's not a good sign, every time I have felt it, I got attacked right after," I continued. "Not all witches can sense magic, it is a rare gift," He said. He had a worried look on his face now. He held out his hand, "let's try again" he said. Once the spell went out, I could feel it, it was right at the border of the cemetery, he accelerated the gas, and we broke through the cemetery walls. My phone began ringing, and we broke the spell immediately. I answered the phone, "he's back!" James said with excitement. "That's great! We are turning around now!" I said, as Conan was doing a U-turn.

Lights came on behind us, I knew it was someone coming after us. They hadn't expected us to do the spell from a distance. I could feel that my magic was weak now, I'm sure Conan was the same, he gave me a worried look. "We won't be able to get away," he said. "Just keep driving" I said, because I didn't know what else to say or do at the moment. The car got closer and closer. It finally pulled up right next to us, it was Misty. "Wow, she came herself this time," Conan said. I let out a nervous laugh. She started doing magic to force us off the road. *Misty is chasing us, she's about to run us off the road.* -Me. *What? Where are you?!* -James. I didn't have enough time to text him again. We got rolled over into a ditch. I was hanging upside down,

I looked over at Conan, he was unconscious, I checked for a pulse and found one, that was one sigh of relief.

I heard footsteps coming along, I placed an invisible spell on Conan. My door was suddenly pulled off of the truck completely. "Sometimes when you want a job done, you just have to go do it yourself" Misty said. I grabbed Conan's invisible hand to channel some more magic from him. I released myself from the seatbelt and cast a spell to throw her back. I got out of the truck and got to my feet. "What are you doing Misty?" I said, angrily, "I have had enough of this!" I yelled. "Oh we're just getting started" she cackled.

I had a sudden burst of power, maybe Hale was sending some my way, I didn't know, but I threw her for a loop again. I kept feeling stronger and stronger. I got closer to her, not scared at all of being hurt. I saw a glimmer of fear pass through her eyes. I put a paralyzing spell on her, I stood over her. "Misty, please tell me why you want me dead" I said to her. She just looked at me, "oh of course" I said and released her head only from my spell. She still just looked at me. "Cat got your tongue Misty? You see how powerful I am, you keep sending your coven to get slaughtered, you are a terrible leader" I said to her. "Maybe I should just go ahead and end you now" I said, more as a thought. "No," she said simply.

My magic wasn't fading, it still felt like it was growing stronger, the feeling of power was intoxicating. I put my foot on her chest and applied just a little pressure. She couldn't feel it because of the spell, but she could see it, there was a new fear in her eyes. "Misty, believe it or not, all I want is to bring all the covens together. Could you imagine all the power we would have? There would be no stopping us Misty!" I said. "It won't happen," she said, simply. "Why not Misty? You would rather die than align yourself with me?" I asked her. "Even if I chose to align with you, there are many more that are against you" she said. "Yes, but the more we have working with us, the more powerful we can be. You are very powerful and yet, no match for me, a witch that just got her powers, just started practicing, and you are nothing compared to me. But, I could help you, I could share my power with you and you with me. We could easily convince the others" I told her. I could tell, she was actually thinking about it.

I heard another vehicle coming, Damian pulled up. "Damian?" I said surprised. "Come on!" he yelled. I looked at Misty lying there, helpless, "I have more than you think on my side already, choose wisely" I said to her. I didn't release the spell, I looked at Damian, "help me get Conan" I said to him. He pulled his car up to the overturned truck and I released the invisibility spell I had placed on him, he started coming to as we pulled him out and put him into Damian's car. "Is she dead?" Damian asked, looking at Misty laying on the ground. "No, paralyzing spell, I'll leave it on until we are out of her reach" I said. He looked at me sideways, like I had done something stupid. "I gave her a lot to think about," I told him. We got into the car and sped away.

"James called me going crazy with worry," Damian said. "You know James?" I asked. "I know David, his brother, he's a good man," he said. I nodded in agreement. "Anyway, he called and begged me to come help you. I sent all the magic I could to you." he told me. "It was a lot, and was no match for her, thank you" I said sincerely. "You should probably call James, let him know that you are okay" he said. "Yeah, well, I lost my phone in the wreck" I said as I checked my pockets. He handed me his "it's the last number that called, in case you don't have his number" he said with a smile. I took the phone, "thank you, seriously, she could have killed me, you saved me," I said to him with a smile.

I used the video feature to call James, he answered right away. He started smiling and laughing and yelling "she's okay!" as soon as he saw me. I saw Levi and Hale pop up behind James. "Yes! I'm so happy" Hale said. "Did you kill the wicked witch of the west?" Levi asked. "I am okay, Damian was a definite life saver, thank you for calling him James. Conan is a bit beat up, but I think he's going to be just fine as well" I said. "I'll see you guys soon, okay? I want to rest for a little while" I said. They all said "okay, see you soon" before I hung up the phone and handed it back to Damian. The wind had died down quite a bit and the air outside, even though it was still frigid, felt a little warmer. "I can't thank you enough," I said to Damian. "Well, I got a feeling you will have the opportunity since Misty knows I helped you and you let her live" he replied. "I think I can win her over," I said, yawning. He laughed, "we'll see about that, you can get some shut eye, I'll wake you up when we are close for directions" he said. I nodded as I closed my eyes.

It felt like I had just closed them when Damian said, "we are close now, I need you to give me direction." I opened my eyes, looked around, it took me a minute to figure out where we were. I kept looking around, then I noticed that we had just passed the road that we needed to turn on. "Turn around, we needed to turn on that road" I said. He looked a bit irritated, but made a U-turn. I looked into the backseat, Conan was asleep, "has he woke up at all?" I asked. "Not that I have noticed," Damian replied. After we turned around and made the turn onto the right road, I asked Damian to use his phone again. He handed it to me, I called James. "We are almost home," I told him. "We have a nice fire going, coffee made, do you want anything else?" James asked. I shook my head, "I don't think so," I said. I hung up the phone.

"Here, pull over here" I said, pointing to the pull over spot. Damian pulled the car over. "It's still really cold out, it's about a thirty minute walk" I told him. "If you can spare any more magic, I can warp us to the house" I told him. He projected his power onto me again, I felt the rush of power, it was like an adrenaline rush on steroids. I nodded at him and took his hand and grabbed Conan's hand with my other and warped us to the house.

We were on the front porch, I looked around, Margo came running up from the forest. I hadn't seen her approach the house before, she growled at Damian. I looked at her, then at him. "It's okay Margo, he helped us tonight" I told her, she stopped growling, but continued to stand there and stare at him. It was still cold out, "would you like to come inside with us tonight, Margo?" I asked the cat. I opened the door and she went inside. "What the heck?" I heard Levi yell. "It's cold out, it would be really rude to make her sleep outside when she wants to come inside, despite what she appears to be, she's still human" I said. "Plus, she doesn't seem to like or trust me," Damian said.

James came running out of the kitchen and swooped me up in a hug. "So glad you are home and safe, I was going crazy with worry," he said. "Thank you Damian," James said. Damian nodded, "my pleasure" he said. James noticed that Conan was on the couch, "is he going to be okay?" he asked. "I think he just needs to rest, we should get him to a bed" I said. The guys insisted that I did not have to help with that, they got him to one of the empty bedrooms and made him comfortable, while I sat down on the couch and rubbed Margo's head between her ears. I was extremely tired, it was like everything caught up to me when I sat down. I wanted to go take a hot bath and relax.

James walked back into the living room. I put my hand out toward him and said, "help me up" with a giggle. He ran over to me quickly, "are you okay?" he asked, very concerned. "Oh yeah, I'm just tired, a little achy, I want to go take a hot bath and go to bed" I told him. "I want to stay with you in your room, I will sleep in the chair or the floor if you like, but I need to be close to you right now" he said, lowly into my ear. "You don't have to sleep on the floor," I whispered back. The thought of him holding me through the night made me relax. I think it was exactly what I needed to hear.

I went to the room where Conan was, everyone was still in there.

I stood in the doorway just listening to them make small talk. “You are staying the night, right, Damian?” I asked. “I should probably get back home,” he replied. “Nonsense, it's late, it’s freezing outside and we have plenty of room and you must be exhausted after all the magic you lent to me” I insisted. “Yeah, I’ll show you an empty room,” Levi said, standing up. “I’m exhausted myself and I am going to bed, I’ll see you all in the morning” I told them, as I walked away to my room. James was already waiting in my bed, I just looked at him and grabbed my bathrobe and went to my bathroom, closed the door, and ran an extra hot bath.

He had fallen asleep by the time I got finished and came back out. I slipped a night gown on and crawled into the bed next to him. I snuggled up to his side and looked at him. I hadn’t woken him up, I kissed his cheek and snuggled up to him as close as I could, it wasn’t very long until I was asleep. I didn’t dream that night, the next thing I knew, I was opening my eyes. I could still feel James next to me, I looked up to see if he was still asleep. He was just looking at me. “Good morning” he said, with a smile. “Are you just watching me sleep?” I asked him. “Yes, I couldn’t help myself, you look so beautiful and innocent,” he said. I rolled my eyes at him.

“So, what all happened last night?” he asked me. “I don’t feel like repeating myself, so I’ll just wait until I can get us all together to explain everything” I said. “I need a new phone, mine got lost in the wreck” I said, thinking of my friends texting me and me not being able to reply after I had just disappeared on them on my birthday. James kissed my forehead, I brought my mouth up to his. He kissed me passionately. After a few minutes of that, I climbed on top of him and we made love. I had never been with anyone like him, he was a passionate, caring lover. When we finished, I rolled over and lay on my back beside him for a few minutes. I could lay here all day in the afterglow, but we had business to take care of, witches to convince to come to our side and all that, so I got up and started getting dressed.

I walked into the kitchen, everyone except for Conan was in there. I looked at them confused, even Margo was sitting by the door. "I think she wants to go back outside," I said, pointing at the door. Hale walked over and opened up the door, it was a sunny day, Margo ran out of the door. "Is Conan okay?" I asked, looking around the room. "Yeah, I think he's in the shower" Hale answered. James walked up behind me. "Good" I said, breathing a sigh of relief. "What's good?" James asked. "Everything, for now" I answered, with a smile. I sat down at the bar with a cup of coffee, and after about fifteen minutes, Conan joined us. I walked up to him and hugged him, "I'm so glad you are okay" I told him. He hugged me back, "thank you for all you did to save us" he said. "I couldn't have done it without Damian," I said.

"So, I wanted us to all be together before I said anything about what happened last night," I said, looking around the room. "What does everyone want to know?" I asked them. For a minute I felt like a pop star at a press conference, the way they all started firing questions at me. I just looked at them. "Why don't you just tell us what happened, then ask for questions," James said with a smile. I nodded while rolling my eyes. "I didn't kill her," I started, "Damian lent me a lot of power. I didn't know where it was coming from, but I knew I could take her down, and I did. I had her paralyzed on the ground and I could have killed her, I chose not to. She is very powerful, I think I showed her how powerful we can be if we work together. She is power driven, so I think I got to her," I told them.

"I think that may have been a mistake," Conan said. "What happened to me?" he asked. "You got knocked out in the accident, I heard her coming, so I put an invisibility spell on you, and I used enough of your magic to free myself from the wreckage, after I got out and we fought for a minute, I felt the surge of magic from Damian going through me" I said. "That would explain why I was so out of it" Conan said. "What do you mean?" I asked. "If you take another witch's magic without their consent, it completely drains them, it can take days, sometimes weeks to recharge" Damian explained. I put my hand over my mouth, "I had no idea! I'm sorry! I didn't know what else to do" I said, almost crying. "I'm not mad, we are both still here, I will recharge" Conan said. Everyone was looking at me, "I swear, I didn't know! But even if I had known, to save you, I would do it again" I said. Conan just gave me a nod.

"You really think Misty will become an ally?" James asked, probably to change the subject, noticing that I was getting uncomfortable. "She loves power, probably more than she hates me" I said, and took a sip of my coffee. "She is old fashioned and set in her ways" Damian said. "I really think that I got through to her," I said again. "We shall see," Conan said. "That we will, I really don't want to hurt anyone else, the power that I had last night, with just Damian projecting his onto me was phenomenal, if more of you did that, I would be invincible" I said. "Projecting magic is my specialty, others can do it, but not completely, like I can" Damian said. "Even so, if anyone else gave me magic on top of what you can do, I would be like a god" I said. Everyone started looking at me like I had said something terrible. "Okay, maybe not a *god*, but very very powerful" I corrected. "Too much magic can also kill you," Damian said. "What do you mean?" I asked. "Your body can only handle so much magic, you are not a god," he replied.

"Damian, I know you have a home close, but would you be willing to stay here with us? Just for the time being, so we can all practice working magic together." I said. "That may be a good idea actually. I'll go get my things today and tell my butler that I will be away for a while" he responded. "Yay!" I said, while clapping my hands and smiling and even bouncing a little with excitement.

My response made him giggle. My family was growing, and I knew soon it would grow even more, the more witches that came over to my side, the better. I would eventually have all the covens working together, I could feel it in my soul, like it was my only purpose for being here. After having coffee, and chit-chatting for a little while, everyone scattered about, doing their own things. Damian left to go get his things, James went to the barn, Hale and Conan were sitting on the front porch, catching up, and Levi went to his room.

Eight

Oh Misty

I walked outside to find James, he was in the barn still. He was brushing Philip. "How is he doing?" I asked, as I walked into the barn. "He's good," James answered. I nodded. The weather felt very nice compared to last night. The sun was shining and the temperature was in the high forties, near fifty degrees. No wind and the sun shining down, made it feel warmer. I walked over to join James, I grabbed another brush and started brushing Philip with him. Philip seemed to be enjoying it, I smiled at James, and thought, 'so this is happy?' Just being in the same place at the same time, doing a simple task, and knowing that others that care about you are near, I had that 'warm and fuzzy' feeling inside, the one that you hear people talk about, but never feel, at least I hadn't. For this moment, I was happy, I didn't know how long it would last and it didn't matter, because all that really matters is the moment we are in, the past cannot be changed and the future never comes, right?

After brushing Philip for a while, we decided to take a walk around the property, he held my hand. "I'm so glad that you let me know what was happening, if you hadn't, you and Conan probably would have been killed by Misty." he said, with his head down. "I know, I'm getting better at this teamwork thing" I said, teasingly. He looked at me and smiled, "yes you are, and you are here with me now because of that" he said. I got in front of him and stopped, facing him. I wanted him to kiss me, and he did, he put his hands on each side of my face and pulled me toward him as he bent down. Every time he kissed me, I got butterflies in my stomach. I wondered if that was something that would last? And then I remembered, not to think about the future, stay in the moment. After a few moments, we stopped kissing and started walking again. "Seriously, you don't know how crazy I was going, when you were in danger, that is something that I have to work on. I want to be with you all the time, to protect you, but I know that isn't possible and I have to trust you to take care of yourself" James said. It almost sounded like he was trying to convince himself of what he was saying. "No one is perfect, we all have things to work on" I told him. "Why didn't you tell me that you knew Damian, or at least knew of him?" I asked. "I didn't think it was important, but David had told me that he thought we would be able to trust him," James replied.

We walked up to the porch together, Conan and Hale were still sitting there. "Mind if we join you guys?" I asked them. "Of course not," Conan said. James and I sat on the porch swing together. "Despite all the bad things, like people trying to kill me, I kind of feel like I've won the lottery with everything else in life, a great house, and great friends to share it with," I said. "We couldn't ask for a better leader," Hale said. "Leader?" I asked, shocked at the word. "Well yes, you will bring all the covens together, be the high priestess over all of them" he said, sounding confused that I was confused. "Don't forget guys, she didn't grow up in our world, she's still learning," James said. Hale nodded in agreement and smiled.

"Nonetheless, she will be an amazing leader, she's already proving to be one" Conan said, "and I am grateful that she was fast acting last night, and I'm still here because of it" he continued. "I'm sorry about stealing your magic, I would have thought twice, had I known it was such a violation. But I probably would have still done it to save you, I would never do that to anyone to hurt them" I said. "I know, like I said, I'm happy that I'm still here" Conan said.

"Well I'm happy about everyone that is here" I said. The sun was starting to go down, short winter days were very annoying, the light half of the year had always been my favorite. A chill started coming over me and I shivered. "Cold? Let's go inside, I'll get a fire going" James said. I nodded in agreement. James' phone rang, Damian had returned and needed someone to meet him at the pullover to bring him to the house, James, Levi and myself were still the only ones that could navigate the glamor that was over the property. I think we would probably leave it that way for as long as possible. James went to meet him and bring him back and put Levi in charge of building the fire. Levi was quiet while building the fire. "Are you okay?" I asked him. "Just a little homesick, this may be the dumbest thing I've ever done" he said, looking at me. "I'm sorry you feel that way" I said. "It's not your fault, it has nothing to do with you," he replied. A flame picked up in the fireplace and he smiled and walked toward the kitchen, he stopped in the doorway and said, "I'm happy for you and James," and then went on into the kitchen.

I sat there on the couch by the fire alone. I was mesmerized by the flames dancing around the wood, and the wood turning red and orange as it was heated. When the front door opened as James and Damian came in, I nearly jumped off the couch because I had been so into the fire. "Didn't mean to scare you," James said, sarcastically. I rolled my eyes at him, "I'm just tired, I'm going to go to bed" I said. I hugged Damian, "thank you for joining us, I'm glad you are here, let me know if you need anything" I told him. Although he had a big box and about four suitcases, I didn't know what else he could possibly need. "Thank you, I think I'll be fine, this will be like a vacation for me" he replied. I smiled as I walked away and went to my bedroom.

James joined me after a few minutes, I assumed that he had helped Damian get all his things into his room. "I'm really tired tonight, will you just lie here with me?" I asked him. "Of course" he replied, as he crawled into my bed. I put my head on his chest and he played with my hair, next thing I knew I was in a dream world again. I looked around for the woman, I didn't see her, but this was all too familiar. I was walking down a street, by the light in the sky, it was either sunrise or dusk. I could see the restaurant coming up in the distance, and all of a sudden, it exploded. "No!" I started screaming and running toward it, all I could think of was the workers and customers inside. James woke me, because he could tell I was having a nightmare, from the screaming and heavy breathing. It was kind of nice to have someone laying next to me, that could save me from the nightmares now. Maybe this was just a regular nightmare? "Shhh, it's okay, I'm here, I've got you" James whispered in my ear, while pulling me closer. I just sank into him.

The next morning, I woke up earlier than I usually did. I couldn't really hear anyone moving about the house, but then again, the walls in the house were very insulated. I opened my bedroom door to go see if anyone was awake. A wonderful smell of bacon and sausage and biscuits hit my nose. For a moment I felt like I was back at David and Sarah's house. I walked into the kitchen to see what was going on. Damian and Hale were in there. "Good morning!" Hale said with a smile. "Good morning, did we finally get someone who can cook?" I asked. "Oh yes! Damian is a *chef*!" Hale said with excitement. "I'm okay, I haven't cooked in years," Damian said humbly. "Well, you are a natural!" Hale said to him. I think Hale had a crush on Damian, I couldn't quite read if Damian was gay, I didn't want to ask and possibly insult him. But then again, he was the one in here with Hale. "Did you cook enough to share?" I asked Damian. "Of course," he replied. I gave them a sleepy nod as I grabbed a plate from the cupboard.

After eating, I walked out of the front door, to see what the weather was like right now, because in Tennessee, that's all you can do, see what it is right now, because it can change on a dime. It felt like it was in the upper thirties to lower forties, so not terribly cold, unless you had to stand out in it with no sunshine. There was no wind either, just calm cool air. James came out of the door behind me, "hey you" he said. "Good morning," I replied. "Are you okay?" he asked. "Yes, why wouldn't I be?" I asked. "Your dream last night," he replied. "Oh, I think it was just a regular nightmare" I said, but in the tone of a question. "Why do you say it like that?" he asked. "I just don't normally have nightmares, and it felt just like the others, when the woman, possibly Valery, was there. But I didn't see her in this one, I even looked around and tried to find her" I explained. "I don't know, this is something strange to all of us, I believe. We should ask the new guy if he's ever heard of anything like this before" he said. "Don't call him the new guy, his name is Damian, and don't forget, he saved my life" I said. "Because I told him to, but yes, I know his name," James replied. I got up to go find Damian, like James had suggested.

Damian and Hale were still in the kitchen, talking and laughing. I think Damian was into Hale, aww, so sweet! I didn't want to interrupt them, so I tried to turn around and leave before they seen me, it was too late, "hello?" I heard Damian say. "Hey" I said, and came around the corner. "Come back for seconds?" Damian asked. "Oh no, it was delicious, but I'm stuffed," I said. "What did you need then?" Hale asked, looking a little irritated that I had interrupted them. I shrugged toward him and mouthed 'sorry' before I turned and looked back at Damian. "James wanted me to ask you if you have ever heard of being attacked in your dreams or someone else controlling them. No one else here has heard of it, and I think they think I am just crazy" I said to him. He looked at me with a confused look on his face. "I think it could be my mom, she's the one that told me to talk to you actually" I said. He had a look of shock on his face, and it looked like all the color suddenly left it as he turned white. "The living can't interact with the dead," he said in almost a whisper. "Yes, I've been told that, but I've also come out of dreams with bruises and notes on my hands" I said. "I'll see if I can find anything on it," he said. I nodded at him, as he walked out of the kitchen and down the hall. Hale gave me a look of disappointment and rolled his eyes, "we were having a little bit of fun, you know?" he said. "I'm sorry, James suggested that I ask if he knew anything, I didn't realize that you two were 'flirting' until I got to the doorway, I was even going to turn around and go back until he heard me out there" I said. Hale smiled, "you really think he was flirting back?" he asked me. "Definitely" I said as I gave him a flirty wink.

I left Hale sitting in the kitchen, smiling like a school boy, to go find James. He was still on the front porch where I had left him. I told him that Damian said he didn't know anything but he was going to see if he could find anything. "Where do they look when they say that they will see if they can find anything?" I asked James. "Old family books? I don't know, you are the witch, not me" he said. I rolled my eyes at him, "that would make sense, I'm sure each coven has their own histories, and individuals have their own as well" I said. "I am going to go take a shower" I said, as I walked back into the house. Hale met me at the door, with his phone and motion silently for me to go into my room with him.

It was Misty, "oh Misty, how are you? Recovered yet?" I asked. "I've thought about what you said, I want to meet with you in person to discuss it more. I give you my word of a truce, for the purpose of this meeting. Come alone, we can meet at the restaurant you worked at before" she said to me. My dream flashed before my eyes, "no, we will not meet there, pick another place" I said. She looked at me with a suspicious look on her face. "They don't know anything of our world, and the fact that they know me, will make them want to hang around wherever I am sitting, I'm afraid they will overhear something that they shouldn't" I told her, it was the best explanation I could give her. She seemed satisfied with my excuse, "we'll meet at the park then" she said simply, not giving me a chance to protest her. "Be there at one o'clock today" she said, before ending the call.

I looked at my clock, it was ten a.m. I called everyone to the kitchen, to come up with a plan. Once everyone was in there, I began telling them about the call. "No," James said. I rolled my eyes, "I'm going, this isn't a vote, but I don't want to go in without a plan" I said. He stood up, to argue more. "Stop, she's right, this is what we wanted to happen, now we just need a plan" Conan said. James sat down, I'm surprised that he didn't just walk out altogether. "I got it," Hale said, "one of you, stay here" he said, pointing to James and Levi, "the other can go and be nearby, but completely out of sight at all times, unless absolutely needed. Then we," he said pointing at the witches, "will be just a bit closer, not too close though, and just 'lend' her" he said, pointing to me, "our magic." Everyone looked around for a moment, like they were all thinking about everything he just said.

"I thought only Damian could do that?" I asked, confused. "No, only I can do it completely, any witch can let you 'borrow' some magic, I can cast all of mine onto you, if I think you need it." Damian explained. "Oh, okay, I get it now" I said. "I think it will work," Conan said. "Great, so we're ready to go?" I asked them. "I want to be the one going this time, I feel like I'm always in the house anymore" Levi said. I knew James would argue and this would cause us to lose more time. "Guys, we don't have time for arguing, we have to go now!" I said, with force. James looked at me and nodded, then he looked at Levi, "don't let anything happen to her" he told him. I was shocked.

We all left the house, Levi went to a store that was near the meeting place, and the witches went to a nearby restaurant, they all gave me as much magic as possible, the rush that went through my body, I felt like a God. I knew that I was indestructible, no one should ever have this much magic coursing through their body. I felt like, with one wrong move, that I could just disintegrate. "Is it possible to have too much magic?" I asked them. "Yes, I told you that before, if you feel like it's too much, we can back off a bit" Damian said. I shook my head, "no, don't do that, I may need all of this if this is an ambush" I said. They nodded in agreement. I turned to leave to go to the meeting. "Please be careful," Hale said. "I will" I said, without turning back around.

I walked to the park, I noticed Levi watching from a shop window across the street, I was afraid that since I could see him, she would also. I sent him a message. *You are supposed to be out of sight!* -Me. *I thought I was, sorry.* -Levi. I continued to walk toward a bench that was in a central location, the bench was empty, so I sat down. After five minutes had passed, I started to wonder if she was standing me up. I pulled out my phone and started to dial her, but she walked up and sat down without saying anything.

"Hello" I said. She looked at me with a puzzled look. "Misty?" I asked. She shook her head, still looking confused. I guess Misty had glamoured someone to look like her. The woman got up and walked away, I continued to sit there, I knew she must be nearby, watching, I just didn't know what she was waiting for. After another five minutes, I was about to just leave, I was getting tired of playing this game. Then she walked up, the real Misty this time. "I was making sure you didn't plan to kill me on sight" she said, as she sat down. "So you used an innocent human as a decoy?" I asked, in a disappointed way. "Does it matter? She's fine, and doesn't know anything happened at all" she replied. "It matters if you want to work with me, we don't put other's lives in danger" I said, in a matter of fact way.

I felt something building in the air, it was magic, "unless you want more of your coven slaughtered, tell them to go now" I said, in a simple tone. She looked at me, confused, "I came alone," she said. Then I felt someone use a spell to attack us. Misty was thrown for a backwards flip, it barely felt like a small push to me. A tallish African American woman came from behind a tree. "You must be Gabriela?" she said, as she approached me. "And who might you be?" I asked. Misty stood up and brushed herself off, "Darcy" she said. I ran through my mind for a moment, yep, I remembered that name from the 'enemy list.' I used my magic and made her sit down on the bench next to me. I looked at her sideways to intimidate her more. Misty walked up behind me, "I could let you use my magic with yours and you could just break her in half right now" Misty said. I saw fear flash in Darcy's eyes. I think she was starting to realize that she made a mistake. "Darcy, did you come here alone?" she nodded to say that she had indeed come alone. "Why would you do that? Do you have a death wish or are you just plain dumb?" I asked her. The spell I had on her was strong enough that she couldn't speak.

"I think the cat's got her tongue" Misty said, teasingly. I released the spell, "don't move, or I will put it back on you" I told her. Darcy just sat there, looking at me. "I think we should just kill her, that was her plan, to kill us" Misty said. I looked at Misty sideways now, "we aren't killing anyone" I said, then looked back at Darcy and added, "unless we absolutely have to." Darcy looked at me, she looked confused, "why would you not kill me?" she asked, simply. It was as if she had been taught that I was a monster and would destroy everyone and everything. And then I realized, that is what they had been taught, all of them, some chose not to believe it, but others didn't know any better.

"Forget what you think you know about me Darcy" I said. "I am not the monster you have been told I am," I added. "Then what are you?" she asked. "I am the one that is going to put an end to all the witch on witch violence and killing" I said. She started laughing. Misty stood quietly behind me, which surprised me. "I stumbled upon a meeting of two of my enemies, and they are sitting here telling me that their plan is to save the world?" she said, still laughing. "Think about it Darcy," Misty said, "we could all unite, and become the most powerful beings in all dimensions" she continued. "Even if we don't always see eye to eye, we still don't have to murder each other" I said. She sat there, not saying anything, just looking at Misty and I.

"I thought the same as you until recently, she could have ended me, but she didn't" Misty said. I looked at Misty, surprised that she seemed to really be on my side. "Even after my witches have done terrible things to her, she still didn't want to kill me," she added. I felt magic building up again, she was going to attack us again. I put the spell back on her, so she couldn't move. "I don't want to hurt you, I'm not going to hurt you, just stop" I said, pleadingly. "You should just go ahead and end me" she said, simply. "Why do you have a death wish?" I asked her. "I won't kill you" I said, when she didn't answer. Misty walked over to her and put a hand on each side of her head. "What are you doing?!" I yelled. "Calm down! I'm just trying to see if I can find anything" she said. I was confused. After a few seconds, she nodded her head, "leave her, she will come after us again as soon as you release the spell" Misty said.

"My car is over here, we can go to my place and finish our discussion" Misty said. I knew the guys would be so mad at me if I went, also, I would lose all the extra power that I was 'borrowing.' "Come on, we don't have a lot of time, haven't I proved to you yet that I'm not going to challenge you?" She asked. After just a little more hesitation, I got into the car. I felt my phone start vibrating immediately. I pulled it out to check it. *What are you doing?!* -Levi. *Her house.* -Me. Then I put it up before she could see anything, at least, I hoped she hadn't seen anything. I kept feeling the phone going off, but I didn't want to pull it out again. "What did you do to her back there?" I asked. "In case you haven't figured it out yet, most witches, especially the high priests and priestess' have one ability that is above the others, mine is I can 'read minds.' She just lost the love of her life, and she definitely wants to be reunited with her" she said. "Oh, that's terrible," I said. "Yeah, we are not going to be her ticket to paradise" Misty said.

"So, how do I know that you really want to join forces with me? How can I trust you and how can I convince the rest of my team that you are genuinely on our side, Misty?" I asked her. "If you are willing, I will perform a chain spell on us" she replied. "What does that mean?" I asked. "It's a binding spell, it will connect our bodies, if something happens to you, it happens to me, and vice versa" she explained. "Is the spell easy to undo?" I asked. "Yes, as long as both of us are doing the spell, it can be undone quickly, if need be. However if only one of us is performing the spell, it would take time and the other would possibly become ill because of it." she told me. "Okay, and what changed your mind?" I asked her. "You did, with your talk of ultimate power and unity of our people. When I was a little girl, I used to daydream that my parents didn't have to worry about an enemy attack constantly" she said. "And, I never had children because the love of my life was a giant, and that was why I hated you so much. You weren't supposed to exist, you went against our laws" she said. "I'm sorry, but I didn't ask to be born. And we will work together to change these outdated laws" I told her. She nodded. We pulled up to her house and went inside.

My phone was going crazy. I simply sent one text out to everyone, *I'm fine.* -Me. "Do you think Darcy will change her mind, like you did?" I asked Misty. "I have no idea, she has never been a friend to me. I really don't know how she will take everything that happened today" she said. "I really don't want to kill anyone, so, for her sake, I hope she can see the benefit of pairing with me" I said. "I can sense that Jason is still alive, will you turn him over now? If I come to stay in your home, will you give me Jason, let me start training him?" Misty asked. "No, that's impossible, I don't want him to die. I will figure out how to reverse the curse" I said, shaking my head. "You mean he hasn't transitioned yet? How is that possible?" Misty asked. "He's in a sleeping spell, he's safe in a hospital far away" I said.

"So, do you want me to perform the chain spell on us?" Misty asked. I nodded, I couldn't think of a better way to prove to the guys that she wouldn't hurt me, she may not be completely trustworthy just yet, but at least they wouldn't worry about her attacking me. "I'll need a little of your blood" she said, handing me a knife and pointing to a cup on an altar. I looked at her sideways. "Just a drop will work," she assured me. I nodded, and poked the tip of the knife into my fingertip. I hoped that this wasn't some kind of trick, but I felt that it wasn't, that she was being genuine. I handed her the cup with my blood in it, and she performed the spell. "I don't feel any different, how do we know if it worked?" I asked. She picked up the knife and poked her finger, mine started bleeding as well as hers. "It worked," she said, simply. "Okay, you are coming back to my place, right?" I said to her, "You really think that's a good idea?" she asked. "I do, especially now that our bodies are 'chained' together, you will need to be protected, as I am" I told her. She nodded in agreement, "let me go get some of my things together" she said, as she left the room.

"I haven't told any of the guys that you are coming back with me" I told Misty as we got into her car to head home. "Wow, don't you think you should do that?" she asked. "We can explain everything to them in person," I replied. She told me to drive, since I knew where to go, even though it was her car. "Do you think Jason will survive the curse? If I never find a way to reverse it?" I asked her. "I'm not sure, I can sense him though, so maybe that is a good sign?" she said, sounding uncertain. "Have you ever dealt with the curse before?" I asked. "No, and I'm not sure where my witches learned the curse, we don't teach it in my coven. She went out of her way to learn it and perform it" Misty said, with a look of worry on her face. "Do you think she learned it from a book? Or do you think she was working with someone outside of your coven?" I asked. "I guess we'll never know, will we?" she replied. "I'm sorry she's gone, she did attack me, and it was self defense, the same for the other one" I said. "I know," Misty said as she let her head hang down.

I pulled the car into the pullover spot. "A glamor?" she asked. I nodded. The sun was beginning to set and the temperature outside was dropping, but I decided not to warp us, we could use the time during the walk to talk more. "I hope you brought a jacket," I said to her. She nodded, looking confused. "It's about a thirty minute walk to get to the house," I explained. She looked at me like I was crazy. "You'll be fine," I said. We stepped out of the car and put coats on, then started the hike into the woods. As soon as we stepped into the woods, I could see Margo walking along the border, but keeping her distance. "Is that a wild cat?" Misty asked. "No, she's a friend. Margo! This is Misty, she is going to help us" I said, loudly. Misty still looked uncomfortable with her following us. "It's fine" I said, to reassure her.

My nose and fingertips started getting uncomfortably cold after only a few minutes, I was second guessing my decision to walk to the house now. "The weather has been really crazy the past few days. I think someone is messing with it somehow and I don't know what their purpose for doing that could be" Misty said, with worry in her voice. "Well, if you really think someone is messing with the weather, we will investigate it, we will figure out who and why" I said. "How?" she asked. "We are a powerful group, getting more powerful with each new member, I don't think there's anything we can't do" I said. "Are you starting a new coven?" she asked me, with a little concern. "No, not a new coven, just a leadership type of coven, only high priests' and high priestess' are a part of it, if the leaders can all come together, then their people will follow" I said. "A coven of leaders? With you at the lead? So, your goal is to be the queen of the witches?" she asked. I suddenly felt like a dictator. "Think of it however you need to, I don't want to hurt anyone, only bring them together." I told her.

I could finally see the house in the distance, across the field. "This looks nice. How did you acquire it?" she asked. "I'm not really sure, I went to another dimension to train, when I came back, it was given to me, and my friends" I told her. "Interesting, which dimension did you go to? Who trained you?" she continued with questions until I started feeling uncomfortable answering. "We will get to that later, I need to introduce you to the rest of the team" I said, nodding toward the house, where *everyone* was now standing on the porch. "Quite the assembly" she said, simply. All of the guys were standing like they were bodyguards, with their arms folded at their chests, feet spread apart. "Are they trying to intimidate me?" she asked me, in a whisper. "Either, you or me, I'm not sure yet" I said. She giggled a little. And I realized that even though I didn't completely trust her yet, that it would be nice to have another female around. I could have 'girl talk' with Hale, but it wasn't the same.

"What's going on? What have you done?" Damian asked. "We are supposed to be a team, why didn't we know that you were bringing her here?" Hale asked, sounding almost hurt. Before the rest of them could scold me, I said, "guys, we are cold, can we please have this discussion inside?" They moved aside and let us pass through the doorway without saying anything else. Once we were inside, we took off our coats and got close to the fire, the guys were all just standing around us. After a few minutes of silence, I said, "guys, I trust her, I am sorry that I didn't communicate with you, to let you know what was going on. Levi saw us get attacked in the park by another witch, he also saw me get in the car with Misty, and I did let you all know that I was okay." "So, why is she here?" Conan asked. "The same reason you are here" I said. "I doubt that" he mumbled under his breath. "How can we possibly *trust* her? How can *you* trust her?" James asked. "We have a spell on us, to prove it, if anything happens to one of us, it will happen to the other" I told them. "You are *chained* to her?!" Damian said, with shock.

"Misty, do you mind stepping out? We need to have a word with Gabriela, alone" Levi said. Misty shrugged her shoulders. "The extra rooms are down that hall" I said, pointing down a hall to the right, "or upstairs" I continued. She nodded and started walking upstairs, the rest of us walked into the kitchen. "Please tell me what you were *thinking*?" Damian demanded. "It was her idea," I admitted. "Of course it was! That would be the easiest way to kill you, chain herself to you then kill herself!" Conan explained. I felt a little worry pass over me, I shook my head, "I trust her" I told them. "Why would you trust her?" James asked. "She fought with me when we were attacked, we talked more at her place, I believe that she wants the same thing we want" I told them. "And the chain spell was to prove to you that she's with us, that she wouldn't hurt me" I continued. "We need to undo the spell," Hale said. "I agree, it's the only way we can really have a little peace of mind, especially with her in our home," Damian said.

"Oh!" I screamed and tumbled to the floor, as my ankle suddenly snapped. I heard a bang come from the other room at the same time. James ran over to me, he had an angry look on his face, "she's already attacking you!" he yelled. "Go get her, tie her up so she can't hurt her anymore until we remove the goddamn spell!" James yelled at Levi. Levi turned and ran out of the kitchen. "I'm sure it was an accident," I told James. He looked at me like he was angry with me,

I hated when he looked at me like that. "Let's get her to her bed, and get her healed," Conan said, looking at Hale and Damian. They took me to my room and healed me as they said, I helped with the spell as well, even though I was in pain. Then I fell asleep.

Nine

Back to 2

I woke up in an unfamiliar room, but the atmosphere was very familiar. James was there, next to me. "Are you awake?" I heard a familiar voice ask from behind the closed door. "Arturo?" I asked. The door opened, "yes darling, it is I" he said. "Is this your home?" I asked, still confused about why I was here. "It is," he said simply. James raised his head. "When I saw you lying next to her, I brought you along, because I didn't want you to wake and see that she was gone and freak out. Plus, you'll have a chance to visit with your brother and sister-in-law and your niece" Arturo said to him. "I have a niece?" James asked, with a smile on his face. "Indeed you do, and she's beautiful," Arturo said. "If you would like, you could head over there, to visit while Gabriela tells me what has been going on" Arturo continued. "I would like to see them also," I said. "That will be fine, later, I brought you here for an update" Arturo insisted. I nodded and got out of bed.

James got up also, pulled a shirt on and kissed my forehead. "How is your ankle?" he asked. "Like nothing happened" I assured him. "What happened? Did you find out?" I asked him. "No, I told the guys to go figure it out and get the spell removed and I stayed with you" he told me. It made my heart feel so full, that he stayed with me, when he didn't have to, he could have just as easily gone to torture Misty with the rest of them. Then I started worrying about Misty, I was sure that whatever happened was an accident. I really did trust her, I couldn't explain how, I just felt it in my soul that she wasn't lying to me. "I hope they don't do anything to her," I said to James. "Oh sure, take her side, she only broke your ankle" he replied, sarcastically.

"I'm sure it was an accident," I said. "What are you two talking about?" Arturo asked, walking into the room. "She brought Misty into the house, and they have a chain spell on them," James told him. Arturo's dark skin almost turned white. "Excuse me?! What are you thinking?!" he demanded. "Exactly," James said, and kissed me on the forehead again, "I'm going to head over to David and Sarah's and meet my niece" he continued, then walked out of the door. I looked at Arturo, "She's on our side, I know she is" I said to him. "Finish getting yourself together and join me in the living room" he said, a little more calmly, but still with force.

I sat down in front of a mirror and brushed my hair, looking in my face, I looked noticeably older. I wondered why? I mean, I knew I had been through a lot in the past few months, but I didn't feel like I should be able to look into a mirror and tell that I have aged. I kept brushing my hair for a few minutes. I was thinking about how Arturo would see everything when I told him, would he be proud? Or would he be disappointed? I smelled coffee, I put the brush down on the dresser and went to join Arturo for some coffee.

"So, you brought your most powerful enemy into, not only your home, but also gave her control of your body? Please explain this to me first," he said. "It's not like that, she wants to help me, we did the spell to prove that she wants to help" I explained. "How?" he said, sarcastically. "She attacked me once, I was 'lent' some extra magic, so I had her on the ground, paralyzed. She knew that I was more powerful, I told her that if we worked together, she could also be extremely powerful, she likes power. I met with her, we were attacked by another enemy, we fought her off, we went to Misty's place, she said that she wanted to help me bring all the witches together," I told him. "And the chain spell?" He asked. "I was worried about convincing the rest of the team that she was on our side, she said she could do the spell to prove it, that if I got hurt, she would get hurt as well" I said. "It seemed like it would work, except no one else was convinced, they think she did it to hurt me" I said.

"And how long has she been there?" he asked. "Just tonight" I told him. I didn't want to tell him about the snapped ankle, because I didn't want to get reprimanded anymore than I already had, but I knew James would end up mentioning it, then he would be angry with me for not telling him myself. "We told her to go put her things away, she chose a room upstairs, and the guys and myself went to the kitchen where they could yell at me for bringing her there and for the chain spell. I was about to go find her and talk with her, and my ankle suddenly snapped" I said, with my head down. "So she already attacked you?!" he said. I shrugged, "it could have been an accident, I'm sure she is being tortured by the guys now" I said, feeling bad that I wasn't there, to find out the truth. "Arturo, I don't know how to explain it, but I trust her" I told him.

He looked at me silently and sipped his coffee. "I hope your trust in her isn't just another spell" he finally said. "What do you mean? Is that possible? Doesn't that mess with free will?" I asked. "Do you think someone that wants you dead cares about your free will? Even if it breaks coven laws, all is fair in love and *war*, my dear" he said. "Can we break any spells that may be on me?" I asked him. "I can try,

I'll need you to go lay down, why don't you just go to the couch?" he suggested. I nodded.

I went and lay down on his couch. "Close your eyes," he told me. I did, I could feel him using magic, moving his hands over my body, like he was a scanning machine. "I can only feel the chain spell and a protection spell" he said. "Protection spell?" I asked. "Probably left over from your mother, she was very powerful, this spell may stay with you for the rest of your life, however, it doesn't make you invincible" he said. I nodded as I opened my eyes. "I look older, don't I? I said to him, he laughed, then got a serious look on his face. "Giant and half/giant life span is shorter than a normal human, sixty years old is the average, plus over usage of magic can also make you age faster" he said. "Well, I guess I only have about five years left," I said, sarcastically.

"You seem different, not your appearance, but your persona, your character, sorry if I'm not finding the right word" he said. "I killed someone" I said, without emotion. He stood, looking at me, not judging, but like he was waiting on me to finish the sentence. "She didn't leave me a choice, it was kill or be killed, she attacked when no one was around to help me" I said. "Understandable, self defense" he said, simply. "I wish it hadn't happened, but like I said, nothing I could do, unless I wanted to die myself" I said. "How is Margo doing?" he asked. "She seems fine, obviously I can't really talk to her, but I see her around" I said. He nodded. "She likes to keep to herself mostly anyway" He said.

"When can I go see David and Sarah and the baby?" I asked. He looked at me, raising one eyebrow accusingly. "What?" I asked, in self defense. "James" he said, simply. I started smiling, "really? What did you guys expect? He's gorgeous" I said. Arturo laughed at me. "David will not be happy about it, I'm just going to tell you that now, if James is a good guy, he will tell him himself" Arturo said.

"What's it to David?" I asked. "James is his brother, he doesn't ever want to see him in pain, and you my dear, are a high risk for that, whether it's your enemies finally getting you, or you just flat out breaking his heart" he said. "Well, I don't plan for either of those things to happen" I said. "No one ever plans for things to happen, that's the problem" he replied. "So, you think David and Sarah hate me now?" I asked. "No, that's not what I'm saying, just saying that David will not be happy about the situation" he replied.

"Tell me what other things you have learned," Arturo said. "I have Conan, Hale and Damian in my corner. Damian has a really helpful gift, he can transfer *all* of his magic to me, and it makes me so powerful that I don't think anyone could defeat me" I said. "That is helpful indeed, but can also be harmful, you going into a fight thinking there's no possible way to lose isn't really a good idea" he said. I just looked at him, "I wish you could feel the power, it's like I'm a god" I said. "Remember, over usage of magic will age you quickly, that's probably why you can already tell that you look older" he told me. It wasn't something that I liked to hear. "Yeah, I guess every great thing comes with great consequences," I said.

James came walking through the door with a smile on his face. "You have to come meet Julie, she's so beautiful, I held her for a good two hours straight, and I still didn't want to give her back" he said. I smiled at him, "yeah, I can't wait, but it's getting pretty late, why don't we go in the morning?" I said. I wasn't super excited to walk into David and Sarah's home since Arturo told me they would be upset with James and I for being together. I wanted the chance to talk to James alone before we went, to see if he told them about us. "Julie is a beautiful name," I said, smiling still. James seemed a bit upset that I didn't want to go over there right now. "We have a good two weeks here, right Arturo?" I said. "Yes, that's how it works," he said sarcastically.

I went to the bedroom that I had woken up in this morning

without saying anything else to either of them. I sat down in front of the mirror and just looked at my reflection. I don't know what I was looking for, someone else? The person I used to be before I found out my whole life was a lie? The person I was before I had to watch the light go out in someone's eyes because of me? I don't know how long I sat there, and I didn't even hear the door open. James put his hand on my shoulder and I jumped. "I'm sorry, I didn't mean to startle you," he said. "It's okay" I said, and put my hand on top of his. I stood up, facing him, I reached up and pulled his head toward mine until our lips met. He started kissing me frantically, like he had been starving for my lips. He guided me to the bed with his kisses and pulled my shirt off in between the kisses. Soon we were on the bed, he was on top of me, I let out a moan of excitement, I wanted him so much at this moment. I ran my fingers over his chest and down his stomach until I touched his hip bone. He let out a moan of excitement this time. I brought my hands back up to his neck, and then I wrapped my arms and legs around him, I let my fingernails sink into his back as he entered me.

When we were finished, we lay on the bed silently for a while, catching our breath. Finally after a while, I asked "did you tell David and Sarah about us?" He was silent, "you didn't, did you?" I said, with just a little bit of attitude. "David told me before we left, not to get involved with you this way" he said in a pleading voice. "So, your plan is to just lie to them? Arturo knows, he will tell them, don't you think it's better if it comes from us?" I said. "I don't know, I just don't want a lecture," he said. I rolled my eyes, even though I was sure he couldn't see. He started snoring. I was so mad at him, how could he just fall asleep in the middle of a serious discussion?! What was wrong with him? I was so mad that I didn't want him touching my skin at all, I scooted to the edge of the bed, he rolled over and put his arm around me. I just lay there, angry, trying to fall asleep.

Eventually, I must have fallen asleep, the next thing I knew, I was opening my eyes to a bright sunny room. James was not beside me, I didn't see him anywhere. I got out of bed and went into the living room. Arturo was sitting there, drinking some coffee. "Where is James?" I asked him. He shrugged his shoulders, "maybe he went back to David and Sarah's house?" he said. "Without me? He knew I wanted to go" I said, disappointed. "I'm sure if he did, he would have a reason for doing so," he said. "How did you sleep?" he asked. "Okay" I said, simply and turned and walked back to the room to change clothes.

After getting dressed, I sat down at the mirror again, to brush my hair, once again, I just stared at myself. It was like it wasn't even me that was looking back. Once again, I was startled by a hand on my shoulder, this time it was Arturo. "I didn't mean to scare you, I was calling for you and you didn't answer, did you not hear me?" he asked. "No, I didn't" I said, looking at him, wondering what was going on. "Have you ever had an issue with this mirror?" I asked him. "What do you mean?" he asked. "Every time I look in it, I get lost, I feel like it isn't even me looking back" I tried to explain to him. He grabbed a blanket from the bed and threw it over the mirror. "No, I haven't had a problem with the mirror, but, let's not take any chances, someone could be using it as a spy glass, or maybe someone put a different kind of spell on it, we will figure it out though" he said, looking concerned.

James came walking through the bedroom door, "what's going on?" he asked. "I could ask you the same thing! Why did you take off this morning?" I asked him, angrily. "You first" he said, moving his finger from me to Arturo. "The mirror is giving her problems," Arturo said as he walked out of the room. "What is your deal? You aren't accusing Arturo and myself of anything are you?" I asked. "I knew it was something magical, and I wanted to know what it was, I can't protect you if I don't know what's going on. You have been hiding quite a lot from me recently, so don't get mad at me for wanting to help you" James lectured. "Where did you go this morning?" I asked, accusingly. "I did what you wanted, I went to David and Sarah's and I told them about us. It wasn't as bad as I thought it was going to be. David was disappointed that I didn't listen to him, I think Sarah is happy about it" he told me.

"Can I go see them today? Meet Julie.." I asked. "Of course!" James said, with excitement. "Great, I'm just going to let Arturo know that we are going," I said, as I slipped out of the room. I looked around the house for a minute before I found Arturo on the front porch. I opened the door and stepped outside with him, "we are going to David and Sarah's, do you want to come with us?" I asked. "No, I will see them soon," Arturo answered. I felt like he was different, depressed, or maybe I just never noticed it before. "Are you okay?" I asked him. He just looked at me with a look that let me know that in fact he was not okay, but there was nothing I could do about it. I nodded to let him know that I understood before I turned to go back inside to find James.

James and I left Arturo's house and headed to David and Sarah's house. I was so excited and happy to see them. As soon as they saw us, they both ran up and gave me a hug. "Where is Julie?" I asked Sarah. "She's taking a nap right now," she told me. "Yeah, it's not good to wake her up, she'll be grumpy until she falls asleep again" David said. "Aww, I bet she's still cute even when she's grumpy" I said. "I made us an early dinner," Sarah said. My eyes lit up, I had missed her home cooked meals. My stomach growled right on que, it was loud enough for everyone to hear so they all laughed at me. We all went inside to eat, everything was the same as it had been when I was here before.

I didn't realize how much I missed them, or the food, or just the simpleness of sitting at this table with people that I cared about, just being near them. After sitting at the table and catching up while eating, for about thirty minutes, I heard a sweet little cry coming from the other room. I looked up at Sarah. "I'll go get her," David said. I smiled at him. Soon the crying stopped. "She loves him so much," Sarah said to me. He brought her into the dining room where we were waiting. She was the most adorable baby, she had brown hair that had the cutest little curls, blue eyes, rosey chubby cheeks, and cherry red lips. She rubbed her eyes as she looked around. James made a cooing sound at her and she giggled. "Hi" I said, waving to her, she hid her face in David's chest to hide from me. "She's not around a lot of new people often, I think it's making her shy," David said to me.

It was a couple of hours before she would let me hold her and play with her, I wasn't angry, it was worth the wait, she was so adorable. "You two will make great parents someday" Sarah said, while watching James and I play with Julie. I let out a giggle, we had not spoken about the future, much less about starting a family. James just ignored the comment. "I'm sorry, I didn't mean to make you uncomfortable," Sarah said. "Don't worry about it" I said, with a smile. It was starting to get dark outside. James looked at me, "we should get back to Arturo's house before it gets too late" he said. I nodded, even though I could sit here and play with Julie all night if she would let me, it was such a difference in my life, to do something as simple as play with a baby.

We told David and Sarah goodnight and I hugged Julie and kissed her chubby cheek before we turned to walk out the door. Julie started crying and put her hands toward us, "she did that to me yesterday" James said. "Aww" I said. "Don't worry, she's going to sleep great tonight, and you guys can come back tomorrow and play some more," Sarah said. I smiled at her, "that will be great" I agreed. We headed out of the door with little Julie crying for us to come back and play. I felt bad, but we were barely out of sight when I heard her stop crying. I just looked at James and smiled.

"Have you ever thought of having kids? A family?" he asked. "Are we really going to have this conversation now?" I asked. "Why not?" he said. "I did before, when life was normal, but not since I found out that life is not normal," I admitted. "So, you've not imagined us with children?" he asked, "later" he added. "No, I haven't, I'm not saying that it won't happen, later, but the way life is right now, I couldn't imagine trying to protect a baby on top of everything else" I told him. "Fair enough" he said, as he took my hand and held it while we walked. "Are there vehicles here?" I asked, I had just realized that I hadn't seen one. "Not motorized, no, if there is more magic, there is less technology. It's like humans somehow still feel that they have a right to be able to do things, like, fly and get places fast, it's like their subconscious remembers, or knows somehow that everything you see, isn't everything. Less magic, more technology and vice versa" James explained. I nodded to let him know that I understood. "So, technology is the best on 13?" I asked, just to confirm. "Yes," he said, simply.

"What is with the mirror?" he asked, like it had been on his mind all day. "I don't know, every time I sit down and look into it, I go into a trance of some sort" I said. He got a worried look on his face. "What?" I asked. "I don't know," he said. "Arturo told me that using too much magic will age me faster too, on top of me being half giant, which apparently they don't live as long either" I said, without stating the obvious, that I would die before I grew old. "We don't live as long as humans or even most witches, once 'the war' is over, you won't have to use as much magic" he said.

Arturo greeted us from the front porch, I'm sure he didn't stay there all day, but it was as though he had, because when we left he was there and he was waiting for us there when we returned. "How was your visit?" he asked. "Great, Julie is adorable," I said, with a smile. "Yes she is, she sure can steal a heart" he agreed. "I'm tired, I think I'm just going to go lay down, if you guys don't mind" I said to Arturo and James. James looked at me confused. “I’m fine,” I told him. “Don’t uncover the mirror, until we find out what is going on with it,” Arturo said. “I won't,” I said as I walked away toward the room.

The mirror was still covered when I went into the room. I put on a night gown, and got in the bed. I could smell the ‘baby’ smell on me, I couldn’t get over how adorable she is.

At some point, I drifted into dreamland. I was on the main street in Moon Springs, the town on 12 where we lived. I didn’t see anyone that I recognized. I was looking around, confused about why I was there. Then I saw Racheal in the distance, I threw my arm up and tried to wave her down, I don’t think she saw me. Someone came up and grabbed my arm and pulled it down, “stop that” a woman’s voice said. I turned to see who it was, it was her, Valery, at least in theory.

“Are you my mom?” I asked her. She looked at me with a confused look on her face. Suddenly her eyes went completely white and she grabbed my arm, “the child will save you” she said in a peculiar voice. “What do you mean?” I asked. Her face went back to normal and she let my arm go. She turned and started walking away. “Who are you?!” I called after her. She couldn’t hear me and continued to walk away. “Valery?!” I called after her once more, still nothing. Someone was calling my name, it sounded far away, but familiar. Then I realized it was James, he was waking me up. I opened my eyes to him, shaking me and saying my name in a scared tone. “I’m up” I mumbled. He let his body fall on top of me in relief. “Are you okay?” I asked him. “Am *I* okay?” He said. “You let out a scream and then wouldn’t wake up, I couldn’t tell if you were breathing or not, you scared the crap out of me!” he said. “I’m sorry, it’s not like I did it on purpose” I said. “I know,” he said, as he wrapped his arm around me in an embrace.

We got up out of bed to go find Arturo, I wanted to tell them both about the dream at the same time, so I didn't have to repeat myself. We found him, sitting at the kitchen table. "Mind if we join you?" I asked him. "Of course not, please," he said, motioning toward the other empty chairs. "I saw the woman in my dream again," I said. I remembered her grabbing my arm, so I looked to see if there was a mark left behind like before, there was. I held my arm up to show them, "she grabbed my arm, and told me that the child would save me" I told them. They both sat in silence, staring at me. "I asked her if she was my mom and she looked confused. I also asked if she was Valery and she ignored me" I told them. "And how can Julie save you?" James asked. "I have no idea," I admitted. "You both assume that the child she speaks of is Julie?" Arturo asked. "I don't know any other children," I said. "Maybe the child doesn't exist yet," he said. "Why would she come to me now about a child that doesn't exist yet?" I asked. "Maybe she got her timeline mixed up," Arturo said. "Are you being serious right now?" I asked. "As serious as possible, since there is no explanation as to why this is happening in the first place" Arturo said.

The three of us continued to sit at the table, we sat in silence, trying to let everything sink in. Just thinking about everything that was happening, trying to make sense of it all. After sitting there for probably thirty minutes, Arturo got up, "I'm going to sit outside on the porch" he said. I nodded at him, "I'll join you" I said. "I want to go back to David and Sarah's today, do you want to go with me?" James asked me. "Of course I do" I said. He nodded, "okay, I'm going to go get a shower" he said, walking away. I went outside with Arturo, "have you made any sense of my dream yet?" I asked him. "No, and I'm not even sure it is a dream, but I'm almost positive that the child she spoke of is not Julie, she doesn't have any powers, nothing really special about her, besides she's a half giant" he said. "So, you think the child is a witch?" I asked. "I do, but only because I have looked into your future as well, I think she is telling you what

I saw as well, the child had powers, but the power isn't what saves you" he said.

"Thanks for being vague," I said, sarcastically. "Everything happens for a reason, if we know too much about our future, we may do something to change it, we shouldn't change something that is meant to happen" he explained. "Then why even look there in the first place?" I asked. "Certain people can look, and be prepared, others cannot handle looking without the temptation of changing, especially to save someone they care about" he said. "Is someone I care about going to die?" I asked him. "I cannot tell you too much about your future, because you have to live it, no matter what" he told me. I nodded, looking down, I understood a little I suppose, knowing that you are going to lose someone and then losing them, is like going through it twice, I suppose.

"We need to discuss what's going on over on 12 more," Arturo said, changing the subject. "What are your plans?" he asked. "I believe that Misty is trustworthy still, even though my ankle got snapped, I'm really eager to get back and have a conversation with her. As long as she is what I think she is, I can use that to get others to see my way" I said. "And if she's not?" he asked. "Then I start over, move on to the next one and get them on my side and get them to help convince others" I said. "You are very naïve," Arturo said. "What?" I asked. "Why would you assume that people who want to kill you are just going to say, 'okay, I'll be on your side now'?" he said. "I realize how it may seem," I said. "I don't think you do, there will be more fighting and more killing, on both sides, you need to be prepared" he told me, as he got up and went inside.

I just sat there, looking out into the forest that was on the side of the house. Why did he keep telling me that someone was going to die? And why wouldn't he tell me who? I felt like he knew, but he didn't think I could handle it. Was it James? I really couldn't handle losing him, not that anyone else was disposable either, I just wish he would tell me, so I could try to prevent it. But of course, that's exactly why he wouldn't tell me. I walked inside to find him. I didn't see him in the kitchen, so I walked into the living room. He was sitting there, reading.

"Why can't you just tell me? Why would anyone be able to see the future if we aren't allowed to change it?" I asked him. "You think I haven't tried, you think I haven't saved someone and watched them die in an accident the very next day?" he said. "My gift is a curse, a curse upon my entire family" he continued. "I'm sorry" I said to him sincerely. He looked at me and nodded, "if I believed there was any way to change the future, I would share it with you, I would help you do it" he said. I nodded, looking down to the floor, feeling ashamed. "What are you guys talking about?" James said, walking into the room. "Just discussing future plans" I said, giving him a half smile because I couldn't find a whole smile inside me. Arturo just sat there, not saying anything.

"Okay, did you want to get a shower before we go?" James asked me. "Sure" I said. I walked out of the living room and into the bathroom. The mirror was still steamy from James' shower, I turned the water on and stepped inside. I started crying, I couldn't control it, something inside me had just had enough, enough of the fighting, enough of the hiding, enough of everything. I let it all out. I must have been louder than I thought, James started knocking on the door and asking if I was okay, I couldn't even answer him. I used magic to unlock the door so he could come in, I needed someone to hold me, someone to tell me that everything was going to be okay. After a good ten minutes of crying into James' chest, I finished my shower and got ready.

After I got ready, we headed out to David and Sarah's house. As we walked, we talked about my breakdown, of course. "You can cry on me anytime you need to, do you want to talk about why though?" James asked me. I shook my head, "thank you, but I don't really know, I think just everything built up and had to come out" I told him. He nodded, "I can understand that" he said. "What do you really think about the dream I had, 'Valery' told me that a child would save me" I said. " I know, Julie, right?" He asked. "That's what I thought, but Arturo doesn't think so, he said that he has looked into my future, he didn't have anything good to say, and that there's no way to stop what's going to happen, so I have to live it basically" I said. "No wonder you had a breakdown, why would he do that? Why tell you anything at all?" James said, sounding like he was getting angry. "Don't get mad at him, it will just cause more drama that I don't want" I said. He ignored me and kept walking.

We walked almost the whole rest of the way in silence. I wasn't sure what he was thinking. I was a little worried that he would have a confrontation with Arturo, and I didn't want that to happen. I didn't want people fighting because of me, that was more stress that I couldn't deal with. When we arrived at David and Sarah's house, David met us by a tree in the field where I had trained. It was crazy how it seemed so long ago, when it had only been a couple of months, it seemed like it had been years ago. "What's wrong?" He asked, as soon as he saw us. "That obvious?" I asked, sarcastically.

We told him about the dream and about what Arturo had said about my future and about my breakdown. "The breakdown is understandable, don't beat yourself up for having a moment of weakness, especially since you are strong all the time, no one can be strong *all* of the time" David said, pulling me in his side for a hug. I put my arms around his midsection, as we continued to walk toward the house. "Sarah cooked again," he told me. "I love her cooking," I said, simply. He smiled, "she'll be happy to hear that" he said.

We spent the day, playing with Julie, and eating. I couldn't imagine bringing a child into this crazy world. It's scary as an adult, how could I explain and train someone when I am just learning? Why was I even thinking about that, it wasn't going to happen, I wondered what child is going to be *my* savior. I wondered how things would turn out with Misty, would she turn out to make me look like the biggest idiot ever? Or was she genuinely on my side? "Do you think we could stay here tonight?" I asked David. "Sure, I don't see why not, just send word to Arturo so he isn't worried" he said. I nodded in agreement, and sent a note, via transport spell.

Ten

The forgotten enemy

I felt more comfortable at David's house, it felt more like home and I felt more welcome. Even though I was brought here against my will, of course, if he hadn't brought me here and taught me everything, I wouldn't be alive right now. The only downside to staying here is that James wouldn't sleep in the same bed with me, he felt uncomfortable doing that in his brother's home. "Yeah, I'm just going to sleep on the couch," he told me. I rolled my eyes at him. I was tired, and I really wanted him to be by my side, but I didn't want him to know how badly, so I didn't argue with him, I just sat next to him for some pre bedtime snuggles.

After sitting with him on the couch in silence for what seemed like hours, but was probably only one hour, I got up, "I'm going to get ready for bed" I told him. Julie had been asleep for an hour or two already. I wanted to give her a kiss on the forehead, but I didn't want to wake her up and have Sarah get angry with me. So, I just went to the room that I had stayed in before, and got dressed for bed. I crawled into the bed, it felt like home. No sooner than I put my head on the pillow, it felt like I was asleep. I had a dreamless sleep that night, it was a deep sleep that I hadn't realized that I needed so badly.

I woke the next morning to the familiar smell of food and coffee. I put my feet on the floor and walked to the kitchen, everyone else was at the table already. I looked at David, "you didn't wake me up this morning" I said to him. "No reason to" he replied with a giggle. I smiled as I sat down with them to eat. "This is delicious Sarah," I said. "Thank you dear" she replied. Julie was sitting in a high chair, gumming a biscuit and making cute baby sounds, like she was trying to join in the conversation. We all made sure to include her for the rest of the time we were sitting there.

After breakfast, David looked at me, "can we take a walk together? Discuss a few things?" he asked me. James looked up, "I'm coming to" he said. "No, I would like to talk to her alone," David said. James looked a bit upset, he nodded angrily and walked away. "Don't throw a tantrum in front of my child James," David yelled after him. James kept walking away without turning around to acknowledge him. "Let me help Sarah get the dishes before we go." I said to David. He nodded, "I'll be waiting on the porch" he said.

After helping Sarah, I walked out of the front door, David was waiting there as promised. "I'm ready," I told him. He nodded as he got up from a rocking chair and said, "great." We started walking away from the house, "I'm sorry that I didn't talk to you about this before" he said. "What?" I asked. "I told James that you two shouldn't cross any lines" he said. "You don't have to say it like that, we are adults" I told him. "I know you are, there are several reasons that I didn't want you to be romantically involved" he said. "I know, it's because I am going to die, and he's going to be devastated" I said. "There's always that possibility, there's also the fact that it's just pure distraction. What if your feelings for each other is the reason for the other's demise? Or worse, what if you both survive this and decide to start a family?" he said. "We haven't talked about that yet, but I did think about it, especially after what Arturo told me. The thought of bringing a child into this world terrifies me" I told him.

He nodded, we continued to walk in silence for a while. "So, you don't think you want children?" he asked, after a little while. "No," I said, simply. "If your enemies find out about the two of you, they will come harder and faster. They will not allow you two to reproduce" he said. "The only people who know are the ones that live with us, Misty doesn't know" I told him. "Any chance that you can walk away from it?" he asked me. "Are you serious?" I asked sarcastically. "Don't tell James I said that," he said. I just looked at him, not agreeing to anything. We walked until we could see the lake in the distance. I could sense something watching me, a chill ran up my spine.

"I had somehow forgotten about them," I said, pointing to the lake. "Oh, they haven't forgotten about you?" he asked, surprised. I shook my head 'no' I could feel how much they wanted me to go into the lake, to never be heard from again. "Usually they don't remember for that long. We may need to do something about it," David said. "Like what?" I asked. "Some kind of spell? Maybe you should go talk to Arturo about it tomorrow, and since they know you are here now, we'll need to keep an eye on you tonight" he said. I nodded, in agreement. Even though I felt ridiculous having to have a babysitter while I slept.

We walked back to the house, James was waiting, sitting on the porch. I walked up to him, "the mermaids still want me" I said simply before walking away. I went to the bedroom that I stayed in while I was there. I noticed that there was no mirror in here. I wondered if it was done on purpose, or just something that got overlooked? I lay down on the bed and rested my eyes. It wasn't long before I fell asleep.

Sure enough I went to dreamland. I climbed out of the window, uncontrollably. I had no idea if it was really happening or not. I jumped a short distance to the ground outside of the window. I heard them singing, it was so beautiful, I wanted to find them, to go to them, to join them. I wanted it more than anything else in the world. A part of me almost felt like it was magic that was being used on me, but no, how could that be? I continued walking through the field toward the forest that was between the lake and myself. There was no one to stop me, even though I felt like there would be. I kept walking. That was the last thing that I remembered, next thing I knew, I was waking up, in the bed, next to James.

He was awake, looking at me. "Good morning," he said. "Did that really happen last night? Or was I dreaming?" I replied. "It happened," he said, simply. "How did I get back to bed?" I asked. "Arturo was watching you, he put a spell on you to make you fall asleep then brought you back" he told me. "Do you remember how you got out?" James asked. "The window" I said, pointing toward it. James shook his head "someone must be helping them, a witch, there's no way they are that powerful" he said. "What do you mean?" I asked, confused. "Go, try to open the window," he said. I walked over and the lock wouldn't even budge, how did I get it open? "Is it possible they have enough magic to unlock it? Open it?" I asked, still confused. James shook his head, "they only have water magic, maybe a little dream magic, but they can't do magic here, on land" he explained. I was still confused, "so you think that someone here is helping them try to kill me?" I asked. "Yes" he said, simply. "After your first night here, David made sure that the window couldn't be opened, unless he wanted it open. He did that with all of the windows because he doesn't want Julie to get out and go exploring and get hurt," James explained.

So, I have an enemy that I didn't know about before, maybe someone had followed me here? But how would they even know I was here? I couldn't make sense of it, even though it was obvious that they weren't working alone. "Do you have any idea who it could be?" I asked James. He shook his head, "no, just know that it's not Arturo because he saved you" he said. I nodded, "even if he hadn't saved me, I wouldn't think it was him" I said. "Well, if he hadn't saved you, you would be dead," James said. "But he did and I'm not" I said. "I don't know if we should stay here, it's no safer here than there" he said. "You don't have to stay," I told him. "What do you mean?" he asked. "If you want out, I wouldn't blame you for leaving, I will tell you now, if you want to run, then run" I told him. "No, no way, I don't know what it is, but I feel like I just can't, I have to be with you, that may seem crazy, but it's the truth" he told me. I snuggled into his chest, "I'm happy that you want to stay, but, it's probably not going to end well" I said. "What do you mean?" he asked. "What will you do when my enemies finally win?" I asked him. "That's not going to happen, stop talking like it is," he said. I could sense anger rising in his voice.

"I'm making you angry? By speaking the truth?" I said, letting the anger rise in me as well. "You aren't speaking the truth! Have you seen you fight?! You are not going down!" he said, yelling now. "I'll not go down easy, but with as many people that want me dead, I won't be able to fight them off forever" I said. "That's why you have people on your side, to help you, when you can't fight, we will! Just like Arturo did last night!" he said, still yelling. There was a knock on the bedroom door that made me jump, I had almost forgotten that we weren't alone. "You guys are going to wake Julie up" David said, without opening the door. James threw himself backwards on the bed in frustration. I sat up and put my feet on the floor and stood up, I felt dizzy and my eyesight went black.

I was lying on the floor, unable to open my eyes, unable to move, but I was fully conscious, I could hear James jump up from the bed and yell "Gabriela!" I couldn't answer him to tell him that I was okay, I felt so bad for him. "DAVID! SARAH! HELP!" he continued yelling, Julie would get woken up for sure now. I heard the door open, "What happened?!" I heard David say. "I don't know, she just stood up and fell down, she won't wake up!" James said, I could hear a sob in his voice now. I wanted to reach up to him, tell him that I was okay, I wanted to wrap my arms around him, comfort him, but I just couldn't move. Someone must have done some kind of spell on me. "We need to get her to Arturo, or get him here, and fast!" David said. I heard Julie start crying from her room.

"Have you ever seen anything like this before?" James asked, desperate for answers. "No" I heard David reply. This was horrible, being completely aware of what's going on, but not being able to interact. I felt someone feel my neck, "her pulse is really weak" I heard Sarah say. NO! I'm fine! I screamed in my head. "NO! NO! Please help her!" James said, through his tears now, I could tell without being able to see him. I didn't like hearing him cry at all, I wanted to comfort him, what the hell was going on? This was obviously some sort of an attack, we definitely need Arturo. I couldn't stand the thought of someone physically attacking now, and I would have to listen and not be able to do anything to help my family.

"I'm going to get Arturo!" David said, "you have to be aware, and watch out for attacks!" he continued, I assumed to James. I heard inaudible sounds come from James, I could tell he was still crying. This was so strange to me, I was so aware, yet so numb, I was trying to think of what kind of magic it could be, so I could fight it myself. I tried healing, but that didn't work. The house seemed quiet, Sarah must have gotten Julie back to sleep. I couldn't feel any presence near me, so I assumed that James must have gone to another room, possibly to watch out of a window for attackers.

After what seemed like hours, I heard Arturo's voice say "where is she?!" "In here," James replied. I heard them walk into the room, and close to me. I felt Arturo 'scanning' my body with his hands, like he had done before. “It’s a spell that paralyzes the body, she’s still conscious in there though, she knows what is going on around her, but she can’t move at all” Arturo said. “We are going to figure this out,” James whispered in my ear. “Can you remove the spell?” David asked. “No, I can’t, we have to find the witch that cast the spell, they have to be near, this spell is strong and takes a lot of magic,” Arturo said. “How close?” David asked. “On the property close” Arturo answered. I heard David leave the room, probably to make sure Sarah and Julie were safe. I didn’t hear anything else from him, so I assumed that they were.

“Is there anything you can do to locate the witch?” James asked. “I can try, she didn’t say anything about feeling magic being used, before she collapsed?” Arturo asked. “No, she just fell,” James answered. I tried to remember if I did feel anything, it felt like it just came from nowhere. I just wanted to get up, help them find whoever did this! But I just had to lie there, with no choice about anything. “I can try to go inside her head, have a ‘mental’ discussion with her,” Arturo said. Yes! I thought, although I didn’t have any information to help them, it would be great to be able to speak with someone. I also didn’t want them to become distracted and vulnerable either.

“Gabriela, can you hear me?” I heard clearly, but not from my ears, from inside my own head. “Yes,” I replied. “Good,” Arturo said. “You are right, I can hear everything that’s going on, but I can’t move. I didn’t feel any magic being used before it happened. I don’t know what’s going on, I wish I could help more. It’s killing me, to lie here and not do anything, not be able to comfort James or communicate at all” I said. “So you have nothing that can help? Not all spells are invisible, did you drink anything outside of this house? Did you accidentally swallow a bug? Anything strange at all?” Arturo asked. “I don’t remember drinking anything, or swallowing anything strange,” I said. “Can I have permission to examine your body? Look for bites.” Arturo asked. This would be awkward.

"I suppose, but I don't recall being bitten by anything either" I said. "I should go now, try to figure out what is really going on here," Arturo said. "Wait! Will you please tell James not to be upset, and I will kiss him so much when this horrible magic is released" I said. I didn't hear a reply.

"Did it work?" I heard from my ears. "It did, she said to tell you to please do not be upset, and she will kiss you soon" Arturo said. Not exactly, but it works I guess. "Does she know what's causing this?" James asked. "No, I need to check her body for bites, she agreed to let me do so," Arturo said. "Do you mind if I do that? And if I see anything, I can call you in to look at it" James said. I rolled my eyes mentally. "No, I know what to look for, you see, witches aren't the only magical creatures. I need to look at her, completely, to see if I can find anything, I only want to help her" Arturo said. "Can I stay in here while you do it?" James asked. "Of course," Arturo answered.

I felt my clothes being pulled off, great, now everyone was going to see me naked. I hoped that David didn't walk in. My shirt came off first, then my bra. "Here!" Arturo yelled. I felt a touch on the inside of my arm. "Kinda looks like a bullseye" I heard James say. "Yes, one big red spot, with a red circle around it, Dragon bite!" Arturo said. "How could she get bit by a *dragon* and not know it?" James asked. They can change shape, including shrinking themselves, they can numb the area before biting, so you wouldn't even feel the bite. I need to check the rest of her, to make sure this is the only bite. And the good news is, I have a cure!" Arturo said. I felt such a relief come over me. "Yes!" James said, with clear relief in his voice as well. I felt my pants come off, and my panties, I hoped I would still be able to look at Arturo after this. "I don't see any more bites, I'll go get the cure and be back as soon as I can," Arturo said. "Will you have David go with you? Just in case there is someone else behind this? I don't want you to get attacked if someone is watching," James said. "I'll speak with him, let him know what is going on and see if he would like to join me," Arturo agreed.

I heard the door close, James started putting my clothes back on. He was such a sweet guy. I hated that he got put through this, I hated that I heard him cry in fear of losing me. Maybe I should try to let him go? I don't think I can, neither of us will just walk away now. With so many enemies, in so many dimensions I started feeling small, how could I possibly win this war? My confidence was shrinking. One little bite and I'm completely out, I guess I was lucky that Arturo knew what to look for and that he has a cure. But would luck always be there for me?

I heard the door to the bedroom open. "That was pretty quick" I heard James say. "I need to take her shirt back off," Arturo said. They took my shirt back off, James hadn't put my bra back on, he probably didn't know how, he only knew how to take it off. I felt a cool sensation on my skin, where he had found the bite on my arm. It felt like some kind of cream or lotion. "How fast will it work?" I heard James ask. "A day or so, depending on how far the poison got into her system," Arturo said. I started feeling sleepy, and I didn't remember anything else until I woke up.

I opened my eyes, they worked! Looking around, I didn't see James or anyone for that matter. I tried to sit up, my body was working, but not completely, I felt so weak, like I had the flu. "James" I tried to call out, but my voice was weak as well, it barely came out as a whisper. Great, I was awake, with no one here now, and I didn't have the strength to get out of bed, or even call out for them to let them know I was awake. I lay there for a little while, hoping strength would just come to me, it didn't. I didn't have enough strength to cast a healing spell either.

Finally after what seemed like hours, the door opened. It was James, I looked at him and smiled the best I could. "She's awake!" he yelled out. He came running into the room and scooped me up and hugged me tight. I let out a little "oh" from the pain. "I'm sorry, I didn't mean to hurt you!" he said. "It's okay" I said, best that I could. "She still needs to heal, we need to get her hydrated and fed," Arturo said. "Thank you" I said to him in my weak voice. "Just rest, darling, you have been through a lot, the poison had almost gone to your heart, you barely survived" he said. I nodded. "How long have I been out?" I asked. "Three days," James replied. I just looked at him, *three days?* And I didn't remember any of it. That must be what a coma is like. I didn't really have the strength to talk, so I stayed quiet.

Sarah walked into the room, she had a saline bag and IV with her. She came over to me with it, and started cleaning my arm and looking for a vein to put it in. She got it in, with no problems. "You're a pro," I squeaked. "I used to run IV's for a hospital," she said. I started feeling better almost immediately, I had never had an IV before, but this seemed unusually quick to be feeling better. "Is that just saline?" I asked, this time in a clearer, stronger voice. "There is a little bit of vampire blood, not a lot, just enough to give you a kick start" she replied. "Wow, I could only imagine what a full dose would do" I said, the back looked clear, that's how little blood there was in it. "Will I have to be extra careful now?" I asked. "You should always be extra careful," she said, laughing. "There is not enough to last, just enough to give you a kick start, like I said before," she said.

Eleven

Back to 12

I felt like getting out of bed in no time at all. My stomach was going crazy, yelling at me, I guess I hadn't eaten in at least four days, so that made sense. I got up out of bed, my legs still felt weak, I suppose because I hadn't stood on them for so long. But they worked for me, nonetheless. I made my way to the dining room, and surprisingly, there was no one in there. I wondered what time it was. "James?" I called out, but tried not to be too loud, in case Julie was sleeping. "He's outside, Alice stopped by to visit with him," David said. "Who is Alice?" I asked. "She's an old friend of his," he said. I shrugged my shoulders. "Why are you out of bed?" he asked accusingly. "I'm hungry," I answered. Arturo stormed into the kitchen, "you get back in bed! We will bring you food!" he yelled at me. I guess James heard them yelling at me and came inside with his friend in tow.

"Gabriela, what are you doing?" he said, joining the gang up against me. "What are you doing?" I asked back, looking at Alice. He was silent, oh no, was he really doing something? I was just saying it, to say it! I looked away from him and walked back to my room, "please bring me some food, Arturo" I said before closing the door. I heard a knock on the door as soon as I closed it. "That was fast" I said, opening the door, it was James, so I started closing the door back in his face, he put his arm up to stop me. "I need to talk to you" he said. "Why?" I asked, starting to cry. I hated crying. "Please let me in, it's not what you think" he said. Too weak to hold the door anyway, I let it go and he stepped inside. He looked at me, this time giving me an angry look. "Alice and I have been friends for a very long time, and for you to accuse me of something in front of her and others, no, I will not defend myself. I shouldn't have to, that was ridiculous" he ranted. "I was ill, and you were outside visiting with another female, how was I supposed to feel?" I asked, trying to defend my feelings. "I stayed by your side for four days" he said, sounding hurt. I couldn't stand hurting him, "I'm sorry" I cried, and wrapped my arms around him. He embraced me back, which made me melt into him. And my stomach growled, very loudly. "Let me go get you some food" he said. "Arturo is bringing me something" I said. "I really am sorry, will you forgive me?" I asked him. "Of course, you also need to apologize to Alice, she'll be here for dinner" he said. "Okay" I said, "if I'm allowed to go to dinner" I continued.

Arturo knocked on the door, and opened it, "I told you to get in bed!" he scolded. "Sorry, Art, it was my fault, don't be mad at her," James told him. "What I tell her to do, is for her own good! I'm not trying to be mean!" Arturo said. I just nodded and went over to the bed and got in it. He had brought me a sandwich, "is this it?" I asked, disappointed. "Sarah has started cooking for dinner, you can have some of that as well, you don't need to eat too much at once anyway, you will upset your stomach" Arturo told me. "Is she allowed to come to the table at dinner?" James asked him. "We'll see," Arturo said. I almost didn't want to go, I felt ashamed of my jealousy toward Alice and didn't really want to see her. I ate the sandwich, like it was nothing and still felt like I needed to eat more. "I'm going to go back outside and talk to Alice," James told me. I nodded, trying to keep my expression blank.

This was boring, just sitting here, in the bed, no one to talk to, nothing to eat. After about ten minutes of just sitting there, looking around, there was a knock on the door. It was Sarah, carrying Julie. "I thought you were cooking?" I asked, surprised. "I'm trying to, this little girl is wanting a lot of attention right now, would you mind watching her while I cook? If you feel up to it of course, if not, I can find David" she said. "Of course I can, I'm just sitting here, being bored anyway, I'd love to watch her actually" I told her. "Great" she said, and put her on the bed next to me before walking out and closing the door behind her. "How are you doing?" I asked Julie in a childish voice. She looked at me and giggled, my heart melted. Julie was very entertaining, I was glad that Sarah brought her to me. I could sit and watch her for hours, she was just so adorable.

There was a knock on the door, Julie looked at me and her eyes got wider. "What is it, silly?" I said to her, she pointed at the door and made cute baby noises. "I know, let's find out who it is, okay?" I said to her, "Yes?" I said, loud enough for whoever it was to hear me. David opened the door, "Sarah told me she was in here, she wanted me to check that you are both okay, do you need a break?" he asked me. "No, I'm fine. I think she is fine too" I said. I got close to Julie's face, "are you fine?" I asked her in my childish voice. She started rambling in baby talk. "She's going to be a talker," I said to David. "Yes, I agree with you," he said. "Okay, dinner will be ready in about fifteen minutes, I think. Will you be joining us?" David asked me. "Ask Arturo, he made me get back in bed earlier" I answered. David nodded, as he walked back out of the room and closed the door behind him. Julie looked confused and started yelling in baby talk again. "Really?" I said to her, so she didn't feel like she was talking to herself. Her facial expressions changed with the excitement in her voice. She had such a personality already.

A few more minutes passed and there was a knock on the door again. It looked like Julie rolled her eyes and I giggled. "Yes?" I yelled. Arturo opened the door. "What's this? I tell you to rest and you are babysitting?" he said accusingly. "I was asleep for days, Arturo, I haven't got out of bed, we have just been talking" I told him. He looked at me suspiciously. "I promise, I haven't even picked her up," I told him. "Do you think you feel up to joining everyone at the dinner table?" he asked me. I nodded, "yes please." David walked in behind Arturo and picked up Julie, she started crying and reaching for me. "Aww, sweety" I said to her. She kept reaching for me. "Don't," Arturo warned. "You don't want to fall and hurt her," he explained. I nodded, "I'm coming, right behind you" I said to her. She stopped crying and laid her head on David's shoulder. My heart melted again. Arturo came to me and offered his arm to help me get out of bed. "Just hold on to me, you are still pretty weak, I don't want you to fall and hurt yourself either," he said. I nodded in agreement.

When we got to the table, everyone was there, waiting. Julie was placed in her high chair. Alice was there, like James said she would be. I felt a little embarrassed by my accusations earlier. "Alice, how are you?" I asked. "I'm good?" she replied. "Good, I'm sorry about earlier" I said. "Don't worry about it, you have been through a lot, it's totally understandable" she replied. "I'm really embarrassed about it," I told her. "No worries, really," she replied. I smiled and started eating, I was still so hungry. "How are you feeling?" James asked. "I am feeling better by the minute, actually" I replied. He smiled at me. "Arturo, can dragons go to 12?" I asked. "They can, they are lizards," he explained. "So, their bites wouldn't have the same effect?" I asked. "No," he replied, simply. "Do you think it's possible that the mermaids had anything to do with me getting bit by the dragon?"

I asked. "Anything is possible, I don't think it's likely as they don't really have a lot of contact. But someone above water could have had something to do with it" Arturo said.

Everyone stopped eating and looked around. "You think there is someone here that wants her dead?" David asked. "Anything is possible, but highly unlikely since there was no attack when she was down. It was probably just something that happened for no reason" Arturo said. I was starting on my third plate, "you probably should not eat so much," Arturo said. I gave him the evil eye and put my plate down. "I made some apple cobbler for dessert," Sarah said. "Yay, sounds amazing" I said, glaring at Arturo. "She didn't eat for like four days," Sarah said, looking at Arturo. "I'm just trying to save you from a stomach ache later, do what you want" he said. I ate some cobbler, and it was delicious.

Everyone seemed to hang around the table longer than usual, maybe to make sure I didn't keep eating, I'm not sure. But after dessert, I quit eating. "Do you think it will be okay if I go out and sit on the porch? I want some fresh air," I said. Arturo nodded his head. "I'll join you" James said, "do you want to join us?" he asked, looking at Alice. She nodded her head and the three of us went outside. I sat down on the edge of the porch with my legs hanging down toward the ground, the taller people could actually touch the ground.

"I came here because I wanted to tell you there are rumors among the giants," Alice said, looking at me. I could tell that she had already told James, he just sat there with his head down. "The giants don't know about you, but someone has told someone, now they are talking, trying to figure out if it's true" she said. "They will come after me too, won't they? If they find out I exist" I said. "Yes," she said, simply. "Who do you think told them?" I asked. "I'm guessing a witch from 12, since they don't really believe the story. If it was a giant or half giant, there would already be a hunt" she said. "Wow, so a witch came here and told them? I must have scared them," I said, with a cocky smile. "It's not something to really be proud of, more hiding and more fighting" James said. "I'm sorry, I didn't mean it that way" I said. "I know you didn't, sometimes I just want this all to be over, to be able to relax," he said. "I guess, my life was just lame before this, and now I have something to live for," I said. They both just looked at me silently.

I heard the door open behind me, David, Sarah and Arturo all came walking out. "Where's Julie?" I asked. "She's sleeping," Sarah replied. "You seem to be doing great now, I am going home," Arturo said, looking at me. I nodded, "thank you so much, for everything" I said. He nodded as he stepped off the porch, "I'll see you before you go back." "Bye" I said. We sat there for a minute, watching him walk away. "He's such a good man, why doesn't he live on 12 with the other witches?" I asked. "Because of his *gift* he prefers to live in solitude, he once lived there, he was engaged, she died and he never saw it coming and so he blames himself for her death. He said he shouldn't be around anyone, he's punishing himself" David told me. "That's sad," I said. "Indeed," David replied.

"I think I'm going to head home, James can I talk to you before I go?" Alice said. James nodded and they walked away. I watched them suspiciously, wondering if I could do a spell to enhance my hearing. "How are you feeling?" Sarah asked suddenly. I jumped at the sound, I had almost forgotten that her and David were still sitting outside with me. She giggled a little, "sorry, I didn't mean to startle you" she said. "It's okay, I'm feeling good actually, no stomach ache either" I said. "Are you full? Now that he's gone, if you want some more food, you can eat," she said with a smile. "No, I'm good," I said, smiling back at her.

James walked back up to the porch, Alice had left. "Are you ready to go inside?" he asked me, holding out his hand to help me up. I nodded and took his hand and jumped off the porch. It was a good thing I waited for him, when my feet hit the ground, I just kept falling. He caught me with ease, "whoa" he said. I found my feet and managed to stand up. "Are you sure you're okay?" David asked. "Yeah, I think I just haven't used my legs in so long, that I forgot how" I said, jokingly. James held my hand all the way inside and to the bedroom. "Maybe I should do some exercises to strengthen my legs," I said. "Why don't you just lay down for now, and rest" James said. "I have rested," I argued. "Please, just get in bed," he begged. "Okay," I said, not feeling like arguing with him.

I got into bed, with no more problems. He lay down next to me, I snuggled up close to him and put my arm over his chest. I could tell something was on his mind, something I didn't know about, maybe it was what he and Alice were talking about? "Are you okay?" I asked him. "Not really, this whole thing just keeps getting more dangerous." he said. My heart sank, I didn't like him feeling disheartened. "I would understand if you wanted to stay here," I said. "I'm not leaving you, I can't believe you would even suggest that, " he said, sounding hurt. I couldn't win, it didn't matter what I said or did. I should let him go, I knew that would be the best for him, I know it would hurt him, but he would eventually get over it, and move on, but I just couldn't do it, I needed him and I was going to be selfish.

"I didn't mean it like that, and you're right, I can't even believe I said that," I said, looking up at him and smiling. He rubbed my head and kissed my forehead. "We do need to talk," he said. I rolled my eyes, but he couldn't see it because my head was below his. I pulled myself off of him and sat up in the bed so I could see his face. "What is it?" I asked. "Alice thinks she should come back with us" he blurted out. I sat there and thought for a minute, I couldn't just come out with a 'no' after I had basically accused them of having an affair. "Why?" I asked. "She thinks she would be of more use there than here, she's also scared that if the giants have too much information, they may find out she is involved somehow and make her 'talk' or try to anyway" he said. "Oh, so, basically she wants to go for our protection?" I asked. He just looked at me. "I don't want her to get hurt because of me, or to get tortured into telling them that I am real. So yeah, if it's the only way we can protect her, then yes she should come back with us" I said, even though I really didn't want her to, but I also didn't want giants coming after me.

"I'm sleepy, let's go to sleep, we can talk more about it tomorrow" James said. I nodded my head and snuggled back up to him with my head on his chest, I could hear his heart beating and he played with my hair. At some point I actually fell asleep. I had a nice dreamless sleep and woke feeling refreshed in the morning. James was still asleep, so I tried to get out of bed quietly and slowly so I didn't fall or wake him up. It didn't work, he rolled over, and said, "are you okay?" "Yeah, I was just trying not to wake you" I replied. He just smiled at me, "we need to practice your ninja skills," he said. I smiled at him, "well, I'm going to go eat breakfast" I told him. He rolled back over in bed to let me know he wasn't getting up yet. I got up and walked out of the bedroom and into the dining room.

Breakfast was ready, as usual. Sarah, David and Julie were already sitting at the table, eating. "Good morning," I said as I entered and sat down at the table with them. "Good morning, is James not up yet?" David asked. I shrugged my shoulders, "he was, but I think he's going back to sleep" I told him. Julie looked at me and started making cute baby noises. "Oh really?" I said to her, to make her believe that I understood her. "Gab!" she yelled out. "She's trying to say your name!" Sarah said, excitedly. "Her first word is going to be *your name*?" David said, in a snarky tone. I gave him a shocked look, "jealous much?" I said. "As a matter of fact, yes, I am," he said. I laughed at him and Julie joined in on the laugh to make the whole scene a little more perfect.

James walked into the dining room, "what's so funny?" he asked. "Maybe if you would get out of bed at a decent hour, you wouldn't miss the funny stuff" David said, as only a brother could. James rolled his eyes and sat down next to me. "Gab!" Julie yelled again. And everyone laughed again. "Is she trying to say your name?" James asked. I shrugged, "sure does sound like it" I said. After we all laughed and ate our breakfast, we went outside to enjoy the fresh air.

"Have you thought about what we talked about last night more?" James asked me. "We have to make a decision quickly," he added. "I know, I think if it's going to protect her and myself, that we should do it," I said. "She'll be here today, we can let her know then" he told me. I nodded, this was going to be a test of our relationship for sure. I would have to keep my jealousy in check. I saw someone walking up on the horizon and got a little nervous, it was just Arturo. I could tell as he walked closer that he looked tired, worn out. I went to meet him so I could walk up the rest of the way back with him.

"Are you okay?" I asked him. "I'm fine, why do you ask?" he replied. "No reason" I said, not wanting to be rude and say 'you look tired.' "Just come to make sure that you are doing well," he said. "I'm good, I feel normal today," I told him. "Good, I'm glad that you are feeling like yourself again," he said, smiling at me. I really felt like something was off with him, he really didn't seem like himself, besides looking tired, he just didn't seem 'normal.' "You don't seem like yourself" I finally got the nerve to say to him. "Just been thinking a lot, I've been considering going back with you" he said. My eyes got wide with excitement. "I said, considering," he told me after seeing my excitement. "So, you haven't made a decision yet?" I asked. He shook his head and let it hang downward.

We reached the house and everyone was still outside, Julie was playing in the grass, a couple of fairies were playing with her. "Can I mention it to James?" I whispered. "Not yet" he grunted back. James looked up at me, "did I hear my name?" he asked. I smiled and shook my head. "How are you, Arturo?" David asked. "I am okay, David,

I need to speak with you in private if you don't mind," he replied. "Of course" David said, getting up, "you look a bit tired, why don't we go inside and rest while we talk." Arturo nodded in agreement and followed him inside. I wondered why he had to talk to David? Was it about what he had just told me? And if so, why did he need to talk to David about it? Maybe it was because 2 wasn't as safe as we once thought it was. And him being here, helped to keep David and his family safe? Suddenly, I didn't want Arturo to go with us. I looked at Julie, an innocent child, playing on the ground, giggling at the fairies flying and dancing around her head.

James said that he wanted to go for a walk, and to see if he could find Alice. I nodded, and he kissed my forehead as he got up and walked away. I looked at Sarah, "sometimes I wish I could just stay here, it's so peaceful, most of the time anyway" I said to her. She smiled at me, "we do have our dangers here, but it's not healthy to always worry about what may happen. Poor Arturo, and his visions, you can see what it has done to him. I am grateful for him though. He put a protection on the property after you were attacked. This is the first time that I have allowed Julie to play out in the yard like this," she told me. "Have you ever been to 12?" I asked her. "A long time ago, for a short time, it seemed like a horrible place, violence and hate everywhere. I couldn't figure out why so many of our kind wanted to be there" she said. I nodded, "maybe we need to be there, to help end the violence and hate, after all, we are part angel" I said. "Do you believe you can end violence by violence?" she asked me. I sat there in silence, she had a point. Maybe I needed a different game plan. I got up and walked over to play with Julie and the fairies.

After playing with Julie for a while, I looked up and saw James walking up, alone. He had a look of worry on his face. I got up and dusted the grass off of me and walked toward him. "What's wrong?" I asked as soon as I got to him. "I can't find her, something isn't right," he said, full of worry. "I asked Theo to come help me look for her," he told me. I remembered that Theo was the other half giant that I had met. "Let me help too!" I said. "I don't think that is a good idea, they may figure out that you are the one they are looking for if they know anything" he said. I was confused, "so we don't know if they know anything, we don't know if they have Alice" I said, trying to make sense of everything.

I could see another tall person walking up in the distance. It didn't look like Alice, so I was guessing it was Theo. "We should talk with Arturo before you guys head out then" I said. James nodded in agreement. We reached the house and James yelled "David!" Arturo and David came outside, "We have giant business to deal with," James said. "I fear that Alice has been taken, we need to get her out, before they get information out of her or kill her." James explained. Theo walked up behind us. "Get Julie inside" David said, looking at Sarah. She jumped up and grabbed Julie, Julie started crying because she had been having so much fun with the fairies. "They won't kill her, but they may try to find ways to make her talk," David said to James.

"Are you sure you don't want me to go?" I asked. "Absolutely not," James said. "Okay" I replied. "Arturo can come with us, you stay here and make sure that Sarah and Julie are safe, we will be back as soon as possible" David said. I nodded at him and went inside with Sarah and Julie, even though there was a protection spell by Arturo around the property, I started working on one around the house as well. Sarah had got Julie to stop crying and she was crawling around the floor now, looking for something to get into. "I think she is looking for the fairies," Sarah said, with a smile. I could see worry in her eyes. "Everything is going to be okay, I can feel it," I said to her. She nodded, "When David was gone to 12, to get you, even though he was only gone for two days at a time max, I still worried like crazy" She said. "I understand," I said, sincerely.

We tried to find things to pass the time, we played cards,

played with Julie, ate, but we were still worrying. "Maybe I can do something to magically communicate with Arturo," I suggested. "You don't want to be a distraction" Sarah said, disapproving of my suggestion. "I won't get in the way, or be a distraction, I just need to know what's happening, before I go crazy" I said. I went to my room to think for a minute, of a way to see what was going on. I heard a noise on the window, it was very light, I walked over to see what it was, it was a fairy. She looked like she was trying to get me to let her in, I couldn't tell if it was one of the ones that had been playing with Julie earlier. "She's asleep," I whispered. The fairy shook her head and motioned for me to come outside. I left the bedroom immediately and headed for the front door. "Where do you think you are going?" Sarah asked, in a tone that I had never heard from her. "Just outside, I'm not leaving," I told her.

I walked around to the window where the fairy had been, she was still there, she flew up to my finger and grabbed it and I could see her tugging it, but I didn't feel it at all because she was so small. "Where are you wanting me to go? I can't leave the property" I said to her. She shook her head to let me know that she wasn't asking me to leave the property. "Okay" I agreed to follow her. We got almost to the edge of the forest when we stopped, there were at least fifty fairies, in a circle. I didn't understand what they were doing, I didn't understand fairy magic, I barely understood witch magic. One of the fairies went into the middle of the circle, and seemingly vanished before our eyes, I let out a gasp, "Oh." The fairies then made a line, they were touching hand to hand, all the way up to my hand. The fairy at my hand, but not yet touching me, closed her eyes and held her head up, I nodded that I understood and closed my eyes, I felt the tiny touch of her hand on my finger, then different scenes began to flash behind my eyelids, like I was moving quickly through the forest.

Suddenly, everything stopped. I could see a huge house, going up to the window, I could see inside, I could see giants, but I didn't know who they were. They had sent the fairy into the giant village, and linked together with her so I could see what she saw. They were smart little creatures. I think the fairy somehow understood that I didn't recognize any of the people in the house, she began to fly around, like she was looking for someone that I would recognize. Wondering if she could take anymore of my suggestions, I thought, I wonder if they are on their way home? The fairy then looked in a different direction, back toward the forest, it would be impossible to tell without going in. She must have heard a noise, so she started flying toward a different house. She looked into the window, Alice was in this house!

She didn't look like she was being held as hostage, she wasn't in any restraints, she was walking around freely. "I'm telling you, if this girl existed, I would know by now" she told someone who was much taller than she was. "There is no half giant half witch, and I would like to know who is spreading these rumors. Because they are probably up to something themselves, and trying to cause a distraction" Alice continued. I wondered where the guys were, Alice seemed to have the giants under control, if they got caught sneaking around, they would be in a lot of trouble. I wish there was a way to get a message to her. There didn't appear to be a way to do that, because it didn't happen. I wanted the fairy to go to the forest's edge. She flew away from the window toward the forest's edge. Just look around, see if they are hiding there, I thought. She flew around the edge of the forest for about ten minutes and I finally spotted something, she stopped.

They were there! They were hiding behind some thick brush. She flew close to them, but tried to stay out of sight. "She's fine, you saw that," David was saying to James. "If she can leave without compromising that she knows anything, she will," Arturo said, agreeing with David. "I don't trust them, they can turn on her at any moment"

James argued. He was being stubborn, he wasn't going to leave without her. "I haven't been around, I can go, act like I heard the rumors and that I want to talk about it with them" Theo suggested. James half shook his head. "I think it's a good idea, neither of us can do that," David said, while pointing at James, Arturo and himself. "I just wish she could come outside," James said. Go back to the house, where Alice is, I thought. The fairy flew back to the house.

"I will go to 12" Alice said, as the fairy landed on the window. "You really think you could handle a mission like that?" the taller person in the room said. "I do, and I know someone who knows a witch here that can help me get there," Alice said. "I don't want you to get hurt," the taller voice said. "I won't, if I think for one minute that the rumors are true, I'll come home and we can prepare," Alice said. Prepare what?, I thought. "That kind of abomination cannot be allowed to exist," the taller voice said. "Agreed," Alice said. "If the rumors are true, there are some of our kind, helping her" the taller voice said. "One of the reasons that I don't believe the rumors, I just don't think that could possibly be true" Alice said. I was impressed by how well she was playing the part, it made me wonder what she had to gain from it? Putting her own life in danger for me? Although I realized she wasn't the only one, I think it was just my jealousy taking over my mind. I tried to block it out so it didn't interfere with the connection to the fairy. "I need some fresh air, I'm going to go for a walk, if you don't mind," Alice said to the taller person. "Don't be long, or I will send someone to look for you" the taller person said in a threatening voice. "I won't be too long," Alice replied, in a calm voice.

She walked out of the door. Follow her, I thought. The fairy followed her. She managed to get to the edge of the woods, still in sight of the window. In case they were watching her, she sat down on the ground facing the house and put her head down so no one could see her mouth move. She was smart, I was impressed. "Can you hear me?" she said out loud. "Yes" a reply came from the woods. "I am fine, I am covering all my tracks, I'm sorry that I couldn't meet you, but I am taking care of things. If I am not there when you are ready to go, just go on without me" she said. "What are you doing?" a voice yelled from the house. "Coming!" she yelled back. I felt a little bad now, she wanted to escape from everything and she couldn't because she was covering for me. I felt the connection spell with the fairy breaking. I was back and the fairies were flying around my head now. "Thank you so much," I told them. I just hoped the guys listened to Alice and started heading home.

I walked back into the house, Sarah looked really worried. "What have you been doing?" she asked. "Playing with the fairies?" I answered. "What do you mean?" she asked, starting to sound more upset. "It's okay, calm down, I saw them, they are okay" I told her. "Are they back?" she asked, looking around me. "No, the fairies helped me see what was going on, they are okay, I promise, *all* of them are" I said. She started to look more relaxed. "You used fairy magic?" she asked, seeming a little surprised. "They invited me, it was all them, I had no idea what was going on until it was happening" I said. A smile went across her face, "I wouldn't tell many about that" she said. "Why?" I asked. "Not many witches have the fairies' trust, so they won't really help witches" she said. "Well, I do have the one that wanted to come with me, she's hibernating because it's cold right now" I said. "True, but even that doesn't mean much, she could have just been using you to get to 2" she explained. "Right" I said, agreeing, even though I knew it wasn't the reason she went. "I'm just saying, watch who you tell, because if the wrong person finds out, they will wage war on the fairies," she said. "I understand," I replied.

Twelve

Back to 2

About two hours had passed before the guys got home. I was starting to worry again, but they must have left right after the spell broke with the fairies. Sarah ran up and hugged David like she hadn't known anything. I hugged James, then Arturo, then Theo, "I'm so glad you guys are back" I said. "Did something happen while we were gone?" David asked, sounding worried. "No, we were just worried about you guys," I said. James pulled me to the side, "I'm not completely sure of what is going on with Alice," he said. "It's okay, I saw everything," I whispered. His eyes narrowed and his voice lowered, "what do you mean?" he said. "It's okay, I will explain in private," I told him. He was looking at me as though I had betrayed him.

"I am going to head home, it is late," Arturo said. "We have an extra bed in the basement, if you are too tired to go home" David said. "No, that's fine, I need to clear my mind before bed anyway," Arturo replied. "If you don't mind, I'll take that bed for the night," Theo said. "Of course not, it's all yours, thank you for going with us" David said. I looked at James and smiled, he still looked like he was upset with me. "Yeah, thank you Theo, I'll see you all in the morning, I'm tired" James said, then he looked at me and said, "are you coming?" I nodded and followed him to the room we were sleeping in.

As soon as the door closed, he whispered in an angry voice, "What did you do?!" "It's okay, *I* didn't do anything, I was trying to think of a spell where I could make sure you guys were okay, and I went outside. The fairies got my attention and they did a spell, they sent a fairy to where you guys were and linked me to that fairy so I could see and hear everything" I explained. He started to look relaxed. "I thought you followed us," he said. "No, I wouldn't do that, when you asked me to stay here, I stayed here." I said. "Alice is doing a really good job of convincing them that the rumors aren't true," I told him. He started to smile now. "I want her to come with us now, I don't want her to have to stay here with them," I told him. He nodded, "she'll do what she can, but if she isn't here, we have to go without her," he said. I nodded, he kissed my forehead. I loved it when he did that. "I hope you never stop doing that," I said. "What?" he asked. "Kissing me like that," I replied. He lifted my head and kissed my lips, it was such a tender kiss at first and then he started kissing me more intensely. He sucked and bit my bottom lip gently, but rough enough that I wanted more, I grabbed the back of his head and pulled down to press him harder against me. He started kissing my neck and I let out a moan. He threw me onto the bed gently, but with force. I took his shirt off and reached for his manhood, I could tell he was stiff, even through his clothes. He let out a moan of excitement at my touch. He started kissing my neck and working his way down, pausing at my breasts. I was so ready for him. He went down my stomach with his kisses, and down further, I moaned, possibly too loudly, but he didn't notice that it was too loud, he didn't stop. I pulled him back up and put my legs around him. He looked me in the eyes before he went inside and said "I love you." That was the first time he had said it, even though I already knew, it was something else to hear it. "I love you too" I replied, before reaching my climax.

After we finished, he fell asleep fairly quickly. I felt compelled to go outside, not magically, I don't think, I just wanted to be outdoors. I walked out of the door quietly, trying not to wake anyone. I stepped off of the porch and onto the grass, it felt wet from dew drops, both moons were clear and beautiful. I sat down in the wet grass, not caring that I would get dirty. I looked around trying to see if I could see any fairies, it was too dark to see anything much, the only light was the light from the moons. I don't know how long I sat there, thinking about what had just happened and feeling warm and fuzzy inside. I heard the mermaids start singing, could they really sense me? I was awake though, I wasn't going to fall for that. "Gabriela!?" I heard James yell from the house. "Yeah!" I yelled back. He came running out to where I was and grabbed me by the arm. "What do you think you are doing?!" he yelled at me.

I didn't know who he thought he was, yanking me up by my arm and yelling at me like I was a three year old, but I pulled my arm back and told him "whatever I want, because I am an adult" in a stern voice. "So you are going to play with the mermaids by choice?!" he said. I looked around, I was somehow at the edge of the woods, "I was just sitting on the ground, I heard them start singing, but I ignored them" I said, confused. "You can't ignore them, you don't have a choice once you hear them" he said, sounding irritated. "Okay, but you still have no right talking to me like I'm a child, and pulling my arm, that hurts," I said in a pouty voice, rubbing my arm where he had gripped it. "I'm sorry, I didn't mean to hurt you," he said. I just looked at him, "I swear, I didn't" he said, in a pleading voice. I put my arms around his midsection to let him know that I forgave him, "let's go inside" I said.

We went back inside and back to the bedroom, trying not to wake anyone in the process. "I'm sorry that I scared you" I said, as I got into the bed. "It's okay, I'm sorry I hurt your arm, is it bruised?" he asked. I held it up, but there wasn't enough light to tell. "I can't see right now," I told him. He snuggled up close to me and put his mouth right at my ear and whispered "I love you." I could feel the heat of his breath when he said it, all I could do was smile. I snuggled in closer to him, before I fell asleep. I fell into the dream state that I recognized as the one where I see Valery or whoever it was.

I was walking down a crowded street, obviously on 12 because there were cars driving by as well. I spotted her, she was walking toward me, wearing a hooded black cape, like a vampire from an old movie. "Aren't you worried you will stand out in that?" I asked sarcastically as she approached. "It doesn't matter, this isn't real anyway" she replied as if I didn't already know. "You have many things to face," she said, as if she was trying to hurry and tell me something. "As if I haven't faced many things already?" I said, sarcastically again. "It will get harder and harder to keep going, seeming like it will never end, but I will tell you there is light at the end of the tunnel and the child, will be the greatest thing to ever happen to the magical community" she said, as she grabbed my arm, the opposite of the one that James had grabbed. I was suddenly yanked from my dream world by a rush of cold.

I was going into the lake! How did I get here?! Something had me, and I couldn't break free. "James!" I screamed, "Arturo!" "David!" It was no use, no one could hear me. This couldn't be it, I felt betrayed by Valery, she had kept me distracted in my mind so I didn't notice them taking over my body! I was going under now, I suddenly remembered Arturo telling me that we could 'borrow' the mermaid's ability to breathe underwater. I tried to relax as much as possible, I was being pulled somewhere, I'm sure it was where they were, so I imagined the power I needed coming to me from the same direction that I was being pulled to. It worked! I was able to start breathing! I almost couldn't believe I had done it!

When I reached the mermaids I was shocked about how ugly they were. I had read about it, but seeing it was another story. There was a group of them around me, with skin tones ranging from light green to dark blue, maybe some purple as well, they had sharp teeth and strange fish eyes, but in the same placement of human eyes. Some of them had snails or other 'feeders' attached to their skin. One merperson came out of the crowd to the front, I assumed it was their leader. They were all so ugly I couldn't really tell genders. "You are a half-breed, you are not supposed to exist, and your blood calls to us" the merperson said to me. "You don't know anything about me, and you will release me unless you are prepared to sacrifice your people" I said, with authority. The merperson laughed, "you are in my world now, it may have taken me a while, but I have you here" he said, with confidence. "I do not work alone, although, with my power, I could" I said, with all the confidence I could.

"How many witches have you lured here to their deaths?" I asked. "And were you able to have a conversation with *any* of them?" I added. The merperson just looked at me. I could tell I was making them think, "If you don't want to be hunted to extinction, I suggest that you let me go back to my friends now, and forget about me" I told them. I could see real worry within all of them now, they started whispering amongst themselves. "I will be the leader of the magical community, an ally like me could do wonders for you" I said. "Can you break the spell upon our kind?" the merperson asked. Now I was confused, I hadn't known of a spell on the merpeople. "Spell?" I asked. "You do not know of the spell?" it asked. I shook my head, "no," I admitted. "We didn't used to look like this, we used to be beautiful creatures, until a witch fell in love with one of us, he was so upset that when she told him that she didn't love him, that he cursed us to look like this, he said to guarantee that no one would ever love any of us, ever again" the merperson explained.

I tried to feel for magic, to see what kind of curse was being used on them. "How long ago was this? I feel like no one on the surface even knows about it" I said. "A couple of centuries, I think," the merperson said. "Can I touch one of you?" I asked. The one that had been speaking came closer, the rest raised their weapons to warn me, and an eel swam between my legs, I let out a scream, it was so snake-like. I hated snakes and spiders! "It's okay, it won't hurt you" the merperson said, "unless I tell it to" it added. I got my composure back, knowing I couldn't lose it again, I couldn't let them see any kind of weakness again. The merperson swam close enough for me to touch, it's skin was slimy and cold. I tried to concentrate on the magic within. I felt a dark magic deep within, it felt cold, and full of pain. I reached inside of the merperson with my magic and grabbed the cold dark magic inside and I squeezed it until I felt it vanish. I heard gasps all around me, I opened my eyes and gasped myself.

A queen was now in front of me, she now looked beautiful, golden skin, human eyes replaced the fish eyes, beautiful crystal blue and deep eyes. Long flowing hair now replaced the spiky blue pegs that had been there before. I heard a scream of terror come from the back of the crowd. Then I saw a light coming toward us from above. "We are under attack!" the Queen yelled. "No! You have to let me go! I'll make them stop! I will come back when I can or send someone else to help the rest of you!" I told the Queen. She nodded, I guess I had earned her trust. I was rocketed to the surface of the water, pushed above the surface and was floating in the air above it. I couldn't breathe! I had to let go of the power I was borrowing from the mermaids. I could see a boat, but I couldn't tell who was on it yet. As soon as I got my breath back, I started yelling "Stop!" to them. I managed to get their attention and the boat started coming toward me. I could tell that James and Arturo were on it, I assumed David was probably driving.

When they reached me, they pulled up under me and Arturo did something to release me from the air that I had been stuck in. James grabbed me up and squeezed me so tight that I couldn't speak. I started grunting to let him know that I was uncomfortable. He released me. "They aren't bad, they are misunderstood!" I said to them. Arturo looked the most confused. "They were cursed a long time ago by a jealous witch," I explained. "I freed the spell from the Queen, right before you guys started attacking, she changed into a beautiful creature right before my eyes, when you guys started attacking I told her to let me go and I would make you guys stop and that I would come back or send someone else to help the rest of them.

James started crying, I felt so bad, he must have been terrified, thinking that I was probably dead. I wrapped my arms around him, "I'm sorry, I didn't go in willingly, I was having one of the Valery dreams, it was like she was distracting me. I woke up when the cold water hit me, and it was too late. I used my instincts and what I had learned, I borrowed the ability to breathe underwater from them" I said. He didn't speak, he just squeezed me tighter. I was right, David was driving the boat, he came out "glad you are safe! We need to head back, get you guys ready to go back to 12" he said. I nodded, James guided me over to a seat on the side of the boat. I looked back, I saw the Queen put her head above the water, I waved at her, she just sank back into the water.

We reached the dock in no time at all. Arturo hadn't said anything the whole ride. "Are you okay?" I asked him. He nodded, "I think it may have been my ancestors that cursed them," he said, sounding sad. "Really? Why do you think that?" I asked. "A family story about a mermaid that tried to lure my great-great grandfather to his death, but he defended himself by transforming them so they couldn't trick anyone ever again" he said. "Yes, that fits, the mermaid's story is that the witch fell in love with the mermaid, the mermaid wouldn't be with him so the witch cursed all of the mermaids to be ugly creatures that no one would ever love again" I explained.

"That would explain why my family has such bad luck in love" he said, "how did you release the curse from the Queen?" he asked. "It's a little hard to explain, but I reached inside of her, with an astral arm, I found the darkness, it was like a ball, close to her heart and I squeezed it until it disappeared" I told him. He just looked at me. I wasn't sure I was explaining it right, because of the look he was giving me, like I was crazy. We all started walking toward David and Sarah's house. I almost dreaded going back to 12, I really enjoyed being on 2. I would miss Julie, I had grown quite attached to her. James still wasn't speaking, I was starting to get concerned that something else was bothering him. "Have you heard from Alice?" I asked him. He just shook his head no.

"If you don't mind, I need you to show me the spell that you did on the mermaid, show me on me" Arturo said, seemingly out of nowhere. "What?" I asked, confused. "I have never heard of such a thing being done, I need you to show me what you are talking about" he said. "But, if you don't have a curse, nothing will change" I said. "But if I do, can you remove it?" he said, as a question. I nodded, "I think I can, yes."

When we got to the house, the first thing I did was take a shower to get the smell of the lake off of me. James was waiting when I got out of the shower. I put a towel over my body and walked over to him, I reached behind his neck and pulled him down until his lips met mine. We kissed a long passionate kiss, until I finally broke it, "we have to finish getting ready to go" I said. He nodded, "I was so scared that I had lost you, and I was mad at myself, because they took you right out of my arms and I didn't even know it" he said with a tear coming to his eye. "I'm okay" I said, as I wiped the tear away.

I walked away to get dressed, James kept standing there. "You need to get ready too!" I told him. He looked at me and smiled, my heart warmed just a little at the sight, and he walked away. After I got dressed, I went to find Arturo, he was outside, on the porch. He looked up when he saw me, "I was thinking we should go to the basement, for more concentration, less distraction" he said. I nodded in agreement. He got up and went inside, and I followed behind him. "I am still amazed that you did this, and that no one has ever shown you. You just knew what to do," he said, as we walked down the stairs into the basement. "You never experiment with magic?" I asked, a little shocked. "I was taught not to" he admitted. "Oh, I guess that's understandable too, you may do something that you didn't intend to do" I said.

When we reached the bottom of the stairs, we sat down at a table, across from each other. I closed my eyes and I went into my mind, to remember exactly what I had done in the water. When I was ready, I opened my eyes and nodded at him, "stand up, here, in front of me" I said. I stood in front of him, like I had the mermaid, and I began. I felt my astral arm reach toward him, then go into his chest. I couldn't sense anything dark there, but it was possible that it could be somewhere else. I pulled my arm back. "What?" he asked. "There is no curse there, if you don't mind, I would like to check your head though" I explained. "My head? Do you think it is safe to do that?" he asked. "I don't know, this is new to me too, but I don't think it will do any harm" I said. He nodded in agreement. I started the spell again, this time, reaching into his head. Again, there was nothing black, but there was something red. I felt like this was pain and I wasn't sure that I should remove it, maybe it was a lesson or a memory. But nonetheless, it stood out to me, I put my hand over it and started squeezing it, it vanished, just as the black in the mermaid's chest had.

When I pulled my hand back, I opened my eyes and looked at Arturo. He was standing there with his eyes wide open. "What did you do?" he asked. "You didn't have a curse, but you did have something blocking you and I removed it," I said. "I feel amazing," he said, simply, "thank you." And he walked away, he seemed to have a little 'extra' pep in his step, he seemed *happy*. I smiled at the thought of him being happy, he was a good man, I respected him as my teacher, as my friend, and I wanted him to be happy. After a few minutes, I followed behind him.

"Which way did Arturo go?" I asked David, since he was the first person I saw when I got out of the basement. "I didn't see him come up," he replied. "Oh, well, we need to find him for the spell for us to go home" I said. "Yes we do," David agreed. I walked outside, I spotted him as he went into the forest. "Arturo!" I yelled. He didn't stop, so I ran after him. I had to warp to the edge of the forest where I saw him enter. Then I followed into the forest. "Arturo!" I yelled again. "Whoa! How did you do that?!" he replied. "Do what? You know how to warp? Don't you?" I asked, surprised that he was asking. "Why are you chasing me?" he asked, changing the subject. "You can't leave, you have to do the spell to send us home" I said. "I was going to come right back, since when are you my keeper?" He said. "Since when do you just take off and not let anyone know?" I replied. "I am a grown man, I'm allowed to come and go as I please" he replied. I rolled my eyes at him, "okay, please get back on time" I said. And I let him walk away, and I headed back to the house.

"Did you find him?" David asked, as soon as I got back to the house. "Yes, he said he will be back later, when it's time for the spell" I replied. "I'm afraid that I may have done something to him that I shouldn't have," I said. "What do you mean?" David asked. "He wanted me to do the spell that I did to remove the curse, because he believed that he was cursed. He didn't have a curse, but I removed something else, and it may have been something that shouldn't have been removed" I said. "What did you remove?" David asked. "I'm not sure, that's my point, he didn't understand the magic I used, and I sure don't, I just used my instincts, but I think maybe I shouldn't have removed anything from him, if that makes sense?" I said. David looked confused, "no not really" he replied. "I'm worried that I may have removed something that affects the way he thinks," I said. "Why did you let him leave then?" David asked. "I couldn't just hold him hostage," I replied.

I walked inside to find James, he was getting things ready for going back to 12, I didn't like to say or even think 'home' around him, because it wasn't his home, his home was here. "Are you excited?" I asked him, while standing in the doorway with my arms folded, smiling at him. "Well, not particularly, to be honest, but I would go into Hell if it meant being by your side" he replied. I melted, I walked over to him and sank into his arms. I proceeded to tell him about Arturo, he wasn't happy with me, of course. He started yelling at me and giving me the same speech that I feel I've heard a million times already. I needed to learn to stop experimenting with magic, I was going to get someone that I loved hurt or killed.

There was a knock on the door, "if you are going to argue and yell at each other, you should probably close the door at least, you are starting to upset Julie," Sarah said. "I'm sorry" I replied, looking down. I walked outside to sit on the porch, hoping to see Arturo or even Alice walking over the horizon. So far, although it was still early, I saw neither of them. James walked out behind me, "I'm sorry" he said, "I know you are already punishing yourself enough, I shouldn't have yelled at you" he continued. "Don't worry about it, you are right, I shouldn't experiment with magic" I replied. He sat down next to me, I looked at him, he was so perfect and beautiful, all I could think was, 'I don't deserve him' I wasn't sure why I thought that, but I did.

He was staring back at me until something caught his eye and he turned his head, "he came back!" he said. I looked and saw Arturo walking toward the house. "I wonder where he even went?" I said, thinking out loud. "Doesn't matter, he's back now" James replied. I nodded in agreement, as I got up to go meet him halfway. I walked toward Arturo, he was definitely different and I couldn't quite put my finger on it. We met midway to the house. "Where did you go?" I asked him. He looked at me sideways, "why are you so concerned with my business?" he asked. "I'm just worried about you, I'm not sure what I did to you" I replied. "You know, I'm not either, but I can assure you that it was something good," he replied, with a smile.

We continued walking to the house in silence. I still wasn't sure that he was okay. He seemed lighter in spirit, he seemed *happy*. "When are we doing the spell?" he asked, when we reached the house. "We are going to wait another hour to see if Alice shows up" I said. He nodded and we went inside. "Can I talk to you for a minute alone?" Arturo asked. "Yes" I said, looking at him weirdly, we had just walked to the house together, *alone*. We walked back outside and went to the edge of the porch, the furthest away from the door. He handed me a letter, "can you give this to Margo for me?" he asked. I was confused. "She's a panther, she can't change to human form" I replied. "I know, she will still be able to understand, she is still in there" he replied. "Okay," I said, and took the paper from him. "Thank you," he said.

I looked up, and saw Alice walking on the horizon toward the house and I let out a squeal. "James!" I yelled, and he came running out of the house. He looked around worried at first, but then he saw her, "Alice!" he yelled and started laughing out of pure joy. I was overjoyed to see him so happy, I was happy that Alice got away from the giants, it was a rare moment to be truly happy and I didn't want the moment to end, I knew it would forever be embedded in my memory.

We all met her at the edge of the porch and hugged her. "I'm so happy that you made it," I said, she looked surprised, she didn't know that I knew everything she went through to protect me, she probably thought I was still jealous of her and James. James hugged her too, "how did you convince them to let you go?" he asked. "I told them I was going to 12 to hunt for the supposed girl and make sure that she doesn't exist, I'm worried that they will send someone to watch me there" she said. "Don't worry, our place is like a fort," I told her, with a smile. Theo had been inside and heard the conversation. "I will stay here and keep an eye on the giants," he said, walking out of the door toward us. "Thank you" Alice said. She let out a little squeal of relief, "I am so happy to be getting away from them, and going somewhere new" she said. I smiled at her, "I am happy to have you join us" I said, sincerely.

When we were ready to go, I said goodbye to Sarah and David. Julie was a little harder to say goodbye to, she would be a toddler the next time I saw her, because of the time difference in the dimensions. It made me so sad to think about it. I wanted to be a part of her life, but I also had things that I had to do. I cried when I hugged her, but I didn't let her see that. The fairies had gathered in the yard, so I walked over to them. "Thank you, for all of your help. Thank you for always helping me, I am forever indebted to you" I said to them. They flew around me in a circle, it was almost like a big embrace. Arturo was standing alone, so I walked over to tell him goodbye again. "Are you sure you feel okay?" I asked as I walked up. "Of course," he replied. "Do you think you could do the spell? Do you think you can remove the curse from the rest of the mermaids?"

I asked him. "You know, I'm not sure, I will practice and work on doing it, but if not, you will just have to do it the next time you are here." He said. I nodded.

He seemed so different, I was still worried about him, and what I had done, something told me that whatever it was, I shouldn't have done it. "I feel like I have been freed" he said, seeing the look of worry on my face. "It's like you took out years of worry, fear, and depression. I remember it was there, but I can't remember what it felt like, because I can't feel it anymore, if that makes sense?" he said. I looked at him sideways, "that doesn't seem like it should be allowed" I said. "Why? Because it's a good thing?" he said. "Well, if what you say is true, why are we just now discovering that it can be done? Why haven't we been doing this all along?" I said. "Does it really matter? And I'm not sure that *I* can do it, maybe *you* are the only one who can perform the magic. Maybe we had to wait for you to be born, before we could have this great gift" he said. "I really don't feel like I am special enough to be gifted with the ability to heal everyone's mental woes," I replied. "Why not, you have seen that most witches have a special gift, why couldn't this one be yours?" he said. "Maybe" I said, "are you about ready to send us back?" I asked. "Sure," he said. We walked over to everyone else.

"Is everyone ready?" Arturo asked as we approached them. James smiled at me, I loved how handsome he was when he smiled, especially when he smiled at me. "Ready to go back to the war we left behind, and ready to win," James said. "I'm ready, ready to be away from the crazy giants, I'm sorry that I didn't do that before now" Alice said. "Levi is going to be upset that we came here and didn't bring him home, he has regretted going almost since we got there" I said. "He needs to learn a lesson, he should not have jumped into your gateway" David said. "That's right, that was very careless, and he should deal with the consequences of his actions," Arturo said. "Okay, well, I think we are ready if you are," I said, looking at

Arturo. He nodded, I hugged Sarah one more time and whispered in her ear, "please keep an eye on Arturo," she nodded to let me know that she heard me.

Arturo began the spell, I closed my eyes and grabbed James' hand with my right hand and Alice's hand with my left hand. Arturo opened the gateway, I opened my eyes in time to see the swirl of blue and purple lights, I closed my eyes again. That all too familiar feeling of nothingness came over me, it was still odd to me, to feel like I didn't even exist, even if it was only for a second or so, and we were back. We were in the field outside the house, it was still dark and cold. I heard a rustle in the woods behind us, I turned to look, it was Margo. I gave her a thumbs up to let her know all was good, "I will see you tomorrow!" I yelled to her as we walked to the house.

"Wow, this place is huge," Alice said as we walked inside. "Oh yeah, fifteen bedrooms and six bathrooms" I said. Her eyes got wide and she said, "wow." "Plus all the land outside, and a barn" I added. "And it's heavily protected by magic," Levi said, walking into the room. Alice went up to him and hugged him. "You guys went home? And you didn't even let anyone know?" Levi said, accusingly. "It wasn't a planned trip, we were taken without even knowing after we went to sleep" James said. Levi nodded, "well, at least you brought Alice back with you" he said as he smiled at her. "Oh what? We aren't good enough company for you?" I asked, teasing. He rolled his eyes. "Will you help Alice find a room?" James asked Levi. "Of course," Levi replied as he picked up her suitcase.

Thirteen

Elves?

It was four o'clock in the morning, James and I decided to lay down and try to get a couple hours of sleep. It really didn't take me long, I guess I was more tired than I thought. It seemed like I just closed my eyes and then James was shaking me, telling me to get up. "What?" I moaned. "We have things to do, we need to find out what is going on with Misty," he said. I had almost forgotten about her, I think that was a spell that my mother had put on me as well, if something was out of sight, it was out of mind. An easy way to forget all the terrible things I would have to suffer through in life? I rolled over, and found the edge of the bed, my feet hit the floor, "I need coffee" I said. "I'll get right on that, your highness," James said, teasing. I rolled my eyes at him and hit him with a pillow. I looked at my cell phone that had been laying on the dresser.

What is going on? First you disappear, now Jason is gone? -Racheal. *I agree, something isn't right.* -Micheal. *We are just really worried about you both, can you please let us know something?* -Anna. The messages had been sent eight hours ago. I had to think of something to tell them. I couldn't bring them into everything, I had to keep them safe at all costs, but how? "Are you okay?" James asked, seeing me staring at the phone. "No, my friends are asking questions that I can't answer. I have to tell them something" I said to him. "Tell them that you have been recruited to a super secret organization as a spy, and you may never see them again" James said, sarcastically. "I would, but it's too close to the truth," I replied, with the same sarcasm. "Let's go make some coffee" I said, getting out of bed.

We walked into the kitchen to find everyone except Misty and Alice. "Where is Misty?" I asked them. "Tied up, we can't just let her wander around until we undo the chain spell" Hale said. "I'll go talk to her after I have some coffee," I said. Suddenly, there was a knock at the door, we all looked at each other. "That's impossible, no one can get through the magical barriers" I said. Another clear knock at the door. "There's no way," I said, not believing what I was hearing. "Someone needs to go look," Hale said. "I'll go," Damian offered. "I'll come with you," I said. James followed us as well.

First we looked out of the windows, neither of us saw anyone. Damian walked up to the door, "hello!" he yelled. No answer. I opened the door, but stayed behind it. "I don't see anyone," James said. "Maybe it was just the wind," I said. "No, look!" Damian said, pointing at the porch floor, just outside of the door. There was an old-fashioned envelope, sealed with a wax seal. James picked it up, "it is addressed to you" he said, looking at me. "Who is it from and how did it get here?" I asked. "Magic" Damian replied, "to the second question anyway." "It says it's from the Elves Faction," James said. "Elves?" I said, confused. "So they weren't actually here?" I asked, confused. "No, they used magic to send it to you, not even knowing where it was going, they must have had a witch send it, unless they sent it from another dimension" Damian said.

Everyone else came from the kitchen to see what was happening.

Alice also woke up and came out of her room. "What's going on?" she asked. "I got a magical letter from some elves, I guess, no big deal" I replied, waving the envelope in the air. "Oh, what does it say?" she asked, sounding genuinely interested. "I haven't opened it yet," I replied. Now that everyone was gathered around, I decided to do just that, open the letter, so they could all see. It said: Dearest Gabriela, We request an audience with you at your earliest convenience. Please reply, on this very same paper within the hour, as we will recall it to us. Thank you, and we look forward to meeting with you. Sincerely, Cori, Queen of the Elves.

"Wow" I said. "I didn't even realize that there were still elves here on 12," Hale said. "What exactly are elves?" I asked. "Exactly what you think, they are miniature people, although here, I believe they range anywhere from 4'5 to 5'5, they are nature loving and nature healing creatures. I have no idea why they would want to meet with you" Damian said. "You think it could be a trap? They have to be working with witches, right? In order to have magic?" I asked. "It's very possible," Conan said. "You should decline," James said. "Or, I could tell them that my friends and I would love to meet with them," I said. "I don't know," Hale said. "Why?" I asked, "what's it going to hurt? I'm curious as to why they want to meet with me" I said.

"What could they possibly offer that you don't already have?" James asked. "Sometimes the best thing someone can offer is loyalty, maybe, I can get them in my corner, if they aren't already" I said. "You have a lot of loyalty, with magic and muscles behind it, here" he replied, pointing around the room. "I know I do, and I love you guys and I am so grateful for you all" I replied. "But you're still going to do it, aren't you? Curiosity killed the cat" James said, putting his hands up in defeat. I wrote on the paper at the bottom, 'My friends and I would love to meet you, let me know when and where.' I put the paper back inside the envelope and laid it back where we had found it.

"I'm going to go talk to Misty now," I said, walking away from the group. I heard footsteps behind me, without looking, I knew it was James. "I want to go alone," I said. "Why?" he asked. "Because, I do," I replied, with an attitude. "Fine" he said, and stopped following. I could tell he was going to be mad at me over it, I didn't care. He had to learn to trust me.

I opened the door to the room where they were holding her, tied up and looking miserable. "Where have you been?" she asked, accusingly. "Healing from a broken ankle," I replied. "It was an accident," she said. "And how am I or any of the others supposed to believe you?" I asked. "I am sorry that it happened, really, and I will gladly undo the chain spell," she replied. "Good, that's a start" I said. "Will you untie me?" she asked. "As long as you know that if you try to run, it won't be good, you *will* get hurt, or worse" I threatened. She nodded in agreement. I don't really know why, but I felt like I could trust her, I felt like she was telling me the truth. I untied her, so she could undo the chain spell. She only had to cut her own finger for mine to open up as well, I let my blood drip into a bowl that she had prepared. After a few minutes of chanting over the bowl of blood and herbs, she looked up and said, "it's done." "Poke your finger, to show me" I said. She poked her finger and a small amount of blood came out, nothing happened on my finger.

"Thank you," I said. "You are more than welcome, I don't want to stay here if no one is going to trust me" she said. "Trust is earned, and since you are coming from the complete opposite end of trust, it will take some time," I told her. "What do I have to do?" she asked. "Just be honest, be helpful, once they see that you are on our side, they won't have a choice," I replied. She nodded her head. "We have another guest, another half giant, her name is Alice. Also, I have been summoned by the elves faction" I told her. "Elves? Why?" she asked, seeming confused. "I'm not sure, but magic was used to get the message to me, so they must be working with at least one witch" I said. She sat there quietly, looking as though she was trying to think. "Maybe they just want protection," I said. "Possibly" she replied.

There was a knock on the bedroom door. "Who is it?" I asked. "James," he answered. "Could you go grab a sandwich and a banana from the kitchen?" I yelled, loud enough for him to hear through the door. "Sure," he replied. "Thank you," she said. "You're welcome, I figured you must be starving, did they feed you at all?" I asked. She shook her head. "I'm sorry, I will have a talk with them, I promise" I said. She smiled at me. "I'm really trying to do the right thing, at least I hope it's the right thing," she said. I smiled at her. There was a knock on the door again. "James?" I asked. "Yes, with food," he replied. "Come in" I said.

He entered and had food as I had requested, he also brought water. I smiled at him. He handed the food and water to Misty. She took it eagerly, I felt bad that they had starved her, even for a day. "I'm going to go talk with everyone, come out and join us when you are ready" I told her. She nodded. I walked out of the room, James followed. "Is the chain spell broken?" he asked. "Yes," I replied.

"I need to speak with everyone please!" I yelled, as I walked into the kitchen. Everyone followed. "First of all, why didn't you give her any food or water? How could you treat someone this way?" I asked, accusingly. "She was a prisoner, until further notice" Damian said. "Did she break the chain spell?" Hale asked, trying to change the subject. "She did, and I just want to say that I trust her, as much as she can be trusted, I told her that she has a lot to prove, I want you guys to give her a chance to prove it," I said to them. They all nodded in agreement. "I'm not sure what's going on," Alice said. "A witch, who was on the other side, says she is on our side now, Gabriela brought her here, and she attacked her, whether it was an accident or not, she broke her ankle" James told her. "Oh, and why are we supposed to trust her?" she asked.

"It was an accident," Misty said, walking into the kitchen. Everyone looked at her. "I'm sorry, and I will do anything to prove that you all can trust me," she said. Everyone nodded, "I'm sorry about tying you up, but we had to, we didn't know" Conan said. "It's okay, I understand," she replied. There was a sudden knock on the door again, everyone looked up. "The elves," I said, looking at Misty, she nodded her head slowly to say that she understood, maybe. I walked to the door and opened it, the letter was laying in the same spot as before, I picked it up and opened it. It said: Your conditions have been accepted, please be at the public park in Moon Springs at noon tomorrow. We look forward to meeting you, Sincerely, Cori.

"Well, that was easy enough," I said. "I am weary of things that are too easy," Damian said. "Doesn't matter, all but one of us will go, one needs to stay here" I said. "Who will stay?" Levi asked. "We will draw straws, make it fair," I said. Everyone nodded in agreement. I cut pieces of paper, all the same size except one small one and put them in my hand, everyone came and took one, Hale drew the shortest one. "Hale will stay here, while the rest of us go," I said. Everyone nodded in agreement. "I have to go see Margo," I said, walking out of the kitchen. I went to my room to find the note that Arturo had given me to give to her. James followed. "You don't have to follow me around, you know" I said, teasingly. "Nothing better to do," he replied. I smiled at him and kissed him. I found the letter and headed outside.

It was a cold day, winters in Tennessee varied, but it seemed like this one was going to be a cold one. I walked to the edge of the woods, where I had seen Margo early this morning. "Margo!" I yelled. I heard a rustle coming from the woods. It was her, she walked up to me, she was such a beautiful creature, I felt bad that she couldn't turn to her human form here. James stood back from us, to give us privacy I suppose, I hadn't told him about the note. "I'm just going to go talk to Philip," he said, walking toward the barn. "Okay" I replied. I looked around to make sure that no one was around and I sat down on the ground, Margo lay across from me.

"We went to 2 for a while," I told her. She looked at me curiously. "Arturo wanted me to give you this letter, can you read it?" I asked her. She pointed at the ground with her nose as if she wanted me to lay it down. So, I opened the letter and laid it in front of her. I didn't read it, I didn't want to invade her or Arturo's privacy. If it was something I needed to know, they would let me know. I turned my head and looked toward the barn, I saw James go inside just as I looked. Margo started growling and it got my attention, I looked at her, "what is it?" I asked. I tried to look, but she picked up the note with her mouth and ate it. "Okay" I said. "Is it bad?" I asked. She got up and walked back into the forest. "I'm sorry, I don't know what it said, I didn't read it!" I yelled toward her. She didn't come back, so I got up and went to join James in the barn.

Alice came out on the porch as I was walking by. "Do you want to come see Philip?" I asked her. "Sure" she replied and followed me to the barn. Philip seemed happy to see her when we entered. She walked up and started petting him and hugging his neck. "It's good to see you," she told him. James walked over to me, "what was that about, with Margo?" he asked. "I'm not sure, Arturo sent a note for her, I didn't read it. It seemed to have pissed her off though. She growled then ate the note and went back into the woods" I told him. "Hmm" he replied. Philip was motioning for Alice to get on his back. "What's he doing?" she said, with a giggle. "He wants you to take a ride," I told her. "I don't want to hurt you, I'm so big," she said. "You are not big, just tall," James said, with a laugh. "I don't think I should," Alice said. "Go ahead, I did it," I told her.

Philip opened the gate and stepped out of the stall, he kneeled down so she could get on. "No saddle?" she asked. "He's not exactly a normal horse," I replied. She got on and he walked slowly out of the barn. "Hold on to his neck!" I yelled, I could tell he was about to start running. And I was right, just as she wrapped her arms around his neck, he took off in a sprint. She let out a yell, I couldn't tell if it was excitement or fear. He brought her back around to us after running in the field for about five minutes. I guess he didn't want her to get too cold. He kneeled down again to let her off, her eyes were wide. "Did you have fun?" I asked her. She scrunched up her nose, "I'm cold" she replied. I could tell she did not have fun, but didn't want to hurt Philip's feelings.

"Let's get inside, I'll build a fire," James said. "I'll make sure Philip is good, go ahead" I told them. I walked with him back into the barn. "I'm not sure she enjoyed that," I told him. He made horse noises, "I wish I could understand you" I told him, with a giggle. "Are you warm enough out here?" I asked him. He nodded his head. At least I could understand that. I pet his nose and said, "good." After I got him settled, I headed back to the house. I was trying to think of something to tell my human friends to keep them from worrying about me, nothing came to mind.

As I walked into the house, I smelled food, someone was cooking! I got excited. I walked into the kitchen, Damian, Misty and Conan were all in there, they seemed to be having fun while cooking a meal. "Smells delicious," I said. They looked up at me. "Thanks," Damian said. "I told Damian that I was quite a good cook, if I do say so myself, and he offered to help, then Conan came in and asked if he could help" Misty said with a smile. I smiled back, "well, I can't wait to eat it" I said, as I walked back out of the kitchen and into the living room, where James was still messing with the fire and trying to get it started. Levi walked in, "let me help" he told James. Everything seemed so perfect, that I just stopped and sat down to take it all in. Alice and Hale came down from upstairs, "What is that wonderful smell?" Hale asked. "Misty can cook, apparently" I told him. "Hmm, is anyone watching her to make sure she doesn't poison us?" Hale asked. I rolled my eyes at him, "Damian and Conan are helping her" I replied.

After a few minutes, Levi had a fire going. "You are just better at doing that than I am," James told him. Conan walked out of the kitchen, "dinner is ready" he said, with a little excitement in his voice. We all went to the kitchen, it was a full on feast, Ham, mashed potatoes and gravy, mac and cheese, corn on the cob, green beans, cornbread and deviled eggs. "Wow, this looks delicious!" I said. "I wanted to fix something special for everyone," Misty said, with a smile. Everyone started fixing their plates, while laughing and teasing with each other. My family was growing, and everyone seemed happy, for the moment anyway, and that's all that really matters right?

After everyone was done eating, I said, "it's only fair that everyone that didn't cook has to clean up." There were a few moans of 'I don't want to' but, everyone did help me clean and do the dishes. I told Damian, Misty and Conan thanks again, and they went to the living room to enjoy the fire. James and I were doing the dishes, everyone else was wiping everything down and bringing us dishes. James kept sneaking little kisses in between people bringing us more dishes to wash. My heart felt so happy and full, I hoped this feeling would never end, although I knew it would at some point.

When we finished the dishes, I told everyone good night, and I told James that I was going to take a nice hot bath. I went to my bedroom and closed the door. I walked into the bathroom and started running my bath. I heard the door open, it was James. "What are you doing?" I asked him. "I'm just going to sit here, unless you need something, like do you need me to wash your hair?" he said. I smiled, "I can wash my own hair, thank you though" I replied. "Okay, have it your way, I'll just sit here and enjoy the view" he said. I went into the bathroom and closed the door. I heard him say "hey, that's not fair" through the door. The bath felt amazing. I couldn't help but wonder how long the happiness would last. I was still trying to think of something to tell my friends so that they could stop worrying. Maybe if I called Racheal and she heard how happy I am, she would convince the others to just leave me alone for now?

"James?" I called out. He came to the door, "yes? Did you change your mind about needing help?" he asked. "No, but I do need my phone, can you bring it to me?" I asked. "Why?" he replied. "I want to call Racheal, try to ease her mind," I told him. "Okay, sure," he said. A few seconds later he came into the bathroom with my phone. I dried my hand with a towel and took it from him, "thank you" I said. He kept standing there, "you can go now" I told him. "Fine," he said, sounding disappointed. I went under my contacts and called her without the video since I was in the bath.

It didn't even get a full ring before I heard a frantic "hello?!" "Hey, Racheal, I am so sorry that you have been worried," I began. "What is going on?!" she demanded. "I am fine, Jason is fine too" I told her, not sure if Jason would be fine. "Are you two together?" she asked. "Kind of, we both took jobs with the same company" I said. "What do you mean? What kind of company?" she asked, suspiciously. "I can't really talk about it, it's a company that's making a new product and I have to keep it secret, that's why I've been avoiding you guys, because I suck at keeping secrets" I said, with a laugh. "And why are you waiting so long to tell me anything? You just let us worry for weeks?" she said. "I am sorry, I didn't know what to say, I was offered a lot of compensation to take the job and I had to decide quickly" I told her. "Please don't be mad at me, I will see you guys again when the job is done" I said. "Okay, thank you for letting me know something," she said. "Will you tell everyone else? I don't want them to worry either, but I don't have a lot of time to have this conversation over and over again" I said. "Yeah, I will tell them," she said. I could hear a little bit of irritation in her voice. "Thank you, and I'll talk to you again as soon as I can," I told her. "Bye," she said. "Bye," I replied.

I laid the phone on a nearby table and sank into the bath water. I felt a little bit of relief, maybe she believed me? But for how long? Would the others convince her that I wasn't being honest? Why did my brain do this to me? Why take something good and make it something bad? James knocked on the bathroom door, "are you okay?" he asked. "Yes, I'll be out in a minute," I replied. I stepped out of the bathtub and grabbed my towel to dry off. After putting on a robe, I stepped into the bedroom. James smiled, I smiled back. "I am exhausted," I told him. "Well, just come here and snuggle up," he said, patting the bed beside him. I gladly laid down next to him and 'snuggled up.'

I was asleep in no time, I was in the dream world where I often saw Valery, if that's who it was. I was in a grocery store, I felt like I was looking for something, but I suddenly forgot what it was I was looking for. I just kept pacing up and down the isles. A hooded woman stepped into the aisle I was in. "Did you do what I told you?" she asked me. "What did you tell me to do? All I remember is you almost getting me killed because you were distracting me" I replied. "Did you heal them?" she asked. "I removed the curse from the queen," I said. She nodded, "good." "You wanted me to almost die to remove a curse? After you went through so much trouble to keep me alive, you were ready to just sacrifice me?" I asked. "No one likes a drama queen sweety. I knew you would be fine and once they knew you could remove the curse, they would never try to come after you again." she said. It was the first time I had heard her speak to me like a mother, like a real mother. I wanted to hug her, but I couldn't move. She grabbed my arm and we were warped to a field.

I didn't recognize the field. There were fireflies everywhere. At least I knew we were still on 12, just in the wrong season, but, I suppose in dreamland, it didn't matter. "Stop thinking too much, you will wake yourself up" Valery said. "Tell me, you are Valery? You are my mother?" I asked. She nodded, "there's something I need to tell you, something that no one else anywhere knows" she said. "What is it?" I said, as she stalled. She started looking around, "I have to make sure we are alone," she said. My eyes popped open. I looked at the clock beside the bed, it was 3:33 a.m. I sat up in the bed, thinking about the dream and what it could have meant. What did she want me to know? And who else could have been there, that she didn't want to hear what she had to say?

James rolled over, when he realized that I wasn't lying next to him, he opened his eyes. "Are you okay?" he asked. "I'm fine, I think," I replied. "What's wrong?" he asked. "I had a dream about Valery again," I said. "What happened?" he asked. "She confirmed it was her, my mom, and she said she needed to tell me something, but then she stopped because she felt like someone was listening to us" I said, almost crying. He grabbed me and pulled me into a close embrace. It felt good, but I was tired of holding so much inside. I let it go, I started bawling my eyes out. He held me perfectly, not too tight, not too loose. He held me until I was done crying, we lay back down and tried to get another hour or so of sleep. He fell asleep, so I just watched him sleeping, until I finally drifted to sleep myself. I didn't return to the dream, just blackness until I heard James saying, "time to get up sleepy head, we have a mission today."

I had almost forgotten about meeting the elves. I rolled over and moaned. The beautiful aroma of bacon hit my nose, "mmmm" I moaned. James laughed at me, "yeah, it's kind of nice having someone here that can cook" he said. I rolled over again, to put my feet on the floor. "Do you remember what happened last night?" James asked me, sounding concerned. I looked at my feet and could tell why he sounded concerned. They were dirty, like I had been walking barefooted through a muddy field. "She said that there was something she had to tell me, something that no one else knows" I told him. "We need to get this figured out, did you ask her why she almost got you killed by the mermaids?" he asked. "She said that she knew I could help them, and that once I did, they wouldn't come after me ever again" I told him. He just looked at me like he was thinking really hard.

"Come on, let's go eat" I said, as I put my feet on the floor. But first, I went to the bathroom and washed my feet. I went into the kitchen, with James following behind me. Misty was cooking, this time Levi and Alice were helping. "Oh no, the kitchen is going to be a mess!" I said, teasing Levi. He smiled at me, "you know you had fun" he said, teasing. I knew that I didn't want to look at James' face right now. "You know I can beat you in a fight, why are you trying to start one?" James said. "Calm down *Romeo*, I was just teasing" Levi replied. Alice looked confused, I looked at her and shook my head to let her know not to ask any questions. Then I walked by her and whispered, "I'll tell you later." "I am so happy that we have someone who can cook," I said to Misty. "Well, I love to cook actually, I grew up with a large family that just got smaller over the years," she said, looking down, "anyway, it makes me happy" she finished.

"It's almost ready, if you want to go round everyone up" Misty told me. "We should get one of those, old-timey triangle things," I said, jokingly as I walked out of the kitchen to go 'round' everyone up. I walked down each hall, yelling, "time to get up! Breakfast is ready!" Doors opened and sleepy people stumbled out. I found Hale and Damian on the porch, I still wasn't sure if Damian was gay and they were becoming a thing. "Hey guys, breakfast is ready," I said to them. They both looked at me and smiled. "Are you ready to meet the elves today?" Hale asked. "That's such a weird question, I mean, I don't know, I guess we'll find out later" I replied.

I thought about it as we walked to the kitchen together, it really was a weird question. It was almost like there were two doors, because there were two possibilities. Behind door number one, a long lost cousin that wants to reconnect. Behind door number two, an enemy that has finally found me that wants to kill me. Which one would I get? Who knows? Of course it became the topic at the table, we had to discuss a plan. "I think all of us being in the park will look intimidating," I said. "What do you mean? I thought we were all going?" James said. "Except me" Hale replied. Everyone just looked at him. He threw his arms up, "just saying" he said. "Your job is important too, someone has to 'hold down the fort," I said.

"I think we should do what we did before" I said, looking toward Misty, "I think a couple of you should come into the park with me and everyone else should remain back, but where they can see what is happening" I explained. "Okay, so who is going into the park with you?" Levi asked. "And, it's not fair to always pick your boyfriend," he added. I could tell James wanted to punch him. "Maybe only witches should go with me, the less they know about what is going on, the better, especially if they prove to be enemies," I said. "Misty and Conan should go into the park with me," I said. Everyone started moaning and complaining, and disagreeing all at once, it was deafening, and I couldn't really understand any one person.

"Hush!" I yelled, they all became silent. "You will all be close enough to help if it comes to that" I told them, as I walked out of the kitchen. I needed to find some aspirin, all of that arguing and complaining had sparked a headache. No sense in using magic for something so small, I might possibly need all my magic in battle later. No one followed me this time, not even James. After I took some aspirin, I went outside to sit on the porch.

Because I had a headache, the cool air felt nice. The front door opened, it was James, "hey, we should get ready to go" he said. I nodded and got up. "Did you all stop arguing and finally agree to my plan?" I asked him. "I guess we don't have a choice anyway" he mumbled. "That's not how I want you to feel either. We are a team, but because we are a mixed team and I am the leader, I need you guys to listen to me" I said. "Oh yeah, only the witches can do anything *special,*" he replied. I rolled my eyes, this was about to turn into another argument. Or I could just walk away, so that's what I did, I walked into the bedroom and closed the door behind me before he could follow.

After I got changed, I came out of the room to meet everyone. We would have to take the truck and Misty's car to fit everyone, it would be too much magic to warp us there, and we needed all the magic we have, just in case. "Since I'm not going, I can warp everyone to the road, then warp myself back" Hale said. "That would be great, save us a lot of time," I said. We all held hands so that he would only have to do it once, although it was still a lot of magic because there were so many of us.

Once we were all in the vehicles driving toward the park we started *fine tuning* our plan. "I want you to be really close, Damian," I said. "Just in case I need you to project your magic on me" I added. "No problem, I can glamor myself as a homeless person," he said. James, Levi and Alice were in the truck, so I gave them a call since I was in Misty's car. "Yeah" James picked up. "Do you guys know exactly where you will be?" I asked. "I'll be in the same department store that I was in before" Levi yelled. "I'll send Alice to the ice cream shop on the opposite side, and I'll be in the gym," James said. "Ah the gym" I said, accidentally out loud, I missed going to the gym. "We have stuff in the basement, remember?" Levi said, referring to some gym equipment that we stumbled upon one day while we were looking around the house when we first got there. "Oh yeah" I said, with a little giggle. "Okay, looks like everyone knows what they are doing, right?" I asked, both into the phone and looking around at everyone in the car with me. Everyone agreed that they knew what they were supposed to do, so I hung up the phone and sat in silence the rest of the way.

We had to park in different places once we got there, so no one would notice us all arriving together. The witches also had to park completely out of sight of the park so no one saw Damian with us as well. Damian got out first and did the glamor spell rather quickly and went ahead of us to the park, begging for change on his way. Once I felt like he was situated, Misty, Conan and Myself started walking toward the park. I made sure I got a glimpse of everyone in their positions on the way.

As we approached the bench, the same one where I had a meeting with Misty, I noticed a short woman sitting. "Is that her?" I whispered to Conan. "I don't know," he replied. I walked up to the woman, "Cori?" I asked. "Yes, dear, you must be Gabriela, have a seat" she said, with a high pitched voice. "Thank you, this is Misty and this is Conan" I said, gesturing toward them. "Nice to meet you all," Cori said. I never would have thought her to be a magical creature. She was about 5'2, blond hair a little chubby, but no pointy ears, absolutely nothing that I could see about her was abnormal except maybe her eyes, they were a beautiful color, golden brown. I would say she was somewhere between thirty and forty years old.

"You requested a meeting, why?" I asked. "There was a lot of gossip about who you really are, I wanted to see if you were a threat," she said. "So you came here by yourself, thinking she may be a threat?" Misty said, narrowing her eyes. "I never said I was by myself, goodness no" Cori replied. I looked around, expecting an attack. "No need to worry, my people will not attack without a reason," she said. "Same" I replied. "So, are there a lot of Elves here?" I asked. "Several of us fled here, years ago, when we started being attacked," she replied. "Attacked by who?" I asked. "We never found out, we just started going missing and we never found out who took the missing ones or what happened to them, we never saw them again. So we came here, made friends with a witch coven for protection and that's how it's been for years. Then we hear of a change coming, you" she said, looking at me.

"Who told you about me? And what do you mean coming? Did someone tell you about me before I knew who I was?" I asked. "Yes, we knew before you did, so we let you get 'settled' so to speak, into your new life before we requested a meeting" she said. "Who is the witch that is helping you?" I asked. "Her name is Pearl, would you like to meet her?" Cori asked. I nodded, to say that I did want to meet her. Suddenly she appeared right next to me, I suppose she had been there the entire time, just using a cloaking spell. Misty and Conan stepped back, they also managed to signal everyone that 'all was good.' "Hello Gabriela," Pearl said. "Hello," I replied.

Looking back at Cori, "so the Elves were in danger, so they came to a dimension where they have no powers to hide?" I asked. "Of course, no one would expect us to do that, it surprises you even now" she replied. "Anyhow, I requested a meeting with you today, to let you know, we are on your side, we offer any services that we can possibly provide in exchange for your protection" she continued. "You want my protection?" I asked. "Yes," she replied. "From who?" I asked. "We are just terrified with the magical war starting here, that soon enough whoever was taking Elves on 3 will find us here" she replied. "And you have no magic here, so what services can you possibly offer me?" I replied. "We make good spies, we can cook, and we make amazing nannies," she replied. "Nanny? None of us need nannies, we may be able to work with you on the spy thing though" I said.

Pearl, who had remained quite suddenly said, "I have grown quite fond of their race, if you were to help me protect them, I would also offer any services I can." "I think we are going to need a second fort" I said, mostly to myself, but out loud. "You have a fort?" Pearl asked. "That's what I think of it as" I replied. "Where do you all live now?" I asked Cori. "We live scattered about, trying to fit in as much as possible, live 'normal' human lives" she replied. "I have an idea," I said. I exchanged phone numbers with Pearl and Cori, "I'll be in touch, soon" I told them. "It was great to meet you," Cori said. And Pearl nodded in agreement. "Likewise, I'm going to speak with the rest of my team, but my plan is to have you both come stay with us, but we need a safe place for the rest of the Elves, let them know, that they may have to go to a safe house soon" I told Cori. "Okay" she replied, I bent down to hug her and I gave Pearl a hug before we walked away.

Fourteen

The army grows

As soon as we were all back in the car, I called James to see where he and Levi and Alice were. "Yeah" he answered. "Are you guys headed home yet?" I asked. "Yeah, we are," he replied. "Okay, we'll just talk back at the house" I replied, and I hung up the phone. "Do you really think it's a good idea to bring them to the house?" Misty asked. I laughed. "It wasn't a good idea to bring you, yet I did it" I replied. She nodded and didn't say anything else.

When we got to the pullover spot, I noticed the truck was already parked. They must have driven really fast. And they hadn't waited for us to arrive before heading to the house apparently, because they weren't here. "Well that's kind of rude," I said, looking at the truck. "It is cold, you expect them to freeze, waiting on us?" Damian asked. I just rolled my eyes at him. "It wouldn't be much if I projected my magic on you for you to warp us" he said. I thought about it for a minute, "I want to walk, give myself some time to think, you guys can warp if you want, I'll be fine" I told them. "I wouldn't feel comfortable leaving you to walk alone Gabriela," Conan said.

"I promise, I will be fine, Margo is out here somewhere" I replied. "James would have our necks if we all left you" Damian said. "I can deal with James," I replied.

It took a little more arguing, but they started getting cold, and decided to go ahead and warp back without me. I continued walking, for some reason, the cold wasn't really bothering me today. I heard footsteps behind me, I turned around to see Margo. "Hey Margo, how are you today?" I asked, knowing she couldn't reply. I hated the fact that they couldn't turn back to their human forms, but they knew when they came here that that's how it would be. I heard heavy footsteps coming toward me, from the direction of the house. It was Philip, he kneeled down for me to get on his back. I agreed and got on. "Did James send you?" I asked. His head nodded up and down rapidly to say 'yes.'

After I got on his back, he started running as fast as he could back toward the house. I kept feeling like I would fly off at any moment. It felt like the ride was never going to end, I was really struggling to hold on toward the end, but we finally came to a stop, James was waiting and he helped me get down. "Why would you tell the others to leave you in the woods and come back?" he asked right away. "It's not like you waited," I replied. "What? You are mad at me for not waiting for you to get home?" he asked. "No," I replied, simply. He started laughing at me and put his jacket over me and his arm around me as he walked me inside, "come on, Levi has a fire going."

The fire was nice and warm, even though, for some reason, I didn't really feel all that cold, I still sat close to it. Mostly, to satisfy James, I was starting to get hot, so I got up and went to the kitchen. James followed me, "are you hungry?" he asked. "Will you stop?" I asked, not sure where it even came from. "Stop?" he replied. "You act like I can't do anything for myself. It gets annoying sometimes" I said. "Me caring about you is annoying?" he replied. "Don't do that, don't turn what I say around" I said. I didn't know why I was being so mean, but it just kept coming. James left the kitchen, I let him go. I found some stuff to make me a sandwich.

A few minutes later, James returned with Damian. I just looked at both of them, I felt like they were coming to ambush me, I have no idea why, but I did. Damian walked up to me, I went into self defense mode and dropped to the floor for a roundhouse kick, I quickly knocked his feet from under him. "What the hell Gabriela?!" James yelled. "I don't know!" I replied. I helped Damian up, he still had a look of shock on his face. "I'm sorry" I said. He just looked at me. "See what I mean? Can you check her?" James said to him. "What are you talking about?" I asked. "James thinks someone put a spell on you, to make you not trust, or like us apparently" Damian said. I looked at him, it did make sense, to explain the way I felt, but who? Pearl? She was the only witch besides the ones I lived with that I had been in contact with.

"I may need help with this, can I get you to come lie down on the couch?" Damian asked. "Can you knock me out for this? I don't want to attack anyone else," I said. "I'll get you some sleeping potion," Damian replied. "Tell everyone to clear out of the living room too, before I go in there" I told him. He nodded. I drank the potion and walked into the living room, everyone had listened, because it was empty. I lay down on the couch and let the black nothingness take over me. I woke the next morning in my bed that I shared with James. He was there next to me, looking at me, smiling. "What?" I asked. "Feel better?" he replied. "I don't know, I think so," I said. "You did have a spell on you, they all worked together to find it and remove it" he told me. "It had to have been Pearl," I said. "Unless it was someone here," he said. "What do you mean?" I asked. "Misty?" he said. I sighed, maybe he was right? How would I ever know?

I got out of bed and took a shower. When I came out, James was still there, like he was waiting for me. "Are you scared to leave me alone?" I asked him. "A little" he admitted. "I think I'm okay," I told him. "I'm hungry," I said. "Me too," he replied. We walked out of the room and into the kitchen. Misty and Hale were in there, cooking breakfast. "Smells good" I said, as we walked in. Misty and Hale both looked up at the sound of my voice. "How are you feeling?" Hale asked. "Better, I think," I said. "I don't understand how anyone was able to put a spell on you" Misty said. "I'm not sure, but I feel like it must have been Pearl, or someone here" I said. Misty and Hale looked at me again, like I was speaking another language this time. I shrugged my shoulders.

"Anyone know where Damian is?" I asked. I felt like I needed to apologize and tell him thank you at the same time. Plus, I felt like he might be able to help me figure out who had put the spell on me. "I think I saw him go outside," Hale said. I nodded, and headed toward the front door. As soon as I stepped out on the porch, I saw him sitting in a chair, alone. "Hey" I said, to get his attention so I didn't startle him. He still jumped a little. "Sorry, I was trying not to scare you," I told him. "It's okay, I was just deep in thought," he replied. "I have a question for you, do you think you could make a truth potion?" I asked. "Probably," he replied. "I think it would be the best way to figure out if it was someone here that put the spell on me" I said. "I think you may be right," he said, as he got up and walked inside.

I sat there for a moment just looking around, I saw Margo at the edge of the forest. I walked over to her. "Are you okay?" I asked her. She laid down at my feet, so I decided to sit down next to her. I rubbed her head and she lay it down on my leg. She rolled over to expose her belly, just like a house cat, I wasn't going to fall for that. She could accidentally rip my head off. "What did Arturo write to you?" I asked. She seemed to get upset that I asked and sat up. "I wish you could tell me," I said. She put her head down like she wanted me to put my hand on it, so I did. I began seeing flashes, was I seeing her thoughts? Was she doing it? Or was I doing it? I concentrated as much as possible. I saw her and Arturo, but they were both younger, they were holding hands, and laughing and sneaking kisses on each other's cheeks. It made me smile. Then it skipped forward a little, they were a little older, I couldn't hear anything, but I could clearly see that they were arguing. Arturo pushed her, and I could tell by the movement of his mouth that he yelled "get out!" I started to pull my hand away. She put her head back on my hand.

This time, it seemed to be right before she came here with me. They were talking, but it seemed they weren't lovers, but friends instead. He hugged her, like he was telling her goodbye, and possibly, sorry. Her head dropped, she still loved him. What had happened? Then she showed me the letter. At least bits and pieces of it. "I'm so sorry for what happened. Gabriela did a spell on me. I'm free now, free to feel whatever I want." I pulled my hand back. "He broke your heart, and now he feels like he can love you again?" I asked her, knowing she couldn't reply. She got up and walked away, I think my guess was right and she felt like she needed to be alone. I walked back to the house.

James was sitting on the porch, apparently he had been watching me with Margo the entire time. "What was that about?" he asked as I walked up. "Nothing" I replied, not comfortable sharing what I had learned with him. "Okay" he said. I walked inside and went to the bedroom. He followed, of course. "Are you feeling okay?" he asked. I nodded, "yeah, I feel okay" I replied. "Good" he said, as he walked up to me. He grabbed my face on both sides and pulled me up for a kiss. It was a passionate kiss, one that let me know he was hungry for more. I put my arms behind his neck and pulled him in closer, harder. I hadn't realized that I was hungry for more also.

I slid my hands down his chest until I reached the bottom of his shirt, which I grabbed and pulled over his head. I ran my hands down over his bare chest this time, down to his stomach, until I got to the top of his pants. I reached further down until I felt his bulge, he moaned at my touch. I brought my hand back up to unbutton his pants. He slipped his hands down under my shirt and pulled it off and started fondling my breasts. I moaned with excitement, as he threw me on the bed, I also let out a giggle. He came down on top of me, kissing my neck, and working his way down, pausing at my breast, as his hands went down and he grabbed my legs and pushed them apart. Before I knew it, he was inside of me, it was like, he couldn't wait any longer. I moaned, it felt amazing, he always felt amazing to me, like he was a perfect fit, I reached climax before he did, but I didn't stop until he was done. I could feel his penis throbbing like it had a heart pounding inside of it. When he finished, he collapsed on me, it felt so good, the closeness, I just lay there. I loved the way he smelled, I can't explain it, except that he smelled like home.

"We should go and see what's going on" I said, after we lay there for a while. "I don't want to, can't we just stay here, let the world fall apart around us?" He replied. "No, unfortunately, we can't," I said. "Alright" he groaned as he got up. I got up right behind him and found my clothes and got dressed. "I'm gonna go make some coffee, do you want some?" he asked. "Sure" I replied, with a smile. He walked out of the bedroom and I finished getting ready. I needed to go talk to Damian about the truth serum, so I walked out of the room to go find him.

I walked out into the living room where Hale and Levi were sitting on the couch. "Have you guys seen Damian? I need to ask him about something" I said. "I think he's in his room," Hale replied. So I walked to his bedroom, the door was closed, I knocked. "Yeah?" I heard from inside. "It's me, can I come in?" I asked. "Sure," he replied. I walked in, he was mixing liquids together, and he also had herbs and crystals lying about on a table. "Are you working on the truth serum?" I asked. "Yes" he replied like he was irritated with the question. "Sorry" I said, throwing my hands up. He just kept working. "You are pretty good at potions?" I asked. "I am when I can concentrate," he replied. "Sorry, I'll go, just come find me when it's done, or if you need me for anything" I told him as I left his room.

I went to the kitchen, where James was just finishing up our coffee. Misty was in there, it looked like she was preparing to cook dinner. "Hi Misty," I said to her. "Hello," she replied. Looking at James, "I'm working on a way to figure out who put the spell on me" I said. "Good, that will be less for us to worry about," he replied. I nodded, "exactly." "The sooner the better, I feel like everyone has me as suspect number one" Misty said. I nodded at her and smiled. I walked out of the kitchen and through the living room and out of the front door. It was snowing! I don't know why I was so surprised, we were well into December now. James walked outside with me, "it's pretty" he said. "Yeah, for a minute, I suppose," I replied. "You don't like snow?" he asked, sounding surprised. "No, winter is the only season I don't like," I replied.

We sat and watched the snow falling for a while, we snuggled close to each other to keep warm and sipped our coffee which was getting cold fast. Damian walked out onto the porch. "It's snowing!" he said, with excitement. I let out a giggle at his excitement. "Yes it is" I replied to him. "I have the potion ready, either of you want to be guinea pigs?" Damian said. "Sure, James will" I said, laughing. "What?!" James replied, while pretending to attack me, but tickled me instead. I laughed until I almost peed myself. "Okay! okay! I will do it! Just stop!" I said, in between laughing.

We got up and followed Damian inside to his room. "It doesn't taste good, sorry" he said, looking at me and handing me a shot glass with a purple, thick, slimy looking liquid inside. I snarled my nose. "I guess it's only fair that I have to drink it, since I'm asking everyone else to drink it, right?" I said, with my nose still snarled, dreading putting that in my mouth. "Okay, first of all, we need to ask some test questions before you drink it, to make sure that it works. I want you to lie when I ask the test questions, understand?" Damian said. I nodded, "yes."

"I'll start with some easy ones, Is your name Gabriela?" Damian asked. "No," I replied. "Are you fifty years old?" he asked. "Yes," I replied. "Okay, bottoms up," he said. I grabbed the shot glass that he was handing me and pinched my nose closed so I wouldn't taste it as much, and I downed it. I almost threw up! I started gagging and trying to hold it down. James started rubbing and patting me on the back gently, "it's okay, just breath" he said. I started taking big breaths and managed to stop gagging. "It's disgusting," I said.

"Okay, I want you to lie to me when I ask you these questions again," Damian said. I nodded. "Is your name Gabriela?" he asked. "Yes," I replied. I put my hand over my mouth in shock, I didn't mean to say that! The effect of this potion was undeniable. "Are you fifty years old?" He asked. "No" shot out of my mouth before I could even think about it. "I think it's good, how long does it last?" I asked. "Not sure, probably around an hour," Damian replied. I nodded. "And is there enough for everyone?" I asked. Damian nodded. "Not just everyone here, but I also want Cori and Pearl to take it," I said. "I have enough," Damian assured me. "Okay, let's get this done," I said.

The three of us walked into the kitchen, Misty was still in there, she was alone. "I'll go find everyone," James said, looking at me. I nodded. "Is the potion ready?" Misty asked. "Yes," I said quickly. "It tastes horrible!" I added. "Oh, so you had some?" she asked. "Yes," I replied. "Well, I suppose that's what a true leader should do, right?" she said. "Yes," I said. "It works," I added. Hale and Conan walked into the kitchen and sat down at the table. "James said we are having a meeting?" Hale said. "Yes," I said. He looked at me awkwardly and I just looked back, I didn't want to talk, not being able to control what I said was frustrating me. I could only imagine a house full of everyone feeling this way, I hoped that there would be no fighting because of it.

James finally returned with Levi and Alice. I looked at Damian and said, "you start." He nodded at me. "Gabriela has asked me to make a potion that will help us figure out who cast the spell on her, if there is an enemy among us, we will know," he said. Everyone looked, most looked confused. "It's a truth potion, it is absolutely disgusting, yes, I took it, yes it works" I said. "This could be bad," Levi mumbled. "Not if we avoid personal questions, we should all be fine" I replied. "After everyone has taken the potion and answered the questions, we should avoid each other until the effects wear off. It is a frustrating feeling not to be able to fully control what comes out of your mouth" I said. Everyone looked at me and nodded, I'm sure that they could all see how frustrated I was just from looking at me.

Damian started handing out shot glasses with the potion inside to everyone. Everyone had the same reaction that I did when I saw it, they all snarled their noses and snorted. "I'm sorry, I couldn't make it taste good, but it does work," Damian said. "Yes it does," I said. Damian held up his glass, like he was cheering everyone, "three, two, one! Bottoms up!" he said. Everyone took the potion. Everyone started gagging, it was about to make me start gagging again. "Just breathe," I told them. After a few minutes, everyone started calming down and just staring at me like they were waiting for me to lead.

I decided to start with Misty. Looking at her, I said, "Misty, did you cast a spell on me yesterday?" "No," she replied quickly. A few people looked shocked, I was relieved. "Conan, did you cast a spell on me yesterday?" I asked. "No," he replied. I quickly moved around the room, asking each person the same question, everyone's answer was the same, 'no.' Once I finished the last one, I said, "That's good that it wasn't any of you, next we will get Cori and Pearl to do the same, if they refuse, we will know it was them anyway." A collective 'yes' came from everyone. "Okay, I think it's best if we separate and avoid each other until the effects of the potion wears off" I said. Everyone agreed and got up to leave the kitchen. I went to my bedroom. James followed me.

"We should play a game," he said as we entered the bedroom. "That's a terrible idea" I replied. "Do you love me?" he asked. "Yes," I said, with a smile. "Do you love me?" I asked him. "I think what I feel for you is more than love, I can't explain it, it is like we are connected in our souls," he said. "Soulmates?" I replied. "Not exactly," he replied. "I'm confused," I said. "It's as if we share the same soul," he said. "How is that possible?" I asked, not necessarily to him, just a verbal thought. I pulled out my laptop and started looking up 'soul mates'. I found one article that said you can have many soulmates. One person says that a soul mate is a soul that you have known in a previous life. And that person could be anyone, in your previous life or this life, friend, lover, family, even an enemy. James was standing behind me reading along with me. "Yeah, that's not what I mean," he said.

He took the computer from me and started searching, after a few minutes he said, "This!" as he handed me the computer. I started reading what he had pulled up. Twin flame, souls that had been once connected and split apart, it said you were lucky if you found your twin flame. "You really think we are twin flames?" I asked him. "Yes, I can't explain my feelings any other way, you literally make me whole," he said. I put my arms around him and squeezed him tightly. He held me tighter, "I wanted you to know that I, more than love you. That's why I'm so protective of you, I'm being selfish, because I don't think I could live without you" he said. I sighed, "we are fighting a war, a magical war at that, and I just learned magic and that all this even exists," I said. "What are you saying?" he asked. "Casualties of war are a thing," I replied. "You sound as if you don't care if you die" he said. "It's not that I don't care, I'm just speaking the truth, because that's all I can do right now" I said. He didn't say anything else, I don't think he wanted to hear any more truth from me.

I fell asleep in his arms. I went to the dream world, where Valery was waiting. It was as if she had been talking to me already even though I was just showing up. "...he said that" she said. I looked at her confused. "Who said what?" I asked. "You never listen to me! That's the problem here" she yelled at me. "I just got here!" I yelled back. She rolled her eyes at me, that must be where I get the habit from. "I have to tell you something, and you have to listen to me, I don't know if I will see you again" she said, desperately. "What?" I asked. "You weren't the second mixed breed," she said. "There is another?!" I asked excitedly. "Not anymore" she said. "You are the first tri..." James shook me and yelled until I opened my eyes.

I looked at him angrily, "I was about to find out something!" I yelled. "I didn't know what was happening. You were yelling and kicking and punching and your hand lit up, like it was glowing!" he said. "What?!" I replied. I looked at my hand, it looked normal. "I was having a normalish conversation with my mother, she was about to tell me something important. It doesn't make sense that I was yelling or kicking or glowing" I replied. "I'm sorry, I was scared that the potion had some kind of effect on you. I was scared," he said. "She said I was the first tri. Before you woke me up, she didn't get to finish and she said that she didn't know if she would be able to come back again" I said, my disappointment coming through in my voice. "I'm sorry" he said again. I got up and walked out of the room to go find another witch.

Conan was the first one I saw. I told him what had happened. "Do you have any idea what she could have been trying to say? What is a tri?" I asked him. "Well the meaning of tri is three, do you think she was saying that you are not only a witch/giant?" he asked. "She did say that I wasn't the second mixed breed. Maybe she was mixed with something else?" I said. "Possibly, she was known for being very powerful," Conan replied. "But what else do I have coursing through my veins? What could she have been? Do you think anyone would know who her parents were?" I asked. "I don't know the answer to any of that," Conan replied. James walked up behind us, I turned and looked at him and rolled my eyes. He dropped his head, still feeling bad. Why did I keep making him feel bad? What was wrong with me? He didn't know, he thought I was in danger, but for some reason, instead of trying to make him feel better, I walked away.

I found Misty in the kitchen, it seemed that was where she was most of the time. "Do you know who Valery's parents were?" I asked her. "No, I never knew who her parents were," she replied. "Why do you ask?" she added. "I think she may have been a mixed breed," I told her. She gasped, "Why do you think that?" "She came to me in a dream," I said. "Has she done that before? Is that a normal thing?" She asked me. "Yes," I said. "I've never heard of the dead communicating with the living, that's the one thing we don't do" she said. "I know, I've heard that before, but maybe it's a clue as to what she is," I said, thinking out loud to myself. "Do any creatures have contact between the dead and the living?" I asked her. "I'm not sure" she replied, shaking her head. I decided to move on to the next witch.

I found Damian in his room. I told him what had happened, what had been said, and that I thought I may have another bloodline within me. "I don't know how that is possible without anyone knowing," he replied. "Did you know her parents?" I asked. "No," he replied. "Do you know anyone that did know her parents?" I asked. "No," he said again. "Is there a test of some sort? Like a magical DNA test?" I asked. "Not that I am aware of," he said. James knocked on the open bedroom door. "What?" I said, looking at him with my irritated look. "I'm only going to say it one more time, I AM SORRY" he said, looking at me. I sighed and looked away. "Don't blame him," Damian said. I rolled my eyes at him and walked out of the room. I supposed it wouldn't hurt to find Hale, and see if he knew anything, so I went looking for him.

I found him sitting on the porch, reading a book. I explained everything to him, then I asked him if he knew anything about it. “It would explain why she was so powerful, but no, I’m not sure what she could have been mixed with,” he said. “Do you know of any way to find out?” I asked him. “Maybe, you can try to tap into it, by using powers only known to a certain species” he suggested. I smiled at him, I kissed him on the forehead, “that’s better than nothing, you are the only one who had any suggestions” I told him. I went back into the house, I wanted to find James, I was ready to forgive him now and make him help me research the different powers of different magical species. I found him pouting in our room.

He looked up when I entered, he didn’t say anything. I walked over and sat down next to him on the bed. “I understand that you thought I may have been in danger,” I said. He continued to just look at me. “I’m not mad at you, I’m just mad that I didn’t get to finish my conversation or even say goodbye to her,” I told him. He still sat there, not saying anything. “My anger was misplaced” I said. “Is it really that hard for you to say ‘sorry’?” he asked. I looked at him for a minute and smiled, “I’m sorry.” He smiled back at me, “did you find out anything?” he asked. “Hale gave me an idea to try, I need your help, if you don’t mind” I said. “Sure, anything” he said, eagerly. “I need you to help me figure out the different powers of different magical species, and I will see if I can do those things,” I said. “Wait, what?” he said. “What?” I asked. “Do you really think that will work?” he asked. “Do you have any better ideas?” I asked. He just looked at me, like he was trying to think of another way.

“Why don’t you like the idea?” I asked. “I don’t want you to get hurt, what if you tap into something that you shouldn’t, what if the other part of you that we don’t know about is bad? Or what if you can’t control it, especially here on 12. Is it really important right now? Can't you just forget about it until we go back to 2 where Arturo can help you?" he said. I sat back and thought about what he was saying. Maybe he was right, maybe I should just not worry about it right now, but maybe it could help us, I didn't know what to do. "Maybe we should have a meeting and ask everyone what they think I should do," I suggested. "Why does it always have to be a team vote? I really just wish you would put this on the back burner for now" he said. "I'll think about it, and for this minute, I will put it on the 'back burner'" I replied. "Thank you" he said, and put his arms around me in a warm embrace.

Fifteen

Finding the truth

At dinner that night, we discussed requesting a meeting with Cori and Pearl to ask them to drink the truth potion. "I can contact Pearl," Misty said. "Yes, do that, just request a meeting. Once we are in the meeting we will tell them what it is about, and see if they will agree to drink the potion" I said. "I think that is a terrible idea, it's obvious that one of them did it, and the other probably knew about it" James said. He really irked my nerves sometimes, he didn't want to make any moves at all, afraid that something would happen. "We will never move forward if we just sit here and do nothing" I said, looking at him. He looked at me silently. "She's right, we can't win a war if we don't fight," Levi said. James looked at him sideways and got up from the table and walked out of the room. Levi continued to eat like nothing had happened.

"Just sent a text to Pearl," Misty said. "Okay" I replied. "So how will we handle this meeting? The same as before?" Alice asked. "I don't see why not, it worked pretty well" I said. "Except someone put a spell on you," Hale reminded me. "Minor inconvenience" I replied, jokingly. "She wants to know what the meeting is about," Misty said. "Tell her we will discuss that at the meeting" I said. "Okay, text sent" Misty replied. We were on dessert which we didn't normally do, before Pearl replied. Misty held up her phone so everyone could see. *Okay, same place, noon tomorrow.* "Okay, I guess we are all set, someone needs to let James know," I said, looking around the table. And then I got up and walked outside, I felt like being alone with my thoughts.

I just found a seat on the porch, it was freezing out, but for some reason I didn't mind. I couldn't help but think how different my life had been just a couple months ago. I had a normal life, lonely, but normal. Now I had this huge family and I was quickly becoming their leader, one of the youngest ones here, and I was 'momma bear'. I couldn't help but giggle out loud at the thought. "What's so funny?" I heard someone say. I turned to see who it was, it was Levi. "Just thinking of the whole situation" I said. "And you think it's funny?" he asked, sarcastically sounding surprised. "Not all of it, but yes, pieces of it are very funny," I replied. "I suppose a bit of it is funny, if you would have asked me a few months ago what I would be doing now, I certainly wouldn't have said being a soldier in a witch war on 12" he said. I could tell he still wanted out, he wanted to go home.

I saw James coming out of the barn, he started walking toward us. "Did we decide what we are doing?" he asked, sarcastically. "Yes, we are meeting them tomorrow, same place at noon, same plan as before" I replied flatly before I got up and walked inside. Levi nor James followed me inside, I figured Levi was telling him what we had been talking about before he walked up. I just wished that I could get James to let go a little more, it seemed like he was getting more uptight about what we had to do, he was getting more and more scared of losing me. I heard a knock on my bedroom door, I got up to see who it was. It was James, "since when do you knock?" I asked him as I moved for him to come inside.

"I didn't know how mad you were at me" he said as he walked in. "I'm not mad at you, I just wish I could make you understand, you are starting to get in the way" I replied. "I don't want to get in the way, I just want to keep you safe," he replied. "I want to try something, can I look into you and see if I can remove your worry?" I asked him. "Do you really think that is a good idea?" he asked. "I don't see why not, honestly, if we can't do something about it, we may have to send you back to 2" I told him. "You really want to get rid of me?" he asked, sounding hurt. "No, but I am the leader and you are starting to get in the way, I can't let someone else get hurt because of you. Personally it would break my heart into a million pieces if I had to send you back to 2 right now." I said. He looked at me, "I'm serious, I need your arms around me, I need your sweet whispers in my ear" I told him. He walked up to me without saying anything and put his arms around me and pulled me closer to him.

"Try to remove it" he whispered into my ear then he released me. I stood close to him, looking up into his eyes, I mouthed 'I love you.' He smiled and mouthed 'me too.' I smiled and closed my eyes to start the spell. I did the same thing that I had done with the mermaid and Arturo, I imagined my 'ghost' arm leaving me and entering his head. I found something, I grabbed it and pulled, it didn't want to move. I tugged a bit harder and it came out. I can always tell when something doesn't belong, it 'feels' like it shouldn't be there. After I had removed it, I stepped back and looked at him. His eyes were closed and he had a slight smile on his lips.

"How do you feel?" I asked him. "Are you finished?" he asked. "I think so," I replied. "I don't feel anything really," he said. "How do you feel about the meeting tomorrow?" I asked. "I'm not opposed to it anymore," he said, sounding shocked. I smiled, "good, that means I can keep you" I told him. "Oh yeah? You get to *keep me*?" He said, teasing as he picked me up and threw me to the bed. He came down on top of me and started kissing me passionately. I didn't realize how much I was craving him, his touch, his scent. Even though it had not been long at all, I felt like I could stay like this forever, live off of his energy alone. "I love you" I whispered into his ear as he entered me. It felt amazing every time, but this time it felt amazing and magical. He was a little rougher this time, but I enjoyed it and every time he saw that I was enjoying it, he got rougher. I suppose he wasn't worried about hurting me physically anymore, that must have been in what I had removed from him as well. I didn't mind at all, it felt more passionate. My orgasm even seemed more intense and he climaxed at the same time.

He lay there on top of me for a few minutes, just catching his breath. He finally rolled off and lay beside me. "Thank you," he said. "For what?" I asked. "I feel like I have been set free. Are you okay?" he asked "Better than okay, that was amazing" I replied, smiling at him. He smiled back and rolled over to face me, he kissed my lips gently. "I love you" he whispered. I smiled at him, "me too" I replied. "I'm going to go see if I can find something to eat, I'm hungry now" he said, getting out of bed. I rolled my eyes at him, "of course you are" I said, sarcastically. "Hey" I said, to get his attention before he stepped out. "Yeah?" he replied. "I'm sorry that you ever felt like you had to hold back, that was amazing" I said, as I winked at him. He put his head down and smiled like I had embarrassed him.

Rayne and Stitch both came through the door when he opened it, I felt like I hadn't seen them in days. They both jumped up onto the bed. "Where have you guys been?" I asked. I got purrs and meows as a response. They kept rubbing against me, "Okay, I missed you guys too" I said to them. They both snuggled up to me and I drifted off to sleep. It was a dreamless sleep, I must have been more tired than I thought, I didn't wake up not even once, not even when James got in bed with me. I didn't wake up until the next morning when James started kissing my forehead and telling me that it was time to get up. I opened my eyes and smiled at him.

"Yes, time to get up, we have to get ready for the meeting today" I moaned as I rolled over away from him. I knew if I got any closer that we wouldn't be getting out of bed anytime soon. "Alice made you something, I put it in the bathroom" James said. "What is it?" I asked curiously. "She said that a warrior leader needs to look the part, so she made you an outfit" he said, with a smile growing across his lips. "Hmm" I replied. I went into the bathroom to see what he was talking about. It was an outfit, soft black leather catsuit, it zipped up in the front and showed quite a bit of cleavage. I put it on along with my black combat boots. I put my hair into a ponytail and walked out of my bathroom back into the bedroom.

"Holy shit!" James said. "Yeah, I'm not so sure about this," I replied. "You definitely look hot!" he said. "I don't need to look hot, I need to kick ass," I said. "Well, can you move in it?" James asked as he stood up and walked toward me. He threw a punch and I blocked it, even though I was surprised. He started to throw another punch and I threw him back onto the bed with my magic. "What are you doing?" I asked him. "Testing you, I think you're good," he replied. I glared at him, before rolling my eyes and walking out into the living room.

Alice saw me first and started jumping and clapping like a child "Yes!" she said. I giggled at her. "Seriously? You think?" I asked. "Oh yes!" she replied. I walked into the kitchen with Alice following me. Levi whistled as I walked by, I smiled and rolled my eyes at him at the same time. "Hot momma" Hale yelled as I walked by him. "Okay, y'all need to calm down now" I said. "How are we supposed to go into a battle with you looking like that?" Levi asked. "What do you mean?" Alice replied. "He means I will be distracting," I replied. "I made that for her, it's very functional, plus it makes her look intimidating" Alice said, sounding a bit like his question had insulted her. "I think it makes her look sexy," Levi replied. "What do you think?" I asked, looking at Misty. "I think it shows your body and muscles well, so in that aspect, you do look intimidating. On the other hand, the guys seem to see you as a sex symbol?" She said, looking around at the guys. "And that will make a good distraction for you to get close enough to kick their butts!" Alice said with excitement. I laughed, but she did have a point.

I decided to wear it to the meeting. We all headed out, same as before with Hale staying behind to 'guard the fort.' Everyone took the same positions that they had done before with one exception. Damian walked into the meeting with us this time, because it was his potion. We walked over to the bench, Pearl and Cori were both there, waiting as promised. "Good afternoon" Cori said, looking me up and down. "What are you wearing?" Pearl asked. "It was a gift," I said. "I think you look nice," Cori said. "Thank you," I replied.

Pearl looked as though she had just noticed Damian. "Damian?" she said. He just nodded his head, silently to acknowledge he heard her. "I'll get to the point, at our last meeting, someone put a spell on me. I asked Damian to make a truth serum so we could figure out who did it" I said. "Everyone that is with us, including Gabriela has taken the potion" Damian said. "I took it first, to test that it worked. Everyone passed, so we wanted to ask the two of you to take the potion to verify that neither of you had anything to do with it" I said.

"If all of your own passed and we were the only other two here, doesn't that automatically make us or at least one of us the guilty party?" Pearl asked. "No, not necessarily, someone that we didn't notice could have done it. Unless you are confessing now?" I asked, looking at Pearl. "I didn't cast any spells on you," she replied. "Good, then you won't mind taking the potion?" I asked. Damian pulled it out to hand it to them. Pearl snarled her nose up, "it looks delicious," she said sarcastically. "It does taste terrible," I replied. "So what are the options here?" Cori asked. "If you refuse the potion, or if you take it and we learn that you did cast the spell, you will be an enemy and we will deal with you accordingly. If you drink the potion and prove that it wasn't you, we will invite you to join our team, and help us figure out who did cast the spell and help us fight and win this war" I explained.

Cori and Pearl looked at each other for a moment, "Okay, we will take the potion," Pearl said, breaking the silence. Damian handed them each a vile of the potion. "Bottoms up, I guess," Pearl said to Cori. They drank it at the same time, Pearl had the same reaction that everyone else did. Cori seemed to not be able to taste it. I looked at her confused. "It's a little gift that we elves have, we can turn our taste buds off" she said, smiling at me. "Wow" I replied. After Pearl stopped gagging I started asking her questions. "Try to lie for this first one" I said to her. She nodded that she understood. "Is your name Pearl?" I asked. "Yes," she said, surprised. "Okay, did you cast a spell on me at our last meeting?" I asked. "No," she replied. "Do you know who did cast a spell on me when we were meeting here before?" I asked. "No," she replied again. I asked Cori the same questions, she gave the same answers.

Damian looked at me like he was confused. "What?" I asked him. "Can I talk to you in private?" he asked. "Sure," I replied. We stepped far enough away that no one would be able to hear us, unless we yelled at each other. "I don't understand, I was certain they would be guilty," he said. "I wasn't, like I told them, it could have been someone that found out about the meeting and snuck in, or close enough to do the spell. We will figure it out together. I want to ask them to come back to the house with us." I told him. He continued to just look at me, "I don't think it's a good idea" he said, "but you are the leader" he added as he walked away. "Where are you going?" I yelled after him. "I'll be in the car," he replied.

I walked back over to the bench where Pearl and Cori were

sitting. "So, are you ready to be soldiers?" I asked them. "I don't fight, it is not in my nature, I cook, I clean, I babysit, but I do not fight." Cori said. "Can you explain what your ultimate goal is, why are you fighting?" Pearl asked. "I'm fighting for peace among the witches, for the ability for them to love and have a family with whom they choose" I explained. "And you will be the ultimate high priestess? Something our kind hasn't had for two thousand years." She said. "I haven't really thought about it, but I suppose, yes, if I can unite all of the covens once again, that would make me the high priestess of the witches" I replied, trying not to sound shocked, because I honestly had not thought about being the supreme leader of a race.

"Can I think about it?" Pearl asked. "I would like to go, all I've ever wanted is protection, to be able to get up and know that I won't be murdered because of what I am and where I live" Cori said. "Great, we will love to have you," I told her. "What is there to think about?" I asked Pearl. "You want to change what our ancestors fought to create, they created it to protect us, and it has worked for two thousand years," she replied. "Did it really? How many innocent babies and children were murdered? And I'm sure their parents as well" I said. "It was what had to be done, to protect our species," she replied. "Are you serious right now? So are you saying that you firmly believe that I should have been killed as a baby? That I shouldn't exist?" I asked her. "You slipped through the cracks, maybe *you* are special, maybe *you* should be here, but that doesn't mean that every creature should be allowed to cross breed and create something that should not exist." She replied. "Maybe I am here to change the world," I replied. She looked at me for a minute.

"You are about to be a part of history, Pearl, you have helped us 'my' side in the past. Now is not a time to try to remain 'neutral.' You have to pick a side, and I would suggest picking the winning side" I said to her. "How do you know you will win?" she asked. "Because I don't have no choice, and it's time for the witches to change. What worked at one time, no longer fits. We have grown, we have evolved." I replied. "I believe in what you are doing, but do you realize how many oppose you?" she asked. "Do you realize how many have already joined me?" I replied. "I don't just have witches, I have shapeshifters and half-giants on my team as well," I told her. I gave a signal for everyone to come to the bench. Everyone started walking up, she looked at everyone, "hello" she said to them. They replied with 'hellos' and 'nice to meet you.'

"Pearl is on the fence about joining us," I said to them. "You are either with Gabriela or against Gabriela, and I don't suggest the latter," Misty said. Pearl looked at her surprised. "Misty has seen the power I have first hand before she decided to join me" I told Pearl. "I don't want to fight you, I don't want to hurt you," she replied. "Like Misty just said, and I have already told you, there is no 'neutral' in this, you have to pick a side" I said. Everyone looked at her, silently, waiting for her to answer. "What will be my part?" she asked. "That is yet to be determined," I replied. "Can I talk to you in private?" she asked me. "Sure," I replied. "I'll meet everyone at the car" I said, to dismiss everyone else. "I'll wait at the edge of the park," James said. I nodded, that seemed fair, Pearl could still be planning on attacking me, though I didn't think that was her plan at all.

Once everyone was out of earshot, Pearl looked at me. "I know I have helped your mother in the past. Something has happened since then. I met Xander, you know who he is?" She asked, looking at me. I nodded, I remembered that he was listed under the 'enemy' category. "We fell in love, he is very stern on his point of view and that you or any other mixed breed should not exist" she said. "Are you still in love with him?" I asked. "I do love him, I would do almost anything for him, but if he knew I was meeting with you now, I don't know what he would do to me" she said, tears coming to her eyes. "You think he would hurt you?" I asked, shocked. "You don't understand how he feels about this," she said, sounding as if she was pleading with me. "Come with me now, I will request a meeting with him myself, and act as though I have kidnapped you" I replied, as a plan was forming in my head.

"What do you mean? He will kill you!" she replied. "And what if he already knows of our meeting? What if it was him that put the spell on me? He could just be keeping you close to get to me" I said. "He loves me, I know he does, he wouldn't follow me, it wasn't him" she replied. I could clearly see that she was blinded by whatever feelings she had for him. She could be right, or I could be right, but if she didn't cooperate, we wouldn't be able to figure it out. "I promise you that I do not want to hurt Xander, I want him on my side. I want all the witches united" I told her. "It's not going to work. He killed his own half sibling! His mother had a baby with a shapeshifter and he killed the baby when his mother was sleeping! He let her believe that it was SID's" she said, starting to cry. "Why do you love him?" I asked. "It just happened. And I think he is just sticking to his beliefs because if he admits he was wrong, he has to deal with the fact that he murdered an innocent child, his own brother" she said.

"I think you should come with us now, we can figure all this out at the house. It's completely safe there. We can talk more and make a plan." I said. "I'm scared," she replied. "I understand that, like I said, I will make it look like I took you hostage" I assured her. "He will eventually find out the truth and then what?" She asked. "I have an ability, I may be able to use it on him, it may sway him to join us" I told her. She looked at me, confused. "I can't really explain it," I said. "I don't think I can go with you," she said. "I like you Pearl, I don't want you to get hurt. Please, come with me, I can protect you and if Xander can't be brought over, you won't have to worry about him anymore" I said. She looked at me as though she wanted to hurt me now. "I told you that I am in love with him, and you are threatening to kill him? How dare you?!" she said, getting angry.

On to the next plan, I didn't really want to kidnap her, but I felt like I had said too much. I couldn't let her walk away and go back to tell Xander everything. I quickly punched her and knocked her out. James saw me do it and came running. I was holding her up, trying not to draw any unwanted attention. "What did you do?!" James said as he approached. "No time to explain, we have to get her back to the house. For now, she is our prisoner" I told him. He gave me a look of disappointment as he picked her up and carried her to the car. I rushed to get in so we could get back as quickly as possible.

"What did you do?!" Damian demanded. "She's involved with Xander, I couldn't have her go back and tell him anything" I said. "What do you mean, involved?" He asked. "Apparently they are in love," I replied. "He's probably the one that put the spell on you," he said. "She seems to not think so, she said he had no idea of our meeting" I told him. He rolled his eyes. "I have a plan, but for right now, she is our prisoner" I said. She hadn't woken up by the time we got to the pull over spot where we parked the vehicles, which was a good thing. I warped her and myself up to the house. Hale was shocked when he saw me dragging her in. "What happened?!" he yelled. "We have a prisoner," I replied.

Cori hadn't seen any of this happen, she had been waiting with the other car. I wanted to hide her before she could see. I didn't want her to not trust me or the rest of the team. "I need to put her where Cori won't find her," I said. "Put her in the last room down that hall, we'll have Cori stay upstairs" Hale suggested. Pearl started coming to. "Help me" I said, looking at Hale. He put his hand on her head and she fell back asleep. "What did you do?" I asked. "Just get her in there" he replied, pointing down the hallway. I nodded and carried her to the last bedroom in the hallway. I tied her to the bed and walked out of the room, I locked it on my way out and put a spell on the door to block sound as well.

I met Cori in the living room. "We have a room for you upstairs"

I told her. "Great, glad to be here, thank you so much for your invitation" she replied. No mention of Pearl, I wondered if she knew about her and Xander? If so, she was loyal, which is a good trait to have in an ally. I watched her walk upstairs as James came in behind me. "Where did you put her?" he asked. I pointed down the hall, "the last room, and Cori doesn't know," I said. "That's not a good idea" he replied. "I don't want her to not trust me or not to feel safe" I replied. "So you kidnap her friend and lie to her, make's sense," he replied sarcastically. "You don't understand, I did what I did because she needed to be saved too" I replied. "Yeah, I'm sure a lot of people justify their wrong doings by making it seem like they were doing something good" he replied. I gave him an evil look and walked away. I wasn't going to argue with him, I knew I was doing the right thing. Whatever she had going on with Xander wasn't a good thing.

I found James, Levi, and Damian and pulled them into the kitchen. "I want to go to 2 tonight. I need to bring Arturo here" I told them. "Damian, can you open the portal?" I asked. "Yes," he replied. "James, I know you want to go, Levi, do you want to go home? Or do you want to see this through?" I asked. He looked at me for a moment, he looked like he was thinking. "I know I've wanted to quit and go home in the past, but I would like to stay, see this through. If that's okay with all of you?" He said, looking around at us. "Of course," I replied. "Yeah, I know things weren't that great when we first got here, but you are my friend, I love you man!" James said. It made me smile to see him being compassionate toward someone besides me, a male anyways... "I have no issues with you staying as long as you want to be here" Damian said. "Alright then, let's go get Arturo," I said, with excitement.

I looked at Damian, "if Cori asks, we just stepped out for a little while, and let her know that I will see her tomorrow. We won't stay very long at all, with the time difference, we only need to visit for a little while, and get Arturo here and take care of business" I said. He just nodded his head to agree. "Alright, we will go grab a few things and meet you outside in about thirty minutes" I said to Damian. "Okay" he agreed. I looked at James and said, "let's go." So we went to the bedroom to gather a few things that we wanted to bring with us. "So are we just going to keep winging this?" James asked. "What are you talking about?" I replied. "You never have a plan, things just 'happen'" he said. I shrugged my shoulders, "it's working so far" I replied. He rolled his eyes at me. After we had a small bag of our things put together, we went outside to find Damian.

Damian was standing on the porch, staying close to the house for warmth because it was starting to get cold out. "Are you ready?" he asked, looking at us. "Yes," James said. "And remember, we'll be back in no time at all!" I said. "I know," he replied. We walked out of sight of the house, since we had not told everyone that we were going. Damian started the spell behind the barn. That familiar feeling of not existing took over my body quickly. Soon we were standing in a field that I recognized, the one where I had trained, the one beside David and Sarah's house. The sun was just starting to come up, so we started walking toward the house. James knocked on the door, David answered, he was surprised to see us and smiled and hugged James and then me. "Is everything okay?" he asked. "Kinda, nothing too serious, we came to get Arturo," I said. "Ahh, okay, well come in!" he said, moving so we could go inside.

"Hey!" Sarah said, surprised but sounding happy to see us. "Hi!" I replied as I walked up to hug her. "Where's Julie?" I asked. "She's still in bed, she will be excited to see you guys," Sarah replied. "Have you guys seen a lot of Arturo?" I asked, looking at David. "No, not really," he replied. "I was just wondering how he has been doing," I said. "He seems good," Sarah said. "Good" I replied, actually feeling relieved. I didn't know what the long term effects of my spell work may be. "Gaga!" I heard coming from the hall, it was the cutest little voice ever! "Hey baby!" I replied. "She's walking and talking!" I said, looking at Sarah. Sarah just laughed. I knew I would miss a lot of her life, because of living in different dimensions, but it kind of broke my heart a little.

Julie ran up to me and I picked her up and hugged her. She giggled and grabbed my hair and showed me that she had my hair, or showed me my hair? I don't know how toddlers think. Either way, she was adorable. "Wanna say hi to James?" I asked her. She pointed at him, "yeah" I said to her. She looked at me and shook her head, no. "My own niece likes you better than me," James said, looking at me. I looked at Julie and made a pouty face. "No!" she screamed at me and started fighting me to put her down. "Okay," I said and I sat her down on the floor, she ran over to Sarah and hugged her leg. "Can we put our bag in the bedroom that we usually use?" I asked, looking at David. "Yes, of course!" he replied. "Thanks" I said, grabbing the bag from James and taking it to the room.

Everything looked the same as it had since I was in there the last time. I sat the bag down on the floor next to the bed and I lay down for a minute, I just wanted to rest. It had been a long day and I wasn't prepared to just go into another day with no rest at all. I closed my eyes and drifted to sleep very quickly. I had a restful, dreamless sleep until I felt someone shaking me. "You gonna just sleep all day?" James said. I moaned and rolled over away from him. "Seriously?" he said. "Fine!" I moaned, not happy, I rolled out of bed. "I let you sleep for like four hours," he said. I gave him an evil look. "I needed more," I replied. He pounced on me and started tickling me, "you don't need more!" he said, teasingly. Then he kissed me, I kissed him back. "We need to go talk to Arturo," I said, in between kisses. He sighed, "I know" he said as he rolled off of me and got out of the bed. I followed behind him.

"Did you have a nice nap?" David asked as we walked into the living room. "I was having a nice nap until I got woken up," I replied, giving James an evil look. "Well, we came here for a reason, we aren't staying long" he said defensively. "I know, I was just teasing, I'm just grumpy because I didn't get my nap out" I said, half smiling at him. He smiled back, but his was a full smile, he looked genuinely happy and that made my heart feel so full. When everything was over, I wanted to come here to live. It was peaceful here.

James and I headed to Arturo's house. The climate here seemed to always be perfect. "Is the weather here always the same?" I asked James. "Mostly, there are slight changes, and sometimes there are amazing storms. Pink and blue lightning strikes, I'm not really sure if they are natural or if someone makes them" he replied. "Sounds interesting," I said. "I was thinking that I would like to live here in the future, when everything is over," I told him. He smiled at me. "I would too, it's a great place to live," he said as he took my hand into his. I got that feeling in my heart again, where it felt full and just pure happiness.

We reached Arturo's house and I knocked on the door. He opened it and looked at us surprised. "What are you doing here?" he asked. "I need your help, I need you to come back with us for a little while" I said. He moved out of the way to invite us inside. "Why what's going on?" he asked. "I took a hostage, Pearl," I said. "Why would you take her hostage? She has always been a supporter of your mother" he replied. "She is mixed up with Xander," I told him. "What? That doesn't make any sense, why would she do that?" he asked. "Maybe he put a spell on her? I don't know, that's one of the reasons why I want you to come back with us" I said. He nodded his head. "So you will?" I asked to confirm. "For a little while, yes," he said. "Thank you," I replied. "I knew I would have to eventually, that's why I considered going with you before" he said.

We sat down to discuss what had been going on, I told him about the spell that was placed on me and how we still didn't know who had done it. "It could have been Xander, if he has a spell on Pearl, he could have followed her without her knowing and done it behind her back" he said. "I agree, I don't know who else it could have been" I replied. "You were smart, you handled it all very well it seems, you are a natural leader" Arturo told me. "Thank you, I feel like I had really good teachers, so I don't want to take all the credit" I said, winking at him. "We taught you how to use magic and fight, not how to be a general in a war, that is something that came naturally to you, and we are all lucky that you are a natural. I feel like that in itself will make this whole thing go a lot faster and smoother than if you weren't" he said. "I agree, I was starting to become too protective and possessive and she performed the same spell on me that she did on you to release it. She was prepared to send me back here if it didn't work" James said, laughing. Arturo smiled. "I'm glad you two can have a laugh at my expense" I told them. "Not laughing at you darling, just amused at your power and beauty" James said, smiling. He actually made me blush, I lowered my head to try and hide it and smiled.

"So, Arturo, do you know a lot about elves?" I asked. "Elves are tricky, they are in the same category as fairies and gremlins," he replied. "I have invited one into the house," I told him. "I don't know if that was the best idea. How long has it been with you?" He asked. "*She* has just moved in," I replied. "I will do my best to figure out if she has good intentions. Why even invite her? What does she have to offer?" he asked. "She has offered home services like cooking and cleaning in exchange for protection. She was with Pearl," I told him. "Like I said, I will do my best to determine her intentions. You need to be more careful about who you invite into the home" he scolded. "Getting mixed signals here, first I'm a 'great leader' now I'm 'not making good decisions,'" I said, rolling my eyes. "Ugh, I hate that, it's a bad habit," Arturo said.

"So when are we leaving?" Arturo asked. "I figured it will be okay to visit at least one day" I said, looking at both of them to see their reactions. They looked satisfied with my response. "Okay then, we will leave tomorrow evening" I said. "Great, that gives me a little time to get some things together," Arturo replied. "We should head back to David and Sarah's place, spend some time with them before we leave," James said. I nodded my head to agree with him. "Will you come over there tomorrow? Or should we come meet you back here?" I asked Arturo. "I can meet you guys over there," he replied. "Great, we'll see you tomorrow then" I said. Arturo grabbed me by the arm to pull me closer and whispered in my ear, "did you give Margo the letter?" I nodded my head and whispered back, "she's hurt, but you may still be able to win her back." He nodded as he released my arm.

James and I headed back to David and Sarah's house. I enjoyed walking with him, our relationship seemed pressured all the time. Except when we were here, alone, just walking side by side. In this moment, life seemed perfect. I wish I could freeze time and stay here with him, forever. Especially when it seemed like he was reading my mind and looked at me with the biggest smile on his face, he was so handsome. "What are you thinking about?" he asked. "Just how handsome you are, and how perfect this is," I said, motioning around with my arms as if to say, everything. "You and your beauty are what makes it perfect," he replied. I stopped, and moved in front of him to make him stop. I reached up to pull his face to mine and kissed him. I kissed him deeply and passionately. I didn't want to stop, but I knew we had to get back before it got too dark, so I slowly pulled away. He let out a moan of disappointment that I had stopped. "I know," I said, agreeing with his moan. He took me by the hand and we continued walking. I suddenly got a strange feeling that we were being watched. I saw a few trees nearby that we could hide behind.

"Go that way," I said, looking at the group of trees. "What is it?" he asked in a whisper. "I think someone is following us," I whispered back. "Shouldn't we just keep going?" he asked. "No, what if it is someone or something bad? We can't lead it back to David and Sarah and Julie" I replied. He nodded and we walked in the same pace we had been walking toward the group of trees. Once we got to the trees, I started looking around, trying to see if I could spot anyone or anything. "You want me to climb up one? See if I can see anything?" James asked. "Sure," I responded. He grabbed a limb and started climbing. He was really good at maneuvering up the tree. I had never seen him climb before, I guess there was never a reason to. He got to the top in no time at all with ease.

He looked down at me and shook his head to let me know that he couldn't see anyone. I felt magic in the air now. Someone was going to attack us, so I got into a fighting position. James noticed me getting prepared to fight and started coming down quickly. "What is it?!" he asked with worry as he hit the ground. "I can feel magic being used nearby" I told him, quietly. A wolf walked out of the woods, into our view. "Emma?" James said. She changed into her human form. She walked toward us, naked. "I didn't mean to scare you guys, I saw you and wanted to say hello, but I was in my wolf form" she said as she got closer. James took his shirt off and offered it to her, she took it, it covered her as a dress would. She smiled at him, "thanks," she said. "How have you been?" he asked her. "Good, a bit lonely since all of our friends except Theo have gone with you" she replied.

"Are you okay?" she asked, looking at me. "I felt magic, like witch type magic, I didn't realize I could feel shapeshifter magic the same way" I said, still worried that there may be someone else nearby. "I didn't see anyone else around" Emma replied, like she had read my mind. I nodded, still not sure that what I felt was her magic. "Can you come to David and Sarah's with us?" James asked her. "Sure," she replied. The three of us continued walking together. "So what have you been up to?" James asked her. "Just roaming around, looking for things to get into basically, I've been spending a lot of time as a wolf. It's freeing, I met another wolf. He has more wolf friends, and he has formed a pack. He offered me a position in the pack, but I told him no, I prefer to be alone." she said. "Why?" I asked. "Why, what?" she replied.

"I'm sorry, you said that you were lonely, and then you said you turned down an opportunity to be with others like you. I don't understand," I said. "Our 'group' grew up together, we've always been really close, like siblings," James said. "I guess I can understand that, that's how I feel about Jason," I replied, knowing that at one point I had a crush on Jason made me a little jealous of how close she was walking to James. She had to have seen us kissing, whether she would admit it or not. "How is everyone else doing?" she asked, looking at James. "Good, Levi was miserable, he's better now, I think because Alice is there now too" he told her. "I've always thought those two would make a good couple," she replied. "They aren't a couple, as far as I know. I think she just helps him feel more comfortable" he replied. I just listened to them silently for the rest of the walk.

We reached the house and went inside, I could smell that wonderful smell of dinner. "Is it okay if we have a guest?" James yelled out. David came down the hallway toward us, "sure" he said. "I think I have some clothes that will fit you, if you like," I said to her. She nodded her head and followed me into the room where we stayed. She shut the door behind her. I found a cute sundress with flower prints that I offered her. She snarled her nose as if she didn't like it. "Sorry, that's all I really have," I told her. She nodded, "thanks," she said and took it from my hand. "You don't like me very much, do you?" I asked. "I don't really know you," she replied. "Do you like him?" I asked her. "What do you mean?" she asked, innocently. I rolled my eyes. "You know what I mean," I told her, narrowing my eyes.

"He's like a brother to me," she said. "I have one of those too, but at one point, I did have a crush on him" I said. "I seen you two kissing, I'm not dumb, and I'm not going to try to come between you. I wouldn't do that," she said. I nodded at her. "Good, we have enough to worry about without having petty stuff added to it" I told her with my eyes still narrowed. She pulled his shirt off in front of me and put the dress on. There was a knock on the door. "Are you two almost done? Dinner is ready" James said, without opening the door. "We are coming" I yelled loud enough for him to hear through the door. He was still at the door when we opened it, she walked out and I grabbed him and pulled him in and shut the door. "I don't want her to come back with us," I told him firmly. He looked at me confused. "I don't trust her, she's not telling us something" I told him. He looked mad and confused now. "Is this another of your jealousy episodes?" he accused. I gave him an evil look and walked out of the bedroom.

The table was full of delicious looking food. Julie was sitting at the table now, without a high chair. "Gabella!" she said, excitedly. I smiled at her, "hi precious!" I said back to her. Emma was sitting at the table, James came in behind me and sat in between her and I. "I would love to go back with you guys and help in any way that I can" she said. I looked at him, with my 'I told you' look. "I'm not sure that is a good idea," he said. I smiled. "Why not? The rest of our group is there" she replied. "Exactly, I don't want to have anyone else to worry about," he replied. "I agree with James, we don't need more friends to worry about," I said. "Besides, you can't even be in your human form there," he added. David and Sarah ate quietly. "I told you, I've been spending most of my time as a wolf anyway," she said. "It's not a good idea" I said, flatly. She looked at me like she was disappointed, but I somehow felt that she wasn't giving up. We all started eating quietly.

When we were finished eating, James and I walked outside.

Emma followed us, she was starting to make me not enjoy my visit. I was starting to dislike her, which I didn't want to do because she was a friend that James cared a lot about. "Seriously, I think I would be happier with you guys," she said. "You will be alone, more so there than you are here," I replied. She gave me an evil look. "I am not trying to come between you two," she said. "It's just not a good idea," James said. Finally, he was taking my side. I felt like he knew that she had a crush on him as well and didn't want the extra drama in our lives. He was definitely getting on my good side, he would probably get laid tonight. She looked at him as though he had stabbed her in the gut. "So, it's a great idea that everyone else is there? But not me?" she said, sounding like her feelings were hurt. "I'm sorry, but we don't have room for you," I said.

"Thanks for dinner" she said and started walking away. "Emma!" James yelled after her. She shifted back into a wolf and ran quickly away. She didn't bother to take my dress off before shifting, she ripped it off with her teeth making sure it was completely ruined. "Good thing I didn't really like that dress" I said, looking at James. He looked like he was upset. I knew he didn't want to hurt her and I felt bad for making him. I grabbed his hand, "it was the right choice, we don't need to worry about her, she'll be fine here. And when this is all over, you can visit her if you want" I told him. He took his hand away from me and walked inside without saying anything. I sat down on the porch instead of following him. I felt like I should give him some space and time to calm down.

David came outside and sat down beside me. "One of the many reasons you two should have never got together," he said. I nodded, "I know you told James to not be with me, why didn't you ever tell me not to get with him?" I asked. "I didn't know you like that, besides, would it have made a difference?" he replied. I put my head down without responding, there was no need to respond, we both knew the answer. We sat in silence for a while. David finally stood up, "for what it's worth, I'm happy for the two of you" he said before walking inside. I didn't feel like going inside and facing James quite yet, I didn't want to fight with him. I spotted some fairies gathering where the forest met the yard, so I walked out to join them. I sat down on the ground close to them, they came over to me and made a circle around me. "Hello" I said to them. They started flying around my head. I felt something fall gently onto my head, I reached up to touch it, it felt like a flower of some sort. I took it off to see what it was, they had made me a tiara from flowers. It was so pretty and I felt so honored, I placed it back onto my head. "Thank you, it's beautiful," I told them. They continued to buzz and dance around me for a while.

"You really think you have time to be a fairy queen?" Sarah said from behind me. I jumped because I hadn't heard her walk up. "Sorry, I didn't mean to startle you," she said. "It's okay, and what do you mean fairy queen?" I asked. "You accepted the position" she said, pointing at the tiara. "Oh, do you think they will be angry with me? I didn't know, I just thought it was a pretty gift" I said. "I think they will understand, just take it off and lay it on the ground," she said. So, I did, some of them looked a bit upset, others looked a bit confused, while the rest picked it up and flew away with it into the forest. "I'm sorry guys, I have to go back to my dimension and be the queen there" I told them. They all flew into the forest after I said that.

I got up off the ground and Sarah and I walked back toward the house. "I never did like Emma, for what it's worth. Something is off about that girl" Sarah said. "What do you mean?" I asked. "I can't really explain it, I hope she doesn't give you guys any more trouble," she said. I sighed, "I hope not too, I'm going to put an extra protection spell on the property" I told her as I stopped and headed back toward the forest. She nodded and continued walking toward the house. After I placed my spell on the property, I walked back toward the house myself. James was sitting on the porch, he watched me walk up without saying anything.

I stepped onto the porch and sat down next to him. He reached over and took my hand and just held it silently for a few minutes. "I'm sorry" he finally said. "For what?" I asked. "I know that she is in love with me, I have never had feelings like that for her though. I do care about her and don't want to hurt her in any way" he said. I nodded, "don't blame yourself for her feelings. She can't go with us, she would get herself hurt to hurt you" I told him. He nodded, "I know" he said. "I want to try to contact Theo, maybe he can keep an eye on her," he added. "Whatever will make you feel better" I said, smiling at him. He smiled back, I was happy that he wasn't angry with me. I took my hand back and got up, I stood in front of him and said, "let's go inside."

I put my hand out to help him up, he took my hand but didn't use it for help. He just held it, I couldn't believe how hard I had fallen for him. I had never felt like this about anyone, maybe he was right, maybe he was my twin flame. I had crushes before, even fallen in love once or twice, or at least I thought I had, I questioned that now. We walked inside, I didn't see anyone else, they must have already gone to bed. We walked into the bedroom still holding hands. He shut the door behind him and turned me toward him. He lifted my head and started kissing me. "I love you" he said, in between kisses. "I love you too" I somehow managed to say.

I reached for his belt, unbuckled it and slid it off. I put my hands under his shirt and lifted that off as well, I loved his muscles and skin tone, so sexy. I started kissing his neck and then went down his chest. I used my tongue on his muscular abdomen. He moaned with excitement which made me more excited. I continued going down, when I got to his pants I unbuttoned them and pulled them down. I kissed his penis gently. I started licking the side and I put the tip in my mouth. He moaned more. I teasingly sucked on the tip for a minute until he couldn't take it anymore and he grabbed my head gently but forcefully pulled me forward until his penis touched the back of my mouth. I slowly sucked and licked, moving my head back and forth. The sounds he was making made me want him so badly. After a few minutes he pulled out of my mouth and picked me up and threw me gently onto the bed.

He went straight for my vagina with his tongue, it felt so good, I moaned as I grabbed his head, I started pulling his hair. "I'm gonna come!" I said. He didn't stop until I orgasmed. Then he made his way back up, he was on top of me and he slid into me. It felt so damn amazing, I let out a moan. I started kissing his neck and chest as he moved in and out. He was breathing so hard and so was I. I was about to orgasm again, he was so damn hot tonight. "Harder" I whispered in his ear. He started moving faster and harder and soon, I was having another orgasm. I moaned with delight. He didn't stop, he wasn't finished, and I was completely okay with that. He kept going and going, "I want you to orgasm one more time" he whispered in my ear. That was so damn sexy, I'm pretty sure that two was my tops, but he managed to top my top that night. I didn't just have one more orgasm, but two more. Then he finally came himself and rolled over onto the bed beside me.

We both lay there, silently until we caught our breath. "That was amazing" I said, rolling over toward him and putting my arm around him. He smiled, "yes, it was," he said. "You should put some clothes on, just in case someone comes in here" he said as he got up and started getting dressed himself. I didn't want to, I wanted to lie there naked next to him, but I got up and started putting clothes on like he had suggested. He lay back down in the bed and I lay back down in the same position with my arm over his chest. I liked to feel his heartbeat. I rubbed his face and neck until he fell asleep. I closed my eyes and followed shortly after.

Sixteen

A little help from our friends

I had a peaceful, dreamless sleep that night. I woke in the morning feeling refreshed and relaxed. James was still asleep when I woke, I started rubbing his face and neck again until he opened his eyes. "You did that to put me to sleep, now you are doing it to wake me up" he said with a smile. "You enjoy it, either way" I said, teasingly. "I enjoy you," he said, rolling over and putting his arms around me. I giggled because he surprised me. There was a knock on the door, "are you guys coming to breakfast?" David asked through the door. I giggled again like a silly high school girl. "Yeah, be right out," James called out. He rolled out of bed and grabbed me and started pulling me out of the bed too. "Ugh, that's not fair" I moaned.

We walked out of the bedroom and into the dining room. "I was about to put everything away, get what you want," Sarah said. I sat down at the table and James sat next to me. "Thank you," he said. I grabbed a biscuit and a piece of sausage and started eating.

It seemed kind of awkward, not knowing if they heard us last night. I wanted to sink into the chair and disappear. But that wasn't an option, we were all adults here, except Julie of course and I didn't see her anywhere. "Where is Julie?" I asked. "She is outside playing, I think she is becoming the new fairy queen since the other one resigned" Sarah said, teasingly. I smiled at her, "I'm sure she will make a more fitting queen than the last one anyway" I said, with a smile. Sarah walked out of the room and it made it a little easier to relax just a little.

"Why are you so uptight?" James asked. "Aren't you scared that they heard us?" I said, quietly. "No," he whispered back confidently. I just kept eating. When I was finished eating I went to find Julie and join in on her coronation. I walked outside, Sarah was right, Julie was over by the forest, surrounded by fairies and they were placing a tiara made of flowers on her head. Julie giggled and tried to catch one of the fairies that was flying around her head. I spotted David in the field, I had a flashback to when I first met James. I couldn't believe he was such a jerk to me then. I got closer to Julie, "mind if I sit down with you?" I asked her as I got close enough for her to notice me. "Gab!" she squealed with excitement. I giggled at her cuteness. I sat down next to her and the fairies flew around both of us, until Julie fell asleep and I carried her back inside.

After I lay her down in her bed, I walked back outside. I saw Arturo walking out of the forest with a bag. I was beyond excited that he was coming back with us. I knew he could help me so much. James was out in the field with David now. I walked toward Arturo to meet him halfway. "Want me to take your bag?" I asked him. He looked at me like I was crazy, "I know I'm older than you, but I can carry my own things, thank you" he said with a smile. "I didn't mean to insult you, I was just trying to be helpful," I replied, trying not to laugh.

"I am so happy that you are coming back with us to help," I said. "I am happy to serve you, you will be our leader, you know?" He replied. "That is the ultimate goal, I suppose, if I don't die trying," I replied. He looked at me very seriously, "dying is not an option, dear" he said. I looked at him and nodded in agreement, even though I wouldn't make a promise to anyone. All I could do was fight and hope for the best. We walked to the house so he could set his things down and then we walked together over to David and James.

"Arturo! Good to see you!" David said, like he hadn't seen him in a while. I didn't ask, but I supposed it was possible that they hadn't seen each other since we were here last. They both had their own lives. "You as well, friend" Arturo replied, putting his hand out to shake David's. James smiled at Arturo to greet him. I walked over and stood close to James, "so what have you guys been doing?" I asked him. "Just talking, catching up," James replied. "Are you guys ready to go?" Arturo asked. "Can we go after dinner?" I replied. "Sure, I don't see a problem with that," Arturo replied.

We walked inside to find dinner was ready. "I wish I could take you with me Sarah, you are such an amazing cook" I said. "Thank you sweetie," she replied. "Misty isn't a bad cook, and she's teaching everyone else to cook too," James said. Sarah looked up quickly, "did you say *Misty*?" she asked. "She has proven her loyalty," I replied to her. "Wow, I would think if you can convince Misty to come to your side that you would have no trouble with the rest" she said. "Well, things aren't exactly what they seem, or what they used to be. I actually have Pearl as a prisoner at the moment" I said. Sarah dropped her fork at that one. "Are you sure you are fighting on the right side?" she asked. "Of course we are, things are just a little different than they used to be or what we expected," James replied defensively.

"Okay, I trust you guys to know what you are doing" Sarah said as she began eating again. "We are doing the best we can, I'm sure we will make mistakes along the way, but we are trying our best to keep them at a minimum" I told her, trying to make her feel better, although from the look on her face, I failed. Everyone was quiet for the rest of the meal. I helped clean up the dishes when we were all finished. "I'm sorry for butting in," Sarah said. "Oh no, don't be sorry, I like having your input. It's just you don't know all the details" I replied. "I know I don't, I'm not there, I just want everyone to be safe. I love you guys and I just couldn't deal with it if anything happened to any of you" she said. I hugged her, "I know, I'm doing everything I can to keep us safe, I promise" I told her. She wiped a tear from her eye and nodded her head as she walked away.

I felt bad leaving like this, but we had to get back. We had to make sure that I wasn't making mistakes. I went to find everyone, David, James and Arturo were waiting on the porch. I walked outside, "I'm ready, whenever you guys are" I said to Arturo and James. "Sarah and I have talked, we think it would be a good idea for me to go back with you, just for a little while" David said. "Why?" I asked. "Extra muscle, extra brains, you can never have too many of either" he replied. All I could think was she didn't trust me, and why was it so important that she was willing to sacrifice her husband, the father of her child? "I don't think that's a good idea" I said.

James grabbed me by the arm and pulled me to the side. "It will give them peace of mind," he said. "I don't want anything to happen to him!" I said, defensively. "Your brother, her husband, Julie's father!" I added. "We will make sure that nothing happens to him, I promise," James said. I knew this was one battle I was going to lose. "What about Sarah and Julie? Who is going to make sure they are safe while he's gone?" I asked. "I talked to Theo, he's going to be here soon, hopefully before we leave. He's going to stay here until David comes back" James replied. "Fine! I'm not happy about it though!" I said as I walked away from him.

I went to find Sarah, she must know, that's why she was so upset about how we are handling things. I walked into the house and found her sitting on the couch playing with Julie. "I didn't know he wanted to come back with us," I said, walking into the room. "He's made up his mind, and I support his decision," she replied. "You don't have to, you can fight him on this," I said, trying to get her on my side. "There's no point, I don't want to fight with him. I trust you guys to keep him safe for us" she said, looking at Julie instead of me. "I guess I don't have a choice in the matter since I'm the only one against it" I replied, walking back outside. I spotted Theo walking out of the forest, I guess it was almost time for us to go.

Theo walked over to greet James, they shook hands and smiled while talking, I was too far away to tell what they were saying. I kept walking toward them, when I got close enough, I asked them when we were leaving. "We're all ready," David said. "You're not even going to go say goodbye?" I asked. "I already said goodbye," he replied. I rolled my eyes, I was so irritated with him, leaving his family here. "There's that attitude," David said with a smile. I wasn't amused with him at all, I just gave him a blank stare. Theo had already walked into the house. We all grabbed each other's hands, in a circle and Arturo started the spell. Soon I felt that familiar feeling of not existing, and then I felt cold air on my skin. I opened my eyes, we were back. It was probably some time between midnight and four a.m.

We walked toward the house, not saying anything, it was bitter cold out, I think we all just wanted to feel warmth again. We entered the front door, the house was quiet, the fire that had been in the fireplace only had a few embers left burning. Nonetheless, it felt warm inside, especially after being outside in the cold air. I showed David to an empty room, I put him next to the one I had Pearl in. I opened the door to the room she was in, she was still there, where I had left her, still sleeping. I turned around to go help Arturo get settled and Cori was standing in the hall. I screamed because the sight of her scared me half to death. James, David and Arturo came running. "What?!" James yelled. "Nothing, sorry, I just got startled" I replied. "What are you doing?" I asked Cori. "I heard people moving about and I came to see what was going on" she replied. "Everything is fine, you can go back to bed," I said. She nodded and walked away. I don't think she saw inside the room where Pearl was, she was standing far enough back that she wouldn't have seen her, I was almost positive of that.

"Is everything okay?" I heard Misty say, as she walked out of the shadows toward me. "Yes, everything is fine, sorry I just got startled," I said. She saw Arturo and narrowed her eyes. "You went back to dimension 2?" she asked accusingly. "Yes, I needed Arturo's help, so I went to bring him back here for a little while" I replied. She just nodded and walked away. David, who had been putting his things up, came out of his room back into the hallway. "I think we should all try to get a few hours of sleep, or at least rest and start dealing with everything in the morning," I told David, Arturo and James. They all looked at me and nodded in agreement. Arturo and David went into their rooms and James followed me back to ours. I didn't feel sleepy, but I did want to rest. I looked at the time, it was two thirty a.m. I lay down on the bed and James lay down next to me. I put my head on his chest and he started playing with my hair, it wasn't long before I drifted to sleep.

I was on a busy street, one that I didn't recognize. I was walking, I was alone, but surrounded by people going their own ways. I started looking around, trying to find anyone or anything that I may recognize. Things seemed a bit more sophisticated around me, cars seemed to be driving themselves, billboard lights were clearer, no one seemed to notice me at all. I heard a familiar voice calling my name, I started looking around, looking for the source, I think it was her, my mom. I couldn't find her, it was like she was trying to reach me, but couldn't. I think I heard her say, "bring Jason back, and watch out for Cori, she will turn on you in a heartbeat." Then I woke up, the sun was up, so I must have slept longer than I had wanted.

I rolled over, James wasn't there. I guess he thought I needed to sleep in for some reason. I got out of bed and walked out of my room, the house seemed quite busy, I smelled food being cooked. Conan, Hale, and Damian were in the living room talking with Arturo. Levi, Alice, and James were on the porch with David. Misty and Cori were in the kitchen, cooking. My stomach growled, so I decided to go to the kitchen. "Good morning" Cori said, as I walked in. "Good morning," I replied. "Sorry about that scare last night," she said. "No worries," I told her. "So, what's on the agenda today?" Misty asked me. I looked at Cori, I didn't feel comfortable discussing things in front of her. "Would you like me to leave so you can talk business?" she asked. "If you don't mind, I just don't want you to have to worry about things that have nothing to do with you" I replied, trying not to insult her. "Of course," she replied, walking out of the room.

After I made sure she was out of earshot, I looked at Misty, "now that we have Arturo here, I would like to go get Jason, and bring him here" I told her. She nodded, his allegiance will still be to my coven, and since I am on your side now, he will be also, if he survives," she said. I sighed, "Is there anything we can do to guarantee his survival?" I asked her. She shook her head, "not that I know of, Arturo may know of something to at least help his odds" she said. I nodded and walked out to go join the rest of the witches to let them know what I wanted to do. I walked into the living room where they were all still sitting and talking.

"Hey" I said as I walked in and sat down with them. "Hi, we were just telling Arturo what all has been going on," Damian said. I looked at him a little confused, I had already told him. Maybe Arturo was just being nice and listening because he didn't want to be rude, or maybe he wanted to hear a different perspective? "Okay, the next thing I want to conquer is, checking Pearl to see if Xander has her under a spell and removing it, if we can. And I want to go get Jason and bring him back and hopefully help him transition" I said. "Neither of those things will be easy," Hale said. "I know," I replied. "Is any of this easy though?" I added. "No, it's not, you're right," Conan said. Arturo just sat quietly like he was absorbing the conversation through his pores. "Breakfast is ready!" Misty yelled from the kitchen. The giants walked inside and headed toward the kitchen, James looked at me and smiled as he walked by. I smiled back at him, "we should go eat" I said, looking around at the witches. We all got up and headed toward the kitchen. I noticed that Cori hadn't come back down, so I yelled up the stairs for her. "Coming" she replied.

We all ate in the dining room, some of us had to stand up to eat, there weren't enough seats for everyone. Everyone made small talk as we ate, not mentioning anything important because of Cori. I started feeling like I had made a mistake bringing her here, I didn't want everyone to feel like they had to hide things from someone here, this was supposed to be our space, our shelter from the enemy, had I brought the enemy in? I needed to get Pearl on our side, that would make me feel better about having Cori here. "How did you sleep last night, Cori?" I asked. "Just fine except when you guys came in and woke me," she replied. "Sorry about that, we were trying to be quiet," I replied. "It's okay ma'am" she said. I gave her a half smile, not knowing if I could trust her made me feel uneasy. "You guys go take care of business, I will clean everything up when we are finished eating," Cori said, maybe sensing that I was suspicious of her, and trying to be helpful.

When we were finished eating, I got Arturo alone and told him about my dream. "I don't understand how she is still communicating with you, or how she's ever managed to do so," he said. "I'm sure we can figure that out later. Right now I want to do what she said, bring Jason back, heal Pearl and figure out where the elf stands" I said. He nodded, "we'll try" he said, simply. "Should we get the rest of the witches and start working on Pearl?" I asked. "Sure," he replied. I walked around finding all of the witches, Misty included and took them to the room where I had Pearl tied up. She was awake, we quickly closed the door and I reinforced the sound blocking spell so no one else would hear what was going on.

"How dare you!" she yelled. "Pearl, will you listen to me please?" I asked her. "No! You kidnapped me and held me hostage, I will not listen to you or anyone else! You will let me go right now!" she demanded. Hale walked over and dropped another sleeping spell on her and she closed her eyes and went limp. "I hate doing this" I said, more to myself even though it was out loud. Arturo walked over to her and closed his eyes and put his arm over her body, like he was scanning. It wasn't very long before he nodded his head, "it is a love spell, a very powerful one at that" he said as he pulled his hands back. "I don't know how to break it," he added. "We have to figure out how to set her free, if we can't do it, we are going after Xander and we will make him take it off" I said, angrily. "How dare he take away her free will, just to use her!" I said, my blood starting to boil with anger.

"Why don't you and a couple of your giant friends go get Jason and bring him back, I will keep her asleep for now, and we will brainstorm and try to figure out a way to get the spell off of her" Hale said, as he grabbed me by the shoulders and pushed me out of the door. I just went, he was right, I needed to get out, cool off, and go get Jason. Of course I wanted James to go with me, so I went to find him. He was with David and Levi on the porch. I walked out of the front door and stood next to him. "Witch business done?" he asked, looking at me. I gave him a funny look, "witch business is never done" I replied. "I need to go get Jason, I want you and one more to come with me in case I need extra muscle" I said to James, grabbing his upper arm and winking. "I would love to go," David said. "I would rather you stay here so I know you are completely safe" I replied smartly. "I can go," Levi offered. I nodded and walked away before David could argue.

I went to my room to grab a few things and a change of clothes just in case we ended up having to stay overnight somewhere again. There was a knock on my door, "come in" I yelled. David opened the door and stepped inside. "I was here for a while before, you know? Watching after you" he said. "I could not live with myself if anything happened to you, you are like a brother to me. You have a daughter to go home to, I didn't want you to come, and I'm not going to agree to you going on a mission" I stated firmly. He hung his head and walked back out of my bedroom without saying anything else.

After getting my things together I went and found James and Levi and we started walking to the pullover spot where we kept the vehicles. I decided not to use my magic to warp us, in case we ran into trouble on the road that I would need to use my magic. I started wondering why I hadn't told one of the other witches to come with us, just in case. But I was fine with them working on one problem while I took care of another. "So, what's the plan?" Levi asked. "We're going to drive to the hospital where we left him and hope that he's still there," I said. "Where else would he be?" James asked. "I don't know, what if he woke up? What if he didn't make it? Or what if he did and he's confused and lost?" I said. "I think you should calm down and not jump to conclusions," James said. "That's why I don't have a plan, I've been trying not to think about it too much," I replied. "We'll go to the hospital, where I'm sure he will still be and we will bring him back here where the other witches and you will help him" James said, trying to get me to feel better.

We finally reached the vehicles. I had already asked Misty if we could take her car, because it was the best one we had right now.

"We need to get some more vehicles, I mean, we have a mansion on a lot of land and we just have this car and the truck" I said. James laughed, "yeah, we'll just steal a couple, no big deal." I rolled my eyes at him. "We should get a bus, seriously though" I said. "I'll not be a bus driver," Levi said jokingly. "You didn't wear the catsuit," James said, sounding disappointed. "I'm hoping that there won't be any fighting," I replied seriously. "Yeah, we know how that turned out last time," he said. "I dealt with it in my normal clothes that time," I replied. "You should call the hospital and try to find out if he's still there," Levi suggested. "Good idea," James agreed.

I didn't want to, I didn't want to hear bad news just yet, but I knew it would be better to find out now if I could, so I started Googling the number. After I found the number I hit the call button, with my nerves frayed and feeling nauseous. "New Orleans East, ICU, how can I direct your call?" a woman's voice said. "I'm looking for my brother who has been missing for a couple of months, I wanted to know if you have any John Doe's" I said. "Yes there are a couple, and one has been here for a couple of months," she replied. "Can you give me a description?" I asked. "No, I'm sorry, you are welcome to come in and see if you know him and help identify him" she said. "What about identifying markings?" I asked. "What do you mean?" she replied. "He had just got a tattoo on his chest," I replied. "I'm not sure," she said. "Okay, thanks," I said as I hung up the phone. Levi and James both glanced at me from the front seat. "It's probably him, all she would say is that he's been there for a couple of months," I said.

We continued driving in silence until my stomach started growling. "Can we stop for some food?" I asked. "Heck yeah we can, I'm tired of driving anyway, one of you can drive next round" Levi said. "I will, because I probably won't be able to drive on the way back" I said, thinking I would have to sit with Jason and watch him. Levi pulled off at the next exit. There was a small diner that we all agreed on. There weren't a lot of businesses off of the exit, but there was a small gas station for us to fill up the car, so we did that before going to the diner. "I don't think you should get out," James said. I glared at him, "I wasn't going to as long as you guys hurry, I can wait until we get to the diner to go to the restroom" I told him. He smiled at me, he was outside, filling up the car and he bent down to my window, I rolled it down and he stuck his head in and kissed me. "What are you two doing? We're on a mission here" Levi said as he walked up to the car. He had gone inside to buy snacks for later. I rolled my eyes at him and he laughed.

He got back in and we continued to the diner. Levi went in to scope it out before James and I followed. He sent a signal that all was clear and we followed. I hated this part of my life, always having to look over my shoulder, always having to have bodyguards when I left the house. I needed this to be over, for my own peace of mind. We sat down at a booth by a window so we could see the car. A short older chubby lady came to take our order. After we placed our order we began making a plan, quietly. "I will glamor us, like I did before. Levi, you should wait in the car so we can make a quick getaway" I whispered. "This is all assuming that he is there?" James asked. "Yes, of course," I replied. "So, how will we get him out?" James asked. "I can glamor us to look like doctors, we will just take him, like we know what we are doing" I replied, with a half smile.

After we finished eating we paid the waitress and got back on the road. I drove this time as promised. I put on my favorite rock/metal playlist and put the pedal to the metal as they say. James grabbed the handle above the window, "slow down! What the hell?!" he yelled. I just winked at him and smiled. For whatever reason, I felt like driving fast and I felt invincible. Levi didn't say anything, he just lay back in the back seat looking totally relaxed. After I merged onto I-20 I slowed down just a little so James would relax a little. It seemed to work, I reached over and took his hand and smiled, he smiled back. “Don’t start getting mushy up there please” Levi said from the back. I gave him an eye roll through the rear view mirror. “We’ve made good time, only three more hours,” I said, looking at the GPS. “I can drive for a little while if you want,” James offered. “No, I’m good, I don’t think I will be able to drive at all on the way back” I replied. “Okay, just trying to be nice,” he said defensively.

“We need to find a witch that can see the future,” Levi said. “Why is that?” I asked. “So we’ll know what to do and when to do it,” he replied. “Yeah, I’m just not sure that is a thing. Because the future hasn’t been written, every little thing we do results in a different outcome, plus knowing doesn’t mean that you can change it,” I said, not wanting to mention Arturo’s gift/curse however you wanted to look at it. “I guess,” he replied. “I mean, have you ever heard of anyone that could actually see the future?” I asked. “No, but I figured witches can do just about anything they want,” he replied. “Just about, but not everything” I said. My phone rang, it was Damian, I answered on video. “Just checking in,” he said. “We are about two and half to three hours away from him still. How are things there?” I asked. “Good, we are just keeping her asleep. Arturo went out for a stroll in the woods a while back” he said, with a little concern in his voice. “Don’t worry about him, I’m sure he’s just saying hi to Margo” I replied. “Okay then, be careful, I’ll check in later” he said and ended the call.

The music started blaring again as I continued driving. “That was nice of him to check in,” James said, breaking the silence. “Yeah, I was starting to wonder how everything was going back at the house,” I replied. “I have to go to the bathroom,” Levi said. I rolled my eyes at him in the rearview again, “you shouldn’t have drank all that soda” I told him. “But I did, *mom,*” he replied sarcastically. “Rest area ahead” James said, pointing at a sign that stated just that. “Fine” I agreed, not going to admit that I needed to go myself. I started slowing down and pulled into the rest area, there weren't a lot of people, a few truck drivers in the back area that was designated for them and an older couple that stopped to walk their dog. I didn't feel a need to be concerned so I headed to the women's room while the guys went to the men's room.

We quickly took care of business and got back on the road with no attacks. "I'm glad nothing bad has happened so far" I said as I pulled back onto the interstate. "Don't jinx us," Levi said. "You're right, I'll keep my mouth shut" I replied. I reached over to turn the music back up, I loved playing it loud, something I didn't get to do a lot anymore since I didn't want to disturb anyone else. "Do you have any snacks back there?" I asked Levi. He threw a small bag of Doritos at me. "Thanks" I said. Looking at the GPS, it now said two hours. The drive was starting to make me tired and anxious. "You okay?" James asked me. "Yeah, I'm fine," I replied, smiling at him.

The last two hours passed uneventfully. I was glad to pull into the hospital parking lot. I quickly did the glamor spell on the three of us so that none of the outside cameras would see the real us. Levi appeared to be an elderly black man while James and I looked like middle aged doctors. Levi hopped into the driver seat, "I'll call or text you when we are on our way out" I told him. James and I got out of the car and walked into the hospital. We walked by several people, patients, nurses, and doctors, luckily no one spoke to us, just nodded to say, 'hi.' We went to the elevator, a sign said that the ICU was on the fourth floor, so that's where we went.

The elevator opened into a waiting room where several people were sitting, some were having snacks, others drinking coffee and looking like they hadn't slept in days and some were just staring off into space with blank expressions. I walked over to a speaker box and pushed the button. "Visiting hours starts in thirty minutes" a voice said. "We are interns from TUL, we lost our badges," I said. I had looked up colleges to get medical degrees in the area and hoped it would work. We heard a buzz and a click of the door opening.

"Come to the nurses station" the voice said over the speaker. We walked through the door. The nurses station was directly in front of us. The sounds of the medical machines beeping and moans of patients was unnerving to me. I could never work in the medical field.

"We don't have any interns on the schedule today" an older white man said from behind the counter. I looked at James and said, "hmm, did we get our schedules mixed up?" "I don't think so," James replied. I didn't see anyone else around, so I used a spell to make him see us on the computer while James distracted him asking about a plant that was sitting on the counter. "Well, I guess we need to go back and talk to the director at the school," I said, looking at James. "Wait a minute, you're on here now. I don't know what happened" the man said. "Oh, okay, great," I replied. He handed us both badges. "Thank you, I am studying coma patients, do you have any of those here?" I asked. "Yes we do, room 444" he said. "Thank you," I said. "His chart is on the door," the man said as I walked away.

James followed behind me. "That was easier than I thought it would be," he said in a low voice. "Let's just get this done before we get caught," I replied. We found the room, the door was closed. I was just hoping that it was him as I opened it. It was him, his hair had grown out, and some of his muscle mass had gone away. They had kept his face shaved for the most part, he did seem to have a five o'clock shadow, but other than that, it wasn't hard for me to recognize him. James was looking in his chart, "they noted that he has a fresh tattoo that won't heal" he said. I pulled his gown down so I could see, it looked the same as it had when I brought him here. "I don't think we will be able to 'walk' him out of the front door," I said. "So, what do you want to do?" James replied. "You go ahead to the car, text me when you are in and I will warp us to the parking lot" I said. He nodded, "okay, I wish we would have had a better plan, but I guess that will have to work" James said. I nodded at him, "go on" I said. He turned and walked out of the room, closing the door behind him.

After about ten minutes, my phone vibrated. *I'm in the car, we are ready to go* -James. I replied with a thumbs up to let him know that I saw it and I was on my way. I grabbed Jason's arm and warped us to the parking lot, hoping I would be at least close to our car. When we landed in the parking lot, Jason's limp body started falling, I caught his head before it hit the pavement. I quickly looked around, I didn't think anyone saw us, I saw a sign with the number eleven on it and quickly grabbed my phone to call Levi. "We are in aisle eleven," I said as soon as he answered. I heard the motor rev up as he pulled out. "I don't see it yet," he said. "Over there!" I heard James say. I felt relieved that he saw me or at least where I was. I could hear the car both on the phone and driving toward me so I laid Jason down and stood up, I saw them so I hung up the phone.

They pulled up, James got out quickly and helped me get Jason into the back seat. I climbed in the back seat with him, pushing his legs out of my way while James got back into the passenger seat and Levi quickly pulled away from the hospital. "Woo," I said, breathing a sigh of relief. "Yeah," James said, agreeing with me. "Can you take these spells off of us?" Levi asked. I removed the glamor spell, we all looked like ourselves again. I was starting to feel tired, I had to be careful the rest of the way home and try not to use magic, so that I wouldn't be completely drained or get magic sickness again. "He looks rough," Levi said, pointing at Jason. "He's alive," I replied, brushing his long hair out of his face. I looked up to catch James giving me an evil look. I just ignored it, I didn't want to defend myself to him. Yes, in the past I did have feelings for Jason, but I was so in love with James that all I felt now for Jason was a close friend or family type of love, but I did still love him. I had known him almost my whole life and I wasn't going to just stop caring about him because I was in love with James.

My phone rang, it was Damian again, I answered on video again. "We got him," I said. "That's great news! No problems?" he asked. "Nothing too big," I replied. "Pearl is still asleep," he said. "Did Arturo come back?" I asked. "Yes," he said, looking around, "although, I don't know where he is right now," he added. "That's okay, I was just wondering" I replied with a smile. "Are you guys coming straight back? Or were you going to stop and rest for the night?" he asked. "We haven't really talked about it, but I think we should come straight back, I don't want Jason to wake up," I replied. "Yeah," Levi said, from the front. "Okay, if you guys need anything, don't hesitate to call," Damian said. "Thank you" I replied as I hung up the phone.

I lay back in the seat next to Jason and drifted to sleep. I must have been more tired than I had thought, when I woke up, we were home. "Wow, we are here already?" I said, stretching. "Yeah, you slept the entire time, I figured you used a lot of magic and that we should let you sleep to recharge," James said, opening my door. "Yeah, I felt tired, but I didn't think I would sleep the entire way. I should call Damian to come help us warp Jason back to the house" I said. "We already called, Arturo is supposed to meet us here actually, he should be here any minute" James said, looking around to see if he could spot him. I heard a rustle coming from the woods and looked, it was Arturo, with Margo by his side. I couldn't help but smile to see them walking together. I wished she could be in her human form so she could talk to him.

He walked up to the car, "warp back together?" he asked, looking at me. "Levi and I can walk, you two warp Jason back together" James said. I nodded in agreement and grabbed one of Jason's arms while Arturo grabbed the other and we warped to the front yard of the house and carried him the rest of the way inside. We lay him down on the couch, and called for Misty to come see him, since she would be his high priestess. "He looks rough, maybe we should have brought him back before now?" She said. "What do you mean?" I asked. "I don't know, I've never seen anyone go this long with the mark without turning or dying" she replied. "He can't die! We have to help him transition" I said. "We'll do what we can," Arturo reassured me. "Let's get him to a room, a comfortable bed and have Hale take the sleeping spell off" Misty said. I nodded in agreement.

We took him to the room next to Arturo's, which was across from the room I had Pearl in. "Anything new with her?" I asked, nodding toward the closed door. "No, we will have to go to Xander, try to convince him to remove the spell," Arturo said. I nodded, knowing that wasn't going to be an easy task. Hale walked up the hall toward us, "you need me?" he asked. "We need you to remove the spell that we placed on Jason," I said, choking back tears, because I knew he could die. He nodded, seeing the grief in my face, he put his hand on my arm, "what will be, will be," he said. "I know," I replied. Hale entered the room with Misty at his side, "best if you wait out here" he said as he closed the door.

Seventeen

Getting them back

I waited in the living room, James waited with me while looking online for used cars. I couldn't sit still, pacing back and forth. After what seemed like hours, but was only about forty five minutes, Hale walked into the living room. "I removed the spell, he's awake, very confused and complaining that the mark hurts" he said. "Do you think he will make it?" I asked, my voice shaking. "I don't know yet," he replied. "Can I go in?" I asked. "I don't see why not, as long as Misty is in there with you" he replied. I nodded my head and started walking toward the room where Jason was. James put his hand on my shoulder, "do you want me to go with you?" he asked. "No," I replied, simply.

I reached the door and opened it. Jason looked up at me. "She murdered Carly!" he yelled, pointing at me. "No sweety, Carly was bad, she did things without consulting me first" Misty told him. "We were in love," he said, starting to cry. I felt bad, he was so confused. "Do you remember who I am Jason?" I asked him. "Yes, Gabriela, I do remember you, what kind of question is that?" he replied, sounding like a smart ass. "Have you told him anything yet?" I asked Misty. "No, I'll let you try to explain it first," she said. I nodded my head at her. "Can I sit down with you, Jason?" I asked him. "If you are going to tell me what is going on, and get me some food, then yes" he replied. I sent James a text asking him to bring food, then I sat down on the bed with Jason.

"Carly was a witch, I am a witch, Misty here is a witch" I said, pointing at Misty. "What do you mean, *witch*?" he replied. "We have magical powers" I said, he was so confused, he didn't remember me telling him about it before we put him in a coma. "No you aren't, I've known you my entire life almost" he said. "I didn't know about it myself until my birthday," I said. "How long has it been since your birthday?" He asked. "Two and half months," I replied. "How?!" He yelled. "The mark that Carly put on your chest, it's a spell that will either turn you into a witch or kill you" I said. He reached for the mark on his chest, I nodded as if to say, 'yes that one.' "I had you put under a sleeping spell to delay her spell" I added. "So, what's it gonna be? Am I going to die? Or am I going to be a superhero?" He asked. "We still don't know, only time will tell, but it won't be a lot of time," I said, looking down.

"This is crazy," he said. "Trust me, I know," I replied. "Show me some magic," he said. I raised my hand and made the light go off, after a few seconds I made it come back on. "That's lame" he said, jokingly. I laughed, "magic isn't really something to play with, it can have effects on the body" I told him. "You mean if I don't die, and I get magical powers, I won't be able to use them?" he asked. "You will be able to use them, but if you use it too much, it can make you sick or kill you" I replied. He rolled his eyes, "can't you just take the spell off?" He asked. "No, we can't, all we can do is wait and see what happens now" I said. "Can I say goodbye to everyone?" He asked. I shook my head, no. "I told our friends that you and I are working on a super secret project and can't talk to them right now," I said. "And they bought that?" he asked. I shrugged my shoulders, "I guess, they stopped texting me" I replied.

"So, how much time do I have?" he asked. Not knowing the answer, I looked at Misty. "I would say a day, maybe less," she said. I cringed, I wasn't ready to lose him. "I wish there was something we could do," I said, starting to cry. "Hey, don't do that, I'm the one in trouble here, not you" Jason said. There was a knock on the door, it was James, bringing sandwiches. "Food! Yes, thank you!" Jason said, getting excited. "Who are you again?" Jason asked as he took the plate from him. James looked at me, "this is James, he's my boyfriend" I said, it felt weird saying it, it was the first time I had said it out loud. "Your *boyfriend*?" Jason asked, as he stuffed half a sandwich in his mouth. I nodded my head, yes. "Thank you James, you don't have to stay, I'll let you know if we need anything else," I told him. He just nodded and walked out of the room.

After eating about half of the plate of sandwiches, Jason handed me the plate and grabbed his stomach, "I'm stuffed now" he said. "How are you feeling?" I asked him. "Stronger actually," he replied. I looked at Misty with hope in my eyes, "it's too soon to tell" she said. "When would he be able to use magic?" I asked her. "The mark will begin to heal, then it will disappear, be absorbed by the body, then he will be able to use magic, if he's still alive" she said. I looked at the mark, it wasn't red anymore but it was still very visible. "Does it hurt anymore?" I asked Jason. "No, not really," he replied. Looking at Misty, "are you sure there isn't something we can try? An ointment or anything?" I asked her. She shook her head, no.

"Do I have to just lay here?" Jason asked. I looked at Misty. "I don't see why you can't get up and walk around," she said. I got up so he could try to get out of bed. He was still noticeably weak from having been asleep for two and half months, but he managed to sit up with his feet on the floor. I put out my arm to help him stand.

"You seem stronger, is it the magic?" He asked. "I've always been strong, there is a reason for that also, but I'll tell you about that after you transition" I said. "I'm weak as shit" he said, laughing. "You will get your strength back after you transition too" I said. He stood up, I pulled my arm back, but was ready to catch him if he fell.

"I think I'm good," he said. He started trying to walk and almost fell, so I caught him. "You are not good," I said. "Yeah, well, I will be right?" He replied. "Yes, you will! And you need to believe that! Don't question it!" I said. "Alright, so, I still have a lot of questions," he said, still trying to walk, slowly putting one foot in front of the other. "Did Carly put a love spell on me?" He asked. "No, if that were the case, it would have broke when she died," Misty said. "Then why do I still have strong feelings for her?" He asked. "I can't believe she's gone," he added, his voice cracking. "I didn't kill her for the record, and it was self defense" I said. "She put the mark on you, therefore, that makes her your maker, your sire, your feelings are related to the mark" Misty explained.

"I'm sure that is something I can help with once you transition and are stronger," I told him. "Who did kill her?" he asked. "It doesn't matter Jason, it had to be done, she wouldn't have stopped until I was dead" I told him. He nodded, but I knew he wouldn't be able to let it go until I removed his attachment to her. He finally made it to the door so I opened it for him. He stepped out and looked down the long hallway. "Really?" He said, sarcastically. "You don't have to, we can get help" I said. "No, I want to," he replied. I smiled, "Of course you do, stubborn ass" I said, still smiling. He managed to smile back.

Alice and Levi started walking toward us. "Why is everyone so tall?" Jason asked. I laughed and said, "that is something I will explain later." "You guys need help?" Levi asked as we got closer. "He wants to try to do it on his own," I replied. "Okay, let us know if you need anything" Levi said, as he and Alice walked away. "She's kinda hot," Jason said, talking about Alice. "Don't" I said, not sure how I felt about the comment. We continued very slowly down the hallway, it took about fifteen to twenty minutes, but we finally made it to the living room. "I recognize this room and that couch," Jason said. "You want to sit on the couch, rest for a bit?" I asked. "Sure," he replied. I helped him over to the couch where he plopped down. "Ah, yes, this is good," he said. I giggled.

"Is Cori cooking?" I asked Misty. "I think so, I told her that I wouldn't be able to leave Jason's side for a while," she replied. "When dinner is ready, I'll help you get to the kitchen," I said to Jason. He nodded his head. "So, I'm feeling a little stronger still, fatigued but stronger, if that makes any sense" Jason said, looking at me. I smiled, hopefully that was a good sign, but I had no idea if it was or not. I looked at Misty to see if she had any answers, but she just shrugged her shoulders. "Can I see the mark?" I asked Jason. "Sure" he said, pulling the top of his shirt down. It wasn't red anymore, it was starting to look like an actual tattoo.

James walked into the room, I looked at him and smiled. I had a good feeling that Jason was going to be okay and that made me feel a little better. "Do you know where Arturo is?" I asked James. "Yeah, he's in the room with the other guest" he said, just in case Cori was listening. "Okay, I'm going to go see if he can come out and look at the mark and give us an opinion" I said, looking at Jason. He nodded his head. I started walking down the hallway to the room where we were keeping Pearl. I knocked on the door so I wouldn't startle anyone. Damian came and opened the door, he moved aside so I could quickly step in.

She was awake, "let me go! There will be hell to pay for this!" she yelled at me. "Why is she awake?" I asked, looking at Damian. "Trying to get her to eat something," he replied. "I won't!" she yelled. "The other situation shouldn't take too much longer, then we can fix this" I said to Damian. He nodded his head and put her back under a sleeping spell. Arturo was sitting quietly in a chair. “Speaking of the other situation, Arturo, would you come look at the mark and give us an opinion?” I asked. Without saying anything, he just got up, he seemed like the old Arturo, before I took his worry away. “Are you okay?” I asked him. “Oh sure, I’m just tired” he said as he walked past me and into the hallway. “He’s in the living room” I said, following behind him.

I followed him down the hallway and into the living room. He walked up to Jason, “can I see?” he said looking down at him. Jason pulled the top of his shirt down again so Arturo could look this time. “The redness is gone, this one little spot here looks to be fading” he said, while shining a tiny flashlight on the mark. My heart filled with joy, “so, he’s going to make the transition?” I asked excitedly. “Looks like it, there’s still a chance that it could go the other way, but I think he’s strong and he’s going to be a great witch,” Arturo said, smiling at Jason. Jason smiled back, “can I do magic yet?” he asked him. “Doubt it, and you shouldn’t try until it is completely gone,” Arturo said. “Why not?” Jason asked. “You could give yourself magic sickness and cause the process to go the other way if you try to use magic now,” Arturo said. I put my hand over my mouth and gasped. “Chill, I won’t do anything,” Jason said, looking at me.

I could tell he was already feeling stronger, he was acting stronger too. Misty continued to sit by his side. I was happy that she had decided to help me instead of fighting against me. Jason needed her and I needed him, he was the closest thing I had to a brother, and I didn’t want to lose him. Cori came into the living room, “dinner is ready” she said in her high pitched voice. “Thank you,” I replied. I put my hand out to help Jason get up, he shook his head, “I think I can do it myself” he said. “Okay” I said, but I stood close in case he needed me.

He got up on his own, it only took a few seconds for him to steady himself and he started walking to the kitchen. I let out a little squeal of excitement. He looked at me like I was crazy. "I'm just happy that you are getting stronger!" I said, with excitement. He rolled his eyes at me, I just smiled back. I followed Jason and James followed me. The food smelled delicious. "Should I go find everyone else?" Cori asked. "No, you've done enough, look at this, this looks delicious!" I said, trying to distract her. Levi walked into the dining room. "Levi, would you mind letting everyone know that dinner is ready? I don't want Cori to do that, she prepared all this herself" I said. "I really don't mind, it's nothing at all," Cori said. I smiled at her, "thank you" I said again. I gave Levi a look to let him know I really didn't want her wandering around the house. He nodded at me that he understood and walked back out of the dining room.

Cori walked back into the kitchen. I followed her, I hadn't had a lot of time to talk to her. I wanted to try to get a feel for her personality. "Thank you again," I said. She jumped a little, "I didn't realize you followed me," she said with a little giggle. "Sorry, I guess we're even now?" I replied. "I wanted to ask you a few questions, if you don't mind," I said. She nodded, "of course not" she said. "How well do you know Pearl?" I asked. "Very well, we've been friends for at least five years," she replied. I nodded, "have you noticed her acting differently recently?" I asked. "Yes, that's why I'm here, she told me that she may not be able to protect me much longer and we needed to get to you for protection. She said the war had begun and I would end up getting pulled into it because of my relationship with her." she replied. "Did she say why she wouldn't be able to protect you? Why do you think she would refuse to come?" I asked, narrowing my eyes.

Cori sat down on a short stool, she looked like she was thinking. "I think she may be involved with witches on the other side of the war" she finally replied. "Why wouldn't she take you to them then?" I asked. "I don't know, maybe she knows she's wrong? Maybe she's acting as a spy" she said. "Or maybe they have something on her, maybe they are blackmailing her or maybe they put some sort of spell on her?" She replied. James came into the kitchen, "everyone is here, ready to eat" he said. I looked at him and said, "coming." I looked back at Cori, "do you want to eat with us?" I asked her. "I really don't like being around a lot of people all at once, if you don't mind, I'll just eat in here" she replied. "Okay, that's up to you. If you need anything, let me know," I said, smiling at her. I didn't want to lose her trust and I just made her question Pearl. I looked behind me as I walked back to the dining room, she was still sitting on the stool, her back toward me, she was definitely an odd person, I still couldn't really tell a lot about her.

"Hey!" Alice said as I walked into the dining room. "Hi," I replied. "Can we eat now?" Jason asked. "Of course, I'm sorry if you guys were waiting for me, I didn't realize I was holding you up" I replied, as I sat down to eat. I sat down in a seat between Jason and James, David was sitting across from me. "Find out anything?" David asked, looking toward the kitchen. I shook my head, "no" I replied. "Food is really good, hope it's not poisonous," James said, putting another bite in his mouth. "I don't think she's going to poison us," I replied in a whisper. "I do feel like she is hiding something though," I added. "So get her to trust you and find out what it is," James said. I nodded as I started eating, he was right, the food was delicious.

"Arturo, will you be able to stay for a while? Help get Jason trained?" I asked. He looked at me, "probably, I can't make any promises though" he said. I nodded, "and you David? Will you help train Jason like you trained me?" I asked. "Yeah, I need to do something useful," he replied. I smiled at him, "at least we found you a purpose, right?" I said. He smiled uncomfortably at me. I didn't really care, I didn't think he should be here, he should be with his family. "Where's that car you drove when you were here before?" I asked him. "I left it in a safe place, do you need it?" he replied. "Sure do," I said. "We can go get it tomorrow or whenever you have time," he said. I nodded my head." I found a sweet blue convertible I want to go look at too," James said. "Okay," I replied, smiling. I hoped that Jason was transitioned soon, and we could get the spell off of Pearl. I knew that was a lot, but I felt like things were starting to fall apart, and I didn't like that feeling.

After dinner, everyone started scattering about, Damian and Arturo, along with Hale went back to where we were keeping Pearl. Jason, Misty, and myself went into the living room. Levi and Alice went upstairs, they seemed to be hanging out together a lot lately. David and Conan helped Cori clean everything up in the kitchen. James went outside, to feed Philip. I sat down on the couch next to Jason again. "I am feeling really good," he said. I smiled, "can I look again?" I asked. He pulled his shirt down, it was noticeably lighter to me now. I squealed with excitement. "I didn't want you to be dragged into this, but you were and I'm just happy that you are going to be okay" I said to him. "You know, this is still all crazy to me, right?" he said. "It's still all crazy to me, so yeah, I get it" I told him.

James walked back inside, he walked over to me and put his arm out to help me up. I got up and followed him to the porch. He looked at me and smiled, then he bent down to kiss me. "I just wanted to get you alone for a minute," he said. I smiled at him. "You need to get some rest, you know? You can't be there for everyone else if you are running on empty" he said. "I just want to make sure that he's going to be okay," I said. "You already know that he is though, right?" he replied. "Nothing is certain, you know that" I said. "You can't stay up all night," he said. "I could, to make sure he is okay," I said, defensively. "I will talk with everyone, they can take shifts watching him and you can come to bed and snuggle with me until you fall asleep," he said, trying to be cute now.

I was thinking about it, but I didn't want to leave Jason, what if he needed me and I wasn't there? But, at the same time, I did feel exhausted, and snuggling with James sounded really nice right now. "Let me go talk to him, make sure he's okay with it," I said. "Okay" James said, sounding defeated. "You can go ahead and ask everyone else if they are okay with your plan" I said. He nodded as he held the door open for me. I walked back toward Jason and James walked toward the kitchen. "Still feeling good?" I asked Jason. He looked up at me and smiled, "yeah, I'm feeling really good, better by the minute" he said. I smiled, "good" I said.

"I think I'm going to try to get some sleep, if you think you will be okay? James is asking everyone to take shifts tonight, keeping an eye on you, making sure you don't need anything" I said. He looked at me for a minute, "I'll be okay, go ahead, go to bed" he said finally. "Why did you hesitate like that?" I asked. "What do you mean?" he replied. I narrowed my eyes at him, "you know what I mean" I said. "I was thinking for a moment of being nosey and asking about your relationship, but, if you are really tired, we can talk about it tomorrow" he said. "He's my boyfriend, I'm in love with him. What else is there to know?" I replied defensively. "I just wanted to talk about it, you are probably my oldest friend, we always talk about our love lives with each other" he replied. "I realize that, but things are different now, I would say I'm more mature now. Besides, there's really nothing to talk about, like I said," I told him. He put his hands up, like I was attacking him, "okay, okay, go to bed, goodnight" he said with an attitude.

I walked away, feeling better about it, he seemed like he was going to be just fine. I knew James would do what he said and have everyone take shifts in watching him tonight. I went to my bedroom and plopped down on the bed. I threw my head back and lay down, I didn't even feel like changing my clothes. How had James noticed I was exhausted before I did? He knew me in a way that I didn't seem to know myself, that was a bit scary. The door opened and he walked into the room right before I was about to doze off. "Hey" I mumbled. "Hey" he replied, crawling into the bed next to me and snuggling like he had promised. I let out a sigh, "are you okay?" he asked. "Yes, I'm perfect now" I said, burying my face in his chest. He rubbed my hair until I fell asleep.

I slept dreamlessly that night, but I could consciously feel James next to me. His every breath made me feel him there. I didn't mind it, it was comforting, I felt protected, I felt wanted, I felt loved. At some point I suppose I stopped feeling him, and slipped into a deep sleep. I didn't wake again until morning, I opened my eyes to see James looking at me and smiling. "What? Am I drooling?" I asked as I rolled over the other way. He grabbed me by the shoulder and rolled me back over, "no," he said with a giggle. "I like watching you sleep, you are beautiful," he said. I buried my face in his chest to keep him from seeing me blushing and smiling. He put his arms around me in a big embrace.

I sat up quickly, remembering everything. "Is Jason okay? Has he transitioned yet?" I asked. "I'm not sure about the transition, he's fine though, no one has said otherwise," James replied. I jumped up out of bed, I needed to go see him for myself. I left the room quickly, without saying anything else to James. As I entered the living room I saw Jason sitting on the couch, he was talking and laughing with Misty. He looked a lot better, my heart was happy. As soon as he noticed me he jumped up and hugged me, smiling. "You look good!" I said. "I always look good, what are you talking about?" he replied. He pulled down his shirt, the mark was almost completely faded now!

"Eeek!" I squealed with excitement. "I know, right?" he said, with all the cockiness he could possibly muster. I pushed him, teasingly, "it's not all good stuff, you know?" I said. "Misty told me, we are in the middle of a war, apparently" He replied. "It is either fight, or die" I said. "You want to explain that to me now?" He asked. "There are other magical creatures, besides witches. All the extra tall people around here are half giants. It has been law for a long time among the magical creatures that they cannot mate and create half breeds" I said. "Okay, so why does that matter?" Jason asked. "Anytime it has happened over the past two thousand years or so, they have found the child and destroyed it" I said, "until now" I added. "What do you mean?" He asked. "Me, I'm a half breed, my father was a giant and my mom was a witch. She was able to hide me with magic, they even killed her to try and find me" I said.

"Wow, why aren't you tall like them?" he asked. "Part of the magic she used, she stunted my growth" I replied. "Misty, how much longer do you think he has until the mark is completely gone and he can start training?" I asked. "Not long at all, the mark will be gone today for sure" she replied. "I will talk with Arturo and David, and of course, I want you to be a part of his training, you are his high priestess" I said to her. She nodded. "The rest of us have another mission that we can't put off any longer" I said. "I want to go on a mission," Jason said. "This is too dangerous for someone that doesn't know what they are doing" I replied. I kissed him on the cheek and walked away to go gather the troops.

I walked down the hallway to the room where we had Pearl. I knocked on the door, Hale opened it, he and Arturo were the only two in there with her, she was asleep. "Jason has almost transitioned, I want to start planning his training and getting her fixed up" I said, glancing at Pearl. "One person will need to stay with her, would you be willing to do that Hale?" I asked. "Of course, whatever you need," he replied. "Arturo, I want you to work with Misty and David and start training Jason. Can you do that?" I asked. He nodded, but seemed a bit disappointed. "We'll all meet in the living room in an hour, to finalize plans, except you Hale, you can stay here with Pearl, if you need a break, take it before Arturo leaves" I said, as I left the room.

I walked down the hallway back toward the living room. Jason and Misty were still the only ones in there, "I need to get everyone radios or something so I don't have to hunt them all down," I said, jokingly as I passed through the living room and walked outside. David and James were on the porch, "hey, guys," I said, as I walked out. They both looked at me, I think they could tell that I was about to assign them jobs or positions. "David, Jason has almost transitioned, I want you to work with Misty and Arturo and get him trained as quickly as possible" I said. "James, we are going on a mission, I'll need you there for muscle," I said. They both nodded at me. "Good, we will all meet in the living room in about forty five minutes," I said as I headed back inside to find everyone else.

I walked into the house without saying anything to Jason or Misty this time. I walked into the kitchen, Cori was the only one in there. "How are you today?" I asked, so I didn't seem rude. "I'm fine, just preparing food," she said. "Great! I'm sure it will be delicious as always, a few of us will be going out today, we are going to try to talk to Pearl again, hopefully she will join us for dinner" I said. She looked at me without expression, "that will be wonderful" she replied. I wasn't sure if it was an elf thing or if it was just her personality, but she never showed emotion, it was like she just existed, never having fun or experiencing anything. "Yes it will" I replied as I walked back out of the kitchen.

I headed upstairs and knocked on Levi's door. "Yeah, come in!" he yelled. I walked in, not super surprised to see Alice in there with him. "We have a mission, I want both of you to come with us" I told them. They looked at me like they were expecting me to say more. "We will all meet in the living room in about thirty minutes," I said. "Okay, sounds good," Levi replied. "Have you guys seen Conan or Damian?" I asked. They looked at each other and shook their heads, "no" Alice said, turning her head toward me. "It's okay, I'm sure I'll find them," I said, walking out of the room.

I walked back downstairs, James and David were now in the

living room along with Jason and Misty. “Has anyone seen Conan or Damian?” I asked. “They were walking around outside earlier,” James said. “Okay, thanks” I said, walking out of the front door. James followed behind me. “Are you sure you are up for all this?” He asked. “What do you mean?” I replied. “You plan to go up against Xander, right?” He said. “Yes, we are going up against him, we have to get him to remove the spell he has on Pearl” I replied. “And I am fine, and I would prefer not to discuss this until we are all together” I said, starting to get irritated with him. “Okay” he replied and went silent.

I spotted Conan and Damian walking along the forest line, they looked our way and I waved my arm to let them know I needed to speak with them. They started walking toward us and we met in the middle. “We are going on a mission today, I want both of you to come with us” I said. They both nodded, “I was wondering when we were going to go” Damian said. “We are going to meet in the living room to discuss all the details,” I said. They nodded and the four of us walked back to the house together.

Everyone except Cori and Hale were waiting in the living room as we walked inside. Jason ran over to me and picked me up and started spinning me around in an extremely excited hug. He was laughing, he sat me down and pulled his shirt down to show me his chest, the mark was completely gone! I squealed with excitement. I hugged him and said, “I'm so happy! I wouldn't know what to do if I lost you!” He squeezed me tight and then let me go. “Everything seems to be coming together,” I said, looking around the room at everyone.

“We just need to discuss a few details,” I said. “David, Arturo and Misty will stay here and start training Jason. Hale will be with the other guest. James, Levi, and Alice will go with Damian, Conan and myself to take care of the other problem” I continued. “I can't wait until I get to go fight,” Jason said. I smiled at him, “you know, you still won't be as powerful as anyone else in this room, they are all high priests and priestesses and I am stronger because of the giant blood in my veins," I told him. He looked quite disappointed, "that's not fair" he said. "Life isn't fair, you know that," I said, smiling at him. After all, we had both grown up as orphans. "I wonder if Cori knows how to cut hair?" I asked out loud. "Why are you asking that?" James asked. I pointed at Jason, "that mess on his head" I said, laughing. Everyone else started laughing with me, Jason picked me up again, this time, throwing me over his shoulder. I screamed, "what are you doing? Put me down!"

"You know what happens when you make fun of me" he said, "No! I have to go! Don't you dare!" I said. He walked outside with me in tow, I knew he was looking for a large enough body of water to throw me in. I saw James, David and Levi walk out behind us. He walked over to the barn, "this will do" he said as he dumped me into the water trough we had set up for Philip. "Ugh!" I yelled. "Can't even play around with you! Jerk!" I yelled at his back as he walked back toward the house. It was all fun and games I suppose, but at the moment I was pretty angry that I was wet and cold.

James walked over and helped me out. "Why didn't you stop him?" I asked. "Wasn't my business," he replied. I rolled my eyes at him and stormed back to the house. I'm glad they were all getting a laugh at my expense. I went to my bedroom to dry off and change into my battle suit, yes the catsuit, so they could laugh some more. As it turned out, it was very comfortable and easy to move in, so it made sense for me to wear it to a fight, whether it turned out to be physical or magical. After changing I walked back out to the living room. Just the people that were going with me were waiting there, I supposed the rest had started their own mission, training.

"Muscles can ride in the truck and witches will take the car" I said, walking past them out of the door. They followed behind me, we walked to save magic, even though Damian could project his magic to me and it made me feel like I had the power of a goddess. It was good to conserve as much as possible for a lot of reasons. "Do we even know where this guy is?" Levi asked. "I was able to look inside Pearl's head, I know where he is," Conan replied. "Okay" Levi responded. We continued walking in silence until we reached the pull over spot by the road. James pulled me into him and kissed my forehead, "be careful, I'll see you on the other side" he said. I smiled at him, "yes you will," I replied. The half giants got into the truck and the witches got into the car and we pulled out onto the road. I knew this would be dangerous, possibly the most dangerous thing we had done so far.

Conan drove since he knew where to go, the truck followed behind us. "How far away is it?" I asked. "About an hour," Conan replied. I nodded and sent James a text to let him know. I sat back in the back seat and tried to relax. Of course I hoped that we would easily sway him to our side, but something told me that wouldn't happen, especially after what Pearl had told me. I hoped that at least no one would die today. I closed my eyes and I guess I fell asleep. The next thing I knew, Damian was telling me to wake up because we were getting close. "Sorry, I didn't mean to fall asleep, I've been extra tired lately, I guess" I said. "It's fine, it didn't bother me at all," Conan said.

"The complex where he lives is heavily guarded. We will need glamor spells on everyone" Conan said. I nodded and put glamours on the three of us. I didn't feel the need to glamor the giants because they wouldn't know what they looked like anyway. We pulled up to a gate where two very muscular men came up to the car. We looked like elderly people, I thought that would look the least threatening. "We are here to cook for the party" Conan said, in a cracked elderly sounding voice. I smiled at how convincing he sounded. "What party?" One of the men said. "The homecoming party for the misses," Conan said. "What misses?" The other man said.

It was clear that this wasn't going to work, Damian grabbed my hand and I channeled his power, I snapped my fingers and they both fell to the ground. Conan jumped out and grabbed one of their badges and used it to open the gate. We drove in, leaving them laying there on the ground. It was just a heavy sleeping spell, they would be okay in about eight or nine hours. The half giants followed behind us. We pulled right up to the front door, parked and got out. We were greeted by more guards with muscles and guns, but apparently they weren't witches, at least none of them tried to use magic to stop us.

It was all too easy for me to put them down. Once the coast was clear, as far as we could tell, we busted through the front door. This place was easily as big as ours, if not bigger. I couldn't see anyone, I'm sure that we had been detected, and Xander was hiding. It wasn't like we were able to make a quiet entrance. "We need to split up in teams of two, one witch, one muscle. James, you can come with me" I said. Everyone nodded in agreement. Conan and Levi went upstairs, Damian and Alice took the hall to the right and James and myself went down the hall to the left.

A voice came over an intercom, "you can look all you want, you won't find me unless I want to be found." "Don't be a coward! We just want to talk to you!" I yelled back. "Then why didn't you just call? Why break into my home if you just wanted to talk?" He said. "I just had a hunch that you wouldn't answer if I called," I said sarcastically. "Like I said, you won't find me, you might as well leave now" He said. "We aren't leaving until we talk to you, face to face, we'll burn this place down if we have to" I said threateningly. I hadn't planned on this happening. I manifested a ball of fire in my hand, I started to throw it at a nearby window curtain. There was laughter over the intercom. I threw the ball of fire and it went out immediately. More laughter, "you think I don't have magical protection on my home?" he said, condescending.

"I will find you!" I yelled, starting to get frustrated. More laughter over the intercom. We kept searching, looking for secret rooms where he could be hiding. "What if he's not even here?" James whispered to me. "He is, I can feel it and we will find him" I said. After about an hour of looking, I decided to try something different. I sent Damian a text message telling him to meet me on the stairs. "We are going to have to do this with magic," I whispered to him. "Agreed, can you do a pinpoint spell to find out exactly where he is?" He replied. "I can with your help. I can do anything with your help" I said. He closed his eyes and I felt his magic going through my body.

I channeled the magic into a spell, a spell to sense anyone in the house. First I found Alice, patiently waiting for Damian to return. I opened my eyes as soon as I saw him. "Behind the bookcase in the living room" I whispered. We sent messages to everyone that we had found him, to come meet us in the living room, but to act like we were giving up. "So, we're just going home?" Levi said, maybe a little too loudly, coming down the stairs. Laugher came over the intercom once more. The taunting made my blood boil, I looked at Damian and mouthed, 'project magic to me.' He started projecting his magic and I used it, to take the protective magic off of the house, I manifested another ball of fire and threw it at the bookcase. This time it ignited and the books were in flames. Within seconds I heard Xander coughing from the smoke.

I put a shield spell on James, Levi and Alice. They began punching through the bookcase wall until they got to the room behind it. Xander tried to use magic against them, but my shield spell protected them from that also. Once they had him contained I used magic to put the fire out. "Well, well, well, Mr. Cocky, all tied up and helpless," I said, walking into the room. He was very handsome, he had light brown hair that curled in the front, blue eyes with thick eyebrows. He had a full beard and mustache but the hairs weren't long. He spat at me. James punched him in the jaw. I looked at James and rolled my eyes. "What? That was just rude, and I'm here to be your muscle" James said, looking at me. I didn't respond, I just looked back at Xander. "Why did you put a spell on Pearl?" I asked him. He looked away. "All we want is answers and for you to take the spell off of Pearl, then we will let you go and leave" I said.

He continued to be silent. Damian started looking around, looking uneasy. "He's not going to talk, maybe we should take him back with us. I don't think it's safe to do it here" he said. I looked around, I couldn't sense anyone else around or anyone using any magic for that matter. But maybe he was right? Maybe we shouldn't give anyone a chance to discover us torturing their high priest. I gave him a nod. "Get him in the trunk" I said, looking at James and Levi. "Although, I'm not sure we should take him back to the house," I said. Everyone looked at me confused. "Where else are we going to take him?" Conan asked. "I don't know, I guess it's the only option, except for the woods," I said. "That may work! Anywhere but here!" Damian said.

They got him to the car and into the trunk, before they closed it, I put a blindfold over his eyes. I didn't want to risk him seeing anything. We got in the vehicles and drove off, leaving bodies of sleeping bodyguards behind us. "So why the hurry to get away?" I asked Damian. "His second in line, he's no one to mess with. If he were to come in and see us, it wouldn't be a good situation" he replied. "What do you mean?" I asked, confused. "Everyone has a second and third in line to take over their covens should they die" he said. "I guess that does make sense" I said out loud, but more to myself.

When we arrived at the pullover spot, we got out of the vehicles. "I don't want to take him all the way to the house, let's tie him to a tree in the woods," I said. I opened the trunk, and he didn't move. I grabbed him by the shoulder and took James by the hand and warped us into the woods. James tied him to a tree and I pulled the blindfold off of him. He still wouldn't look at me. "Why did you put the spell on Pearl?" I asked again, angrily. He looked away. James punched him in the face. I didn't want to have to do it this way, but he wasn't giving us a choice.

"Let me talk to him for a minute alone," I said, looking at James. "I don't think that is a good idea," he replied. I wanted to try the 'good cop/bad cop' routine, I looked at James, narrowing my eyes, "I didn't ask you if you thought it was a good idea" I said. "Fine, I'm not going very far though," he replied. I heard someone coming up behind us, I looked around, it was Margo. "She can stay with me, I'm sure she would love to rip someone's head off if need be" I said, looking at James. He rolled his eyes at me and walked away. Once he was at least fifty feet away, I got down on one knee in front of Xander.

"I know you have seen the power I have, why would you still want to stand against me? You can fight with us, all of the witches can be united again" I said. He looked at me this time. "You are a disgusting creature that needs to be done away with" he replied, and I could tell that he meant it from the look on his face. "I can help you, I can take away the things inside of you that make you so miserable" I said to him, softly. "You are garbage, and I will never fight with you or for you" he replied. "Why did you put the spell on Pearl?" I asked again. He looked away again. I knew he wasn't going to tell me, and he wasn't going to remove the spell either.

I looked over at James and waved him to come back. Margo just sat, watching us. I looked at James and shook my head to let him know that I didn't get anything out of him. "Margo, watch him for a moment please" I said. She stood up and licked her lips, "don't eat him" I said, then added "yet." When we were out of earshot, I started whispering to James, "he's not going to be easily convinced. He wants to kill me" I said. "Ask Damian, if we kill him, will the spell be broken" James said. I looked at him, I hadn't thought about that, but he was right, it may be the only way. I sent a text to Damian and asked. He responded with, "it should, is there no other option?" I replied with, "I don't think so."

We walked back over to Xander, Margo backed off a little and lay back down, still watching us. "I'm done with this, you know it's over for you right?" I said. He didn't lift his head or acknowledge that I said anything at all. "You could have joined us, but it looks like you have made your choice," I said. He still didn't move. I looked at James, thought for a moment on how and who I wanted to kill him. I looked at Margo, she stood up and licked her lips, she looked eager to do the job. I looked back at James and he nodded his head as if he knew what I was thinking. We both moved and I motioned for her to go over to Xander. She walked over, slowly. He looked up once as he saw her approaching, he managed to get one short scream, "NO!" out before she ripped his head off. Blood squirted everywhere from his aorta, after she threw his head about six feet away. I grabbed James by the arm and warped us back to the house.

Upon landing a few feet from the porch, I let go of James and ran inside. I went straight to the room where Pearl was being held. I didn't knock, I busted in the door with a rush. Hale stood up in shock at me busting through. She was still under his sleeping spell. "He's dead, wake her up!" I said. He looked confused for a moment, then he woke her up. She opened her eyes and looked around. She looked at me, she was silent for a few moments. "I'm sorry" she said, sounding weak. "You have nothing to be sorry about," I replied. "How do you feel?" Hale asked. "Hale, I'm sorry, I said horrible things to you" she said. "Like Gabriela said, you have nothing to be sorry about, you were under a monster's spell" Hale said. "We took care of the monster, you are free now" I said, with a smile. She gave me a knowing look and smiled back. Looking at Hale, I said, "will you help her get ready to come out and get some food, help get her strength back?" "Of course," he replied. I walked out of the room.

"Meeting in the living room!" I yelled, while walking down the hallway, hoping that everyone would hear me. I got to the living room and started pacing back and forth while waiting for everyone to get in there. Everyone started coming in, including Cori. "I'm sorry, Cori, you don't need to be here, but Pearl will be joining us for dinner tonight" I said, looking at her with a smile. She walked away, into the kitchen. After the swinging door closed behind her, I threw a sound blocking spell over it. Once everyone was in the living room, except Pearl and Hale I began talking. "Xander is dead, the spell he had on Pearl is broken, anyone that can help her for the next day or so until she gets her strength back, I will be very grateful for that. She will be a great asset for us."

"But now Oscar will be the new high priest of the Moon coven. He's been known to be just pure evil, even more so than Xander," Damian said. "Yes, we will have a new, possibly more dangerous enemy, but we have a lot of strength here" I said, pointing around the room. "How is Jason doing?" I asked, looking at Arturo, even though Jason was sitting on the couch. "He's doing fine, he's not going to have as much magical power as most of us do, considering most of us are high priests or priestesses, or like yourself being half giant, or like myself being a sole practitioner most of my life," he replied.

"I think it would be a good idea for us to start training together as a team, learning each other's magical strengths and weaknesses," I said. "That's a very good idea," Arturo said. Everyone else in the room mumbled their agreement as well. Pearl and Hale entered the living room. He was helping to hold her up. I felt bad, her condition now was my fault, but I didn't know what else I could have done. I walked over to her. "I'm sorry for holding you as a hostage, I didn't want him to take you and kill you. Cori doesn't know that you have been here, I told her you were joining us for dinner tonight" I said in a lowered voice, close to her ear. She looked at me and smiled and nodded. I only hoped she didn't hold any ill will toward me, I hoped that she really did understand that I only did what I did to protect her and the rest of us.

Eighteen

Oscar's threat

Cori showed no emotion when Pearl walked into the dining room to eat dinner with us. "Good to see you, friend," she said to her plainly. I looked at Pearl with a confused look. She looked back at me and smiled. After Cori went back into the kitchen, Pearl looked at me and said, "elves don't really show emotion, it was branded as a weakness by them a long time ago." "Hmm, that explains a lot," I replied. "It's not that they don't feel, but they don't show it" she said. "I get it, I think," I replied. We sat down to eat, everyone was making small talk until the room was full of the loud hum of a bar.

"Do you think we need to go see if we need to dispose of the body?" James whispered in my ear. "I'll see if Margo is around after dinner," I whispered back. He looked confused, I just smiled at him. I knew I could see into her mind. So after dinner, I walked outside, and over to where the woods met the yard. I looked around and listened. Arturo walked out and over to where I was standing. "I'm looking for Margo," I said as he approached. "Why?" He asked. "She was the one that did the deed today, I need to check in with her and see if there is anything we need to do, like get rid of any remains," I said. "Oh, well, I doubt that there are any remains if Margo took care of him," he said. "I still want to check in with her," I replied. He nodded his head and sat down on the ground. "She'll smell us and come if she's near. Her sense of smell, is exceptional" he said. I nodded and sat down with him.

It was surprisingly not too cold, but a chill was definitely starting to come over as the sun set. James walked out of the front door, I waved at him to let him know he could come over and sit with us. Once he got to us, he sat down close to me and put his arms around me. He made me feel warm, it was nice. "So, what are we doing?" James asked. "Waiting to see if Margo will come to us," I replied. "Oh, okay" he said. The three of us just sat there, quietly for a while. I heard a rustle from the woods behind us and looked around. Margo was standing there, I motioned for her to come over. She just stood there, staring at Arturo. "Is she mad at you?" I asked. "I'm not sure," he replied. She finally walked over and lay down next to me.

"We were wondering if there were any remains left to get rid of," I said as I put my hand on her head. I started seeing flashes of blood, meat and bones. I could see her crunching the bones, snapping them into pieces. She ate the meat from his bones. Then I saw when it was done, there were only a few puddles of blood on the ground. I took my hand away and nodded at her. She rolled over on her back just like a house cat that wants you to rub it's tummy so it can claw your hand and arm. "I'm not falling for that one," I said to her. I didn't think she would really attack me, she probably wanted me to feel how full her belly felt after eating Xander.

"Is it supposed to rain soon?" I asked out loud. James pulled out his phone to check the weather. "Tomorrow evening" he replied. "Why do you ask?" Arturo asked. "All that's left is a little blood, I think a good rain will take care of that" I replied. He smiled, "the perfect killing machine" he said, more to himself than anyone else. Margo got up and walked away. "I think she's still upset with you," I said, looking at Arturo. "I don't blame her, I shouldn't have sent that letter to her, I should have just left her alone. I think she was finally at peace with the past and I had to go and shove it in her face again" he said. "You both deserve happiness, and I hope you can find it" I replied. James didn't have any idea what we were talking about, so he sat quietly with his arms around me.

It started getting colder, so we decided to go back inside. I wanted to find Pearl and see how she was feeling. I found her in the kitchen, talking to Cori. "How are you feeling?" I asked, walking through the door. "I'm feeling better, thank you for what you did for me" she replied with a smile. "Of course" I replied, I didn't want to say too much in front of Cori, I couldn't afford to lose her or anyone else's trust at the moment. I think Cori sensed that I wanted to speak with Pearl alone, she excused herself and went upstairs. "Do you want to stay in the same room?" I asked Pearl. "That's fine" she replied and then she broke down, she started crying so hard she almost fell. I caught her and hugged her, I held her, rubbing her head and back to try and soothe her. Her body shook with her sobs. I knew what it was like to be strong all of the time, even through your own misery. I knew exactly what she was going through.

She finally stopped crying enough to speak. "The things he did to me, and made me believe that I enjoyed it!" she yelled. "I'm sorry, he can't hurt you anymore, or anyone else," I replied as calmly as I could. "I wish I could have seen him in his last moments," she said. I didn't say anything, just kept trying to soothe her and calm her down. "Oscar is a terrible person," she said after a few moments of silence. "So I keep hearing," I replied. "We will take care of anyone that gets in the way, don't worry. This is the winning team here and we'll gladly accept others that truly want to be here. And we will get rid of the ones that don't. Murdering of innocent children has gone on for too long, it will not continue" I said, my voice rising as I spoke. She nodded and wiped the tears from her face.

"Feel free to take a shower or bath or whatever you need, make yourself at home. This home is all of ours. This is our safe place, we are safe with each other and the protection spells all around us" I said. "Thank you, I don't know if I can make my mind stop long enough for me to feel safe," she replied. "I might be able to help you," I said. She looked at me curiously. "There's this thing I can do, I can remove emotional stress along with anything else that may be causing you to not be able to move forward" I said, not knowing how else to explain it. She looked at me and nodded, "yes, you can try," she said, sounding as if she wasn't sure she believed me. "Let's go to your room," I said. I walked down the hall with her, by her side, with my arm around her so she knew I was there for her, physically and emotionally.

Once we got to her room, I walked her to the bed, she sat down and I sat down on the bed beside her. "Close your eyes and try to relax," I said. She nodded and closed her eyes. I closed mine and started the spell. I reached inside of her, there was more pain inside of her than I had seen inside anyone else. I started working on removing it, this was just around her heart, I hadn't even looked at her head yet. I removed the red energy, then looked inside her head. There was more there as I had suspected there would be. I heard a knock at the door that made me break concentration. Pearl opened her eyes and looked at me, there seemed to be light behind her eyes again. I smiled at her. I went to the door to see who had knocked. It was James, "I was worried about you, I didn't know where you went. I've been looking everywhere" he said. "Is something wrong?" I asked, getting worried at the tone of his voice. He just looked at me, like he didn't want to speak in front of Pearl.

"It's okay, she's a part of this team now" I said. He nodded,

"Oscar sent a video message to Damian," he said. I nodded, dropping my head. I wasn't ready to fight the next one this quickly, but I suppose that's just how things go, right? I looked back at Pearl, "you can come if you want, or you can take a bath and just relax" I said. "I'll come, it's not like he's attacking us right now, I know him, he likes to taunt his prey" she replied, looking disgusted. We followed James into the living room where everyone else was waiting. Pearl was walking on her own and appearing stronger and looking better than she had before dinner.

Damian pulled up the video on his phone. Oscar was a very muscular black man with short hair. When he spoke, it was exactly what I expected him to sound like, a deep threatening voice. "I don't know what you did to Xander, but his death will not be in vain. We will avenge him and we will continue doing his work. We will hunt down and kill any abominations. Laws were passed long ago and we will uphold them. Gabriela, you are no exception, orders to my people are to kill you on sight. As for the rest of you, you will get your punishment for protecting her, then you will all die as well. I don't make empty threats, I'll see you all soon." The phone went black, everyone just looked around at each other for a moment.

"He can't get to us here, we will just have to find him first" I said, breaking the silence. "He won't be easy to find either," Pearl said. "We will continue with the original plan, train together, learn each other's strengths and weaknesses. That's how we will become the best, that's how we will defeat our enemies" I said. Everyone just looked at me and nodded in agreement. "I think we should all get some rest and we will get started first thing tomorrow" I said. I felt more like everyone's mom than their leader, telling them to go to bed, but I wanted to go to bed and there was really nothing else to be said at the moment about the threat. I looked at Pearl and asked her if she was okay. "Yes, I really do feel better, thank you for whatever it was that you did" she replied. "I didn't really get to finish, are you sure you are okay?" I asked. "Yes, I'm gonna go take a bath like you suggested and I will feel wonderful" she said. "Okay" I said, smiling at her.

I walked into the bedroom and James followed me. He grabbed me by the shoulders and turned me toward him, "no one is going to hurt you" he said. "I'm not really worried about me," I said. He gave me a weird look. "I don't want anything to happen to any of you," I added. "You are worried about us? After watching that video, you are worried about *us*?" He said, acting like it was the most ridiculous thing he had ever heard. "Of course, you are all my family now and he threatened all of you" I said. He didn't seem like he wanted to keep arguing with me, he pulled me into him and squeezed me in a bear hug. "I'm really tired, I want to go to sleep," I told him. He released me and nodded. He kissed my forehead and said, "I'm gonna grab a snack, I'll be back in a little while." I nodded, even though I got the feeling that he was lying to me. But I didn't want to argue so I just got into the bed as he walked out of the room.

I felt like I fell asleep as soon as I lay down, I had been more exhausted than I had thought. Or maybe it was because of all the magic that I had been using. I never even noticed James getting in bed next to me. I had a dreamless sleep and when I opened my eyes again, it was morning. James was there next to me, awake and smiling at me. "What are you looking at?" I mumbled, sounding grumpy. "You and all your natural beauty," he replied. I rolled my eyes, I knew I was a complete mess with my hair going every which way and I probably had dried drool on my chin. I rolled over and stretched, that felt amazing, I must not have moved all night.

I smelled the scent of bacon and my stomach growled. I looked at James, "have you been out there yet this morning?" I asked. "Not yet, sounds like everyone is up though," he replied. I rolled over to get up and he grabbed me and pulled me back down. "I'm hungry" I whined. He kissed my forehead and then kissed my nose and then kissed me on the lips. My stomach growled very loudly. He pulled away from me and smiled. I smiled back and said, "I told you, I'm hungry." "Fine" he grunted and pushed me teasingly.

I got out of bed and walked out of the bedroom. The only person in the living room was Jason. "Good morning, your highness," he said. I rolled my eyes at him, and said, "is breakfast ready?" "I think it might be, everyone else is already in there," he replied. "Why aren't you?" I asked. "I'm just not that hungry, just sitting here thinking about everything," he said. "Are you okay?" I asked. "Don't you wish we could go see our friends? Go to the gym? Go to work?" he replied. "I know, this is a totally different life that neither of us asked for, but we have to see this through, we cannot contact our friends at all. That would put them in danger for sure. We are lucky that you survived, I can't risk losing any of them." I said.

"I totally understand, I just wish things were different. I know that they aren't and I have to accept it, I guess I just wanted to talk to you to see how you accepted it. But I understand now, I don't want anything to happen to anyone because of me" Jason said. "I'm sorry that you were brought into this, maybe one day we can return to halfway normal life, but right now, this is what it is," I replied. Then I walked into the kitchen to get my breakfast. Everyone looked up at me, some said, "good morning," some said "hello" and some just smiled. "Hey everyone, how are you guys doing?" I asked, so I didn't seem rude. I really just wanted some food and hoped no one started a conversation with me immediately.

I got lucky or maybe everyone noticed how vigorously I was putting food on my plate and decided to let me eat. After I finished eating, James walked in, he smiled at me and I smiled back. Shortly after him, Jason walked in, I guess he decided he was hungry finally. James got a plate and sat down next to me. "Feel better?" He asked. "For sure," I replied, rubbing my belly. "So, do you have a plan for us yet?" Damian asked. "We will respond to his video with a video of our own, to start" I said. "And then what?" James asked, sounding like he didn't like the idea. "And then we continue with the original plan of training together and getting stronger as a team" I replied.

"I'm ready to make the video whenever you are," I said, looking at Damian. "Okay, we need to do it somewhere with a neutral background so we don't give him any clues at all of where we are," Damian replied. We chose one of the empty bedrooms that had plain white walls. I sat in a chair against the wall while Damian filmed. "I don't want to have to wipe out your whole coven, but I will also do what I have to do to make sure that the murdering of innocent children stops. I'm not scared of you, if you could see what I'm capable of, you wouldn't be making threats at all, you may even choose to join me, like others have. My team is strong and getting stronger and better by the day, if you still choose to go against us, you will join Xander. I have no problem ridding the world of murderers. I'll be seeing you soon."

Damian stopped recording when I finished talking. "What do you think?" I asked. He shrugged his shoulders, "I don't think it's going to scare him, but it will let him know that you aren't backing down" he replied. "Who is next in line after him?" I asked, knowing that I would have to kill him. "I'm not sure, but I can find out," Damian replied. I nodded my head, "I hope they are more open to change than Xander and Oscar" I said, as I stood up to walk out of the room. "You want me to go ahead and send this? Or would you like to show everyone else first?" Damian asked. "We can show everyone, then send it," I replied.

He followed me out of the room and we walked to the living room where everyone was waiting. "Video is finished, we are going to let you all see it before we send it" I said. Damian played the video for everyone. James looked at me like he was disappointed. "What?" I asked him. "Nothing," he replied. I was starting to think that the emotions I took away from him were coming back, but he didn't want me to know or to send him away. I looked at Damian and said, "send it." Damian nodded as he clicked the send button. I clapped my hands together, making some of them jump. "Let's get started on training now" I said, with excitement.

"We should all partner off together with a different partner everyday. I know that Damian and I work great together. How is Jason doing in training?" I asked, looking at Misty. "I think it would be good for him to branch off with others, we are always here if he has any questions," she replied. I nodded, "okay, I will partner with Jason today then" I said. James looked disappointed again. "Everyone should pick someone to work with that they haven't really spent a lot of time with and we will switch up everyday" I said. Conan and James teamed up, Hale teamed with Pearl, Misty teamed with David, Damian teamed with Arturo which left Levi and Alice together for the first day.

We would all learn each other's strengths and weaknesses, and we would learn to work off of each other's strengths and strengthen each other's weaknesses.

Nineteen

Strengthening the army

Jason and I decided that we would go outside to work, it was a nice day, the sun was shining and it was around sixty degrees out. You could feel spring in the air, even though it was only late February. We walked out and chose a spot near the barn. “So, what do you think your strength is?” I asked him. “I can do some magic, but apparently not a lot, I think my physical strength is my strength” he replied. “Okay then, so you would say that magic is your weakness?” I said. “For sure,” he said. I thought for a minute, I wondered if I could project magic to him the way Damian did for me?

“I’m going to try something” I said and put my hand on his shoulder. I closed my eyes and imagined power leaving my body and going into his. “Whoa!” he yelled. I opened my eyes, he was floating! I wasn’t expecting that. “What do you feel?” I asked. “Powerful, like I can do anything” he replied. “So you feel like you can do *anything* and you decide to *float*?” I said. “It was like I had to do something and that was the only thing that came to mind” he said as he lowered himself back down to the ground. “You aren’t super man, you don’t need to fly" I said. He laughed at me. "I'm serious! What if you fall? Everything can't be fixed with magic, you know?" I said, sounding like a mom.

"So, what did you do?" He asked. "I lent you some of my power, Damian has done it for me a few times and I feel like a god and like I can do anything" I said. "That's how I felt," he replied. "I wouldn't think you would be as powerful as I am when it happens to me though" I said. "Why not?" He asked. "I am naturally stronger than you because I am half giant and a natural born witch" I said. "How do we know I'm not something? I was an orphan too, I didn't know my parents, maybe I am part something magical too" he suggested. "You never know," I replied, not wanting to argue.

"I think I may have some other magical blood in me as well, I think my mother may have been a mixed breed that managed to slip through the cracks of the murderers" I said. "Why do you think that?" He asked. "I've seen her in my dreams, she's spoken to me, and the last time I saw her, I think she was about to tell me that she was. But she said that she may not be able to contact me again and I haven't seen her since" I explained. "So you can talk with the dead?" He asked. "I don't know, all of the witches say that is impossible, no one has ever spoken with a passed loved one" I replied. "What if she's not dead?" He asked. I looked at him, "what do you mean?" I asked. "What if she's hiding somewhere and she can only communicate with you through dreams? That's what it sounds like to me" he said.

"How? And where could she be?" I asked. "I don't know, I don't know a lot of things yet, but if I find anything in those boring books that Arturo is making me read, I'll let you know" he replied. I nodded my head, I understood how boring Arturo could be as a teacher, but I also knew he was one of the best teachers. "Let's go eat lunch," I said. He nodded and we walked inside. I guess everyone had the same idea as they all started pouring into the kitchen. Cori had prepared sandwiches and fruit salad for everyone. "Thank you so much," I said to her. She nodded, and said, "of course ma'am." "If you ever want a day off from everything, just let me know, we are all grown, we can take care of ourselves" I said to her. "Oh no, I take care of you and you take care of me" she replied as she walked back to the kitchen. She was so odd, but I didn't think she was a threat. I think their whole race was just misunderstood, but I didn't know any other elves so it's possible that there were bad ones out there I suppose.

After lunch Jason and I headed back outside, to the same small clearing. Someone had let Philip out of the barn to roam around. "Whose horse is that?" Jason asked. I laughed, "he's James' friend, Philip. He's a shapeshifter" I said. "Oh, I've learned about them, they can't change into human form here, right?" Jason said. "Right, there is a black panther here as well, her name is Margo and she is actually the one that killed Xander, bit his head right off and ate him" I said. Jason flinched a little and looked grossed out. "What?" I replied, teasing. "Nothing," he replied. We decided to start fight training.

"Don't take it easy on me" I said, teasingly. "I didn't plan on it," he replied as he came at me. I dodged him easily and dropped down to the ground for a roundhouse kick and knocked him off his feet. "Don't take it easy on me either," he said, sounding like his ego was hurt. I put out my hand to help him up, instead, he grabbed my arm and used his legs to throw me over him and onto my back. "Ouch" I said after I landed, but it was more my ego that was hurt than anything else. He laughed and jumped up to his feet. We kept it up for a couple of hours before I decided we should do some book training as well. I hadn't read everything myself so it wouldn't hurt anything to read a couple of hours instead of continuing to beat each other senseless for two more hours.

He agreed and we walked inside. I had some books and so did

he. I told him to pick one from his. He picked one about vampires. I hadn't read it, I didn't really see a point in reading it since they weren't a threat to us. "Why do you want to read that one?" I asked, confused. "I'm just fascinated with them, I want to learn all I can," he replied. I shrugged my shoulders and said, "okay." We sat down in the library and started reading the book together. "So how do you become a vampire?" he asked after we had read for a few minutes. "If you die with vampire blood in your system you become one" I replied. He nodded. "It's not something you want to do, you would have to live eternity in another dimension and never see anyone you know again" I added. He just looked at me with no expression.

I didn't really learn anything new about vampires from reading the book, but it seemed like he did. Everyone started gathering around us and the chatter became too loud to concentrate. "I guess everyone else is done training for the day?" I asked. They all looked at me. Cori came into the library and said, "dinner is ready." Jason put the book up and we all went to the dining room to eat. The food was delicious as always, I was starting to feel sore from the fight training. James started pointing out bruises on my arms. I leaned over to Jason, "we forgot one thing, healing each other" I whispered. He nodded his head, "we'll do it after dinner" he replied.

After dinner Jason and I went to his room to do the healing spells on each other. I did him first because I knew he couldn't do it as well as I could normally, much less when he was injured. He did okay with his, I still felt a little sore, but the visible bruises went away. After he finished the healing spell, he leaned in and kissed me. He kissed me on the lips, a very passionate kiss. I pulled away and slapped him in the face as hard as I could. "How dare you!" I yelled. He grabbed his face where I had smacked him. "I won't heal that for you" I said as I walked out and slammed the door.

James had heard me yell and was running toward me. "I'm fine," I said as I walked right by him. I went to the bedroom and slammed the door. James came in a few minutes later. "What happened?" He asked, seeing that I was still upset. I just looked at him. I didn't want to tell him, I didn't want him to be jealous, I didn't want him to be angry with Jason or with me, I didn't know what his reaction would be. "Please tell me, or should I go ask Jason?" He said. "No," I replied. "No, you won't tell me or no, don't ask Jason?" He asked. "It's nothing" I said, with a pouty face. "Then why won't you tell me?" He asked. "Just drop it, please" I said, using my whiny voice. He walked over to the bed and stood next to me.

I looked up and smiled, I knew a way to get him to stop talking about it. I raised his shirt and licked his stomach. He let out a moan of excitement. I unbuttoned his pants, pulled out his penis and put it in my mouth, I felt it harden and grow inside my mouth and I moaned to turn him on more. "Oh my god" he said as he got even more excited. He pulled away from me and pulled me up off of the bed, he pulled my shirt off and tossed it onto the floor. He put his mouth against mine and just breathed into me, as he pulled my bra off. I bit his bottom lip and he threw me onto the bed. I gave him a seductive smile and he came down on top of me. I let out a moan as he went inside, he always felt so good, it was that perfect fit.

After we both climaxed, we lay there next to each other, catching our breath. "That was amazing, but I haven't forgotten," he said after a few minutes. I rolled over so that my back was facing him. "I said it's nothing and I don't want to talk about it, I handled it" I told him. "Okay" he said, sounding defeated. I hoped that he really would let it go, we didn't need added drama on top of what we already had to deal with. I couldn't believe Jason, why would he do that? He has never kissed me, and there was a time when I would have loved it, but not anymore. I was so in love with James, everything about him is absolutely perfect in my eyes. I couldn't imagine my life without him now, it's like we were always destined to be together, we just had to cross dimensions to find each other.

I lay there until I fell asleep, another dreamless sleep, it was almost as if I closed my eyes and then woke refreshed in the morning. I rolled over and James was still asleep, he was usually awake before me. I put my arm over his chest and kissed his cheek. His eyes twitched and opened. He looked at me, smiled and kissed my forehead. I smiled back at him. "I love you" I said. "I love you too," he replied. I got up out of the bed and said, "we better go eat and get ready for another day of training." I was thankful knowing that I wouldn't be working with Jason again.

We walked out of the bedroom together and went to the kitchen. Almost everyone was already there, ready to eat. All that was missing was Levi and Alice, and they joined about five minutes later. After we finished eating, I said, "I'll work with Pearl today, does everyone else have their partners for today?" "I think I'm going to work with Jason today," James said. I looked at him, narrowing my eyes. "What?" he said, like I shouldn't be looking at him suspiciously. "Nothing," I replied. As we all got up to go begin, I walked by James and whispered, "just train, no need for any drama." He looked at me and shrugged his shoulders, I rolled my eyes and walked away with Pearl.

Pearl was a much stronger witch than Jason, of course. And she was feeling a lot better now, I also felt she wanted revenge, and since she couldn't get it on Xander, Oscar would be a good replacement. Her strongest magical ability was magic detention, meaning, not unlike myself, she could feel it when magic was being used nearby. When we joined hands we could both feel the magic that was being used all around us, we could almost feel every detail, like what kind of spells were being used. It could come in handy, and it was definitely good to know we were capable of doing it. I decided to train the same way as I had with Jason, so next we went inside for some reading. We could fight after lunch.

We read a book about fairies. "I have a fairy here with me," I told her. "Where?" she asked. "In a jar in my room, she's hibernating until it's warm enough," I replied. "That's amazing, so the fairies really like you then?" She asked. "Yes, I suppose, I mean, I never had an issue with them and they came to me in a dream to communicate. They did try to make me their queen once and I, not realizing what was going on, let it happen until I was told what was happening. Then I took off my tiara, they seemed a little upset, but not angry. Then they choose David's little girl after that" I said, with a laugh. "They were just choosing you to represent them to our race, not as their queen to stay with them and rule, you are still that person to them" Pearl said. "Hmm, that's good to know," I replied. "Lunch is ready" Cori said, from right beside me. I jumped because I hadn't heard her come into the room. "Sorry" she said and walked back to the kitchen.

I looked at Pearl, "does she do that on purpose?" I asked. "Does it happen a lot?" She asked with a smile on her face, she looked as though she was trying not to bust out laughing at me. "It's happened a few times now," I said. "Maybe? Maybe it gives her something to laugh about when she is alone at night" Pearl replied. "I'm about to start doing it to her, see if I can get a reaction out of her," I said, jokingly. "I wouldn't do that," Pearl replied. "I was joking, but why not?" I asked. "It would shame her if she showed any emotion, including being scared," she replied. "Okay, I don't want to shame anyone" I said as we walked into the kitchen.

Baked chicken strips and garden salad today, and it was delicious. I was a little nervous about the fight training with Pearl, I didn't want to hurt her. I've only trained with men and Margo until now. And Margo was only for a minute and since she was in cat form, didn't really count anyway. "How are you feeling about fight training?" I asked Pearl. "I'm fine with it, don't worry about me, just because I'm a little bit older than you doesn't mean that I can't defend myself or kick your butt" she replied. I gave her a cocky smile, "we shall see about that" I said. We walked outside to find a place to fight, James and Jason were in the spot that I had used with Jason yesterday. They didn't appear to be having any issues from where I was standing. Maybe James didn't say anything to him, and maybe they were actually getting along. That would make me happy, even though I was still angry with Jason for what he had done.

"Let's go over there," Pearl said, pointing at a place near the woods. I nodded and followed her. We walked past Arturo and David, "hey, I gathered and shaped out sticks for fighting, they are in a pile over there if you want" David said, pointing towards the woods. I saw the pile of sticks he was talking about. "Thanks" I said, as we continued walking by. We went over to grab a couple of the sticks and went to our chosen spot to begin. "Have you ever used these in fighting?" I asked her. "A long time ago, but I'm sure I'll remember pretty quickly" she replied, winking at me. I think I was starting to really like her, she was sassy. She was right, she had no problems picking it up again, or keeping up with me. We both landed a few blows to each other and we both blocked fairly well. After beating and defending until we were both pretty bruised up, we decided to heal each other and call it a day.

We were walking back toward the house, talking and laughing and James came to meet us. I looked up at him, "everything okay?" I asked. "Yeah, sorry, I just wanted to walk with you guys, is that okay?" He replied. I smiled at him, "sure" I said. "So how was today for you guys?" He asked. "Fun," Pearl replied. I smiled. I was glad that was her answer. "How was your day?" I asked. "Interesting," he said. I rolled my eyes, I didn't want to deal with the drama, I knew I would have to eventually though. We walked into the house without saying anything else. I walked into the bedroom so I could go to the bathroom and get cleaned up before dinner. James was waiting on the bed when I came out of the bathroom.

"What did he say?" I asked, rolling my eyes. "He told me he

kissed you, and you slapped him and haven't talked to him since. He apologized to me, and I told him that he needed to apologize to you" he said. I nodded. "Why didn't you just tell me?" He asked. "I didn't want drama, I didn't want you to start a fight with him," I said. "Not that I didn't like what you did instead of telling me, but I don't want you to be afraid to tell me things. I'm not a crazy person that's just going to start a fight," he said. "I'm sorry" I said, crinkling my nose up as I spoke. "Just trust me from now on?" He said. I nodded, "okay" I replied.

We walked out of the bedroom and went to the kitchen to eat with everyone. Everyone ate quietly, and seemed like they were all pretty tired from training. I suppose that was the way it should be, I was just used to everyone talking and the hum of chatter. It seemed eerily quiet. I tried to break the silence by asking "how was everyone's day?" I got a few shrugs and okay's and everyone went back silent. I felt like I needed a way to keep them motivated. I felt like a terrible leader because I didn't know what to do or say at that moment.

I went to my bedroom, feeling defeated. Stitch and Rayne were in there, I wondered what they thought of everything. I wondered if I could read their minds the way I did Margo's. I tried, but it didn't work, I suppose because they are just normal cats, not shapeshifters. James came into the room. "What's wrong with you?" He asked. I sighed, "I feel like everyone feels defeated, I need to think of a way to keep them motivated" I said. "I think everyone is just tired, they aren't used to this, I don't think anyone feels defeated. And I also think this is exactly what we need to be doing" he replied. I nodded, "I hope so," I said.

He got into bed with me and the cats left. I snuggled up to him, I just wanted to be held. He put his arm around me and pulled me close, I put my head on his chest and listened to the sound of his heart beating until I fell asleep. I had a normal dream that night, and by normal, I mean, not magical. I dreamed that I was riding in a blue convertible, James was driving. It was weird, because I felt like I didn't know him, like I had just met him. I looked at him and said, "Do you believe in magic?" He looked at me and smiled like I was joking, and said "you mean like card tricks?" I looked back at him, confused, and shook my head and said, "never mind."

I opened my eyes to see that James was awake and smiling at me. "Why do you do that?" I said, turning my head the other way. "Because you are beautiful and one of my favorite things is watching you sleep" he replied. I blushed, "I had a crazy dream," I said. "Did you see her again?" He asked. "No, it was a normal dream, but it was crazy," I replied. "Oh, okay, want to talk about it?" He asked. "No, it was just crazy, no need to talk about it. Did you ever check on that car for sale?" I replied as I got out of bed. "Not yet, I haven't had time," he said. "You should probably make time, if you want it. It will be sold to someone else if you don't" I said. I went to the kitchen, everyone was already in there, and the normal chatter was back. I guess James was right, everyone was just tired yesterday, it made me feel better about what we were doing. Jason walked up to me and said, "I'm sorry for what I did, I don't know what came over me." "Just don't let it happen again and we will be fine" I replied with a smile.

After we ate, we teamed up in two's again. I got David today, which I thought was pointless since he is the one that trained me how to fight and he can't do magic, but I did it anyway. "You know since you can't do magic, I'm gonna make you read magical books with me for half of the day" I told him. He scrunched his face up at me to show me he was displeased with my statement. "Don't you miss your family?" I asked. "I have been back to check in with them several times," he replied. "Oh" I said, surprised. "Yeah, Arturo has taken me back and forth," he said.

I felt a little better toward him now, I didn't realize how much of a grudge I was holding on him for leaving his family behind. I didn't understand how someone could do that, growing up as an orphan made me really judgy on people who did that. "How are they?" I asked. "Great, Sarah understands that I want to help you win this war. Julie is growing like a weed and sweet as sugar" he said. I smiled, "I can't wait to see them again" I said. Then we walked outside, to find a place for fight training. It was even warmer today than it had been the past few days. The warmth of the sun on my skin felt amazing. We went to the area where he and Arturo were the day before and began our fight training with the sticks.

After a while, I asked, "do you think we should try other weapons?" "What do you have in mind? I mean, we already have magic" he replied. "I don't know, I am just getting bored with playing with sticks," I said with a smile. He laughed, and said, "I can always just start punching and kicking you." "You can try," I snarled. It was weird how I always felt like he could be my brother and now I'm with his brother. So I guess that did make him my brother, that made me feel warm inside. After kicking each other's butts for a while, I healed our scrapes and bruises and we went inside for lunch. James walked up to me and kissed me on the forehead. "How's it going?" He asked. "Good" I replied, smiling up at him. "Okay, see you tonight" he said, and walked away.

At least he knew he didn't have to worry about me when I was with David, I could definitely tell his mind was at ease today. After we ate lunch, David and I found a book about dragons to read. I was actually curious, since I had been bitten by one and don't even know how it had happened. Obviously they can shrink themselves, apparently to the size of an ant, but their bites are still powerful. Of course, if it had wanted to kill me, all it would have had to do is remain in it's full size and swallow me whole, or just cook me with fire. "I wonder why I got bit?" I said, it was more a thought although I said it out loud. "It is odd, I still think someone could have sent it to bite you" David replied. I looked at him, still confused, because I was in dimension 2 when it happened and not many knew that I was there or who I am.

I wasn't as tired after today as I had been, probably because I didn't really use much magic. I wasn't as hungry as I normally am either, but I joined everyone for dinner and ate a little anyway. James sat beside me like he always did, everyone was quiet again. I didn't feel as bad as I had the night before because I could see it in their faces that they were all just tired. I just looked around and smiled whenever anyone made eye contact. "I just wanted to say that I am proud of everyone and we are doing great. And if any of you need to talk to me or need me for anything, I'm here" I said, because I felt like I had to say something, I did mean it though. Everyone looked at me and smiled, or said 'of course' and continued eating.

After dinner, I went to my bedroom, James followed quickly. "Hey you" he said, in a silly voice. "Did you get into the wine?" I asked with a smile. He laughed, "maybe just a smidge" he replied. I smiled at him and let out a little giggle. He sat down on the bed next to me, I could tell he was sleepy and the wine made his eyes look drowsy. I patted on the pillow to tell him to lay down. He smiled at me and put his head down on the pillow. I put my head on his chest and he started snoring. I couldn't believe how fast he fell asleep, it made me smile and I was laughing on the inside. He would never be able to hang with me on Broadway. I eventually fell asleep as well, I didn't have any dreams that night.

When I opened my eyes in the morning, I looked around for a minute, James wasn't there. I got up and went to the kitchen, feeling hungry because I hadn't eaten much the night before, he was sitting at the table. He looked at me and said, "good morning. I didn't want to wake you up, you looked like you were sleeping peacefully and my stomach started growling too loud so I decided to come eat." I smiled at him, "it's okay" I replied. I sat down next to him and started eating. After breakfast we split into teams of two again. I was working with Arturo today. I felt like it would be much the same as yesterday, except I would be using magic today.

Arturo and I walked outside, it was a bit cooler today than it had been yesterday. "The weather here is quite weird," Arturo said as we walked around the property, looking for a place to work. "Yeah, I grew up here and it still surprises me every year. Sometimes the seasons don't want to change, and sometimes they change on que it seems," I replied. He sneezed. "Yeah, allergies are terrible too, you should take something before it makes you get sick" I told him. "I can't wait to get back home," he said, jokingly. I laughed. We found a spot and started fight training, I hadn't done this with him so it was interesting. He liked to cheat and use magic, which was fair I suppose since that's more than likely what the enemy would be doing.

"I don't mean to pry, and you don't have to talk to me about it if you don't want to, but what happened between you and Margo?" I asked. "I was young and dumb, I fell in love with her, and when she fell in love with me too, it scared me. I was afraid we would be attacked even if we didn't reproduce because of the laws. I was also afraid that she would want kids and I didn't want to stand in the way of her having a family so I broke it off with her" he said. I was a little shocked that he told me so much. "It hurt me a lot, and I never found what I had with her again," he added. "She is hurt, but I think you may still have a chance," I replied. He smiled, but tried to hide it from me, which made me smile.

Fighting with Arturo was fun, I wish I had done it before. We trained in fighting until lunch time. After lunch we read, I found a book on unicorns which were apparently extinct now. "Could a shapeshifter be a unicorn?" I asked. "I suppose anything is possible, that's what my mother always told me anyway when I asked her silly questions," Arturo replied with a smile. I rolled my eyes at him.

"Well, I try to keep an open mind about things," I said. "It's not a bad trait" he replied simply.

After reading we started magical training. Arturo, of course, was good at scanning people and things for magical spells placed on them. He showed me how to do it. It was a combination of how I remove trauma and sensing magic. I wasn't as good at it as he was, but I could do it. When we combined our magic, we both felt more powerful. I didn't feel like a god, like I did when Damian projected his magic to me, but still more powerful than I did alone.

"You need to be careful of how much magic you use. I know I've told you before, using powerful magic can age you faster and giants already have a lower life span than most" Arturo said, while plucking a gray hair from my head and showing it to me. "I need to find out about my mother, but I don't know how," I said, changing the subject. "You really think she was part something besides witch?" He replied. "Yes, I do," I said. "And, even more than that, I think she could still be alive, or at least was," I said. He gave me a curious look. "Did anyone see her die? Did anyone see her body?" I asked. "Not that I know of," he replied. "Dinner is ready," Cori said. Making me jump again, I hadn't heard her come into the library where we were working.

After she walked out, I looked at Arturo and said, "I swear she does that on purpose." "What? Cook dinner? I thought that's why she was here," he replied. "No, sneaking up on me and scaring me" I said. "Did you hear her come in?" I asked him. "No, I wasn't paying attention," he replied. "What do you think of her? Do you get any bad vibes?" I asked. "No, not really, I don't really get anything from her," he said. "Have you ever spent time with an elf? Pearl says they don't show any emotion at all, that they view it as a weakness and it would greatly shame them even if it happened by accident" I said. "I have not and that could be a reason why some think they are bad" he said. "That's what I thought too," I said. "I would just keep doing what you have been, don't really talk about anything around her," Arturo replied, as we walked out of the library to go eat.

It seemed that everyone was getting used to training, the normal chatter was back. I smiled at everyone as I entered the dining room. "How was your day?" James asked. "Great, how about you?" I said. He just smiled at me and patted the chair next to him for me to sit down. "I heard from Leticia, high priestess of the forest moonrise coven today," Hale said. "Oh, really? What did she have to say?" I asked. "She wants to work as an ally on the outside. She says she's always disliked Oscar and she heard that he had taken over the moon coven and his plans to fight us and kill you upset her" he said. "Should we trust her? Now is no time to bring new people in, they could be working for him" I said.

"I trust her, and you're right, we shouldn't bring anyone new in now. But if she wants to work as a spy on the outside and get information on what he is doing, without giving her information on what we are doing, I don't see how that would hurt anything" he said. I nodded, "Don't give her any information and I don't see an issue with it" I said and started eating. The normal chatter started again, and I noticed that Arturo looked uncomfortable. I gave him a look to ask what was wrong without saying it aloud and drawing attention to him. He shook his head and started eating. He walked out as soon as he was finished eating. Maybe he wanted to see Margo?

I went to the front door and looked out of the window. He was standing at the edge of the lawn where the woods began but I didn't see Margo, so I went out to check on him. "What's wrong?" I asked as I walked up, he was facing the woods with his back toward me. "Forest moonrise was the coven I was born to, it just touched a nerve, that's all" he replied. "Do you know Leticia?" I asked. "No, I do not," he replied. I heard a rustle in the woods, "is that Margo?" I asked. He didn't reply but she walked out into view. "I'm just gonna go inside, and get ready for bed, good night" I said, as I walked away. She probably only came out because I was there, but I wanted to give them some privacy.

I went inside and went to my bedroom. James was already in there, he was petting Stitch. I smiled, "I always thought you didn't like my cats," I said. He looked at me, with a look of confusion. "Why would you think that?" He asked. "I've just never seen you pet them or show them any affection" I said. He shrugged his shoulders and said, "I just came in and he followed me and jumped up on my lap, so I was just petting him." I sat down on the bed next to him and Stitch came and sat on my lap. "Traitor" James said, to Stitch. "What do you think life will be like when this is over?" I asked him. "What do you mean?" He asked. "Everyone will go back to their own covens, we won't have to look over our shoulders all of the time, but what will we do?" I said. He laughed, "you think too much, we will live, travel, do whatever we want," he said. I smiled, he lay down next to me and I snuggled up to him and put my head on his chest. I loved being near to him, I loved how he smelled and I loved hearing the sound of his heartbeat. He started playing with my hair and soon I fell asleep. I had a dreamless sleep, and when I woke in the morning, he was still in bed with me, looking at me and smiling.

We got up and went to eat breakfast. I was a bit excited for the day. I would be training with Alice, at least she was someone new to work with. She seemed excited to work with me as well. After breakfast we quickly went outside to find a good spot before everyone else got out there. We found a place near the barn, before we started, we let Philip out. She put her arms around his neck and gave him a hug, then she started petting him. "I miss you buddy" she said to him. "I've got so much to tell you," she added. I smiled. I knew she could tell him now, but it seemed like it was something personal that she didn't feel comfortable saying in front of me.

"I have a question for you," I said. "What is it?" She asked, sounding nervous. "The catsuit, why?" I said. She laughed, "it was actually

James' idea, but he asked me to make it" she said. I rolled my eyes, "well, thanks, it is kinda nice in a fight and I feel like a badass" I said. We both laughed about it for a few minutes before we began fighting. She was strong, probably stronger than myself. She was also very agile for her size. "Do you do this often?" I asked. "I had brothers growing up," she replied. I nodded as I dropped down for a roundhouse kick. I wanted to drop her to the ground at least once, but she quickly jumped to miss the kick. We were a good match for each other, neither got the better of the other but we went at it until lunch time.

There was nothing to heal, so we went straight to lunch. After lunch we went to the library to find a book. The book we decided on was on magical spells. We sat down on a leather loveseat and started reading. I had to throw in some girl gossip as well, I wanted to get to know her better. "So, you and Levi are together?" I asked. She blushed, "we are complicated" she replied. "What does that mean?" I asked. "I don't really want to talk about it" she said, scrunching her face up. "Okay" I replied and we continued to read. Now I was even more curious about them, I guess it was my nosey nature, but I didn't press for answers. Noticing that it was almost time for dinner, I put a spell on the door for an alarm to ring in my ear if anyone entered. I wasn't going to let Cori scare me today. She never came, James sent me a text to let me know when it was time to eat.

Twenty

Continuing to train

After dinner, I wanted to take a walk, the weather was getting so nice, and I wanted to be out in it. I wanted to go out with my friends, I knew that wasn't possible yet, so I just took a walk around the property. I went for a ride on Philip, then I went into the woods and found Margo. I sat down on a log near her and she walked up to me. I felt like she wanted to tell me something so I put my hand on her head. She showed me Arturo sitting with her earlier and she put her paw on his leg. She was showing me that she forgave him. "Aww, that is great, he is a good man," I said. She lay down on the ground and started rolling around. "I wish I could turn you back to your human form" I told her. Her head went up and she looked toward the house, "someone coming?" I asked. She kept looking, finally I heard footsteps walking toward us. Shortly after I heard the footsteps I could see that it was James. I waved my arm so he would see me.

"What are you guys doing?" He asked as he walked up. "Just having some girl talk" I replied, smiling at Margo. She got up and walked away. "Looks like girl talk is over, did I see you riding Philip earlier?" He asked. "Yes, why do you ask?" I replied. "No reason, it's just a bit weird to me I guess" he said with a little giggle. "Are you about ready to head inside?" He asked. "Not really, but I guess I have to eventually. I think I'm getting a touch of cabin fever since the weather is getting nice" I replied. "Hopefully we will be ready to get rid of the threat soon," he said. "He's not the only threat, I have got to get them to see how the old laws should be done away with" I said. "I think the only way is the way we are doing it now, by force," he said. "I don't want to be a dictator," I replied. "I know, and once you are the Grand High Priestess, you can rule however you see fit, but we have to get them in line first" he said. I smiled at him and he put out his hand to help me up. We walked back to the house together, he put his sweater over my shoulders because the night chill had begun to move in.

I went straight to my bedroom, I picked up the jar that the fairy was in. I couldn't see her, but I whispered, "not too much longer until you can come out." James walked in and noticed me holding the jar, "I forgot about the fairy" he said as he sat down on the bed. "I haven't, I feel bad for her, I didn't realize she was just coming here to sleep" I said. "She wanted to come, don't feel bad about it," he replied. I smiled at him and walked over and kissed him. It was a long passionate kiss, as if I had been craving his kiss and not realized it. He threw me on the bed and we made love for hours. I felt like I would never get tired of this, of him. I slept really well that night, no dreams, and when I woke in the morning he was there, smiling at me. This time I didn't ask him why, I just smiled back.

I stumbled out of bed, to go eat breakfast. I was working with Levi today. I was a bit anxious that it would end in some kind of drama, but I didn't let it show. Levi didn't seem excited to work with me, we walked outside to find a spot for fight training. "You okay?" I asked him. "Sure, just never excited to beat up on a woman," he replied. I rolled my eyes, "don't think of me as a woman" I said. "Yeah, okay, how am I supposed to do that?" He asked. I punched him in the face, "does that help?" I asked. "Ouch" he said, rubbing his jaw. I shrugged my shoulders and said, "what are you gonna do about it?" He came at me but missed, I laughed to taunt him. "You shouldn't have assumed that you could kick my butt just because I am a female," I said. "Clearly" he replied.

He finally got a blow or two in on me, but nothing serious, I still think he was holding back. Maybe he was afraid of repercussions from James, he didn't need to think that way. If we are going into a fight, we have to fight, no holding back. After lunch, we went to the library to do some reading. He wanted to read a book on necromancy, which was fine with me. I hadn't studied it yet. Something about raising the dead and controlling them, like your own zombie army didn't sit right with me, but it seemed to excite Levi. Probably because he is a guy, it's okay for me to think that since he thought I couldn't fight because I'm a girl.

"So, are you and Alice a couple?" I asked him, to see if he would talk to me about it. "A couple of cool kids," he replied with a smile on his face. I laughed at him, "agreed" I said. "You should learn this," he said, pointing at the book. "You think I should raise the dead and have an army of zombies?" I asked. "You would control them, it's not like it's actually people, their souls are gone" he replied. "How do you know that for certain?" I asked. "It's just a corpse, once we die, it's just a body," he said. "Where does the soul go? Since you know so much." I said. "I'm not sure, but it doesn't just stay in a rotting corpse," he replied. "What do you believe?" He asked. "I believe in reincarnation," I replied. "Then why are you asking me?" He said sarcastically. I rolled my eyes at him as Cori managed to sneak in and make me jump again, "dinner is ready" she said. Levi gave me a weird look, "did you just jump?" he asked. "She does that to me almost everyday," I replied. He laughed as we got up and went to the dining room.

Dinner was uneventful, with the normal chatter of everyone talking about how their day had been. It started clouding up outside and a light rain began, so I couldn't go for a walk today after dinner. I decided to go sit in the living room. Levi followed me in there, "do you want me to build a fire?" he asked. "No, I mean, fires are nice when it's cold, but I'm comfortable," I replied. "Okay, just thought I would ask" he said as he walked upstairs. Alice followed him about five minutes after. I wondered why they were trying to be so secretive? I don't think anyone else here would mind if they were together.

James joined me on the sofa. I snuggled up to him, I didn't care if anyone knew that we were a couple. Jason came into the living room, "mind if I join you guys?" He asked. "No, I don't mind," I replied. "I wish we could go out, go to a bar or something" Jason said. "I know, me too," I replied. "What is with you guys?" James asked. "Sorry, in a world that doesn't have a lot of magic, us normal people are used to finding distractions from everyday life" I said. "Well, what else do you do besides get drunk?" James asked. Jason and I took turns naming off our favorite pastimes. "Golf" "Swimming" "Bowling" "Going to the movies" "Concerts" "Okay, maybe we can get something set up here, games or something to do in the evenings, maybe even set up a big screen outside to play movies on the lawn?" James suggested. I smiled at him, "that sounds really nice, I don't want everyone to get too comfortable and lose focus right now though" I replied. Jason got up and walked away, seeming irritated with my answer.

"I'm sleepy, I think I'm going to go take a relaxing bath and get ready for bed" I said, as I got up and kissed James on the forehead. I went to the bedroom and into the bathroom and started running my bath. I always ran my bath water extremely hot, I usually looked like a lobster after a bath because my normally pale skin would be red. It felt nice though, it helped me to relax. Rayne made her way into the bathroom with me. She would always sit on the edge of the tub and watch me. I always wondered what cats thought of humans sitting in water. They must think we are completely nuts. My anxiety was starting to act up, voices in my head telling me that I should just give up, throw in the towel before one or more of my friends ended up dead. I knew I couldn't listen, I didn't have a choice, this wasn't just about me, it was about doing what was right, moving the world forward.

James walked into the bathroom. "Are you going to stay in here all night?" he asked. "I could stay in here forever, it feels nice," I said. "You know what else feels nice?" He asked. "What?" I asked with a smile. "These arms around you" he replied in a teasing voice. "You're right, I'm getting out now" I said with a smile. He walked out and came back in with my bathrobe. "Aww, thank you" I said, still smiling. "You're welcome" he replied, winking at me. I went to the bedroom and sat down on the bed. James sat down behind me and started massaging my shoulders. "Thank you, I've been kind of tense," I said. "No problem, you want to talk?" He asked. I shook my head, "no, it's not important, just everything that's going on" I said. "I do want my snuggles that I got out of the bath for though" I said. He lay down and I lay down next to him and put my head on his chest.

I fell asleep quickly, I started dreaming immediately. I was in the same place as I had been the last time that my mom had contacted me. I started looking around for her. I didn't see her anywhere. I walked up one side of the street and back down the other side. I just kept looking, it was like she had created the space, but couldn't get to me. Then I thought, maybe she left some other clue? But what? I started looking in cars passing by, on the sides of buildings.

I noticed a mural on the side of one of the buildings. I recognized what it was right away. The painting started with a fiery spiral coming out of what looked like a chimney, the spiral turned into a tail and then talons. Great wings spread out. It was a phoenix. What did it mean though? Did it mean anything?

I woke from James nudging me. I groaned at him and gave him an evil look. "You were groaning," he said. "Don't wake me if I'm dreaming" I said, angrily. "I'm sorry," he replied. "Did you see her?" He asked. "No, but I saw something, I don't know what it means, I think it is a message from her" I told him. "What did you see?" He asked. "A painting of a phoenix," I said. He looked at me like he was confused, "I don't know what that could mean" he said. "Me either, probably why I was groaning, I was getting so frustrated" I said, "sorry I snapped at you" I added. "It's okay," he said. It was still early but I could see that the sun was starting to come up, so I didn't try to go back to sleep.

I walked outside to sit on the porch. I didn't see anyone else yet, I heard Cori moving about in the kitchen, getting breakfast started. It was still a bit chilly outside, but the fresh morning air smelled nice. I saw Margo sitting at the edge of the woods, something else caught her eye, or ear, she turned and ran back into the woods. After a little while, I started hearing people talking and walking around inside. Conan and Hale came out and joined me on the porch. "Nice morning," Conan said. I looked at him and smiled, and said, "yeah, it's not bad, feels nice."

We sat there and talked for a while and James joined us, he sat close to me and put his arms around me. "Do you think Arturo is up yet?" I asked no one in particular. "Not sure, why do you ask?" Hale said. "I need to talk to him about something," I replied. "If it's something magical, you know we are witches too, right?" Conan said. "I know, I just didn't want to add anything onto either of you right now" I said, trying not to offend them. "It's why we are here,"

Conan said. Thankfully, Arturo walked out and joined us at that moment, I just didn't want to repeat myself, I knew no one would have answers. "Speak of the devil and he shall appear," Hale said, looking at Arturo and smiling.

"You were talking about me? I hope it was good." Arturo said, teasingly. "Always," I said, with a smile. "So, I had a dream last night. It was one of the dreams where I usually see my mom. I didn't see her this time, so I started looking around for her, or for a clue. Something caught my eye, it was a mural painted on a building of a phoenix," I told them. "Any idea what it could mean?" I asked them. They all looked like they were trying to think. "Maybe she's trying to let you know that we will rise," Hale said. I smiled at him, but I didn't think that was what she was trying to say. "You think she is trying to tell you that she is, or was, part phoenix?" Arturo asked. "I don't know, is it possible?" I asked. "I don't know the answer to that, I have never met a phoenix," Arturo replied. "I learned that they don't reproduce, they are just reborn when they die. So how can anyone be part phoenix?" I asked. Cori stepped out on the porch and said, "breakfast is ready." Before anyone could answer. She didn't scare me this time, win for me.

I was a bit excited, today I was training with Damian. The feeling of having ultimate power like a god was addicting to say the least. After breakfast, I headed outside with Damian for fight training. He didn't take it easy on me, he was probably my most worthy opponent so far. By lunch, I was bruised and broken, literally, fractured my ankle. It was an easy heal with our powers combined. By the time I got to the dining room for lunch, I felt brand new. "Sorry if I was too hard on you," Damian said. "No, don't be, my enemies aren't going to show mercy or take it easy, that's what I've been trying to get through to the rest of these dopes," I said, teasingly. Levi overheard and rolled his eyes at me. After lunch we started magical training, the part that I was really looking forward to.

"Hale told me about your dream," Damian said. I looked at him, waiting for his opinion. "Has she ever said anything to you that could be about the future?" He asked. I thought for a minute, "she did say once that, 'the child would save me' or something like that" I replied. "Hmmm" was his reply. "Is there a prophecy about me?" I asked. "Not that I know of," he said. "Damn" I replied. He laughed at me. He projected his magic onto me, I wasn't sure what to do, so I did what Jason had done and started levitating. I went higher than I meant to, of course. I shot up way too far, above the house, above the trees. I am scared of heights so I started to panic and fall. I just knew this was it, this was how I was going to die. I was falling so fast but it seemed an eternity before Damian caught me by retracting his magic and using it to stop my fall only a couple of feet from the ground.

"What the hell?!" He yelled at me. "I don't know," I replied. "You couldn't think of anything else but flying?!" He continued to yell at me. "I'm sorry, just feeling all that magic coursing through my body, I had to release it somehow" I said. He nodded, "please just don't ever do that again" he said. "I don't plan on it, don't worry" I replied. He let out a nervous giggle and said, "James would have killed me if you had died." I just gave him a look to let him know that I was sorry for scaring him.

After that, we went inside to read for the rest of the day. We found the perfect book, *The History of the Phoenix*. I found one reference that really got my attention, it said, one story says they are able to change into people or other birds. I pointed it out to Damian. "If they can change into people, then my mother could have been part Phoenix, and if she is or was, maybe she's still alive somewhere!" I said excitedly. "I still think it's a stretch, if she were alive, don't you think you would have actually seen her by now? Not in a dream, but don't you think she would be here with you?" Damian said. "If she could, yes, but what if she can't?" I replied. He just looked at me, then he looked over my shoulder to let me know someone was there. "Is dinner ready?" I asked without turning around. "Yes ma'am it is," Cori replied. I rolled my eyes and closed the book.

I eagerly told Arturo about the discovery I had made about the Phoenix. "I have heard that story before, when I was a child my father told me about it. He said that it was a young man that seemed to have amnesia, he didn't know where he had come from, he had just woken up in the desert, hot, thirsty and naked. When provoked, he would throw fire and burn whole villages down. And when they shot him with an arrow through the heart, his body started smoking and burst into flames. After it finished burning, a tiny bird emerged from the ashes and flew away. No one ever saw him again, in either form" Arturo said. "So, why couldn't it be possible that my mom was or is part Phoenix?" I asked. "I guess anything is possible, but if so what does it mean?" Arturo replied, looking very thoughtful. "If you figure it out, let me know," I said.

After dinner I went to my bedroom, James followed soon after. We lay in bed and snuggled. "How was your day?" He asked. "I don't really want to talk about it, it was exhausting," I said. Not wanting to tell him that I had a broken bone, almost killed myself, and I didn't want to talk about my mother anymore. "You can throw fire pretty well, maybe you are part Phoenix," he said. I just looked up at him, he kissed me on the forehead and then I just laid my head down on his chest and fell asleep.

I had a dreamless sleep that night. When I woke in the morning James was still snuggling me. I looked at him, smiled and said, "I love you." "I love you too, did you dream at all?" He replied. "No," I said, simply. We got up to go have breakfast. I was working with Misty today. I almost hoped she would take it a little easy on me after the day I had yesterday. While we were having breakfast we were all discussing how everything was coming along, everyone seemed to be feeling more confident and that made me feel good. "I feel like I learn something new everyday, plus I'm getting stronger, physically and magically," Jason said. I smiled at him, and whispered, "me too." He laughed, and I laughed with him, but I was serious.

After breakfast Misty and myself went outside for fight training, we chose the spot near the barn. Philip was roaming around, it was a very nice day, warm with sunshine. We used the sticks in our fighting, she was strong. And since we were both witches, we used some magic as well. When it was time for lunch, we healed each other and went inside to eat. After lunch we worked on magic training, not that she needed it. She was very powerful, I can understand why me seeming to have more power than her had scared her to come to our side. "Honestly, I have no idea why I'm so powerful, and I had never met anyone that was more powerful than myself until I met you," Misty said. "Now that you know that the power wasn't all mine, do you regret your decision?" I asked her. "No, I don't, and it doesn't matter that the power doesn't come from you, the fact that you can hold it, harness it, and use it is seriously astounding" She replied. "Why do you say that?" I asked. "Some would drop dead from that much power coursing through their body" she replied. I looked at her astonished, and learned something new yet again.

After magic work, we went to the library. I found a book on elves, "Mind if we read this one?" I asked her. "No, that's fine," she replied. We sat down on the sofa next to each other and began reading. I didn't really find any helpful information in the book, nothing I didn't already know. Apparently the most distinct characteristic of an elf is that they show no emotion, and physically their eyes can be strange colors. Cori's eyes were a golden brown, they looked a little strange but not inhuman. "Have you checked on the rest of your coven since you have been here?" I asked Misty. "Yes, I call them daily to make sure they are okay and aren't causing any trouble" she replied with a smile. "Do they hate me because of Carly?" I asked. "They are upset that she is gone, but I have explained to them that things have changed now" she replied, simply. I nodded. A voice right near my ear said, "dinner is ready." I jumped again as I turned to Cori and said, "thank you."

Dinner was uneventful, just the normal chatter. I was feeling exhausted, it was such a nice evening that I couldn't just go to bed without enjoying a nice walk around the property. I managed to sneak out alone. Philip was still grazing in the yard, I walked up to him and started petting his neck. He lowered himself, wanting me to get on. "I don't know, I'm pretty tired," I told him. He snorted and neighed and remained lowered. "Fine, just for a few minutes," I said as I climbed onto his back. He took off slowly then started trotting. I giggled as he started to gallop faster, the wind felt nice as it blew my hair back. I was becoming a pro at horse riding, I wondered if I could ride a normal horse? After running around the property a couple of times he walked back toward the barn and let me off. I pet him and smiled, then I hugged his neck, and said, "thank you." He nudged my back as I walked away and I turned and smiled at him again.

I walked over to the edge of the yard where the woods began and sat down. Looking up at the treetops. It was relaxing, so I lay down, and I guess I had been more tired than I had realized because I fell asleep. I woke up to what felt like someone rubbing my arm with sandpaper. It was Margo, she stopped when I opened my eyes. I guess she had been worried about me. I sat up, "I'm okay, I guess I just fell asleep" I told her. She started rubbing against my back and making small growling noises. "I'm sorry if I worried you" I said, as I rubbed her head. She lay down on the ground next to me. Movement toward the house caught my eye, I looked and saw that Arturo was walking toward us. The sun had just set and the light of dusk was fading as was the warmth of the day.

Arturo sat down next to Margo. He looked at me and said, "how are you?" "I'm fine, why do you ask?" I replied. "You don't seem fine,"

He replied. "I am, I mean, as fine as I can be," I said. "What does that mean?" He replied. "I mean, with everything that's going on. My life went from normal to extraordinary pretty quickly. And not to mention all the people that want to kill me and a mom that I'm now not sure if she's really dead or not. I'm just exhausted" I said. "Maybe we should take a day off from training?" He suggested. "No, I don't think we shouldn't do that, maybe we will have time to take one day after training" I replied. He nodded, "spirit of a warrior" he said. I smiled at him. It was now completely dark out, but I noticed a figure walking toward us, it was James.

He walked up to us and sat down next to me. "Still missing the *normal* things?" He asked. "What normal things?" Arturo asked. "He's talking about things that I used to do for fun," I said, looking at Arturo. Arturo just nodded his head and turned his attention to Margo. "Why don't you take her back with you the next time you and David go?" I said. He looked at me, "do you think she would want to go?" He asked. "Just let her know where and when to meet you, if she shows up, then she wants to go," I said. He nodded. "And how is it that you can go to different dimensions so often? I thought it took a lot of power and should only be done every few months or so?" I asked. "Being a solo practitioner most of my life helps," he said. James stood up and put his arm out to help me up. I took it, and we walked back to the house together.

We went straight to the bedroom and sat down on the bed. He started massaging my shoulders, it felt amazing, I hadn't even realized how tense I was. "So Margo and Arturo?" He asked, almost sounding like he was talking to himself. "Yes, what's wrong with that?" I asked. "Nothing, nothing at all, I just never even imagined the two of them together" He replied. "Arturo broke both of their hearts when he broke up with her, he did it because of the laws that we are fighting to break now" I told him. "I wouldn't care a bit about any stupid laws, no way I could ever leave you" he replied. I turned around and smiled at him. He kissed me, I put my hands behind his head to pull him closer into me. It wasn't long until we were making love, after we finished we lay there silently, holding each other.

As exhausted as I was, it took me a long time to fall asleep. I lay with my head on James' chest, listening to his heartbeat. He started snoring lightly, so I knew he had fallen asleep. I was so glad that I had found him, but I started to think about David's concerns. I was a target to so many, if I was killed, what would that do to him? I tried not to think about it, and I certainly didn't plan on getting killed. I now had an army behind me and I knew that the army would grow before it was over. And once this was over, and I was the Grand High Priestess, and the laws were changed, would we be able to relax then? Or would we always be looking over our shoulders for that one enemy that we didn't know about? At some point my mind eventually stopped and I drifted off. I had a dreamless sleep, and when I woke in the morning I was still sleepy, but I got up anyway because that's what I had to do.

I didn't feel very hungry, but I went to breakfast anyway and nibbled on some of the food, hoping that no one would notice that I wasn't really eating. I was working with Hale today and Conan tomorrow, how did I end up with all the witches back to back? I was pretty sure that was what was making me so exhausted, using so much magic. "I have a question," I said to Hale. "I'll try to answer," he replied. "How is magic not like a muscle? Like using it everyday should make you stronger magically right?" I said. He just looked at me like he was confused. "I feel exhausted from using magic daily," I said, trying to explain what I was talking about. "Witches are born with how much magic their body's can handle, you have been taking on other's magic as well. That can kill some witches," He replied. "So I've heard," I said as I got up from the table.

We walked outside to begin fight training. "We don't have to use magic today, if you need a break from it" Hale said. "That wouldn't be fair to either of us, the whole point of this is to learn to fight together, use our brains together and to use magic together" I said. "But if it's hurting you, how does that help any of us?" He replied. "It's not hurting me, I'm a little tired, we will rest after tomorrow" I told him. He reluctantly gave in and we used magic. When it was time for lunch, we healed each other's scrapes and bruises and went inside. It was strange to me that we could heal the outside and I could heal other's emotional trauma but I couldn't be magically healed from my exhaustion.

After lunch we went to the library, I found a book on spells and magical projection that we sat down to read together. "What do you think about necromancy?" I asked Hale. "Why are you asking?" He replied curiously. "I was having a discussion the other day about it with Jason," I said. "How do you feel about it?" He replied. "I don't like it, I think it's a bad thing" I said. "Depends on the intent of the user, just like with any magic. If the intent is bad then it's bad, but if the intent is good, then it's good" he said. "How can it be good?" I asked. "Raising the dead to fight for a good cause would be good, don't you think?" He replied. "No, I don't," I said. "Then we can agree to disagree, I see no point in arguing," he said. I didn't reply, I could tell he was set firmly in his ways.

I found a passage in the book under magical projection that said several witches had died taking in too much magic at once. I pointed it out in the book and said, "do you think I am in danger of doing this?" "You should be able to feel if it is too much," Hale replied. "How? How will I feel it? All I feel is god like when Damian projects his magic to me" I explained. "You are very strong magically, it would probably take a lot more than one witch projecting magic to you to kill you. Although, you can still do damage to yourself" Hale said. "I know, the aging thing, apparently that is already affecting me," I said. "I hope that when this is over, we can all live in peace and not have to worry about using too much magic or any if we choose not to," Hale said. I looked at him and smiled. I hoped that too, but I had a feeling that this wouldn't end soon. "Dinner is ready," Cori said from right beside me. I let out a little grunt with my jump this time. I really wasn't expecting her.

Dinner was just the same as it always was, the normal chatter. I was extremely tired and still not feeling very hungry. I nibbled on my food again and excused myself early. I went straight to my bedroom this time. I would love to go outside and frolic with Philip and sit with Margo, but I was just too tired tonight. I lay down on the bed and Rayne and Stitch jumped up to cuddle with me. I drifted off in no time at all. I had a dreamless sleep, James didn't even wake me when he came to bed. I woke in the morning feeling rested, thankfully. James was lying next to me, still asleep. I managed to get out of bed without waking him. I decided to go for a run before breakfast since I didn't get out the night before.

The sun was just starting to come up and there was a light fog low on the ground. I noticed an unnatural light out of the corner of my eye. I turned to see what it was, it was a bluish light that I recognized immediately. Suddenly, Arturo, David and Margo appeared and the light disappeared. I smiled and waved at them and continued my jog. It made me happy that Margo had gone with them. I couldn't wait to ask her how it went. The air was still chilly, but it felt nice on my face. I started sweating and took off my sweatshirt that I had on over a tank top, I threw it on the porch as I ran by. People were starting to wake up and move around now. Conan and Hale were sitting on the porch and James walked out, he waved at me and I waved back. I ran a couple more laps before I decided to stop.

I walked up to the porch where James had sat down with Conan and Hale and took the empty seat next to James. He tried to put his arm around me, but I pushed him away and said "I'm hot and sweaty" with a smile so he didn't get offended. "I just wanted to sit here to cool down for a minute before I go get a shower" I said. He shrugged and pulled back, but whispered in my ear, "you know I don't mind if you are sweaty." It sent a shiver up my spine, in a good way. "I'm working with you today, Conan," I said. "Yes," he replied. I smiled. "I got a lot of rest last night, I hope you are ready" I said, teasingly. "I think I can handle it," he replied. I giggled as I stood up to go inside to take a shower before breakfast.

After my shower, I joined everyone in the dining room. "As long as nothing happens, we will take tomorrow off before we start planning our next move" I said to everyone. They all seemed happy about the announcement, smiling and cheering. I smiled with them. I knew everyone else had to be just as tired and worn out as I was. Arturo seemed to be in very good spirits, smiling and laughing with everyone. He and Margo must have made up, I smiled at him. I was feeling more hungry today as well. After breakfast Conan and I went outside to start our fight training.

I shouldn't have teased him, he was certainly not holding back. I had to really bring the defense, possibly more than I had with anyone else. After going at it for about an hour I started to lose momentum and he managed to get a good hit with his stick right on the side of my face, I heard my jaw crack. The look on his face told me it was bad, really bad. Then I felt the pain, I couldn't close my mouth. I let out a gargled blood curdling scream. He immediately cast a spell to numb my face and said, "sit down, I'll start healing you!" I looked at him, not able to feel my face and sat down, like he had said. He sat down across from me and closed his eyes.

I noticed James was walking up behind Conan quickly. "What the hell?!" He yelled when he saw my face. "I'm trying to heal her," Conan said, sounding irritated. I waved to tell James just to go, but he came and sat down next to me and put his hand on my leg instead. I wanted to give him a look that I didn't want him there, I didn't want him to see me like this, but I couldn't feel my face so I couldn't. Conan started the healing spell, I still couldn't feel my face, but after a minute or so, he opened his eyes and said, "there, all better!" I still couldn't talk because my face was numb, so I motioned around my face with my hand. "Oh! Of course, sorry!" Conan said as he took the numbing spell off.

I touched my face and moved my jaw to see if it worked. "All good" I said and smiled at Conan and James. "Please don't break her again" James said to Conan as he got up and walked away. I looked at Conan and "wow" was all I could manage to say. "What? I didn't do it on purpose, you failed to block" he said. "I know," I said with a little giggle. We decided to move on to magic training. We took turns casting spells, I practiced working with more elements since I could conjure fire pretty well. I tried water, it took me several tries but I finally got it. Then I conjured a wind tunnel. I decided not to mess with Earth quite yet, I didn't want to accidentally cause a major earthquake. We kept working with magic even after lunch. When there was only about an hour left before dinner we finally went to the library to read.

I found a book that I recognized, the one on magical creatures that I had read before. I decided to read it again. We sat down on the sofa and opened the book. It opened directly to the Phoenix chapter. "Wow, maybe that's a sign," I said. Conan rolled his eyes at me, and said, "not everything means something." I snarled my nose up at him and rolled my eyes. We started reading, but I didn't find anything new. I noticed that it was getting close to dinner so I started being more aware of my surroundings. I still didn't hear her come in until she was right at my ear saying, "dinner is ready." Of course, I jumped again. I was getting so irritated with her, but I didn't let it show. I had a feeling that if I let her know that I was irritated with it, she would try even harder to do it.

Everyone seemed a little lighter, a little louder, a little happier tonight at dinner. Maybe it was because we were taking a day off to relax and celebrate tomorrow? Maybe it was because they were feeling better as a team? Everyone seemed to be getting along well, that was a plus. After dinner, I went outside. It was a very warm day and the evening sun felt amazing. I sat down next to the woods, hoping Margo would come join me. After sitting there for a few minutes she came out of the woods and stood in front of me. “Hi!” I said, excitedly. I pat the ground next to me to tell her to come sit with me. She walked over and sat down. “So, you went home with Arturo for a while?” I asked. She put her head against my arm, so I put my hand on her head and waited for the visions to start.

Twenty-One

Keeping a promise

I put my hand on Margo's head, she showed me when they landed on dimension 2. She was in human form, of course, and naked. Arturo had some clothes ready for her to put on. They said goodbye to David and he walked away. Arturo grabbed her face and started kissing her. I squealed a little with excitement for them. I suppose that was all that I needed to see, she pulled away. I smiled at her and said, "I'm so happy for you two." She rubbed against my back the way a house cat would. I giggled at her. James had found me, I looked up to see him walking toward us.

"Mind if I join you?" He asked as he approached. "I don't mind at all," I said with a flirty smile on my face. He sat down beside me and said, "it feels nice out this evening." "Yes it does" I agreed. Margo got up and ran into the woods. Either we were boring her or she heard something moving around like a deer or rabbit that she would make her dinner. James and I lay back on the ground and looked up into the sky. "The view of the stars from here is breathtaking," James said. "I agree," I replied. "Do the stars not shine on dimension 2?" I asked.

"The light from the double moons pretty much drowns it out. You have been there" he replied. "I don't really remember seeing many stars, maybe just some of the brightest, like it is when you're in a city here," I said. "Yeah, that's pretty much how it is. This is really beautiful" he said. "I think the two moons are beautiful," I replied. "I think you are beautiful," he said right before he kissed me.

"I think we should go back to dimension 2, rest up before we go to battle" James said. I looked at him, slightly confused. "What? It's not going to hurt anything, we will only be gone for a night. If we go tonight, we will be back by the morning and still enjoy another day off with the rest of them" he said, looking toward the house. I thought about it for a moment, it did sound like a good idea, but at the same time, I was worried about losing focus. It was almost like he could read my mind from the look on my face. "It's okay to take a little break, we won't be putting anyone in danger," he said. "What about losing focus on what's happening? I know two weeks without having to think about the impending war will dull what we have been working so hard on for myself" I replied. "You could never be dull in any way," he argued. I rolled my eyes at him. "I will randomly attack you to keep you sharp," he said with a sly smile. I smiled back at him, "okay, we can go, but, I don't know if we should stay for two weeks" I said. "Okay, fair compromise, I suppose, whenever you decide to come back, we will come back" he agreed.

We went to find Arturo and David to let them know of our plans. They agreed to let us jump with them to 2 and we would stay at David's house. I went to find Levi and Alice to see if they would like to join us. "No, I don't want to go back there right now, I think that would be too dangerous for myself. I feel like I barely got away from the giants the last time," Alice said. She looked at Levi like she was waiting for his answer. "I don't need to go back right now either," he said, looking at her. "Okay, I just thought I would offer," I said, as I walked out of the room because it felt awkward.

I went back outside where James and Arturo were standing close to the barn talking. "Hey" James said with a smile as I walked up. I smiled back at him and said, "Alice and Levi don't want to come with us. Do you think we should take Philip? It would give him a break from being in horse form for a while" I suggested. James looked at Arturo, "I don't see a problem with that, Margo will be going, so we might as well take Philip too" Arturo said. I smiled, I was getting a little excited for the little get away. I walked into the barn and walked over to Philip. I put my hand on his head, "we are going to 2 for a little while for a little get away and we are taking you with us" I said. He lifted his head and let out a snort, it sounded like an agreement and I smiled at him.

I went inside to get my things ready. I went to my room, Rayne and Stitch were laying on the bed. I lay down for a little while and cuddled with them. They purred as I took turns petting them. I noticed a movement from the corner of my eye. It was the fairy! She had woken from her winter slumber. I walked over to the dresser where the jar was sitting with the firefly inside. She was crawling around the glass. The nights were still very chilly and I hadn't seen any other fireflies yet, so I was concerned about letting her out just yet. And I didn't want to let her out into the house, I was scared the cats would kill her. "I think we need to wait a little while longer before you go out, it's still a bit cold out" I said to her. The firefly just crawled around the glass. I was sure she understood me, but had no way to communicate back with me.

I sat the jar down and started packing a bag. I decided to put the jar in the bag and take her back to 2 with us. I kept finding James' clothes, it seemed that he had more in here than I did, I giggled. I didn't pack his things, he could do that himself. After I finished getting my bag together, I went out into the living room. James and David were sitting there. "I got my stuff ready," I said. James looked at me and smiled and nodded and got up to go get his things together. “Are you two officially living together?” David asked after James had left the room. “I suppose we are, all of his stuff is in my room, well, I guess I should say, ‘our room’” I said, with a giggle.

David looked at me with a blank face. “You still don’t want us together, do you?” I said. “It’s not that I don’t want you together, I just fear that it is not a good union. You shouldn’t mix business with pleasure” he replied. “I love him and I would do anything to protect him. And I won’t let our feelings for each other get in the way of what has to be done” I said. David looked at me and nodded, “what’s done is done, there is nothing I can do about it now. And he loves you too, by the way” he said. I looked at him and smiled. I felt my stomach growl so I went to the kitchen to find a snack.

Cori was in there preparing dinner, she looked up when she noticed me come in. “Dinner will be ready in about an hour, ma’am” she said. I smiled at her, “I was just looking for a little snack” I said, picking up an apple and taking a bite. She turned and continued with what she had been doing without saying anything else. After eating the apple, I walked out of the kitchen. Damian and Hale were now sitting in the living room with David. I didn’t want to tell everyone about us leaving, so I didn’t say anything about it. David seemed to pick up on what I was thinking and didn’t say anything either.

“So, we are going to relax and party tomorrow?” Damian asked. “That’s the plan, we all need a little break,” I replied with a smile. I felt like I was betraying them by not telling them. I didn’t want the majority of the team to go with us, I was afraid if everyone lost focus, it would lead to us getting defeated and possible lives lost. James came out of the bedroom and I quickly looked at him and slightly shook my head to let him know not to say anything, he gave me a slight nod back that he understood. “So, do you guys have any ideas for fun stuff to do tomorrow?” I asked, looking at Damian and

Hale. “Relaxing sounds fun to me,” Hale replied with a smile. “Of course we will do that too," I said with a giggle.

“I am going to go start relaxing now as a matter of fact, maybe a nap” I said, with a smile as I walked into my bedroom. I didn’t want to be around other people at the moment. I didn’t want to let it slip that we were leaving tonight. I knew that they wouldn’t know that we were gone, but it still felt like I was betraying them. I walked into the bedroom and lay down on the bed. Stitch jumped up onto the bed with me, purring. I started petting him and his purrs got louder. It startled me and I jumped a little when the bedroom door opened. Stitch jumped down and ran out as James came in. He walked over to the bed and sat down next to me. I put my arms around his waist without sitting up.

“Are you okay?” He asked, petting my head. “I feel like I’m betraying the others by not telling them that we are leaving, but at the same time, we can’t let them go. I can’t let everyone lose focus on what lies ahead. And what lies ahead is bothering me, we have no idea how things are going to work out” I replied. “Well, I’m not too worried. We have a very strong and capable leader. We have all worked hard to learn each other’s strengths and weaknesses. And I simply don’t see anything wrong with a little, well deserved escape before the storm hits,” James said. I looked at him and smiled, “I wish I had your confidence about everything” I replied. “It’s okay to be scared, I would be willing to bet that the bravest warriors in history had to fight their own insecurities and fears before going into battle” he said, trying to reassure me. I looked at him and smiled, just the fact that he was trying so hard to make me feel better, made me feel better.

I could smell food and knew it must be close to dinner time. I sat up, kissed James and said, “let’s go have dinner.” “You should probably tell Levi and Alice not to tell the others that we are leaving,”

James suggested. I looked at him and nodded, "you're right" I said. I walked out of the room and saw Levi and Alice walking down the stairs, I walked toward the stairs and met them at the bottom. "Hey, I would appreciate it if you don't mention that we are leaving tonight to anyone else," I whispered. They both nodded their heads and we walked to the kitchen together. The food was amazing as always, the chatter seemed extra loud with everyone being excited just to have a little fun and relax the next day.

After dinner I walked out to the front porch to sit and watch the sunset. Damian joined me. "You think it's a good idea to take a day off?" He said, in a tone that suggested that he didn't think it was a good idea. "Really? You think that we don't deserve a day to rest, a day to play, just one day before we start fighting?" I replied. "I was just asking," he said, defensively. "Why? What is your reasoning?" I asked in a firm tone. "I just don't think taking our minds off of what we are doing for a single moment is a good idea," he replied. "I understand where you are coming from with that, I have struggled with it myself, but I truly believe we are doing the right thing, just one day, everything will be okay" I said, smiling at him. He smiled back, let out a sigh and said, "you're probably right." He got up and went inside and I followed. I went to the bedroom to make sure I had everything ready. We would be leaving in a couple of hours.

I double checked my bag and looked around the room, I didn't see anything else that I would need. I still felt like something was off, maybe it's just that I had never planned a trip to 2, I had always been kidnapped and taken. I giggled to myself at the thought. It would be a nice break, I told myself. I had never taken an actual vacation in my life. It was strange enough for me to 'come home' to this gigantic house instead of my tiny apartment. And to live with so many other people when I had lived alone since I was eighteen. Everyone was great though, and they really felt like family to me, not that I had much to compare it to. Before, Jason was the closest thing I had to family. I felt warm and happy inside. I couldn't possibly think about losing any of them now, it would crush my soul. I would do whatever I had to do to keep them all safe and happy.

I knew they would be safe here for the night, the protection around the property was strong even without my magic in it. I had to let go of my fears, of needing to be where they were, that wouldn't always be possible anyway and I needed to get used to it. I wondered if I told James that I had changed my mind, if he would just kidnap me and take me anyway so that I could still go but not feel guilty about it if anything were to go wrong? Probably not, he respected me too much to do that now. I heard the door opening and turned to see him walking in. "You good?" He asked. "Yeah, just still struggling with the whole thing, I'm trying to get over it though" I replied. He smiled at me, "I won't force you to go, if you are really against it, if you really don't want to do it, you don't have to go" he said. "I want to go, I just can't help feeling guilty and I'm not even sure why" I replied. "It doesn't matter then, just let it go," he said with a smile. I smiled back and nodded.

When everyone started settling down and going to their rooms, those of us who were leaving met outside by the barn. Everyone got there before Arturo, but he came along shortly after mumbling something about how he had to use the restroom. I looked at him funny and giggled. Margo let out a growl. "Sorry, love," he said, looking at her. We all joined hands in a circle to quickly perform the jump before anyone saw us. The usual feeling of nothingness and we were all standing in a field. I could see David's house in the distance. Philip and Margo were both in human form and naked. Arturo grabbed a trench coat from his bag and handed it to Margo and then he pulled out a gray blanket and handed that to Philip so they could cover themselves.

I took a deep breath of the fresh non polluted air then I let it out. It was a good decision to come here, I could feel it already. The tension was leaving my body and I felt an excitement come over me to see Julie and Sarah. I hugged Margo and smiled. She smiled back and said, "what was that for?" "I just wanted to hug you, I haven't got to see you in this form in a while," I replied with a smile. "Oh, sorry, for me it's no difference what form I am in, I feel the same. But I guess if I look at it from your point of view, I can see how it is different for you" she said. "Same," Philip said. I walked over and hugged him. He smiled at me, "so you like riding?" he said, teasingly. "Don't be rude," James said. "What?" Philip said, looking at James like he didn't know what he was talking about. I just smiled because I didn't want them to start fighting.

"Are you going to your place?" James asked Philip. "Yes, I need clothes anyway, but I would like to join you guys back here for a day or so before we go back, if that's okay?" Philip said, looking at David. "Sure, sure, no problem," David replied. "We may not stay the whole time, so I think it is a good idea for you to be here, in case we go back earlier" I said. He nodded, "No problem, James knows how to get in touch with me, I'll just be heading home now then, see you all in a few days," Philip said as he walked into the forest. "We are going to head to my place," Arturo said, with his arm around Margo. I smiled at them. "Okay, you guys have fun" I said, with a wink. I didn't think it was possible as her skin is, but I saw Margo's cheeks turn pink. After they walked away, James, David, and myself, walked toward David's house.

Julie was outside playing, and as soon as she noticed us, she ran toward us. "Gabby! Daddy! Jay Jay!" She yelled. She was getting so big, and she was so adorable. I had not heard her address James in any way, Jay Jay was a cute pet name for her uncle. As soon as we were close enough, I knelt down and put my arms out and she ran to me. I hugged her tight, "I missed you!" I told her. "I miss you!" She replied. I let her go so she could give her uncle and dad a hug. She had seen her dad a lot since she had seen James and I. I think that's why she hugged us first. Theo came out of the house, he saw us and waved. We waved back, then Sarah came out, she walked toward us and we met a few feet from the house. She hugged and kissed David, then she hugged James then me.

"I'm so happy you guys are here!" She said, excitedly. "Me too!" Julie said. I bent down and picked her up, she put her arm around my neck and put her cheek to my cheek. It made me smile, this child loved me for no reason at all other than I was here. The unconditional love of a child is something I had never experienced or thought of. Holding her, I understood her, I understood parts of my past from when I was a child. Maybe this was what my mom had meant when she said 'the child would save me.' David took Julie when we got to the house, "you guys can go put your things in your room" he said. "I'm going to head back to my place if you're going to be here for a few days," Theo said. "Yeah, sure, thank you for all that you are doing," David said to him. Theo looked at him and smiled, "I'm happy to help, it's good to feel needed and that you are doing something useful, you know?" Theo replied. David patted him on the back and Theo walked out of the front door. James and I walked into the bedroom, which was way smaller than what we had on 12, of course, but it was still nice. We started putting our things away and I yawned.

"That's the only bad part, spend a whole day there, come here before bedtime and spend another whole day before bedtime" James said, laughing. "Yeah, well, I may just have to take a nap, we are here to rest aren't we?" I said. He pulled me into him and kissed me. "Yes ma'am we are," he said, when he pulled away. I smiled at him, and said, "don't call me ma'am, that's weird." He laughed at me and smacked my butt playfully. "Watch it buddy," I said, teasingly. There was a knock at the door. I looked at James to suggest he answer it. "Yes?" He said. David opened the door and came inside.

"I just wanted to come make sure you guys are good, do you need anything?" He asked. "A nap" I said, yawning. "Same here" he replied with a smile. "I don't want Sarah to know too much about what is happening, if you don't mind not talking about it in front of her?" David said. I gave him a sideways look. "I just don't want her to worry about us," he said, putting his head down. I nodded, "I'm not going to lie about anything if she asks, but I won't volunteer any information" I said. He nodded. "I won't say anything," James said. "Thank you," David said, looking at him. "I'm just gonna go, let you guys get settled, Sarah is excited to cook a big dinner for us" David said with a smile as he walked out.

"That was a little odd," I said, looking at James. "Not really, he doesn't want her to worry, what's odd about that?" James replied. "I don't know, I guess I just don't like being asked to hide things from people," I said. "You aren't really hiding anything, you just aren't sharing. Think of it like we are secret agents, leading double lives," James said, winking at me. "Wow, that's actually not far from the truth" I replied, as I continued putting our things into the dresser. I came across the jar, the fairy was in her natural form and she was asleep. I didn't want to wake her, but also wanted to make sure she wasn't dead, so I ran my finger down the side of the jar. I didn't want to tap on it, afraid that would hurt her ears.

She lifted her head and looked at me, then she stretched and yawned. "Sorry, I wanted to make sure you were okay. We are on 2" I said. She jumped up, realizing that she was in her natural form and flew to the top. I opened the lid and she flew out. She flew up to my face and kissed me on the cheek. I smiled at her as I walked over to the window and opened it, with a little struggle, so she could go see her fairy family. "We will be going back in two weeks, tops, maybe sooner, if you still want to go back with us" I said. She nodded and waved at me as she flew outside.

I sat the jar on top of the dresser and left the lid off. "I think she'll be back," James said. I must have looked sad. "I'm not worried about that, I feel bad about taking her from her family, taking anyone from their family. Theo, Philip, everyone pretty much is giving up so much to help us, to help me" I said, as I sat down on the bed. "Because it's the right thing to do, you are going to change the world, reunite the dimensions. Everyone wants to be a part of that, trust me, you aren't forcing anyone to do anything" James said. I looked at him, and put my arms around his midsection. "I'm so scared that someone will die," I said, without looking up. "We will do everything we can to keep that from happening, but they know there is a chance, we are fighting a war and our enemies are ruthless" he said. "That doesn't make me feel better," I replied. He kissed the top of my head.

I walked over to the bed and lay down, "I want to get a couple hours of sleep" I told him. He nodded at me, kissed me on the cheek and said, "I will leave you in here, I'll come back and wake you in a couple of hours" he said as he walked out of the room and closed the door. I didn't lay there long before I fell asleep. It seemed like no time had passed at all when I felt someone gently shaking me. I opened my eyes and saw James bending over me. "Hi," he said. "Hi, just a little more sleep," I said as I rolled away from him. "Dinner is almost ready, you can get lots of sleep tonight" he said. "Ugh, fine" I said as I rolled out of bed.

The sun was low in the sky, soon I would be able to see the moons, one of my favorite things about 2. I followed James out of the room and into the kitchen. The food smelled and looked amazing as always. I sat down at the table in between James and Julie. Julie smiled to let me know she was pleased that I sat next to her. I fixed a plate and started eating. "David says you may not stay a whole two weeks? I was wondering why?" Sarah said. I looked at her, smiled, and said, "I just don't want focus on what we are doing to be lost." "Oh, okay" she said, seeming satisfied with my answer. It was the truth, I didn't lie so I didn't feel bad about my answer.

After dinner James and I went outside, he knew that I loved the moons. He brought a blanket so we could lie down and enjoy the view. I felt like I fell more and more in love with him everyday. The moons were at about eighty-five percent. I looked over at James, his silhouette in the moonlight, made him almost look like a statue. He looked back at me, "what?" he said. "Just admiring your beauty in the moonlight," I replied. He laughed at me. "What? It's true" I said. He turned and kissed me. It was a long passionate kiss that made me tingle inside. I moaned from excitement and he pulled away and smiled at me.

"We shouldn't get too excited out here, we don't know who may be watching" he said, looking toward the house. "Is there somewhere else we could go? I would love to make love to you under the moons," I said. He rolled over on top of me with an excited laugh. He started kissing and sucking on my neck, getting me more excited. I moaned louder and then he stopped. "Seriously, we don't know if anyone is watching, I will figure out something before we leave though" he said as he rolled off of me and lay on his back next to me, catching his breath. I let out a sigh of disappointment. "Don't do that," he said. "Well, you got me all hot and bothered," I replied.

I heard something in the wind that distracted me, I got silent and still so I could tell where the sound was coming from. "What is it?" James asked. "Shh," I replied. He started looking around and looked like he was ready to fight. I put my hand on his arm and shook my head 'no.' He looked at me like he was confused now. It was a beautiful sound, someone was singing, but I still couldn't tell where it was coming from. I looked at him, confused that he couldn't hear it. I concentrated harder, it was coming from the lake! "The mermaids!" I said, sitting up quickly.

"What are they doing?" James asked, sounding worried. "Calling to me, they know I'm here, I told them that I would come back and remove the curse on the rest of them" I replied. "How are you going to do that?" James asked. "I'll have to go into the lake, I'll do it the same way as I did the first one, it's the same thing that I did to you to remove your worry and anxiety" I explained. "How long will it take? How will I know you are safe?" James asked. I looked at him, "I don't have a death wish, I'm not going to do something that I think is dangerous" I replied, a little insulted by his questioning. "Okay" he said, throwing his arms up to indicate he was surrendering.

"I'm going to head to the lake, if it will make you feel better, you can go get Arturo and tell him what I am doing" I said. "You're going now?! It's dark!" James said, sounding like he was getting upset. "Would you rather me go willingly? Or would you rather them call me out in my sleep again?" I said, in a matter-of-fact way. "I can watch you in your sleep!" He yelled. "You couldn't before, and that's okay, their magic is strong." I said. I could tell he still wasn't convinced, so I put my hand on his arm and said, "I promise I will be okay, it will be better if I go now, willingly. We don't want them to think that I am trying to avoid them and not help them, I don't need any more enemies."

James sat there looking straight ahead, instead of looking at me for a long moment. We were just wasting time arguing. "I am going, like I said, if it will make you feel better, go get Arturo," I said as I stood up. I started walking toward the lake, I looked back and James still hadn't moved, he was still sitting in the same position, looking off into space. I continued to walk toward the lake, I couldn't let personal feelings get in the way of business. I didn't want to hurt him in any way, but he had to learn that everything we do is dangerous. He had to learn to let go when need be.

The closer I got to the lake, the louder the singing became. The moons reflecting in the water was a beautiful sight. I heard a loud splash come from the lake. "Hello?" I said, nervously. The mermaid that I had removed the curse from appeared from beneath the surface. She smiled at me. "I'm sorry that it has been so long, I have so much that I have to do, but I am here now" I said. She motioned for me to come into the water. I put one foot in, the water felt nice. I started walking in further. She swam closer as I walked deeper. Her golden skin sparkled in the moonlight. She truly was a beautiful creature. When the water was at my neck, she swam up to me and took my hand in hers, I could feel her magic entering my body and the air started feeling thick. I could still breathe, but it didn't feel natural.

I put my head and nose under the water to take a breath, that felt much better. "They are all gathered, and waiting for you" she said, with a smile. I followed her, it felt like we swam for thirty minutes before we got to everyone. I went to work immediately, removing the curse from them, one by one. I watched them turn from scary monsters into beautiful creatures. Each of them was overjoyed by their transformations. I couldn't help but to think, what an evil witch he must have been, to turn a whole race into monsters. I was happy that I could help them now. When I was about halfway finished, I started feeling drained and I knew that I would not be able to finish all of them tonight.

I started looking around for the queen, she was sitting above us on a throne, watching. I waved at her, she waved back. I motioned for her to come down, she shook her head and motioned for me to keep going. I shook my head at her, trying to tell her that I couldn't. She put her hand up. She got off of her throne and swam down to me. "What is wrong?" She asked. "I'm feeling very weak and drained, I need to go home and rest and recharge. I will come back and finish the rest tomorrow" I replied. She looked dissatisfied. "I will come back," I reassured her. She still just looked at me. "I came tonight, didn't I?" I said. "Fine, but our race is one that you do not want to start a war with" she said. "Of course not! I have done nothing to your people except help them!" I said, defensively.

She threw her arm up violently and I shot up to the surface, I felt her magic leaving my body. Treading water, I looked around, I was in the middle of the lake and I couldn't see anyone waiting for me. I was a bit disappointed that James had not gone to get Arturo. I guess I really upset him. "I can't come back to help you if I drown!" I yelled. One of the mermaids that I had helped tonight, popped up beside me. She took my hand and dragged me to shallow water, closer to the shore. I looked at her and said, "thank you." She smiled and nodded and swam away.

I walked the rest of the way to the shore, and I noticed someone come out of the woods. It was James, he didn't say anything, but he stood there with a blanket to put around me. We walked back together, he was still silent. "I didn't have the energy to remove the curse from all of them, I will have to go back tomorrow" I said. He looked at me with no expression and didn't acknowledge that I had said anything. "Why are you acting like this?" I asked. He just put his arm around me and pulled me closer to him in a sideways embrace.

"Seriously? You aren't going to talk to me?" I said. "I don't really know what to say. You don't listen when I talk, what I say doesn't matter, so why should I say anything?" He replied. I felt hurt by his words. "That's not true, there are just certain things that I have to do that you can't be there for," I said. "So don't ask me to speak on those things" he said. "Okay, that's fair I suppose. But it would be nice to have someone to talk to about it, I guess I will go talk to Arturo tomorrow before I go" I said. From the way he was acting and the way that I felt, I was worried that this would stand between us, that was not something that I wanted.

The next thing I knew, I woke up in the bed. It was morning, James was pacing at the side of the bed. "What's going on?" I asked. "Arturo! She's awake!" James yelled. "What happened?" I asked, confused. "You fainted while we were walking back" James said in a way that made me feel like he was reprimanding me. "Okay" I replied defensively. Arturo came into the room, he came to me and started scanning my body the way he had done before. "She seems fine, I think she just over used her magic and was already exhausted on top of that" Arturo said, looking at James. "I'm fine," I said, narrowing my eyes at James. "Good," James replied.

"I'm going to stay for dinner," Arturo said, as he turned and walked out of the room. James just looked at me for a moment. "I'm happy that you are okay," he finally said. "Thanks" I replied. "What's your problem? Why have you been acting so weird?" I asked. "I think it's the spell you did to remove my worry and anxiety. When it would normally show up, I shut down instead" he replied. I looked at him, that made sense I suppose. I nodded at him. "I suppose that I can't be upset with you then, right?" I said with a smile. He walked over to the bed and sat down next to me, then he bent down and kissed my forehead. "You can be if you want, but I hope that you aren't," he said. I hugged him and said, "never." We got up from the bed. "Wait, Arturo said 'dinner' . How long was I out?" I asked as I felt my stomach rumble. "Just a day," James replied. "Wow, I have to get back out there this evening," I said. James didn't reply. I would talk to Arturo about what had happened and what I still had to do. We walked out to the kitchen. Sarah was just finishing up putting everything on the table and sitting Julie. Margo was there too, so I walked over and gave her a hug. "I'm glad you are okay," she said. I smiled at her, and said, "thanks." Julie insisted that I sit next to her, which I had no problem doing.

"So, do you want to tell us what happened last night?" David asked, looking at me. "Well, I definitely wanted to talk to Arturo about it, but I suppose I can tell everyone," I replied. Everyone looked at me with anticipation except James, who continued eating and only paying attention to his food. "James and I were outside enjoying the night sky when I heard someone singing. It took me a minute, but I figured out that it was the mermaids and then I remembered that I had promised to come remove the curse from the rest of them. So I went to the lake and was met by the queen, she took me down to the rest, I only got about halfway done before I started feeling exhausted. She wasn't happy about it, but let me go on the promise that I would be back tonight to finish. She gave me a warning that I didn't want to start a war with them." I told them.

"She certainly doesn't sound very grateful for what you did for them," Sarah said. I looked at Arturo, waiting to see what he would say. "Maybe you shouldn't go back," he said. "Why? I mean, I know that I was threatened, but if they hold to that threat and come after me or any of you, I just couldn't live with that" I replied. "Maybe we can stall somehow, find out more about them before you restore the rest of them," Arturo said. "How? I am supposed to be back tonight. They have taken me before, if I don't go, they will make me go," I said. Arturo nodded his head, "maybe I should go with you then." Margo looked at him with a look of disapproval. She put her head down when she noticed that I had seen her give him the look.

"No, I don't think you should go down with me, but, maybe you could be somewhere close? And if I needed you, I could send a signal." I said. "I really think I can finish the rest tonight without too much of an issue, I was just exhausted from lack of sleep yesterday" I added. "To free a race from a supposed curse that has plagued the magical community for ages is something that we should have thought more about," Arturo said. "What do you mean?" I asked. "What if it was a punishment, not a curse. What if they lied about why they were transformed" he said. I shook my head, "I think it's the other way around, they were wrongfully cursed and they have been retaliating against witches because of it. And even though I am helping them now, they have not been able to trust witches for so long, that they still find it difficult to do so" I said.

"You may be right, and I may be right, is the risk worth it?" Arturo said. "I think it is, I would rather have allies than more enemies,"

I replied. "Okay, we will go down to the lake after dinner," Arturo said. "I will get the boat," David said. After we finished eating, Arturo, David and myself went outside. Everyone else stayed inside, including James. The boat was already in the water, tied to a post at the end of a boardwalk. "I will send any signal that I can at the first sign of trouble," I said, looking at Arturo. He nodded, "David and I will be in the boat," he said. "The middle of the lake is where I feel like we were last night" I told them. "I wish we had a more accurate pinpoint of where you will be," David said. I looked down, "sorry, I'm not that good with coordinates" I replied. "It's okay, I just hope we can get to you in time if we need to" David said.

"I understand that, and I wouldn't blame you if something happened. This is my choice, and it's something that I feel like I need to do" I told him. "Yeah, well, James wouldn't be understanding if something happened to you" David replied. I looked down again, he was trying to make me feel guilty and it was working. But it didn't matter, I had to do this, I didn't want to start a war with the mermaids. I noticed someone in the water was watching us. I smiled and waved at the queen. She was still pretty far out in the lake.

I started walking into the water and I turned around and waved at David and Arturo like I was telling them goodbye. They took the hint and nodded at me and walked away, into the forest, out of view. I continued walking toward the queen. After noticing the guys had walked away, she started swimming toward me. When she reached me, she put her hand out and I took it, I felt her magic going into my body and dove under the water with her. "You are later than I expected," she said. "I just woke up, I told you last night that I was too tired to go on, I didn't realize how tired I was and I fainted on the way home" I told her. "You are rested now? You can finish the rest?" She asked. I nodded, "I'm pretty sure I can," I replied.

She dragged me down faster until we reached the rest. Most of the ones that I had already cured were not here. It made me wonder where they might be and I started worrying about Arturo and David being on the boat in the lake. I felt like I just needed to get to work, get it finished and get out. So, that's what I did, they formed a line and I started removing the curse from them, one by one. After a while, I started feeling the exhaustion setting in again. I looked up, only a few left. I needed to finish this, I couldn't stop now. I started wishing that Arturo was here, so I could use his magic. I tried to sense him, but I was too far down in the water.

The queen noticed that I started slowing down and swam down to me. "What's wrong?" She asked. I shook my head, "just feeling drained" I replied. She narrowed her eyes at me. "You will finish, there are only four left," she said. I nodded, "I planned on it" I replied. I continued to the next mermaid. I kept going, somehow I found the strength. I felt like I didn't have a choice, leaving just a few would somehow have been just as bad as not showing up. As soon as I finished the last one, feeling dizzy, I turned to the queen. "I need to go home now," I told her. "There are things that we need to discuss," she replied.

I must have fainted again. I woke up in a cave, still underwater. It was dark, there appeared to be bars around me and I started to get scared. "Hello?!" I yelled. I didn't hear a response. "Hey!" I yelled again. "What's going on?" I yelled out into the darkness. "Shhh! You are going to wake everyone" a voice whispered. "Good!" I yelled. "Seriously" the voice replied. Then she came into view. "I need to go home!" I yelled again. "Have my friends come to look for me? Did you hurt any of them?!" I demanded. "The other world cannot find us unless we want to be found" the mermaid replied. "How long have I been out? They will be worried sick about me" I said, lowering my voice this time. "You have been resting for one night, I think," she said, putting her finger on her chin to indicate that she wasn't really sure.

"Are you serious?!" I yelled. "What is going on?!" I heard another voice yell from outside of the cave. It was a voice I recognized this time, the queen. "Uh oh" the other mermaid said as she swam away. The queen came into view. "I need to go home, please," I said to her. She glared at me for a moment. "Please, I have done everything you asked me to do. I need to get home, my friends will be worried" I said calmly. "You disturbed my sleep for nonsense, you could have waited to go until I woke" she replied. "I am sorry, when I woke up, I didn't know what was going on or where I was," I said. "You are safe here, your friends haven't been harmed," she replied. "I understand that, and I am very grateful to you for that, but, can I please go home now?" I asked again.

She started looking around, "where did Jilly go?" she asked. I assumed she was talking about the other mermaid that I had been talking to. "I'm not sure," I said. "I'm here" said a voice, coming from just outside of the cave. "Will you escort the witch to the surface?" the queen asked. My heart felt lighter, relieved. "If it is your wish ma'am" Jilly replied. The queen nodded her head and Jilly swam over to me and took my hand. "Thank you" I said, looking at the queen. "You cured my race, I don't usually do favors, but you have helped us, but don't ever assume that I owe you anything" she said. "Yes ma'am" I replied, not wanting to make her angry.

I just wanted to go home and hopefully never have to deal with the mermaids again. Jilly and I started swimming toward the surface. Once we reached the top of the water, I felt the mermaid magic being recalled from my body. I looked around, hoping to see anyone, but it was dark so I couldn't really see anything. Even with the light of the two moons shining down on us. I looked at Jilly, and said, "can you please help me get closer to the shore?" She looked at me and nodded. She took my hand again and we started toward the shore.

When we were about halfway to the shore from the center of the lake I heard someone shouting my name. "I'm okay!" I yelled back.

Jilly looked at me with a look of terror. "I have to go, they will kill me without hesitation" she said as she dropped under the surface. I continued to swim toward the shore. I heard the boat motor start and felt a bit relieved. I started treading water where I was so I could manifest a fireball to give my location. I threw the fireball straight into the air and the boat started coming toward me. I felt relief again that whoever it was, had seen it before it disappeared. When the boat reached me, I realized it was James, he put his arm out to grab me and pull me in.

He threw a blanket over me and held me. I started crying, I wasn't sure why, I think it was more because I felt bad for putting him through so much worry and pain. "Are you hurt?" He asked. I shook my head 'no.' "I'm sorry, I know everyone must have been worried. Something happened out of my control" I said. "You're here now, safe," James said. I nodded, "let's go home" I said looking at him. He nodded and helped me take a seat before starting the boat and heading toward the dock. When we reached the dock, he got out first then turned to me and handed me his arm to help me out. "Gabriela! Thank goodness you are safe!" Arturo yelled, walking toward us. I walked over to him and hugged him, "I'm sorry to cause everyone worry" I said. "Just happy you are safe," he replied

The three of us started walking back toward David's house. I explained to them what had happened during the walk. "We started looking for you, but we couldn't find anything, no trace of magic or life," Arturo said. "They have a protection shield so they can't be found," I explained. "We thought about just firing into the water, but we were scared that we would accidentally hurt or kill you," James said. "Yeah, I'm glad you didn't do that. If any of you had been hurt trying to save me, I wouldn't have been able to live with myself" I said. "You are here, you are safe and so is everyone else, so everything worked out" Arturo said.

David and Sarah were sitting on the porch, they both got up

and ran to me and hugged me and let me know how happy they both were that I was safe. “I’m just wet and tired,” I told them. “Of course, go ahead and get cleaned up and dried out, we will see you in the morning,” Sarah said with a smile. I nodded at them. “I’m going to head back to my place, let Margo know that you are safe so she doesn’t worry anymore” Arturo said. I nodded at him. “Give her a hug for me,” I said. He smiled at me, “will do” he said as he turned and walked away.

James took my hand and led me into the house. “I will run you a warm bath,” he said. I smiled at him, “thank you, that will be nice” I replied. After a nice warm bubble bath, I went into the bedroom. James was lying in the bed, still awake, waiting for me. I smiled at him and I crawled into the bed next to him and snuggled up close. He put his arms around me and pulled me into him. It wasn’t long until I was asleep. I had a dreamless, restful sleep. When I woke in the morning, I felt refreshed. I stretched and smiled. The sun was coming in through the window and it felt nice and warm. “Good morning,” James said. I smiled at him, “yes, it is,” I said.

I smelled something delicious and my stomach growled. He smiled at me and said, “let’s go eat.” I smiled back and rolled over to get out of the bed. We walked to the kitchen together. Julie was very happy to see me, as usual, I sat between her and James. “So happy you are back here with us,” Sarah said. “I’m sorry I worried everyone so much, it’s over now, I don’t have to go back and deal with them anymore” I said. “Stop apologizing Gabriela, you did something you needed to do, you are safe now, it’s over, like you said” David said. I nodded silently at him and started eating.

Twenty-Two

Fun in the moons

After breakfast, James and I went outside to enjoy the beautiful day. We held hands and walked. There was a nice warm breeze blowing, everything seemed alright, if only for the moment. "I wish I could have been there with you," James said. I looked at him and smiled, "let's just let it go, it's in the past now" I told him. He smiled at me and bent down and kissed me. His kisses gave me butterflies like I had never known before. I couldn't imagine them ever going away as long as he always kissed me like this. It was as if every kiss was our first kiss. He pulled away and grabbed my hand, "come on, I want to show you something" he said. I looked at him and smiled excitedly.

He took me to a clearing in the woods that was open, there was a tent set up. "What is this?" I asked. "This is so we can have some privacy, I figured you can do a spell to hide us magically and we will be completely alone to do as we please," he said, grabbing me by the waist and pulling me into him. I smiled at him, "I love you" I told him. "I love you," he replied. "The moons are going to be full tonight" he said, winking at me. I put my arms around his midsection and hugged him tight. “Good thing that werewolves aren’t real,” I said jokingly. He laughed at my silly joke, another reason to keep him.

“Come on” he said, as he dragged me toward the tent, “I want to show you the inside.” “Okay,” I replied with a smile. He opened up the tent and bent down to go inside. It was beautifully set up. A bed was in the center with sheer curtains hung around it. Flowers and candles set up on shelves along the tent walls. “I even got a cooler for chilled wine and water so we don’t get dehydrated,” he said, pointing to the corner. “What about food?” I asked. “We can go back to David’s for meals if we want,” he replied. “And to shower of course,” he added. I smiled at him and said, “Sounds wonderful.”

“We should head back now for dinner and get whatever we want to bring with us,” James said. I nodded at him and he took my hand again as we started walking back toward the house. “Thank you for being so amazing, I feel like I don’t deserve you” I told him. “Why would you feel that way?” He asked. “I don’t know, maybe childhood trauma?” I replied. He just nodded, and bent down and kissed my forehead. I think that was the best response he could have given. He didn’t pressure me to explain, he just made me feel loved and that was something real to me. He made me feel complete, something I had never felt before. If the rest of the world could have what we had together, the world would truly be an amazing place.

When we were a few feet from the house I could smell dinner. It smelled amazing as always. Julie was playing outside in the yard and David was sitting on the porch. Arturo and Margo were sitting with David on the porch as well. Everyone looked happy, smiling and talking with each other. Margo smiled and waved at James and I. She got up to come meet us, she hugged James and then hugged me. I smiled at her, “I just love your hugs,” I told her. She smiled and blushed a little as she pulled away. “What did you guys do today?” She asked. “I took her to show her a camp that I set up for the two of us," James said. "Oh, that sounds fun," she replied, winking at me. I smiled and put my head down as I felt my face get hot, I was the one blushing now.

After dinner, we hugged everyone and told them bye and that we would be back by in the morning. Then we headed to our cute little campsite in the woods. The moons were rising and I felt a tingle of energy coming from them. This was going to be an amazing night, I could feel it in my soul. We walked silently, holding hands until we reached the campsite. I quickly put up a spell to keep us hidden. James motioned for me to come inside the tent. "I think we should put a blanket down out here" I told him. He looked at me and smiled and went inside the tent, he came out a few seconds later with a plaid blanket.

He lay the blanket down on the ground and smoothed it out as flat as he could. I walked over and he grabbed me by the hand and pulled me down. He started kissing me as if he had been craving me for a long time. The butterflies in my stomach went wild. I took charge of the kiss, pushing him down to the ground as I climbed on top of him, straddling his midsection. He moaned with excitement as I moved down to his neck with my tongue. I reached behind me and felt his hardness and he moaned again. Then he took charge again, rolling me to the ground and laying on top of me, my legs wrapped around him.

I moaned with excitement as he started kissing my neck. He slowly moved down, pulling my shirt off then my bra. He kissed and licked my nipples as I got more and more excited, my whole body felt like it was tingling with butterflies. I moaned louder. He moved down to my stomach, running his tongue up and down. He moved back up and kissed me again. I could tell that he wanted to make tonight last, and that was okay with me. I rolled him over and got back on top and started kissing and sucking on his neck as he moaned. He grabbed my butt and squeezed, making me moan. I slid downward and unbuttoned his pants. I pulled his penis out and I licked the top and the sides without putting in all of the way into my mouth. He moaned with excitement.

Before I had a chance to put it all of the way into my mouth, he took charge again and threw me gently onto my back. The moons were high above us now, even if I didn't know about magic, and if I could only see one moon, it would have still felt like magic was happening, a natural magic. He pulled my pants off and slid my panties off, using both hands. He moved slowly, sliding them down my legs and eventually reaching my feet, then he tossed them into the night. He came back up to my lips and kissed me even more passionately, if that was possible.

I put one arm around his neck and explored his body with the other hand. He had one hand on my chin and started exploring my body with his other hand. We both moaned with excitement. All I could think was I wanted him inside me, I knew it was going to feel so amazing. He started moving down my body again with his tongue. All I could do was moan, moan with pleasure, moan with anticipation and excitement. When he reached the magical spot and ran his tongue over it and around it, I moaned louder and louder. That made him more excited as he started to move faster and faster. I reached one climax, staring up at the moons.

He smiled at me as he came up and lay down next to me. I rolled over, facing him, smiling back at him. I started rubbing his chest and stomach with my hand. Then I reached down and grabbed his penis again, he was still hard as a rock. He moaned with excitement as I started kissing his chest while rubbing his penis. I moved down slowly until my mouth was at his penis, I took it into my mouth as he moaned with excitement. His moans made me moan more. I sucked hard and moved my head up and down, feeling him hit my throat until he pulled me off and threw me back down on my back.

He climbed on top of me and entered me slowly, teasingly. I

wrapped my legs around him and pushed him into me. He moved faster and it felt so amazing. I was in ecstasy, moaning with pleasure until another climax was reached by me. He climaxed shortly after then he lay on top of me and kissed me, still passionately, but not as passionately as before. He moved his mouth close to my ear and whispered "I love you" into it. The words combined with feeling his hot breath in my ear gave me butterflies again. "I love you" I replied, in a whisper, but a little louder than he had said it, because my mouth wasn't right at his ear.

He rolled over and lay beside me, we wrapped our arms around each other and fell asleep, right there, naked, under the two moons. We slept there all night, wrapped in each other in the open. We didn't have to worry about anyone or anything seeing us because of my spell, not even a spying creature such as a mouse could see us. I had a dreamless light sleep that night, still aware that I was lying naked under the moons with James' legs and arms wrapped around me. He seemed to be in a deep sleep, lightly snoring and not moving.

As soon as he moved in the morning, I slid out from under him and he woke up. He lay there, for a minute just smiling at me without saying anything. His hair had fallen out of it's normal ponytail and was going every direction, he looked a bit wild but still handsome. I smiled at him and said, "good morning." "The best morning," he replied. He started to get up but looked like he was having problems. He looked at me and said, "I'm a little stiff from sleeping on the ground." I giggled at him, "you're just getting old" I said, teasingly. I stood up and put my arm out to help him, he took my arm and pulled me back down.

"I'll show you old," he said. I giggled as he tickled me then he kissed me which ended up in a morning quickie. After that, we both got up and found our clothes, got dressed and headed to David's house to eat and shower. "Are we coming back here tonight?" I asked. "That's the plan," James replied. "Okay, I'm going to leave the protection spell up" I said. He nodded and took my hand and we started walking toward David's house. We walked silently, just enjoying being near each other.

As we approached the house, we noticed David sitting on the porch. He was just sitting in a rocking chair enjoying the morning. He waved when he noticed us walking up. I waved back at him. "How was camping?" David asked when we reached the porch. I'm sure my face turned bright red. "It was great," James said. I just smiled and nodded in agreement. "Well, breakfast should be about ready if your guys are hungry" David said, changing the subject after he noticed how uncomfortable I was becoming. "Great" I said as we followed him inside.

Julie was excited to see me as usual, I just loved that little girl so much. It seemed like she got more adorable everyday. I sat between her and James as usual. "Fairy said, no leave yet" Julie said, looking at me. I looked at her confused, then I looked at Sarah "she talks to the fairies?" I asked. "They chose her as their correspondence with the giants" Sarah replied, shrugging her shoulders. "What do you mean, Julie?" I asked. "She said no leave yet" Julie said, sounding irritated, which made her look even more cute. "Okay" I said, to appease her.

Arturo and Margo walked in the front door. "Hey guys! There's plenty of food here if you're hungry" David said. "Sure," Arturo said, pulling a chair up for Margo before sitting beside her. "Did you guys have fun camping last night?" Margo asked. I smiled at her, blushing again, and said "yeah it was great." She giggled a little quietly. I rolled my eyes at her and continued eating. James didn't seem to be affected by the conversation at all. I nudged him with my elbow. "What did I do?" He said defensively. I just smiled and put my head down and continued to eat.

After breakfast James and I went to take showers and everyone else, besides Sarah went outside. Sarah stayed inside and cleaned up the dishes. After our showers, James and I went to join everyone else outside. Julie was with the fairies and David, Arturo and Margo were all standing in the field talking. I wanted to see the fairies and try to figure out the message they were trying to get to me, so I joined Julie while James joined the others. “Hey there” I said as I approached Julie. “Hi Gabby,” she replied. “Can I sit here with you?” I asked her. She nodded excitedly and patted the ground beside her.

I sat down where she had suggested. “Is the fairy here? The one that said we couldn’t leave yet?” I asked. The fairy flew up to my face and kissed my cheek. “I guess so, how are you?” I asked, knowing that she couldn’t reply. “I need to know why you don’t want to go yet, if you need to stay here, that will be okay. But I can’t guarantee how long we are going to stay” I told her. She shook a finger at me and flew over to Julie’s shoulder. “She said, it’s im-port-ant” Julie said to me. I sighed, wishing I could communicate with the fairy myself.

“Horsey!” Julie yelled suddenly, pointing toward the field. I looked, she was right, it was a horse, but not just any horse, I recognized Philip right away. “Let’s go see the horsey, " I told her. She got up excitedly and started running toward the field. I got up and followed at a normal speed. James and David were standing close to Philip and Sarah was walking toward them, closer than Julie and I were. David and James were smiling and patting Philip. Julie got to them before Sarah and I because she was running. I wondered if she had never seen a horse before?

She stopped a few feet away from him and just stared up at him with her big brown eyes. Philip just looked at her for a moment and then he put his head down close to hers. She smiled and looked at David for guidance. “Go on, pet him,” David said, smiling at her. She raised her hand and started rubbing his head between his eyes. “Oh my,” she said. I couldn’t help but to smile, she was the cutest kid I have ever seen. Philip noticed me standing in the distance and started nodding his head like he wanted me to come closer, so I did.

He nudged me like he did when he wanted me to ride. I shrugged my shoulders at him. "Why?" I asked with a giggle. He replied with another nudge.

"Gabby ride the horsey!" Julie exclaimed. I smiled at her and said, "okay." I could never disappoint her or tell her 'no.' Philip kneeled down and I climbed onto his back. He took off slowly and went into a gallop. Julie was giggling and jumping excitedly. "Do you think you could hold onto her if I hand her to you?" David asked, talking about Julie. "Sure, Philip, you have to go slow though," I replied. David handed her up and she squealed with excitement. I sat her in front of me so I could hold her. I rubbed Philip's neck and said, "okay, go slowly."

Philip walked around with the two of us on his back for about thirty minutes. I noticed everyone was talking and for a moment, I felt paranoid. I have no idea why, but I felt like they were distracting me from something. I hoped I was wrong, I was their leader after all, any plans needed to go through me. They couldn't be planning something without me. "David!" I yelled. He looked my way and I motioned for him to come take Julie. He walked over and grabbed his daughter by the waist and set her down on the ground. Philip kneeled down so I could get down.

"What were you guys talking about?" I asked David. "Oh, nothing in particular, just chit-chatting," he replied. I looked at him with a suspicious smile. "I promise, what do you think we would be talking about?" He said, noticing my look. "Not sure, it just seemed like you were discussing something important," I said. "No, we weren't," he said, starting to sound annoyed. "Okay" I said, throwing my hands up, surrendering. He gave me one more look of annoyance before turning to walk away.

I walked over to join everyone and Julie, seeming to be over the horse now, walked back over to the fairy circle. James put his arm around me and pulled me close. "Have fun?" Arturo asked, looking at me. "Sure, Julie enjoyed it," I replied. Philip came out of the barn in his human form. He walked over, smiling and put his arm around me too. "I haven't got to spend much time with you in this form" he said. I smiled at him, blushing a little. It was odd that I was always riding around on his back and we barely knew each other.

"So, what were you guys talking about?" I asked, looking at James, innocently. He smiled, "We were discussing having a bonfire tomorrow night" he replied. "Sounds fun" I said, with a smile. "Yeah, that's what I was thinking, a little fun never hurt anyone" he replied with a handsome smile. "We should really be thinking of getting back and getting down to business. Putting it off will not make it any easier, in fact, I think it will make it tougher on us" I said, trying not to sound like a Debbie downer. Everyone just looked at me with a half smile, as if to acknowledge that I was right. James put his arm around me and we started walking toward the house.

Dinner was delicious as always and after some friendly chatter everyone headed to their rooms to get some rest. James and I headed back to our camp. I was going to let them have their little party or bonfire or whatever they had planned, but then we had to get back. My instinct told me that being in another dimension at this time was not a good idea. We needed to be with the rest of the army, both for our own protection and for theirs. If anything were to happen to them while we were away, I would never forgive myself. I tried not to think negative thoughts, after all, we haven't been gone that long and the house is very hidden, still something was telling me to get back as soon as we could.

When we reached the camp, James lit a fire and we snuggled up in our sleeping bag near it. He started massaging my back, not in a sensual way, but, actually massaging out stiffness that had built up. It felt amazing. At some point I fell asleep, I guess I hadn't realized how tired I was. I had a dreamless sleep and woke in the morning with James still lying in the sleeping back with me. The fire had burned out, only a small amount of smoke rose from the ashes. I rolled over to see that he was awake. I kissed him and whispered, "we need to get everything packed up and head back to David and Sarah's." "I know," he whispered back. He kissed me before unzipping the sleeping bag and standing up.

After we got the camp packed up, and made sure the fire was completely out, and I removed the protection spell, we headed toward the house. I could still see one of the moons in the sky, the other had already set. The sun was already over the horizon and shining brightly. The walk back was mostly silent, with a little bit of small talk here and there. When we came to the edge of the forest where David's lawn began, I could see that Arturo and Margo were sitting on the porch along with David. I threw my arms up to wave hello, all three of them waved back. I would never take it for granted how I had found all of them, how they were a part of my life now, how they were my family now and always.

"Hey, how did you all sleep last night?" I asked as we approached the house. "Wonderful," David replied. "Good, good," Arturo said. Margo just smiled and nodded her head. "Great. So after the bonfire tonight, we should get back" I said, trying to sound as friendly as possible so I didn't alarm anyone. After all, just a sense of feeling like I needed to be back wasn't anything major and I didn't want them to feel threatened. Everyone just nodded and smiled the same way they had last night when I mentioned it. I guess they understood, maybe they all had this anxious feeling, but no one wanted to talk about it. As if saying it aloud would give it more power, and who knows, being that we are magical creatures, I suppose that it could.

"Breakfast is ready" Sarah said, sticking her head out of the front door. I smiled at her and watched as her smile faded while looking at David. She knew right away, just by looking at him that we were going to be leaving soon. I could see worry come over her face. Everyone got up and started heading inside. I grabbed David by the arm and held him back from going inside. "We'll be right in," I said to James as he turned to see if I was behind him. After the door closed, I looked at David and whispered, "you can stay here, you don't have to come and fight in a war that isn't yours to fight and possibly get hurt or killed. You have a family that loves you very much and they need you." He looked at me and smiled and patted my hand which was still on his shoulder, "I do have to go with you, I made a promise to protect you a long time ago and I'm not going to break that promise" he whispered back.

I felt guilty, his promise wasn't made to me and I really would prefer him to stay here with his family so I would know that he was safe. But I wouldn't deceive him, and sneak off without him, because I knew he would never do anything like that to me. He was truly like a brother to me, as Sarah was like a sister and Julie was my niece. We joined everyone else at the table. Julie cheered with excitement as we sat down. I smiled at her and told her to "eat up." "I need you to tell the fairy friends that we will be leaving tonight," I said to Julie. She shook her head 'no' and continued eating. I wasn't going to argue with a child while we were eating, so I didn't say anything else about it. I would take her out to them when we were finished.

Sarah was quiet throughout the meal, everyone else just seemed to be making small talk. I was starting to wish that we had not come here in the first place at this time. In my mind, it was just too dangerous, too distracting, the team needed to stay focused on what was coming. We couldn't get caught off guard. I could almost hear James' thoughts in my own mind, "they may be upset now, but they know you are doing the right thing for everyone." I looked over at him and he smiled at me and nodded. That was strange, how did that happen? "I had Arturo do a spell to link our minds," James' voice in my head again. I didn't like the idea whatsoever.

I imagined a link between our heads, a gray string of energy, ever flowing, and I cut it. "Why did you do that?" James said, aloud. "How dare you invade my brain without my permission" I said, sternly. I cast a glare at Arturo, he put his head down. "What is going on?" David asked. "Arturo did a spell for James that invaded my personal space" I said, as if I couldn't believe either of them would do such a thing, and to be honest, I was finding it hard to believe.

"Did someone put you guys up to that? Did someone else tell you that you should do it? I'm really confused right now, because that seems like an enemy move" I said. "Honestly guys, what in the world *were* you thinking?" David said. Neither of them spoke, it was Margo who came to their defense. "Arturo would never do something to hurt you, Gabriela. He was trying to help James, he thought it would help in battle, not having to yell plans through enemy ears" she said. Looking at James and then at Arturo, I said, "are you sure no one told you to do it? You haven't had any dreams? We can't have the enemy getting this close and that spell was just an invasion of privacy, are there no laws against magic like that?" I asked, mainly looking at Arturo now.

"No, there has never been any set rules on magic, except for not cross breeding" Arturo said. I looked at him and nodded, "well, there is about to be, when all is said and done, we can't have people living without rules, because apparently you don't realize right from wrong?" I looked at him with a confused look on my face to let him know that I still couldn't understand why he would do such a thing as I spoke. "I understand that you are upset and I understand why. I'll not cast another spell like that again," Arturo said. I could tell that he desperately wanted me to drop the subject and I didn't want to continue to make him feel uncomfortable so I just looked at him and said, "okay."

When we were all finished eating, I took Julie outside to play. I needed her to get the message to the fairies that we would be leaving tonight. I walked with her, holding her hand until we reached the edge of the forest where she had played the day before with the fairies. I sat down and she sat down across from me. "You needed a break?" she asked me. I smiled at her, and said, "yes, I did." The fairies didn't seem to be coming out, I wondered if they would if I was here. Maybe I should just wait until later, I knew at some point today, she would be playing with them.

"Where did you want to go?" I asked her. "The water," she replied. I cringed a bit, "why would you want to go to the water?" I asked her. "To play!" she yelled with excitement. "Does your mommy and daddy let you go to the water?" I asked. "No, Gabby does," she replied, pointing her finger at me. "Why would you think that?" I asked her. "Your friends live there," she replied. This day was too weird, even for my life. "Why do you say that? I don't have any friends that live at the water" I told her. "In the water" she said. "Listen, Julie, the things in that water are not my friends. If they come to you, don't listen to them, they are trying to trick you into doing something" I told her, hoping she understood.

She looked at me for a moment and started shaking her head, "no they want to tell you goodbye before you leave" she said, looking confused. "I don't think so sweetie, they aren't very nice creatures, I helped them to become a little nicer, but I still don't believe they are that nice," I tried to explain. "They are friends," she said as she looked toward the water. I knew better than to sit and argue with a child, and no matter what I said, she wouldn't understand. I got up and took her by the hand and started walking back toward the house. She yanked her hand out of mine and said, "no! We have to go the water!" "It's okay sweetie, we'll go in a little while, I feel tired, I think I need a nap first" I told her as I faked a yawn.

She reluctantly took my hand again and we walked back to the house together. As soon as Sarah saw my face when we walked in, she knew something was wrong. I shook my head at her so that she wouldn't do or say anything in front of Julie. "Did you guys have fun playing outside?" Sarah asked with a confused look. "No," Julie replied. "I felt tired, so I came back to take a nap before we go explore some more," I said, indicating for her to follow me to my room. I almost wish that I hadn't broken the connection with James so I could tell him to watch Julie while I talked to David and Sarah about what had happened.

James was sitting on the couch, not looking at me, I guess he assumed that I was still upset with him, and I was, a little, but Julie's safety came before any kind of pettiness that might be going on. "James, can I speak with you for a moment in private?" I asked. He looked at me and stood up, without saying anything he walked toward me. "The mermaids are up to something" I whispered quietly in his ear. He looked at me with narrowed eyes and then looked over at Julie who was now sitting on the floor, near us playing with some dolls. He looked back at me and I nodded my head. "Will you please keep an eye on her while I speak with Sarah and David?" I whispered. He nodded his head.

I looked toward Sarah who seemed to be getting anxious and mouthed, "bring David," and I looked toward the bedroom where James and I slept. She nodded her head and walked away silently. It didn't take them long to get to the room. Once they were inside with me, I shut the door and cast a spell around it to keep anyone from eavesdropping. I could tell they were both anxious to know what was going on, so I didn't waste any time. "I took Julie out to speak with the fairies for me, to let them know that we would be leaving tonight" I began. They both sat quietly, waiting for me to give them bad news. "When we got to the edge of the forest, I sat down, but Julie wanted to keep going. I asked her where she wanted to go and she informed me that I needed to visit my friends in the water." I continued.

Sarah put her hand over her mouth as a small gasp of horror slipped out. "I tried to explain to her that they are not my friends, but she can't comprehend that. They have gotten to her somehow and now I am worried as I am sure you must be right now" I said. "Is that all that she said?" David asked. "She said that I needed to go tell them goodbye before I left, I'm taking this as a threat to her. David, please talk with Arturo and see what he can do to remove their connection to her." I said. He nodded in agreement. "I will go to the lake and see what they want, I will tell them to leave her alone" I said. "I don't think that is a good idea," David replied. "I don't know what else to do, I need assurance that they won't do her any harm, I need to see what they want from me" I said.

"And what happens when they take you again?" David asked. "I am pretty charged right now, plus, I will let whoever wants to come with me, join" I said. David nodded. "Except you two" I added. David looked at me with a confused look now, "I think you should both keep an eye on Julie, make sure they don't lure her to the water" I added. "They are going to kill you" David said, he said it with no emotion, his words sounded as cold as the water and they chilled me to the bone. "I haven't fought powerful witches to be killed by mermaids," I said. "Do what you have to do to make sure Julie is safe," Sarah said. I nodded at her, "of course, and if I have to die to ensure that, I would gladly do so" I said as I looked toward David. He continued to look in the other direction, refusing to look at me.

"They could be spying on us through Julie, using her somehow, so be careful what you say around her," I said. David nodded his head, he looked so defeated. Sarah nodded her head that she understood, still having a look of fear on her face. "Okay, I suppose I will grab James and have him come with me. I'll have Arturo use magic to protect Julie," I said. They both just nodded as they walked out of the bedroom door. I didn't know what the mermaids had planned, I couldn't believe they had gone after a child to get to me.

As soon as Julie saw me come into the living room she ran toward me. "We going now?" She asked. "In a little while, I have to do something with your uncle James first" I told her. She looked sad, so

I asked her, "is that okay with you? It's something really important." "Okay" she replied, with a little cheer this time. James played along by smiling at me and pretending to know what I was talking about. "Is Arturo here?" I asked James. "I think he and Margo are in the field, getting things ready for tonight," James replied. "Great, I'll just talk to him on the way out. We should get going so I can get back and go do what I need to do with Miss Julie" I said, winking at her. She giggled at me. "Sarah, David! James and I are leaving for a little while" I yelled loud enough so they could hear me from the kitchen. Sarah came into the living room and picked Julie up. Julie rubbed her eyes and yawned. "I guess it's nap time huh?" Sarah said as she carried her to her bedroom. Once we were outside, I spotted Arturo, I walked over, pulling James with me so I could explain to everyone what was going on.

"I am sure I can see if she is under a spell and remove it, then put a protection spell on her, and I will join you to make sure you are safe," Arturo said. "I will stay and eat anyone who tries to come onto the property while you are gone" Margo said. I gave her a crooked, evil smile to let her know that I liked that idea. "I'm going with you," James said sternly. "I knew you were going to come, I wasn't going to stop you" I replied. "We need to move fast," I said, looking at everyone. "Where is she now?" Arturo asked. "Sarah was putting her down for a nap as we were walking out, I told them I was going to ask you to help" I replied. He nodded, turned and kissed Margo and walked toward the house. Margo looked at me, nodded, then walked into the barn, where I assumed she was storing her clothes so she could transform into the lethal panther. And that was exactly what she did.

When she came out, she started running along the property line, patrolling. I hoped for everyone's safety that no one decided to try and visit in the next hour or so. Arturo came out of the house and motioned for us to come walk with him. We caught up to him quickly. "They did have a spell over her to spy on us, on you," he said, looking at me. I nodded, I already knew that's the only way they could have known that we were planning to leave tonight. "I removed the spell, it was the only one that I found on her, and I put a protection spell on her," he said. "Thank you, it's so petty that they used a child" I said. "At least they didn't hurt her," James said. "I know," I replied, looking down, trying not to let the image of what could have happened pop into my head.

We moved quickly toward the lake, it seemed that we reached it in no time at all. I put a hand into the water to let them know that I was here. After that, I quickly linked to Arturo and James so we could communicate silently in our minds. They both nodded at me after realizing what I had done. *Yes, I guess it can come in handy in certain situations.* I thought. They both nodded to let me know that they had 'heard' me. I nodded back. A splash in the water caught my attention. *Act friendly, unless we're provoked.* I thought. I recognized the mermaid as the one who had been swimming around the cave when I woke up underwater last time. I smiled and waved at her. She swam closer.

"Why did you bring back-up?" She asked when she was close enough to speak. "Back-up?" I asked, trying to look innocent. "These guys?" I said, pointing at James and Arturo, "they are friends of mine, just as you are, they wanted to meet the mermaids and I thought you guys would like to meet them as well" I said, improvising. The mermaid looked at me with a confused look, I started to worry that she didn't believe me. I didn't want to start a fight where there wouldn't have been one. I could never tell how the mermaids would act, I think that they just did things differently from other races. "Could be thought of as an act of war" the mermaid said. "So could putting a spell on a child to spy on me" I replied, I didn't want to start a fight, but I wasn't going to lay down and take a beating either.

"I don't think the queen will be happy if I bring your friends," the mermaid said. "Well, how about, we will wait here, and you go explain to her that I brought my friends to meet her and we will wait here until you come back" I said. "You know what they say about the messenger, I think I'll bring you with me now and you can tell her that you brought friends, and if she agrees to meet them, I will come back for them." she said. *I think it's the only choice guys, I don't want to start a fight, I'll make the link as strong as possible and hopefully it will still work when I am down there.* I thought. *No, please don't.* I heard James' voice in my head. *Just let her go, the longer we stand here the more awkward it's going to become.* Arturo's voice interrupted.

"What are you doing?" the mermaid asked, sounding suspicious. *I have to go now.* "Alright, I'll go with you and you can come back for my friends when the queen agrees," I said as I walked into the water toward her. *Please be careful.* James' voice said. *Be safe.* Arturo's voice added. I didn't acknowledge that I heard them, I just kept walking toward the mermaid. When I reached her she quickly took me by the hand and I felt the mermaid magic enter my body and we quickly went under water. We reached the little community in no time at all. The mermaid held my hand until we reached the queen. "Madam," I said, bowing my head. "It's good to see you again" The queen said.

I looked at the mermaid that had brought me down, then looked back at the queen, "I bought a couple of friends that would love to meet you" I said. She looked around, "where are they?" she asked. "We didn't think it was a good idea to just bring them down unannounced, I wanted to ask your permission" I replied. "You want me to give you permission to bring other land walkers in and show them where we live?" She asked suspiciously. "Or you could come to the surface and I can introduce you. I have learned that you can never have too many friends," I said. "That may be so, but our race hasn't survived all this time because we are naïve," she said. "I didn't think you were, you may do things a bit different than others, but naïve never crossed my mind when thinking of you" I replied, trying to choose my words carefully.

I couldn't hear James or Arturo, I was positive that the protective mermaid magic was blocking the connection. I had to convince the queen to meet with them quickly, because I feared that this could all turn south and an unwanted fight could emerge. "Ma'am, have I not always kept my word to you? I give you my word that my friends are your friends, you have nothing to fear and only protection and loyalty to gain" I said. "Nonetheless, as their queen, I have to protect my people, I cannot allow anyone into our home. I will however, with back-up, go up and let you introduce me. Just know that if any harm comes to me or any of my people that it will be seen that every witch alive will drown in this lake" the queen stated. "Of course ma'am" I agreed, lowering my head to bow.

Five mermaids swam up by her side, I assumed they were her bodyguards. "Are you ready, Gabriela?" She asked, looking at me. "Yes ma'am" I said, with a smile. Two of the bodyguards swam ahead of us, two on each side and one in the back as we headed toward the surface. I concentrated on the link as we rose higher and higher. Finally I heard James' voice, *Gabriela? Where are you, please say something so that we know you are okay!* I responded quickly, *I'm fine, we don't have much time, the queen is coming up with bodyguards, I told her that you are just here to meet her, so please, smile and be friendly when you see her and I am with her also.*

When we reached the surface, we could see James and Arturo on the shore. They started waving and smiling just as I had told them to. The queen looked my way after seeing them. I smiled at her. "Are these the same people who tried to find our home before?" She asked. "They only tried to find me when I was missing, they did not succeed," I replied. "I know they didn't. So, why should I befriend them? Just because they are your friends? They don't seem very smart, if my intent was to kill you, you would have been dead already and they could not have stopped me. So again, what can they possibly offer to me that I don't already have?" She said. "They are land walkers, they can protect your people from outside sources," I replied.

She seemed to think for a moment and then said, "My people have survived this long because we are smart and we keep out of other's business and keep others out of our business. Anytime any of us have gotten involved with another species it has not worked out for our best. So, knowing you is knowing one too many of another species. What are you anyway? I know you are a witch, but I sense something else as well." She said, looking at me suspiciously. Arturo had apparently cast a spell to amplify his hearing, his voice popped into my head, *don't tell her! You are a witch and that is it!* "No ma'am, I am nothing else. I am just a witch" I replied.

"Why are you lying to me? I don't like being lied to, do you know what it means when someone tries to lie?" She said, in a threatening way. "I'm no.." I said, before she interrupted me with, "It means you think I'm stupid." "No ma'am, I'm not lying to you, please, I have no reason to lie" I pleaded. "Of course you do, I know the laws, I know that interbreeding between species is illegal and any child born of such is to be destroyed immediately. My only question is how did you slip through, I don't even care what you are mixed with, but if I had to guess, I would say giant, even though you aren't that tall, it's the only other species that I am very familiar with and you do seem familiar" She said.

Arturo, what do I do? I thought and looked toward him. *Don't look at me! She is not dumb she will figure out that we are communicating!* Arturo's voice said. I quickly looked back at the queen, not sure what to do or say. *Tell her you don't know what she's talking about.* Arturo said, more calmly. "I'm afraid that I don't know what you are talking about, I just learned that I am a witch and that other dimensions and magical creatures exist, I grew up as an orphan" I said. After a moment of silence the queen seemed to grow softer, a little smile even formed on her face. "That, I do believe," she said. I breathed a sigh of relief. *Don't get too comfortable babe*. I heard James' voice say. I smiled more because of him, but I looked at the queen.

I wanted this whole thing to be over more than anything, I hated feeling out of control. "You came here to reprimand me for using the child to get to you" the queen said. "I would never, however want to ask that you not involve her again. She has nothing to do with anything that is going on. She is just an innocent child." I said. "I didn't harm her, nor would I. I simply used her as a messenger" The queen said, narrowing her eyes. "I understand that, but please try to understand how that made us feel, imagine if I did that to one of your young" I said.

"Is that your mate?" She asked, pointing at Arturo. I gave her a confused look. "No, he is not my mate," I replied. I knew that from the look on my face that she could tell I was a bit offended. "I didn't mean to offend you, so the other one there?" She asked, pointing at James. "No, actually, I don't have a mate," I said. "But you fancy that one? You would prefer him over the other one?" She asked. I was starting to get nervous, I was scared she was about to hurt James to get a point across to me. "They are simply friends, and bodyguards, just as you have" I said. I didn't come here for a battle but I was always ready to fight if I needed to. Even though I hadn't trained in the water and I was out of my element, I felt a sudden surge of power. Arturo had projected onto me.

We had to resolve this quickly. "Madam, I did not come here to disrespect you, or to harm you. But, I'm afraid if you keep going the way you are at the moment that I will have no choice" I said, in a firm way. She looked into my eyes, "so you have a weakness? And it's easy to see, you will never be able to see mine. That is because I would rather die than see the one I love die" she said, calmly. "So what? Are you trying to teach me something?" I asked, a little easier and a bit confused. "Yes, you care deeply for the child that I used as a messenger and it shows and that half giant there, it would destroy you if you saw him killed" she replied.

"Your enemies will get to you through them, be aware of what is going on around you or you will lose your war" She said. I felt my muscles untense. She was trying to help me in her own weird way, but I understood exactly what she was saying. "You are wise ma'am" I said. "I had to show you, because, if I just told you, you would not have believed me," she said. I nodded and bowed my head, "thank you" I whispered. "I want you to win, you have helped us and I don't know any other way to repay you. But, again, I am not stupid or naïve, and you should not expect your enemies to be either" she said. I nodded my head so she knew that I understood.

"I did summon you here to tell you goodbye, until we meet again," she said. I smiled at her, "until we meet again" I replied. The queen and her bodyguards sank into the water and I swam toward the shore. I broke the link between James, Arturo and myself. "That was intense," James said, as he put his arm out to help pull me up. "Yeah, it sure was," I agreed. "They are such a strange race," Arturo said. "Only strange because they aren't the same as us, she is very wise" I said. "I agree, just odd," Arturo said. "So, now that I know what she showed me today, what can I do about it?" I asked aloud to no one in particular. "I can't just stop loving the people that I love," I added.

"Maybe you can, when the enemy is near, think of something they have done that made you angry, be angry with them to save their life," Arturo said. "Maybe that will work, if they have made me angry," I replied. James put his arm around me, "I guess I need to work on pissing you off then" he said, teasingly. "Don't joke about serious things, please" I said. "You're irritated, my plan is already working" he said, winking at me. I couldn't help but to smile.

We walked back to the house, David and Sarah met us in the yard. I hugged them, "everything is okay, they won't hurt Julie," I told them. "They just wanted to show me that they could get to me through the people that I care about, and that my enemies would be able to do the same," I explained. "Can you guarantee her safety?" Sarah asked. "They won't hurt her, they had no intention of hurting her." I replied. I looked up and saw Julie coming out of the front door. "She's up," I said, pointing toward the house. We all started waving at her like she was our favorite person in the world and we hadn't seen her in awhile. She smiled and waved back excitedly.

"You went to see your friends?" She asked innocently, looking at me. "Of course, I did," I replied with a smile. She smiled back as she threw her arms round my legs. I bent down and picked her up and squeezed her tight. I tickled her side and she giggled and said "stop it Gabby." I never felt so much like a slave as I did around her, I think she could literally ask me to do anything and I would do it, just for her, just to see her smile or hear her giggle. I looked at James and he was smiling at me, I smiled back. He walked over to me and put his arm around me and whispered, "you are so good with her." He almost sounded like he was surprised by it.

"Almost party time!" Margo's voice yelled from across the field. I looked at her and waved as I said, "let's do this!" We all started walking toward the field where a pile of wood was stacked ready to burn. There was a smaller open fire where food was being prepared as well. Arturo was there as well as Philip and Theo. James put his arm around me as we walked. For a moment, everything felt right in the world, like this is how everything was meant to be. I felt that everything we were doing now was taking us toward a better future and my heart felt warm and happy.

Margo was wearing a beautiful red silk dress that hugged her curves nicely. Arturo walked in not too far behind, he was wearing a red suit and looking sharp. "What were you guys doing?" James asked more to himself with a smile. "We were just talking and dancing in the moonlight, it's a nice night" Arturo said, as he walked by, putting a hand on James' shoulder as he passed. I just looked at him and smiled. I was so happy that he was able to reunite with Margo, they were such a lovely couple.

Margo made her way around the field, being social and letting everyone know that she was there before making her way back to where James and I were and sitting next to me. Arturo was at the bar fixing them drinks. I turned toward Margo because I felt she wanted to tell me something. She held up her hand to show me a ring. "Oh my goodness! That's beautiful" I said with a squeal. "So you guys are getting married?" I asked. "Sort of, it will be a handfasting ritual. After we have won this war, we will be together forever" she said with a confident smile. I smiled back at her, this was just another reminder for me that I wasn't the only one affected by the outdated rules. There should be no reason why a witch and a shapeshifter shouldn't be together if they choose each other.

The party was amazing of course, lots of laughter, lots of fun. Everyone seemed happy, if only for the moment. When the party was over, we started saying our goodbyes. "I wish David would stay, but I know he won't. I promise, I won't let anything happen to him" I told Sarah as I hugged her. She nodded and gave me a smile as she pulled away, "I know" she replied. Julie had fallen asleep, I carried her to her room and put her in her bed and gave her a kiss on the forehead. "See you soon princess" I whispered. She smiled as she rolled over and snuggled her teddy bear.

Twenty-Three

Back to war

After saying my goodbyes, I walked back out to the field where everyone was waiting. The fairy flew up to me and landed on my arm. "Will you be returning with us?" I asked. She nodded her head to let me know that she was indeed returning with us. When I reached everyone, I took my backpack down so I could find the jar for the fairy. I found it rather quickly and she flew inside. We didn't waste any more time. Arturo opened the portal and we went through.

It was dark, but warm when we came through on the other side. Everything seemed quiet and calm. We weren't far from the house. We all walked quietly inside. I looked at the clock on the mantle, it was twelve thirty-four a.m. We were only gone a few hours. It didn't seem that anyone was awake, we all went to our rooms, quietly so we didn't disturb anyone else. Once I was in my room, I set the fairy jar on the dresser, inside a box so that the cats wouldn't knock it down. Then I lay down on the bed. James came and lay down next to me and pulled me as close as he could.

I loved the feeling of being wanted, I felt like my whole life I wasn't wanted. I guess growing up as an orphan will do that to you. I knew it wasn't necessarily true, I knew that my friends cared for me, I knew that coworkers had cared for me. But this was different, I couldn't explain how he made me feel. I guess the closest thing to an explanation is, he made me feel whole. I knew that he was important in my life, and that he would always be a part of it. We drifted off to sleep wrapped in each other's arms. It was another dreamless sleep for me, somehow I felt that I would never dream again and I wasn't sure if that was a good thing or a bad thing.

I woke to the sound of Cori knocking on the bedroom door and saying that breakfast was ready. I rolled over and moaned, I was still sleepy and didn't want to get out of bed just yet. "Come on, we should join them," James said. "I know" I replied in a whiny voice as I rolled out of bed and grabbed some clothes to change into. James got up as well and walked into the bathroom and turned on the sink and splashed water onto his face.

We walked out of the room together and headed to the kitchen. I was a bit surprised to see everyone was there. They had already begun eating. "Sorry we are late" I said with a smile looking around. "Oh, no worries" "You're fine" were a few of the replies that I heard. "Everyone must be excited for today, I suppose?" I said. "Yes, I think everyone is," Levi said, with a smile. I smiled back, "good, I'm sure it will be fun, we just have to keep what is going on in the back of our minds, because we can't forget completely" I said, trying not to sound like a party pooper. "Of course," Alice said.

After we finished eating, everyone headed outside. All of the men started setting up a couple of makeshift bowling lanes. It didn't take them long at all and they weren't terrible either. We had fun for a few hours with them. Until Cori called to everyone to come eat lunch. We all walked inside, a few were teasing each other about how much better they were or how they had 'kicked their butt' everyone was smiling, everyone was happy and everyone seemed to be relaxed. I smiled because that was the goal. One normal fun day before we figured out our next move.

After lunch we all went to the library which had been decorated to look like a bar with a stage and a karaoke machine. I smiled and giggled. "You have to sing for us," Jason said, looking at me. "No, you know I'm terrible," I said, laughing. The truth was, I was terrible, but I loved singing anyway, music had always been a big part of my soul. Suddenly everyone was chanting "Gabriela! Gabriela!" "Fine! But you will all regret this" I replied as I stepped up and took the microphone. Everyone clapped their hands and cheered for me. I picked the Fleetwood Mac song, The Chain, as the song I would butcher.

Even though I was terrible, everyone still clapped and cheered when I finished, some even yelled "encore!" "I don't think so, let someone who can actually sing have a chance to entertain us" I said, smiling as I walked off the makeshift stage. I sat down next to James, "I don't think I would know any of this music. I haven't spent a lot of time here" he said as I sat down. I smiled at him, "If you want to sing, just go sing anything you want, there are no rules" I told him. "Maybe," he replied, smiling at me.

Damian and Hale sang a duet together, a Hall and Oates classic. Everyone continued enjoying themselves, smiling, laughing and enjoying a few adult beverages. It seemed like no time at all when Cori suddenly appeared to let us know that dinner was ready. We all went back to the kitchen to eat our dinner. Everyone continued to smile and laugh. The chatter was loud and full of life. We decided to have a calmer night and just play a few rounds of poker and have a few more drinks.

I didn't mention anything about the war, I felt that tomorrow morning would be soon enough for that. Cori just couldn't go a day without giving me a startle, she appeared close to my ear and whispered, loudly, "would anyone like any dessert?" After jumping and catching my breath from the scare, I replied, "not I" with a tight mouth. James giggled at my expense. "Glad you find it funny" I replied, teasingly, then I laughed along with him. "What are you guys laughing about?" Misty asked, walking up behind us. "Just the fact that the elf likes to constantly startle me" I replied, still laughing. "Hmmm, I've heard that elves do that to people they become attached to" she replied in a serious tone. "Lucky me" I said, still giggling.

After Misty made her way around the room, she circled back to our table and sat down next to me. "I know this is supposed to be a fun, no worry day, but I have an uneasy feeling. I'm scared that something more terrifying than we could have imagined is heading our way" she said in a low voice so that no one else would overhear. I looked at her, surprised by what she had said. "Maybe I shouldn't have said anything," she said, after a moment of silence between us. "No, you have every right to tell me your fears. I'm sorry, I just don't know what to say. Is it instinct? A premonition?" I asked. I could feel James leaning in on our conversation now. I wasn't sure if he had heard from the beginning or not.

"Will you come for a walk with me Misty?" I asked, so we could get away from everyone else. James started to stand up, so I put my hand on his shoulder and shook my head. "Let us go talk alone," I whispered to him. He gave me a look of disapproval but sat back down. Misty and I walked outside toward the barn. I saw Margo at the property line, stalking back and forth. It was a nice warm night. After we were far enough away from the house, I sat down on the ground and patted the ground next to me to tell Misty to sit next to me. "Isn't the grass wet from the dew?" She asked. "Yes, but what difference does it make? We can wash our clothes and we can use magic if they get stained" I replied with a giggle. I was feeling a bit light headed from the adult beverages.

She smiled and sat next to me on the wet grass that was surely staining our clothes a bright green color. "I had a dream," she started. "It felt so real, you were gone, we were all trying to find you. It seemed like a lot of time passed and we started losing hope, that you must be dead" She said. "Did you find me?" I asked. She looked down and shook her head, "no, I woke up, we didn't find you, and I don't know if you were dead or alive" she said. "Well, if I go missing, just try to look back at the dream for clues. Were there any at all? Anything to say, who might take or kill me?" I asked, feeling my buzz slip away as fear started replacing it. She shook her head again, "no, nothing, it was as if you had just vanished." She said.

We both sat there next to each other in silence for a few moments. "Have you had prophetic dreams before?" I asked. "Once or twice and I wouldn't have said anything, but the dreams have the same feel to them, and this felt like one of them for sure" She said. I nodded, "I don't think we should say anything to the others until we know a little more. I don't want everyone getting paranoid. Was I gone when the dream began? Did anything lead up to my disappearance?" I asked. "You were gone when it began, that's another reason why it scared me so much. You were gone and we were searching for you, that's all I know" she replied.

"Okay, we will keep it to ourselves like I said before" I said as I stood up. "We should get back inside before they come looking for us," I added. She nodded, "I didn't want to keep it to myself, and I'm sorry I don't know more" she said as she took my hand and I helped her to her feet. "It's okay, it's not your fault that you didn't see more," I said. "That's one reason why I told you, I think we should tell someone else, maybe they will have an idea to figure out more, like inducing a dream state in me or extra protection for you," she said. "We'll talk more about it tomorrow" I said, nodding my head toward the house where James was walking out of the front door. She put her head down and nodded. We walked toward the house.

"I was wondering where you disappeared to," James said. "I told you that we needed to talk in private," I replied with a smile. I wasn't sure what to do with the information I had just received, there wasn't much to go on and I didn't want to put the team in a panic. So, for now, especially for the rest of the night, I would smile and pretend that I didn't know anything, which was pretty much true, I didn't really know anything. I could tell from the look on James' face that he would question me later. For now, I would lie to him, I had to protect him and the others. Misty already knew, but I could keep it from the rest. "I think I need some more wine" I said with a smile as I walked past James and into the house.

After a few more drinks together we all went to our rooms to get rested. I told them we would have a meeting in the morning about what our next move would be. As soon as James and I got to the bedroom and closed the door he started asking me questions. "What was Misty saying?" "Why did she seem upset?" "Does she know something that we don't?" "She just needed another woman to talk to," I replied. "I'm not sure I believe you," he said. "Believe what you want, if it was something you needed to know, I would tell you" I replied feeling a bit heated. "I don't want to argue with you," he said, sensing that I was getting upset. "Then don't, just forget it" I replied.

I knew the best way to take his mind off of something was to give him something else to think about, so I started taking my clothes off. "You are trying to hide something aren't you?" He asked curiously. I guess he was catching on to my tactics. Nonetheless, instead of replying to him, I just walked over and unbuckled his belt. Then I raised his shirt and started kissing his chest and his hard stomach. He let out a moan and I knew I had won, for now. After we both climaxed we both passed out, him before me. It was another dreamless night for me. It was as if I closed my eyes and then opened them and it was morning.

When I opened my eyes, I looked over to see James staring at me. "What is it?" I asked. "You are beautiful and I like looking at you," he replied. I smiled at him, even as what Misty had told me the night before crept back into my head. I'm sure my smile faded, James looked alarmed. "What's wrong?" He asked in a stern voice. "I'm not sure exactly, but we need to have a meeting with everyone," I replied. He nodded his head in agreement as he got out of bed without saying another word. I got up and got dressed as quickly as I could. I didn't like not telling him first, but I felt like him finding out with the rest of them would be the best thing right now. I knew he would be upset with me for not telling him, but he has to learn that just because we are lovers doesn't mean he gets inside information before anyone else.

He walked out of the room before I did, I followed a couple minutes after. I walked out to see that he was already gathering everyone into the living room. I smiled at him, and he smiled back, I guess maybe he did understand. When Misty walked in the room, I motioned for her to come stand next to me, she did just that. When everyone was in the living room, I began, "Misty had a dream, and I am going to let her share it with you all." I sat down and let Misty talk. She spoke loud and clear, like she had training in public speaking. She told them all what she had told me the night before and when she was finished speaking, it seemed as though everyone started asking questions all at once. I stood up and held my hand up to stop them. "I asked her all these same questions last night, what she told us is all that she knows," I said.

Misty stood there for a moment, "I'm sorry that I don't know more, maybe there's a reason I was only shown a little" she said, sounding ashamed. "You don't have to be sorry, you haven't done anything wrong" I told her. Then I turned to address everyone else, "unless anyone has an idea of what we can do to prevent this from happening, we will continue doing what we have been doing and what we were planning to do." I could tell that James was upset by the look on his face.

"I don't think we should just continue as if we know nothing," James said. "Well, technically we don't know anything, not anything that would make me change my course of action" I replied. "You are clearly in danger," he said with a stern voice. "I will excuse you from our mission if need be" I replied in a more stern voice. He looked at me with a hurt look in his eyes and walked away. I knew it wouldn't be the end of the discussion, he had to go think of what he could say to me that would make me change my mind before we continued.

Twenty-Four

The next course of action

My next course of action was to send a spy into enemy territory. We had to figure out what was going on with the other side. Then maybe we could figure out how to save my ass from being a missing person. But deciding who to send was bugging me. Cori would of course be my most dispensable player, but she was no warrior, nor would it be fair to send her to her death and more than likely not gain any information. Conan and Hale and Misty and Damian and Pearl are all known high priests and priestesses so Oscar would know right away that they were only there to spy. Levi, Alice, David and James are all too tall, he would know right away that they are half giants. That left Jason or Arturo. Arturo is very powerful, he could possibly pull it off, but what if he didn't? I couldn't afford to lose him. And Jason, he was just too new at all of this, no way I could send him.

A lightning bug landed on my hand, as if on cue. Of course! I said aloud. "Can you do the same spell that you did on 2?" I asked the bug. The bug just walked around on my hand. "Can you show me what you see from afar?" I asked, trying to be more specific. The bug just continued to walk around on my hand. Maybe she didn't have her powers here in this dimension. I just watched the bug crawl around my hand for a few minutes, meditating on what I should do. Nothing came to me and she flew off of my hand and over to the window. "I suppose it is warm enough for you to go out now, if that's what you want" I said aloud as I opened the window just enough for her to go out. "Be careful please!" I added as she quickly flew outside.

I stepped out of the bedroom to see if I could find Arturo. James passed by me heading to the bedroom with his head down and didn't even acknowledge my presence. I guess he was still pissed off at me, but I didn't come this far to just give up. I walked down the hallway toward Arturo's room. When I reached it, I knocked. No answer. Conan popped out of his room and said, "I think he went outside for a walk with Margo." I looked at him and smiled and said, "Thank you." "You're welcome, anything I can help you with?" He asked. I shook my head and said, "I don't think so, but if I need you, I will come find you." I smiled at him and walked away.

I didn't want to wait, so I went outside to find Arturo and Margo. It didn't matter if Margo knew, she couldn't tell anyone anyway. It took a few minutes, but I finally spotted them at the edge of the woods. Arturo was sitting on the ground and Margo was lying down next to him with her head in his lap. It wasn't hard for me to imagine her as her human form, probably because I knew her in both forms. I walked toward them waving to get their attention so that I didn't startle them. Arturo waved back to let me know that he saw me.

"Hey! Mind if I sit with you guys? I have some things I need to speak with you about," I said as I approached. Arturo waved his hand over the ground next to him to let me know I could in fact sit with them. "What's going on?" He asked as I sat down. "I want to send a spy into enemy territory" I said. He immediately looked at me like I had said the craziest thing. "Hear me out" I said before he could speak against it. "I've gone over my options, and the best one is the fairy and the second best would be you" I said. Margo raised her head and glared at me, I could tell she wasn't happy about what I had said.

"I would prefer to send the fairy, with her gift of sharing sight with me, but I can't communicate with her here at all. I tried speaking with her and all she did was crawl around on my hand. Do you know if she can use her magic here? The way she did on 2?" I asked. "I'm not sure, I will try to communicate with her, where is she?" Arturo replied. "I'm not sure, she wanted to go outside so I let her" I replied. "Oh," Arturo replied. "And, what are we trying to learn from sending in a spy?" Arturo asked. "I would like to figure out why I'm going to become a missing person," I replied quietly.

"And another thing I wanted to speak with you about, James, I have done spells to keep him from letting his emotions interfere, but his emotions are too strong it seems, I'm afraid he will do something to compromise what we have to do" I said. "There's nothing I can do about that, I don't think you should exclude him or push him away because of it" Arturo replied. "So I shouldn't do anything about it?" I asked, a little shocked. "He wouldn't let anything happen to you, he would die for you," Arturo replied. "That's what I'm afraid of. As much as I know he doesn't want to lose me, I couldn't stand to lose him either" I said. "You both knew what was happening when you became emotionally involved, or you should have, I know you are young but you are far from dumb. And you were even warned against it by David but you both still followed your hearts instead of your heads, it's too late on that matter now, what's done is done" Arturo said. I nodded my head as I lowered it, feeling a bit ashamed.

"I guess you're right, I can't argue," I said, quietly. "It's okay, I know how you feel," Arturo said as he patted Margo on the head.

She rolled over and pushed her head into his hand harder. They were so cute, even in her cat form you could tell how much she loved him. I noticed that James was walking toward us. "When the fairy comes back, I will bring her to you so you can try to communicate with her and see if my plan is possible," I said as I stood up. "I'm going to go talk with James," I added as I walked away.

I started walking toward James. As soon as I was within reach of him, I grabbed him around his midsection and squeezed as hard as I could. "I'm sorry I've been such a bitch to you" I said. "It's okay, I understand" he replied as he pulled my head toward his and kissed me gently. "I know that we have a mission, I know that you are the leader of this small army and I don't want to get in your way" He said. "I know, I should have more faith and trust in you." I replied. "From now on, I will trust you more," I added. "What were you speaking to Arturo about?" He asked. I had to tell him, no more secrets.

"I want to send a spy into enemy territory so I can try to prevent me from becoming a missing person" I said. He nodded, "that sounds like a good idea, anyone in mind?" He asked. "The fairy," I replied. "The fairy?" He repeated. "If we can figure out how to communicate with her and if she can use her magic here, then yes" I said. "And who is the backup plan?" He asked. "Arturo," I replied. "We can't afford to lose him," James said. "We can't afford to lose anyone," I replied. James just nodded his head and pulled me into him in an embrace.

After standing there holding each other for a moment, we walked inside without saying another word. I decided to call a meeting and let everyone know what was going on. I had a team for a reason and I couldn't keep things from them. They were all here because they wanted to be, because they believed in what we were fighting for and because they believed in me. After I explained my plan, I finished with, "I am so grateful for each of you, and I am sorry for the way I have acted. I hope that you can all forgive me and not hold a grudge, I promise you that I will never act that way again, we are a team." Everyone smiled at me.

"We can help with communicating with the fairy," Hale said, motioning toward all the other witches. "Yes, and we can give her magic if hers doesn't work here" Misty added. I smiled, "Of course, why didn't I just come to you guys to begin with?" I said with a laugh. "Anyone know how we can find her? Or do we just wait for her to return?" I asked. "We can do a scrying spell to locate her," Damian said. "Okay" I said, nodding my head. I hadn't used scrying magic before, but I was always willing to learn new magic.

Damian sat down at a table in the library. "I need a map of the area," he said, looking at me. "I don't have a map," I said. "Would a picture work?" James asked. "Yes that will work," Damian replied. I looked at James, confused. "Google maps," He said. I smiled at him and said, "of course, I love technology." James went into our room and came back out a few minutes later with a printed picture of the property. You couldn't see the house or the barn, it just looked like a clearing in the woods. "I love magic too" I said as I took the picture and handed it to Damian.

"Couldn't we just summon the fairy?" Conan asked. "Yes, if this doesn't work, we will try that next," Damian replied. He laid the picture down on the table and took a rock on a string and held it over the picture. He started humming and mumbling what sounded like a spell. The rock started to swing and before long, it dropped onto the picture. "That looks like where the barn is!" I said, excitedly. Damian, James and myself went outside to the barn to see if we could find the fairy. Phillip was outside in the field, it was a nice sunny, warm day. The barn door was open so Phillip could go in and out as he pleased, we walked inside and started looking around. Dust went into my nose and made me sneeze.

After looking for about thirty minutes, we all met back in the middle of the barn. "She's probably sleeping in a hole somewhere. Fairies are night creatures," Damian said. "Should we summon her, or should we wait until night?" I asked. "Probably better to wait for night, she may not be too willing to help if we pull her from a deep sleep" Damian replied. I nodded. "We may as well go have some lunch then" James said, putting his arm around me. I smiled at him as I let him guide me out of the barn and back toward the house.

Cori had fixed some sandwiches and fruit salad for lunch. I walked into the kitchen where I found her cleaning and preparing to cook dinner. "Do you ever take a break?" I asked her. "No need, I would rather just keep the warriors fed so they can defeat the bad guys and I can have a somewhat normal life," she replied. I smiled and nodded at her as I left her to her cleaning. I walked back to the dining room and grabbed some fruit salad. Everyone ate more quietly than normal. I guess everyone had a lot on their minds.

After eating lunch, James and I went outside to hang out with Phillip. I brushed his mane and tail as James talked to him, filled him in on everything that was going on. By the time I was finished his tail and mane were super soft. He nudged my back with his nose as I turned to walk away. After he got my attention he kneeled down for me to get on his back. I handed the brush to James and said, "why not?" I climbed onto Phillip's back and put my arms around his neck as he took off in a sprint. I was getting better at this, and I loved the feeling of the wind hitting my face and my hair flying as he ran faster.

After we galloped around the property about three times, Phillip walked back toward the barn where James was still standing and waiting for us. Conan walked up from the other direction as Phillip stopped and kneeled down for me to dismount. "Hey guys," Conan said with a warm smile. "Hey, what's up?" I replied. "Nothing much, I was just admiring the way you ride. I used to ride a little when I was younger" Conan said. I smiled at him, "I don't think I'm much of a rider" I replied with a laugh. "Nonsense! You are a natural!" Conan argued. I just smiled and blushed.

"We should get inside and work on the plan" I said. Conan smiled and nodded and James put his arm around my waist and we walked inside. James and I went straight to the library and Conan went to gather the other witches. James and I just sat down at the table and waited silently for the others to join. I could tell he was getting anxious, as was I. After a few minutes of waiting, the door opened and everyone started walking in.

I started with, "I think we should go ahead and summon the fairy." Everyone nodded and agreed. "James, you don't have to stay if you don't want to, but you are welcome to, of course" I said as nicely as possible. "I'll stay," he replied with a smile. The witches started cleansing the space and then we formed a circle so we could begin the summoning spell. Misty had brought a chocolate chip cookie, a silver spoon, and a bell for the spell. Conan placed the items in the middle of the circle, "now all we have to do is join hands, and meditate, imagine the fairy in the circle" he said.

We all joined hands and began the ritual. With my eyes closed, I imagined the fairy waking from her nap and flying out of the barn, and toward the house. I imagined her coming in the bedroom window that I had left open, then going under the closed bedroom door and to the right, then coming under the library door. "It worked!" James said. I opened my eyes and looked, the lightning bug was sitting on the cookie, seeming to be enjoying a nibble or two.

"Great! Now we need to start working on setting up communication with her," I said. "I think I know a spell for that, I'm going to set up a mental connection with you and her," Misty said, looking at me. I nodded, "okay, sounds good, let's try it," I replied. Misty placed her left hand over the lightning bug and her right hand over my head and started to mumble an incantation. When she stopped mumbling, I opened my eyes, I looked at the lightning bug. "I don't feel any different, how do we know if it worked?" I asked. "You would be able to see through her eyes." Misty said, looking down. I tried to see through the lightning bug's eyes and I couldn't. "I don't think it worked, is there something else we can try?" I asked. Cori popped up and announced that dinner was ready, making me jump out of my skin yet again.

"Let's discuss it at dinner, maybe try again a little later," Hale said. I nodded, "James, will you go get the jar for the lightning bug?" I asked. "Of course," he replied. "We need to work together and make this happen, I have an important mission for you" I said as I put her into the jar after James returned with it. I sat the jar on the table and went to dinner. "I think we all need to focus more, and the fairy has to let us in too," Arturo said. I looked at him and nodded. "I'll try to talk to her, but I'm not sure if she can understand me," I said. "I don't see why she wouldn't, if she ever could, Margo and Phillip can understand us in their animal forms," Arturo replied. "You're right" I said as I stuffed a fork full of food into my mouth.

After dinner, we all headed back into the library. I brought the jar with the fairy inside as well. I opened the lid and she crawled out onto my hand. "We need you to do something very important for us, we are going to give you some of our magic so you can help us, okay?" I said to the bug. She seemed to understand, somewhat, I suppose. She flew off of my hand and into the circle we had prepared earlier. "See, I told you she could understand," Arturo bragged. I just smiled at him and let him have his win. We circled around the fairy like we had done earlier. Misty started the same spell as earlier.

Somehow, this time it worked! I could see through the lightning bug's eyes inside my mind. It wasn't quite the same as it had been before on 2, but I was pretty sure it would work. "It's working guys!" I exclaimed. Everyone seemed to breathe a sigh of relief all at once. "Thanks everyone, I will communicate with the fairy on what I need her to do now. I will keep you all updated on what's going on" I said.

Everyone went their own ways and I put the fairy back inside the jar and went to my room, James followed.

I opened the jar and the fairy flew out and landed on my hand. I could see myself through her eyes so I knew the magic was still working. "We should drive her close to the complex," I said. James looked at me like I was crazy, "that seems dangerous," he said. "How else will she know where to go?" I asked. "Ask Arturo, maybe he has a better idea," James said. "I can disguise us, so we won't be recognized, we'll just drive close so that I can show her where to go" I said. As I heard my own voice repeating everything I was saying in my mind like an echo.

"What's wrong?" James asked. I must have had a weird look on my face. Instead of saying it out loud, I wrote it on a piece of paper: every sound is echoing in my mind. He just looked at me and nodded. I was starting to get a headache and feel lethargic from it. I picked up the pencil once more and wrote: we need to hurry and get this done quickly, I don't like the side effects. James nodded again that he understood. I put the fairy back in the jar and walked toward the door.

Once we were outside, I grabbed James by the arm and warped us to the vehicles. He gave me a sour look, I guess I had taken him by surprise. I just shrugged my shoulders at him. We got in Misty's car thinking it would be the least noticeable. James started driving toward the complex where Oscar and his crew were staying. When we were close, he pulled over. "You need to drive by it, I can let her out of the window and make this quicker" I said. He shook his head, no. "We need this to work," I pleaded. He threw the car into gear angrily and did as I asked.

He stopped at the corner, I nodded at him, rolled the car window down and took the lid off of the jar. "I need you to go inside, find the witches and just let me hear what they are saying" I said to the bug. She flew out of the window, toward the complex. We drove away, after we were about a mile away, I told James to stop. He found a safe place to pull over where we wouldn't look suspicious in a grocery store parking lot.

The parking lot was busy with people. "You should go inside and pretend to shop, I need to concentrate anyway. I will get in the back seat and lay down so we don't draw any unwanted attention" I said. "I don't want to leave you alone," James replied. "I'll be fine," I said sternly. He narrowed his eyes to let me know he wasn't happy and exited the car. I crawled into the back seat and lay down to concentrate on what the fairy was seeing and hearing.

I could see, she was on a lamp post about twenty-five yards from the front door. She wasn't moving, probably waiting for an opportunity to get inside. There didn't seem to be a lot of movement going on. There were guards posted at the front door, but as of this moment, no one was going in or coming out of the doors. I decided to try something, I thought something to the fairy, *go around to the other side.* It worked, or by coincidence she left the lamp post and went to the side of the house.

There didn't seem to be any open doors or windows on that side either. *Keep going around, check all sides of the house.* I said to the fairy in my mind. She was listening. She flew around to the back of the house, someone was coming out of a door, but she was too far away to try to get inside before it closed. *Go close to the door, maybe he will go back inside soon,* I said. She flew over to the door and landed on a security light above it. *Now we just wait,* I said to her.

The car door opened and I sat up with a jolt. It was just James. I looked at him with narrow eyes. "I've just been walking around forever, I can't just keep walking around without drawing suspicion" he said defensively. "Fine, I have a feeling it's going to be a while anyway, she hasn't even got inside yet" I replied. "Steak out mode, I suppose," James said. "I did buy us some water and snacks just in case" He added, throwing a bottle of water and some chips at me. I drank some of the water and pushed the chips aside. "Don't distract me, I need to concentrate, I can communicate with her telepathically and tell her what to do next" I said. James just looked impressed and nodded as he got comfortable. I lay back down in the back seat.

Finally after what seemed like an hour, a man started walking toward the door. *Get ready!* I said to the fairy. As soon as the door opened, she flew inside. She seemed to get pushed by the pressure of the air from the door and fall to the floor, but she quickly recovered. The room was huge, she followed the man that had come through the door. He went into an adjacent room where I could see Oscar sitting at a table. The fairy landed on a chandelier that hung above the table.

"Anything yet?" Oscar asked the other man. "Not yet, we are still looking, I know we will find it," the man replied. "Then why have we not found it yet?!" Oscar yelled. "They haven't been seen by anyone, as soon as they mess up and come out, we will follow them back" the man said. "They aren't stupid, you need to stop assuming that they are!" Oscar replied. "We are not assuming anything, sir," the man said. I knew they were talking about us, they were looking for the farm and not having any luck. At least I knew our location was safe, for now.

"What are your plans when we do find them?" The man asked. "That's none of your business, the less people that know, the better" Oscar replied, more calmly now. I knew that we weren't going to get anything else out of this. *Get out as soon as you can,* I said to the fairy. She flew back toward the door that she had snuck into. She landed on the trim above the door. "Who is using magic?!" Oscar yelled. "I have no idea," the other man replied. "Someone is, I can feel it, everyone here knows the rules! Has someone penetrated the complex?!" Oscar yelled. "No, there's no way," the other man replied. "He can sense magic being used, he can't find her can he?" I asked, looking at James. "I don't know," he replied. "We have to get her out as soon as possible," I said. "I'm sure she will be fine," James said, trying to calm me down. "They are witches with the same knowledge as us, they know that lightning bugs are fairies!" I said as I began to cry. "Don't lose focus Gabriela, guide her to safety" James said calmly. I nodded and wiped the tears from my face. I lay back down to concentrate better. I could see that the fairy was still sitting on the door trim. Several people were now walking around, searching, some of them had guns ready.

Just stay hidden, don't move until the door opens, then get out as quickly as possible. I told the fairy. I heard a vehicle pull up next to us, I looked up, it was the pick up truck. Arturo, Jason, and Hale walked up to the car. "I had a feeling that you may need some help. And why would you just take off and not let anyone at the house know what you were doing?" Arturo asked. "I had to go, I will explain later, but it should have been an easy mission," I replied. "Nothing is ever easy, you need to learn that," Arturo scorned. "Okay, you can 'dad' lecture me later, right now, our fairy is in trouble" I said.

"What's going on?" Arturo asked. "We sent her into the complex, Oscar could sense magic being used, now he and all of his people are searching for the source of it" I said. "And where is the fairy?" Arturo asked. "She's hiding on a door trim, waiting for an opportunity to escape" I replied. "That may not happen," Arturo replied. I shook my head, "no, she will get out!" I replied with tears forming again. "We need to get back to the house," Hale said. "No! I'm not leaving her!" I said, with tears now running down my cheeks. "We should have made a complete plan," Arturo replied. "Punish me if need be, but not by leaving her, she is in there for us!" I begged. Hale put his hand on my forehead and the next thing I knew, I was waking up in my bed.

I immediately tried to make contact with the fairy, no use, I was too far away. I stormed out of my bedroom, Jason was the first person I saw so he was the one that I went off on. "How dare you guys do that!" I yelled. He threw his arms up, "hold on, I was just there, I didn't do anything" he said. Arturo walked into the room. "We have to go back and get her!" I yelled. "They are looking for us, we can't just go right to them," Arturo said, calmly. "What if it was you?! Would you want me to leave you?!" I yelled. "Yes," he replied, still calm. I shook my head, "no, I can't, we have to go back" I pleaded.

James walked into the room. "James, please! Please! We have to go back for her!" I begged. He put his head down. "You can't hold me prisoner here, I will go by my damn self!" I yelled as I stomped off. I went back into the bedroom. I threw myself onto the bed and cried. I couldn't let her die, this was my idea, it would be all my fault. Rayne jumped onto the bed to comfort me. She rubbed her head into mine and snuggled up to me. I heard the door open, I didn't bother to look up, I knew it was James. He sat down on the bed next to me. "She may have gotten out, we don't know. She seems pretty smart, maybe we will see her in a few days," he said.

"She doesn't know her way back even if she did get out" I said. "Arturo is right, what we did was dangerous. We should have made a solid plan with the rest of the witches before we just took off" he said. "I couldn't wait, the noise in my head was nauseating," I replied. "I understand honey, there's nothing to be done now, except wait and see if she comes home" he said, trying to calm me down. "It's all my fault" I said as I started crying uncontrollably. He pulled me into him, my head in his lap and rubbed my head as I cried, and I knew they were right, there was nothing else to do.

I cried until I fell asleep. I didn't even realize I was asleep and I heard a familiar voice. It was my mom. "Everything will work out, trust me," her voice said. I couldn't see anything, only darkness. "How do you know? Where are you?" I asked. "I'm always here baby, even if I can't talk to you or see you. I can see everything," she replied. "I need you," I said. "I'm here baby." Then I woke up. I couldn't tell if it was real, if I had really spoken to her or if it was my brain's way of helping me cope with everything.

Twenty-Five

Rescue mission

I decided that I couldn't just let it go, I had to do something. I knew it would have to be on my own, and that I couldn't tell anyone, they would only stop me. I couldn't let an innocent friend die because I made a careless mistake. I wouldn't let her go that way. James woke up and rolled over. "How are you feeling?" He asked. "Like I murdered a friend" I replied. He just reached over and pulled me into him. I could hear his heartbeat, it was all the comfort that I could ask for at a time like this.

Someone knocked on the door. "What?!" I yelled. "It's me, can I come in?" Arturo said through the door. I didn't really want to see him so I remained silent. After a few moments, James said, "come in." I raised my head and looked at him with narrowed eyes. He shrugged his shoulders and gave me a look like, 'what am I supposed to do?' Arturo walked inside, "I am truly sorry about what took place yesterday" he said. "I can't do this, I can't just lose friends and be okay with it" I replied. "I know, and I know this doesn't help, but it does get easier," Arturo said. "No, I refuse to accept this," I said. "We have to think about the whole, not just one," Arturo said.

"Save it, it doesn't matter what you say, I am not okay with this," I said sternly. "You have to be, we cannot do anything about it, it happened, we can't turn back time" Arturo said. "All we have to do is go get her, get close enough that I can reestablish the connection, locate her, rescue her and come home" I said. "Get it out of your mind, it's not going to happen, we need to focus on what to do next," Arturo said. Going against my own gut, I kept arguing. "I can't focus on the next mission when the last one isn't finished" I said. "It was a fool's mission and it is finished. That's it, the end," Arturo said, starting to sound irritated.

I knew I was never going to convince him that we had to go back for her, so I just shut up. I would have to do it on my own. I just looked blankly at Arturo until he felt uncomfortable and left the room. After he left, James looked at me and said, "babe, please, let this go so we can move on from it," I just looked at him blankly, hoping he would leave the room too, no such luck. I refused to talk more about it to people that I knew wouldn't help me, so I kept my mouth shut and started secretly planning in my head.

I grew up alone, I had been alone my whole life, I could do this. It hurt a lot, because I had become used to having people there for me, people on my side. I knew I could do this all by myself though. I had to pretend that I was going to let it go, it was the only way they would leave me alone. I started crying again, bawling my eyes out, James pulled me into him to comfort me. I tried to take my mind off of the issue for the time being, but I wasn't giving up and I was going back for her.

Someone knocked on the door again. "What?!" I yelled. "Breakfast is ready," Cori said. "Thank you" I replied, whipping tears from my face. I thought that was odd, why didn't she just pop in like she usually did? Was that her way of showing sympathy? I got up from the bed. "You coming?" I asked James. "Yeah" he replied. We walked out of the room together and into the dinning room to eat. I tried to eat, but I didn't feel hungry even though I knew I should be. I still picked up the fork, scraped up food with it and put it in my mouth. It had no flavor to me. All I knew was that I had to get the fairy back.

Everyone gathered in the library after breakfast. I couldn't even concentrate on what they were saying. Something about invading the enemy before they could invade us. "I don't feel well, I'm just going to lay down," I said. They all looked at me, some with sympathy in their eyes, others with worry. "I'm sure I'll be okay after a nap," I added. Some of them gave me a sympathetic smile, others just looked away. I could tell they didn't care, she was nothing to them, but she was something to me.

I went to my room and started making a plan. I wish that I had at least one of them to help, but I knew that I didn't. I could get help though still, Phillip, I could ride him out, he would help me, I knew he would. I might actually have to warp us out of here, but I could do it, I knew I could. I could warp us out, ride him until I could make contact with the fairy, then we could go rescue her and come home. They would probably never even know we were gone. I had a feeling my room was being watched, so I didn't leave it, not until I had the plan all together.

I knew that I had to keep everything inside. I wanted to tell James, so he didn't worry when he realized that I was gone. But I knew that I couldn't, he would stop me, he would tell Arturo at the very least and *he* would definitely stop me. All I knew was I had to do my very best to get the fairy back. I felt inside that she was still alive and confused about me just leaving her. But I hoped that she would know that I wouldn't do that willingly and that I would be back for her. I decided that my best alibi right now would be to lay down and try to take a nap. So I did just that and to my surprise, I fell asleep. It was a dreamless sleep this time. I woke up what seemed like an hour later, James was beside me on the bed, he was asleep.

I nudged him just a little to see if he would wake, he did not. I looked outside, it was dark. I looked at the clock, it said, ten thirty-three. I slid out of the bed as quietly as possible and went into the bathroom and closed the door. I decided to wear the catsuit to hide better, plus it was in the closet in the bathroom. I locked the bathroom door from the inside and quickly got changed. The bathroom window was just big enough for me to climb through and it was about five feet from the ground.

After I put my hair in a bun, I slid the window up as quietly as possible and slithered out. I hit the ground hard enough for pain to shoot through my body, but I didn't break anything and I knew the pain would pass quickly. As soon as I hit the ground, I remembered Margo and Philip, I couldn't let them see me, they would alert the others. So I warped to the property line by the road where the vehicles were. I had decided that taking Philip would be too risky. Thankfully, the keys were inside Misty's car, it was the most quiet vehicle.

I got in, started it up and headed toward Oscar's complex. I knew that I couldn't drive right up to it, so when I was about three miles away, I found a place to pull over. It was an apartment complex that wasn't gated. I parked and tried to make contact with the fairy. Either the spell had worn off, or she was still out of range, I refused to think of the other possibility. I tried for a little while longer, no use, I couldn't reach her. I got out of the car and warped to the grocery store where we had parked before.

I sat down next to a tree and tried to make contact again, but still couldn't. The spell must have worn off. Unless she had gotten out and started making her way home, again, I refused to think of the only other option. The smart thing for me to have done at this moment would have been for me to abort the mission and return home. I couldn't do it though, I couldn't just let her be a sacrifice to my cause. I started walking toward the complex along the forest line, hiding behind trees. I was so pale skinned that the moon's glow reflected off of my exposed skin, seeming to make me glow.

I walked along the forest line for what seemed like an hour, although I'm sure it was much less time. I didn't see anyone, not even a regular human the whole way. I was now directly behind the complex, I tried once more to make contact, still nothing. I noticed a guard walking around the complex, doing circles, he seemed to be the only one. I had to be careful, I knew that Oscar could sense when magic was being used. So, I would have to use my human skills to maneuver the situation.

I crouched down behind a tree a few feet inside the forest to hide. The night air was a bit chilly but not too bad, it felt nice out. Under different circumstances I could imagine lying outside and star gazing with James. I shook the thought from my head, so I could focus on the task at hand. I had to think of a way to distract the guard without using magic. I noticed a pile of sticks lying on the ground. I could start a fire and run when he came. Not sure if that would work, I would probably make too much noise. He would probably call for help the minute he saw the fire.

Every idea I could think of, I could think of several reasons why it wouldn't work. If I could use magic, this would be so much easier. I could use magic as long as I could out magic all of them. So I started thinking of a way to do just that. I could start the fire, and then warp myself to the house. It would set off the magic alarm so I would have to quickly get into the house, search for the fairy and get out. But what happens when I don't find her quickly? Would I be able to walk away and leave her behind? I was starting to doubt my decision to come here in the first place. I should just go back home, but I couldn't, something inside wouldn't let me.

An idea came to mind, I could use an invisibility spell. Oscar would sense the magic, but if I was invisible, he couldn't possibly find me, right? Well, I was certainly going to try. After all, I had come all this way already, I couldn't just go home now. I performed the spell on myself, invisibility was a tough one, because I could still see myself, but I was sure that it worked. Lights came on outside and alarms started sounding off. I would step out of the forest into sight to make sure they couldn't see me and if they could, I would warp myself as far as my magic would take me.

I stepped out of the forest, careful not to make any noise. I was in the light now, within sight. I could see people running around with guns, but they didn't see me. This was a good thing. I didn't walk too close to any of them, I didn't want them to hear me breath or see my footprints as I walked in the grass. I walked to the door where I had last seen the fairy waiting on the door frame. I stood beside it and tried to make contact with her again, but it didn't work. It was possible that the spell had worn off or even that she broke it to keep from being found.

I waited by the door for maybe ten minutes and finally it opened. I slid inside before it closed. I quickly ran my fingers over the door frame, she wasn't there. I looked around and didn't see anyone, so I whispered, "fairy, are you here?" I didn't see any movement. I suddenly noticed that I felt different, I felt like my magic wasn't working anymore. It was like it was being drained from me. I quickly reached for the door, it wouldn't open. "You are really dumb enough to walk right into my house? And alone at that?" I heard Oscar's voice come from an intercom.

I froze. Two men came into the room and grabbed me. I fought, and yelled at them to let me go, but it was no use. Oscar had somehow disabled my magic, I was helpless. The two men took me into an office where Oscar was sitting behind a desk, he motioned for me to sit in a chair across from the desk, like I was a welcomed guest. I looked at him and shook my head, no. "Sit!" he yelled. One of the men grabbed my arm and pulled me to the chair and threw me into it. "Fine, I'll sit," I said, matter-of-factly.

"Let me introduce my colleagues, this is Vance," Oscar said, pointing to the guy on his right. "And this is Parker," he said, pointing to the guy on his left, the one that had thrown me into the chair. "You can't just hold me hostage, they are on their way to find me as we speak," I said, as threatening as possible. "Makes no difference to me, who is looking for you, they'll not find you unless I want you to be found" Oscar replied, calmly. I just stared blankly, trying not to show fear. "I could just kill you now and hand your dead body over to your clan, what then?" Oscar said. "They would have revenge, that's what" I replied smartly.

"You act like you aren't afraid to die," Oscar said, sounding genuinely curious. "Why should I be?" I replied. "No matter, death is not what I have in mind for you at this time, it would be far too easy for you anyway, it seems," Oscar said. I could feel myself going numb, I couldn't sit in the chair anymore, I was sliding down toward the floor. Vance and Parker came and grabbed me by the shoulders and held me up. "What did you do to me?" I asked, possibly letting a little fear be heard in my voice this time.

"I have reason to believe that Valery is still alive. Has she been in contact with you?" Oscar asked. "No," I replied. "So, we are going to do this the hard way then? Oscar said. I watched him open a portal and 2 shadowy figures slithered through, I watched them slither inside Vance and Parker, I assumed they were demons. The now possessed Vance and Parker picked me up and carried me down some steps. It looked like I was going into a classic dungeon. Grey brick walls, steel bars, no windows, only torches for light. They threw me inside one of the many cells, shut the door, locked it and walked away.

I lay there, not able to move until Oscar came down after a few hours and removed the spell that made me numb. "I just realized, we can't torturer you if you can't feel anything, now can we?" He said as he laughed at his own sick joke. "You don't have to do this, we can all work together" I said. He started laughing uncontrollably, like I had said the funniest thing he had ever heard. "No we can't, we were divided long ago by the existence of your kind, mixed breeds," he said after he stopped laughing. "And besides that, you weren't trying to work with me before, when you broke into my house," he added.

"I wasn't going to hurt you" I said, knowing it wouldn't make a difference. "And my people will come for me, and I can't say *they* won't hurt you" I added. He started laughing again. "They will never get through, and if they do, I have plenty more cells down here" he said. He started to walk away. "Wait!" I yelled, "Why did you ask me about Valery?" I heard him stop, but I couldn't see him in the darkness. "Because, she will get her punishment for bringing an abomination into this world, she deserves it more than you do, it wasn't your fault you were born after all, it was hers." he said, sounding more quiet than normal, or maybe it was just because he was so far away.

I heard him walk away. I was alone in a creepy dungeon. He was right, I didn't ask to be born, but I wouldn't turn against my mother. Even if I wanted to, I didn't know how to find her or if she was truly alive. I sat down in a corner in the cell and put my back against the cold brick wall. I started meditating, and trying to use magic, I couldn't. I knew I wouldn't be able to, but I had to try. I pulled my legs up and rested my head on my knees, somehow I managed to fall asleep.

I was awakened by a loud sound, I'm not sure what it was, but I could see Vance and Parker standing outside of my cell, or the demons that had possessed them were. Vance was tall with sandy blonde hair and Parker was dark skinned with dark, straight hair, if I had to guess, I would say he was Hispanic. Parker was handsome, I suppose Vance was too if you liked light haired men. They were both muscular and looked like they could be soldiers. I wondered if they knew what was going on, or if they had any control at all, or if was just all demon in control.

"What's the plan Oscar?" Vance said in a deep voice. "Torture her until she talks or dies" Oscar replied. I knew they would kill me either way they weren't just going to let me leave here, looks like it's going to be a slow painful death for me. Parker opened the door to my cell and he and Vance stepped inside. At that moment it was as if time slowed down for me, I knew it hadn't, but it's the only way I can describe the feeling that came over me. They both started hitting me, hard. I fell to the floor, screaming in pain. There were moments when I blacked out from the pain. They beat me for what seemed like hours, until I heard Oscar's voice somewhere in the background say, "take a break, we don't want to kill her on her first day."

They stopped beating me and walked out of the cell. I couldn't move, I was sure some ribs were broken, and possibly other bones in my legs and arms, but I wasn't sure. I closed my eyes and retreated far into my own head, I could see James, smiling and looking so beautiful with the sunset reflecting in his eyes. I could see Julie, laughing and playing with the fairies. I could see Arturo and Margo, sitting together under a tree. I could see myself riding Philip, I could even feel the breeze on my face and feel my hair blowing in the wind. I started drifting in and out of consciousness. I tried to focus on all the beautiful things in my life, but darkness would take over, either way, the pain seemed to be getting less painful and more bearable.

After a few hours, I woke suddenly. Oscar healed me, completely. "Don't worry, we'll do it again shortly," he said. "I Can't have you dying on me on the first day, that wouldn't be any fun, now would it?" he added. "You son-of-a-bitch!" I yelled. "Just fucking kill me!" I screamed. He laughed and walked away. I lay down on the floor and started bawling, feeling sorry for myself for the first time in a long time. I had learned long ago that my life was hell and I would just have to deal with it, but recently I had been given hope, I had been given love and now it was all gone and the hell had returned.

I knew it was my own stupid fault that I was here, I could be safe in my bed right now, with James' arms around me, but I had to go be brave and to be honest, I would do it again to save a life. But, I hadn't saved anyone and only got myself killed. At least the mystery of how I became a missing person was solved now, at least for me. I couldn't see how I could go through this everyday, possibly multiple times a day, maybe I could trigger the demons somehow and make them just kill me. That was my only escape plan at the moment, death. I could hear footsteps coming toward my cell. I braced myself and prepared for the pain.

Vance and Parker entered my cell, they immediately started beating me. The first blow broke my jaw bone, so much for trying to trigger them with words, I didn't have time to think of anything else, they were pounding my head, my back, kicking me in the ribs, and legs. They seemed to be triggered already by something, maybe they would just go ahead and finish me this time. "That's enough boys!" Oscar yelled. Vance landed one more kick to the side of my head and blackness took over.

I heard a familiar voice in the darkness. "Gabriella, oh no, what has happened to you?" Valery's voice said. "They won't let me go, they are beating me, they want to know where you are, but they are going to kill me eventually, I just wish they would get it over with" I replied. "No, you have to hold on, help is coming," she said. I was awakened by a kick to my side. My vision was blurry when I opened my swollen eyes. Oscar was standing over me, and a few seconds later, I was healed again. "No, please, please just kill me, get it over with. Valery is dead, just kill me and end this" I begged. He laughed and walked away.

This routine continued for days, weeks, months except the part about Valery, I didn't see her again. Day after day I was beaten to the brink of death and brought back so they could do it again and again and again. I began to wonder if my people had given up, maybe had a mock funeral without a body? I hoped that they had, I hoped that they weren't continuing to worry about me, I hope they gave themselves closure. Everyone deserves closure, something I knew that I would never have. I wondered if I would be able to communicate with anyone when I was finally dead, tell James and everyone else that I was sorry for what I had done.

One day, after I had been beaten and healed by Oscar I asked him "why won't you just kill me?" "Because this is too much fun" was his reply. He was truly the most evil person I had ever known, I would never have done this to him before and if by some miracle I managed to escape, I would still never do this to him, I would kill him as fast as I possibly could, to rid the world of his evil presence. I would make sure he could never do this to anyone else, ever again. Somehow, in my heart, at that moment, I felt that I would have that chance. I didn't know how or when, obviously most of all, how? Maybe it was just my subconscious trying to keep me a little sane, by giving me some sort of hope.

It was strange, but I began to get used to the pain, somehow it didn't hurt quite as bad when my bones snapped in two or when a size twelve boot landed hard on my head. I didn't think it was possible to get used to something like this, but here I was, being more tolerable by the day. Maybe Vance and Parker would notice and tell Oscar, the only solution would be to go ahead and kill me, right? Turns out that I wasn't right about the killing part, they started burning me with fire and liquid acid. My skin peeling away or disintegrating from my flesh. This was a new pain that I wasn't used to and it felt like the first day I was captured all over again.

Retreating into my own mind, my own good memories is the

only thing I could do. And once all possible hope had left, even the hope for death as a release, I just lay there on the floor, when I wasn't being beaten. I didn't eat the garbage they tried to feed me, I didn't drink the horrible water they tried to give me. It was as if I died, but I was still breathing. I knew once I began to tolerate the new torture method they would just find another. How could this become my life? I couldn't even cry anymore, I tried to will myself to death, but death refused me.

I couldn't understand how anyone could be so cruel to another living creature, even one they disliked. I don't like spiders, I usually catch them and put them outside, but if I must kill one, I do it quickly, I don't torture it for eternity. I just knew that if by some miracle I did get out of this, Oscar would pay for what he was doing to me. I lay down on the floor and awaited my next beating.

They came in shortly after I had managed to drift to sleep and began my daily torture. I didn't even scream anymore, I didn't have any screams left inside of me. I just took it, it did still hurt, but the hurt had become normal. They beat me, and burned me until I blacked out once again.

Twenty-Six

The funeral

This time, when I woke, I wasn't healed. I couldn't move because of the broken bones and blood was still leaking from me onto the ground. My vision was blurry and I had to fight to stay conscious. But I heard a familiar sound, unless I was hallucinating, it was Margo's growl. Then I could have sworn that I heard her scream before the darkness took me over. When I came back again, I heard other familiar sounds. I heard David's voice and James' voice. Either I was finally being rescued or I was finally dying, I wasn't sure which yet. I tried to yell out, but no sound would come out. I couldn't get enough air into my lungs because of the broken ribs. I saw a stick laying on the ground close to me, one that they had used to beat me with, I managed to pick it up and throw it against the bars to make a noise. "Down there! I just heard something!" I heard someone say, I couldn't tell who it was as I slipped back into the darkness.

I woke slightly a while later and I felt the sensation of being carried. I tried to open my eyes, but I couldn't. "We have to get her home now! So we can heal her before she dies!" I heard someone say before the darkness took over again. The darkness didn't want to let me go this time, I felt like I was floating, I couldn't see anything and I couldn't hear anything. Maybe this was finally my end, at least I wouldn't have to suffer anymore like I had the past few months or however long it had been. But surely I wouldn't spend eternity like this, in complete nothingness.

Somehow, my eyes finally did open. When I looked around, I couldn't believe it, I was home! I moved just a little to see if the pain was gone, it was, I was rescued and healed. I didn't see anyone, I sat up in the bed and started bawling my eyes out. James must have heard me, he came running in from the bathroom. He put his arms around me and squeezed me, "you're home now, it's okay" he whispered. I cried harder because of how much I had missed him, how much I had put him through and he was still here, comforting me. "Shhh, it's okay" he whispered in my ear.

When I finally managed to stop crying I asked, "how did you guys find me?" "We can talk about all that later. Just let me hold you right now" James replied. I didn't have any arguments with that. He could lay here and hold me for the next week and I wouldn't complain. I had missed him so much and I know that he had missed me too. "How long was I gone?" I asked. "Two and a half months," he replied simply. I just nodded my head. It had seemed like at least double that, but I had no real sense of time. They probably did the whole routine of beating me and healing me twice a day for the entire time I was held captive.

"Do you need anything? Food? Water?" James asked. I shook my head 'no' "just you, you are all I need right now." I replied. "I'm so sorry" I said as I began crying again. "I know, it's over now, you are safe, please just try to relax," he replied. I nodded my head and then lay down on his chest. I could hear his heart beating, I had missed this so damn much. I knew now just how lucky I was and I also knew that I would never test that luck again.

"Is Oscar dead?" I asked after we had laid there for a while in silence. "We will talk about everything that happened later," James said, sternly. I nodded as I drifted off to sleep in his arms. What a change that was. I felt safe, for the first time in months, and I knew that no one was going to hurt me for the first time in months. I slept peacefully. I didn't wake up until the next morning. James never moved, I'm not sure if he didn't want to disturb me or if he was as exhausted as I had been. When he realized that I was awake, he started gently rubbing my back. I looked up at his face and smiled, something I didn't think I would ever do again. He kissed my forehead and said, "let's go get breakfast."

I looked at him and I must have had a terrified look on my face because he looked alarmed all of a sudden and said, "what is it?" "I'm not sure I can face everyone right now after what I put everyone through" I replied. He sat back down on the bed with me. "There is something I should probably go ahead and tell you," he said with difficulty. "What?" I asked, feeling very concerned from the way he spoke. "Not everyone made it back," he said. I covered my mouth and started crying, "who?" I asked through the tears. He pulled me into him and whispered, "Margo."

"No! No! No!" I screamed as I cried uncontrollably. Someone started knocking on the bedroom door. "We'll be out shortly" James said, loudly enough for whoever it was to stop knocking and walk away. "Please say it's not true" I cried. "We all knew what we were getting into when we signed up for this. She was a true soldier. She was the one who finally found your scent. We tried to save her, but it was too late. It was almost too late for you too" James said. I couldn't stop crying, I couldn't stand that someone was dead because of me. And not just anyone, someone I loved, someone that Arturo loved and someone that was loved by many.

"How is Arturo taking it?" I asked, still crying. "It's only been a few days, he sits by the woods a lot and doesn't really talk to anyone much" James replied. I cried more, how could I have taken away his soul mate? This was all my fault, I was sure he would hate me, and I wouldn't blame him if he did. "We should go get breakfast, no one is angry with you, they are overjoyed that you are back and safe" James said. "I don't think I can do normal right now" I said as I collapsed back into the bed. "Fine, I will go get you a plate and bring it back to you in here" James said. He turned and walked out of the room.

I wasn't sure if I could even eat, I wasn't given any edible food or drinkable water the entire time I was held captive. When Oscar healed me each day, or twice a day, he healed me completely, even the starvation and dehydration. I got up and walked to the window and looked out from the side so no one would see me. I could see Arturo, sitting by the woods where he and Margo used to sit. He was just staring off into space it seemed. I went back to the bed and cried more.

James walked in with a plate of food on a tray with a glass of water and a glass of orange juice. He sat it down on the nightstand next to the bed. He sat down on the bed next to me and started stroking my head. "I can't, I just can't," I said. "It may take some time, but you can, and you will," James replied. I shook my head no and continued to cry. Somehow I cried until I fell asleep again.

When I opened my eyes, the sun was a lot lower. James was still next to me. I sniffled and rubbed my eyes. I looked over at the night stand, the tray of food and drink was gone. I wondered if James had taken it back to the kitchen or if Cori had come and taken it out. I remembered why I had cried myself to sleep again. I started crying again. James sat up and put his arms around me. "This won't bring her back" he whispered in my ear. "I just can't accept it, it just can't be true" I said, through the tears. "I wish it wasn't true too," James replied.

"You really need to try to eat something," James said. I think he was just trying to get my mind off of what had happened. "The funeral is tomorrow, I'm sure you want to go, right?" he asked. I nodded my head. "Is it going to be here?" I asked as I wiped tears from my cheeks, it didn't help because they kept falling from my eyes. "No, we are going back to 2 to put her to rest, then we will come right back" he said. I nodded my head, "It's fitting for it to be there" I said. "Will you try to eat?" James asked. I looked at him and nodded. "Do you want to go to the dining room? Or would you like me to bring you some food in here?" James asked. "Bring it in here" I replied.

James looked at me and nodded, with a defeated look on his face then he kissed my forehead and walked out of the bedroom. I sat down on the bed. I would avenge her, she did not die for nothing. I would finish this war and bring peace and unity to all magical beings. That was the promise I made to myself and to Margo and I would do everything in my power to make it so. Thinking of power made me wonder if my magic had been restored. I pointed at a hair brush on the dresser and moved my finger, it moved along with me. So I knew my magic had been returned.

James walked in carrying a tray with a plate of food and a glass of water. I took the food and ate slowly, the water, I drank rather quickly and he refilled the glass for me and brought an extra glass also. After I ate and drank a lot of water, I looked at James and said, "Do you think Arturo will speak with me?" "I'm sure he will, but do you think that is a good idea right now? I think you should wait until after the funeral" he replied. I nodded my head, he was right, I would probably just start bawling my eyes out. I just smiled at James and nodded my head, it was still weird to me how it seemed he could read my mind even without a spell connecting us.

After we finished eating, James took the dishes back to the kitchen. I decided that I wanted to take a bath and try to relax a little. I went to the bathroom and started running my bath water and started to undress. James had come in and I hadn't heard him because of the water. When I turned around and he was standing behind me, it startled me and I had flashbacks which caused me to scream. "Shh, it's okay, it's just me" he said as he put his arms around me. I started bawling again. "Shh," he continued as he rubbed my back.

He reached over and turned the water off, "your bath is ready" he said, still trying to get me to calm down. "Thank you" I said through my sniffles. "And I'm sorry that I'm acting this way," I added. "You don't have to apologize, what happened, happened and we will get through this. I am here with you, and for you and I love you" he said. "I've put you and everyone else here through so much," I said. Still holding me, he replied, "it's over now, you went through a whole lot more than we did." "Your bath is gonna start getting cold, you should hop in and relax the best you can, I'll stay with you if you want" James said. I nodded my head, "yes, I would like for you to stay with me."

I stepped into the bath, it felt nice. James added some Epsom salt and started rubbing my back with a washcloth. I didn't deserve him, he was so good to me and I literally ran away from him and he had no idea where I was or what was happening to me. I started crying again at the thought. "Do you think you should try doing some magic to help you?" James asked. "I don't know," I said through the tears. "What about the spell that you used on Arturo and myself?" He suggested. "I don't know if I can do it, maybe one of the other witches can try" I said, although I didn't feel like I was ready to see anyone else just yet.

He nodded his head, "I'll go talk to them when we are done here if you like." "Okay" I said, I didn't know what else to say, I couldn't argue with trying to get better. After my bath, James handed me my bathrobe. I slipped it on and walked into the bedroom and sat on the bed. "I'm gonna go see if anyone wants to try the spell, okay?" James said. I nodded my head silently. James walked out of the bedroom and shut the door behind him. I wondered if I had anything black to wear to the funeral tomorrow, but I didn't feel like getting up to look.

James came back about ten minutes later with Misty. I couldn't look up, I didn't want to face her. "Hey" she said in a friendly voice, almost like she was speaking to a child. "Hello" I replied without looking up. "It's okay, we don't have to talk right now, if you want to just lay back on the bed, I can start the spell" Misty said. I lay down on the bed without saying anything. She began running her hands over me, about a couple inches away from my skin. I wanted this to work, I wasn't sure that it would though.

"Relax," Misty said, calmly. I closed my eyes and tried my hardest to relax. I could feel her working her way into my mind. "There is a lot, I will remove all that I can," she said. I didn't respond or move. I wanted it all gone, but if she could remove any of it, I would be okay with that for now. I started relaxing naturally, she must have already removed some of it. I started feeling lighter, I almost felt like I could smile.

I was almost asleep. I was so relaxed when I heard James say, "are you okay?" Then I heard a shuffle and a thud. I sat up. Misty was laying on the floor. "I tried to catch her," James said, looking panicky. "Is she breathing?" I asked, trying to stay calm. James put his fingers on her neck to feel for a pulse. He looked at me and nodded his head, and said, "she just passed out." "I guess it was too much magic at once for her to handle," I replied. "Will you carry her out and ask the others to help, tell them what happened?" I said. James nodded and swooped down to pick her up and carry her out of the bedroom. It was odd to me that what she had done had taken so much out of her, she was very powerful.

A few minutes later he came back into the room alone. "Is she okay?" I asked. He nodded, "the others are taking care of her, they said not to worry, she will be fine" he replied. He walked over to the bed and sat down next to me. I don't know what came over me, but I started attacking him, in a sexual way. I grabbed his hair and pulled his head back and started kissing him frantically. He wasn't going to let that happen, being the dominant one, he grabbed my hands and put them behind my back and forced me onto my back with his chest.

I didn't mind, I just needed him so bad at that moment. I needed to feel him inside me. I managed to get one hand free and I reached for his cock and squeezed while I sucked on his neck. He let out a moan of excitement and ran his hand up my shirt and squeezed my breasts. I unbuttoned his pants, "I need you inside me" I whispered in his ear. He kissed my neck and started taking my pants off. I moaned with excitement. When he entered me, it was almost as if it was my first time, minus any pain. And when I came, it was as if I had entered another dimension even though I was still here in bed with him.

We lay there next to each other silently for a while. "That was amazing," he said, finally breaking the silence. I just rolled over and put my head on his chest. He started rubbing my hair, it felt nice. Everything seemed to be falling back to where it was supposed to be. I must have fallen asleep, the next thing I knew, James was waking me up saying that it was time to go to the funeral.

Twenty-Seven

Making a mends

I got out of bed and looked in my closet for something nice to wear. I felt numb, it was like I had cried so much that I couldn't cry anymore. I found a black broomstick skirt and a dark gray blouse, and I started getting dressed. James came up behind me and put his arms around me, "are you okay?" he whispered in my ear. "No," I replied. He didn't push for more, he understood that I wasn't okay and that I obviously didn't want to talk about it. After we got dressed and looked the best we could, we went to the living room to meet everyone.

Everyone gave me my space and didn't try to speak to me. They could tell that I still wasn't quite back just yet. We all walked outside to make the jump to 2 where Margo would remain forever. The jump was quick, per usual. We landed in a field, I could see David's house in the distance. I noticed that Arturo wasn't among us. "Where is Arturo?" I whispered to David. "He is already here, he has been for a while," David replied. I nodded and looked down at the ground so he wouldn't say anything else. I didn't know if I could handle speaking anymore, and I didn't want to have a meltdown.

"We will be ready for the funeral in about an hour," David announced loudly to everyone. "Gabby, you and James are welcome to go to the house while you wait, Sarah and Julie will love to see you both" David said. I looked at James and nodded, he put his arm around my waist and we started walking toward the house. I noticed Julie playing outside as we approached, she was playing with the fairies. How could I tell them that I lost the fairy that came with me, after I had promised to keep her safe? I started to feel a panic rising inside me.

James must have felt me tense up, "let's just go inside" he said. I nodded. I would never get over his ability to read me and to respond appropriately. He was my rock, now more than ever, but somehow I knew he would only get more durable as I needed it. I looked up at the house and saw that Sarah was standing in the door waiting for us. I tried to smile, but I don't think it worked, as she didn't respond.

She held the door open as we walked inside. She came in behind us and gave each of us a hug. "It's good to see you both, although not under these circumstances" she said. I nodded and gave her another attempted smile. She hugged me again, "don't beat yourself up over this, I heard what happened. I know that any of them would have gladly have done what she did to save you" Sarah said. "That really doesn't help, it's bad enough that we lost her, but to think of losing anyone else, I just can't" I said, as I started crying.

James put his arms around me and pulled me into him. "I didn't mean..." I heard Sarah say. "It's okay," James said, cutting her off. I cried for a little while, then I excused myself to the restroom so I could clean myself back up. When I came back out, Sarah and James were sitting on the couch having tea or coffee. Sarah stood up when she saw me. "Would you like some coffee?" She asked. I nodded, "yes

I would, thank you" I replied. She disappeared to the kitchen and came back quickly with a cup of coffee. I sat down next to James to drink it.

"Your outfit is beautiful," Sarah said to me. "Thank you," I replied. "Should we start walking down to the lake?" James asked Sarah. "Yes, just let me get Julie," She replied. Sarah stepped outside to get Julie. I looked at James, "the funeral is at the lake?" I asked. He nodded, "we have a bit of a different sort of ritual when it comes to funerals here" he said. I didn't ask anymore questions, because I knew I was about to see it first hand.

Sarah came inside with Julie. Julie immediately ran up to me and hugged me. I didn't know if she understood what was happening. I hugged her back, she was too big now for me to pick her up. "I'm happy you are here Gabby" Julie said. "I'm happy I am here too sweetie" I replied. She held one of my hands and James held the other as we left the house and headed toward the lake.

We walked quietly all the way to the lake. When we got there, I noticed some people were already sitting down on them. There was a canoe type of boat on the lake and I noticed that Margo was inside of it. "Viking funeral?" I whispered to James. "Sort of, we don't set it on fire, we just let it drift out until the mermaids drag it down" he replied. I must have had a horrified look on my face, he continued to explain more. "It's believed that they prepare the soul for it's next life, before they devour the body," He said. "What?!" I said, a bit loudly, causing everyone to look our way. "It's what we do with all of our dead, you do believe in reincarnation don't you?" He asked. "Of course, but what of the souls in other dimensions?" I asked.

"I'm not sure if non magical beings get reincarnated." He said looking down. "So, we are all the original magical beings?" I asked. "Yes," He replied. "So, what do they do to prepare the soul?" I asked. "They release it, with their magic" He said. "Okay, so this is what will happen when I die?" I asked. "I don't want to think about that, but yes, if your soul is to come back, you will need a funeral like this one" He said. "So, you are saying that if I don't want to reincarnate, I could just have a normal funeral?" I asked. "Yes, I suppose that's what I am saying. I don't want to talk about this anymore" he replied.

I spotted Arturo standing alone by the lake. "Excuse me for a moment" I said to James and walked away without further explanation. I walked over to Arturo as quietly as possible. I didn't want to startle him, but I didn't want anyone else to walk up on us either. I walked up and stood beside him so he could see I was there without saying anything. I wasn't quite sure what I was going to say just yet, but I knew I had to speak with him. He turned and looked my way, then looked back out toward the lake.

"I'm sorry" I said, quietly. "I know," he replied, just as quietly. We stood there for what seemed like forever without saying anything, just looking out into the lake. "I would give my life to bring her back if I could," I finally said. "I know, but that would defeat the whole purpose wouldn't it?" Arturo replied. "What do you mean?" I asked. "She died so that you could live, did she not?" he said. "I know, this is all my fault and I wish I could just take it all back, everything. I wish I didn't even exist" I said.

"Nonsense, you have more purpose here than anyone I have ever known. We are all fighting a war with you and for you. Of course there will be casualties and you are fooling yourself if you believe otherwise. We all joined this fight knowing that we may not live to the end and I know, if she were to rise from the dead at this moment, she would do it again" Arturo said.

I stood there for a moment, thinking about what he said. I knew deep down that it was all true. Why did it have to be me? Why did I have to save the world and meet a new family just to watch them die? I wouldn't wish this existence on anyone. I always knew that I was destined for something bigger than myself, but I could never have imagined this.

"Can you forgive me?" I asked him. "There is nothing to forgive," he replied. He reached out and pulled me into a hug. It felt nice. I started crying. "She will find her way back to us, I know she will," he whispered into my ear. I pulled away and smiled and nodded my head. "You're right, she will" I said, wiping tears from my cheeks. "They are starting," he said, pointing to the water. "Okay, I better go back to James. Oh, one more thing, I promise you this now, she will be avenged" I said with a smile, then I walked back toward James.

James reached out for me as I got closer, I smiled at him and he smiled back and seemed to relax. Several people carried the boat to the water, just as people carried coffins to the gravesite. They pushed the boat, carrying Margo out until the current picked it up and carried it out. Once it was far enough out, the mermaids came up and tipped the boat so that her body fell into the water. There were several moans and cries from the attendees. But I didn't have any more tears left in me at the moment. I only had a rage that was building inside of me. Oscar had to die, for what he had done to her.

Everyone mingled for a while, sharing stories of Margo. They had all known her a lot longer than I had, my favorite memory of her was when David had her surprise attack me during training. Then I realized that was the first time I had met her. Sarah walked up to me, "some of you are leaving tonight, I was hoping I could talk you and James and of course, David into staying just one night. I'll make dinner and we could all spend a little time together" she said. I thought about it for a moment, then I nodded my head and said, "that sounds nice." She smiled, "wonderful! I'll see you back at the house when you are ready. I'm just going to go find David and let him know" she said as she walked away.

I looked up at James and smiled, "you don't mind staying one night do you?" I asked him. "Not at all, whatever keeps that smile on your face" he replied. I still couldn't believe how lucky I was to have him, things like that just didn't happen to me. He took my hand and we started walking toward Sarah and David's house. I noticed that Arturo was standing in the same spot as earlier. I stopped, James looked at me. "Can you wait just a few minutes, I want to go talk with Arturo again" I said. "Of course," he replied.

I walked away quickly, toward Arturo. It was starting to get dark, I could see one of the moons rising already. "Arturo!" I yelled to get his attention. He turned around. "Are you staying the night, or are you heading back?" I asked him. "I hadn't even thought about it to be honest, I guess I was just going to do what everyone else is doing" he replied, blandly. "Well, David, James and myself are staying the night. I think the rest are heading back. I'm sure David and Sarah wouldn't mind if you would like to join us" I said. He nodded, and said, "okay whatever you think." I didn't want him to be alone right now, I wanted him to be around people who loved him. I put my arm around his shoulder and we started walking back toward James.

As we got closer to James, I said, "Arturo is joining us tonight." James nodded and smiled, "that's great, glad to have you" he said. The three of us headed toward Sarah and David's house together. None of us spoke on the way, just enjoyed each other's company. The lights were on when we got to the house, James just opened the door without knocking.

The first thing I noticed was the wonderful smell, Sarah was already cooking. The second thing I noticed was the warm feeling, it just felt safe here. Sarah came out of the kitchen to greet us, then she returned to cooking. David was playing a matching card game with Julie in the living room. As soon as Julie saw me, she ran up and grabbed my hand "come play with us Gabby," she said as she pulled me toward the game. "Now, Julie, you should ask her if she would like to play, not try to make her play," David scolded. Julie looked up at me with a pleading look on her cute little face. "It's okay, I will play for a little while," I said.

Julie giggled at my response and continued to pull me over to play. "Gabby, you don't have to if you don't feel up to it" David said to me, low enough so Julie wouldn't hear. I smiled at him, "it's okay, really" I said. He smiled back and said, "okay." The three of us sat down on the floor and started matching cards, David and I let Julie have the most of them of course. James and Arturo went out to sit on the porch. After a while, Sarah came to tell us that dinner was ready.

The meal was amazing as usual, plenty to go around. I noticed that Arturo wasn't eating much and he had such a lost look on his face. Every time that I have experienced heartbreak, I always find distractions to keep me from thinking too much about it until the pain is bearable. So I started trying to think of a way to distract him from his pain. The only thing that came to mind was drinking. "Would you like a glass of wine, Arturo?" I asked. He looked up, surprised to hear his name spoken. "What?" He replied. "Would you like a glass of wine?" I repeated. He shook his head as he lowered it down and said, "no thank you."

I couldn't stand seeing him go through this, he lost the love of his life, his soulmate, his twin flame. It was breaking my heart all over again, but I was happy that he decided to stay with us for the night. I had a glass of wine, and then another and another. I wanted to kill the pain inside me. Then I made a very terrible decision, I cast my feelings onto Arturo, I made him drunk against his will. It didn't take the others long to notice that Arturo was suddenly talking and even smiling, telling stories of his youth.

James pulled me out into the hallway, "what did you do?" he asked. "I just wanted to help him feel a little better" I stuttered, followed by a hiccup. "But what did you do?" James repeated. "I shared my buzz with him," I said, followed by another hiccup. "You shouldn't have done that," James said. "But why?" I asked. "Because, you don't do things like that to people without their consent" James said sternly. I put my head down, "I'm sorry" I said. "I'm going to help you to bed, then I'm going to make sure that Arturo is okay before I join you" James said, sounding frustrated. I just put my head down and let him lead me into the bedroom that we normally slept in when we stayed here, I kicked my shoes off and fell into the bed facedown. James rolled me over and said, "I'll be back in a little while" and then he left the room. I passed out before he returned.

I didn't dream, but I woke up feeling refreshed the next morning. James was lying next to me, still sleeping. I sat up quietly, trying not to wake him. I walked over to the door and slowly opened it, I looked back and he was still sleeping. I slipped out of the door. I smelled coffee, so I went straight to the kitchen. David and Sarah were at the table. Sarah smiled at me and said, "have a seat, I'll grab you a cup," as she got up and walked into the kitchen. David looked at me, "I am disappointed with you" he said. Then I remembered what I had done. I put my head down, "is he okay?" I asked. "He is still sleeping," David replied. I nodded, Sarah returned with a cup of coffee and sat it in front of me. "Thank you," I said. I stayed quiet and drank my coffee.

After sitting with them in silence for a while, I decided to go sit on the front porch. The morning air was nice, there was a light dew on everything. I knew what I had done was wrong. I would be lucky if Arturo didn't hate me forever. Why did I keep wronging him? Was I doing it on purpose? Was I some kind of karmic return for him? The door opened and snapped me out of my thoughts. It was Arturo, he walked out and sat in the chair next to me. He had a cup of coffee as well. "I'm so sorry about everything, I don't know what has gotten into me" I said. He nodded but didn't reply, he just sipped his coffee. I wished he would say something, anything, but I didn't push, I just sat there and finished my coffee.

After a while, the door opened again, this time it was James. "David and I are ready whenever you guys are," he said. Then reality hit me, we had to go back and finish a war, we had to end this nonsense. I looked at him and nodded. Arturo stood up, "I'm ready" he said, simply. I stood up as well and said, "let's go." I went inside to make sure I had everything and said goodbye to Sarah and Julie. Julie started crying and saying, "don't go," which made things a little harder. But I walked away and met everyone else outside. We quickly warped back to 12. We landed between the barn and the house, it was still dark.

Twenty-Eight

Back to business

We walked into the house, the clock said 3:33 a.m. I wasn't sleepy as I am sure none of us were, but the house was quiet, so we all went to our rooms so that we didn't wake the others. After James closed the door we sat down on the bed. "I'm sorry about my behavior last night, I don't know what I was thinking" I said. "Did you apologize to him?" James asked. "I did, I don't know if he has forgiven me, but I did tell him that I was sorry" I replied. James nodded his head. "I think we just need to focus on what we are doing next," James said. I nodded in agreement.

I sat there, quietly for a moment, meditating on what needed to be done. Obviously the final result would be Oscar would be dead, payback for what he had done to Margo. But how were we going to get there? His army is strong and they are smart, add in magic and it seems almost impossible. But I couldn't think like that, it was either him or me and at this moment, he was winning. I wouldn't let that happen, I wouldn't lose anyone else. I would be the hero they were all hoping me to be, or I would die trying at least.

Once the sun started to rise, we could hear and sense movement in the rest of the house. We came out of the room and into the dinning room. I could smell food being prepared by Cori. I walked into the kitchen, "can I help you with anything?" I asked her. "Oh no, of course not," she replied. "Okay, I'll be in the dining room if you do need anything" I said. She nodded and returned to cooking. I walked back into the dinning room. People were starting to pile in. Jason and Hale were there and Alice walked in the same time I did.

"I'm glad you guys made it back okay," Alice said, looking at James and I. "Yeah, we've been back for a few hours," I said. "Did Arturo come back?" Hale asked. And I suppose that was the question on everyone's mind because they all looked at me anxiously waiting on my reply. "Yes, of course he did," I said. Everyone seemed to breathe a sigh of relief. I was a little confused. I know that he lost someone very important to him, but why would he not return? We all had a mission, why would they think that it was even an option for him not to return?

As everyone else started joining us and the table started to fill up, Arturo finally came in and sat down. Everyone seemed to get quiet. Cori started bringing food into the dinning room and we all ate, quietly. When we were finished eating I stood up. "I know things have not gone as planned recently," I said loudly to get everyone's attention. Once everyone was looking at me, I continued. "We can and we will win this war. Oscar will pay with his life for what he has done. I know most of you have been in this world longer than I have, and I didn't ask for the role I have been given. But I accept it and I will do everything in my power to make sure no one else is hurt by this evil man. We will work together, just as we have trained," I said.

"When are we attacking?" Misty asked. "We will make a plan on our next move now," I said. Everyone seemed to come alive, they looked excited and I had a warm feeling inside. I knew they weren't blood thirsty killers, but at the same time, they were tired of living in fear and they were ready to end this once and for all. "Okay, do we know if they are still in the same place?" I asked. "I can go stake it out and find out," Arturo said. I nodded, and he got up and left without another word.

I looked around at everyone else and said, "Does anyone have any ideas on what we should do now?" "We can go ahead and get a plan going for attack, assuming they are in the same place until we find out otherwise" Jason said. I looked at him, impressed. He had taken this life on head on, he didn't ask for it, just like I hadn't, but here he was, ready to fight a war that he never would have even known about if he hadn't been changed. "That's a great idea" I replied. "I don't really know a lot about the complex, the place is huge. I saw the backyard, a study and the dungeon" I said.

"We were able to get in to get you out" James said. "Right, so we know we can get in, but so do they now" I replied. "So it may be dumb to assume that they would still be there" Misty said. "Do they have a safer place to go?" I asked. "They have several," Misty answered. "Is it possible for them to attack us here?" Alice asked. "The farm is cloaked by magic, I suppose it is possible for them to find a way around it, but very unlikely" Hale replied. "I think that if it is a possibility, that we should also prepare for that scenario" I said. Alice smiled. Levi put his arm around her shoulder and smiled as well.

"We need to start setting up defense here," Damian said. "I had a dream, it may have just been a dream, but I did see us fighting here. My mind could have just been using familiar scenery so I don't really trust it" Misty said. "Do you remember what happened in the dream?" I asked. "Not really, it was probably just a normal dream anyway," Misty replied. I nodded, "It's fine, no matter where it happens we will kick their asses," I said, with a smirk. Everyone started laughing and cheering. I was glad that I could get their spirits high again. Something that we had been lacking as a group.

"I think Alice and I can work on setting up some traps around the property, a witch's help with magical traps would be great as well" Levi said. "I can help with magical traps," Damian said. "Okay, that's great, you guys can go ahead and get started on that, no sense in waiting around" I replied. Alice, Levi and Damian walked out of the room. "Should we wait for Arturo to return or go ahead with an invasion plan?" I asked, looking around at the remaining crowd. "I think we should go ahead a start," Misty said.

Misty looked uneasy, I wondered if she knew it would be soon? Maybe she was a little scared, maybe she wasn't telling us everything about the dream? She had been right before, too bad there was too much blank space in her dreams. "Misty, is there anything we can do to help your dreams be more detailed? Like some sort of herb or spell we could use to help you see more?" I asked. She shook her head. "She doesn't want to, she's too scared," Hale said. Misty lowered her head. "Seeing things doesn't mean you can change it," Misty said softly. "It's okay, it would be nice to know when and where, but it's okay. Eventually we will know and we will fight and we will win!" I said. Misty smiled.

"You should talk to Arturo about being able to see future events, he can see things sometimes too," I told Misty. I knew there must have been something in her past that made her afraid of that power. Something terrible that she couldn't talk about, maybe Hale knew what it was, maybe that's why he was tormenting her about it now. To change the subject back to what it needed to be, I started talking about raiding Oscar's complex. "I don't think waiting for the cover of night will give us an advantage. I think they will expect us at night, so daylight will be the best time to go" I said.

"What did you learn from sending in the fairy?" Hale asked. It hurt a little to be reminded of that, "not a lot really. Oscar can sense when magic is being used, so we need to not use magic until we are inside" I replied. Everyone nodded. "We need non magical weapons then" Misty said. "I think the giants can help a lot with that, their strength alone is a non magical weapon. Guns are too loud" I said. "If we got guns, we could also get silencers," Hale said. "Don't they still make noise though?" I asked. "These people are trained well in all areas, we have to be as cautious as possible, we won't lose anyone else" I added.

We all knew the time was approaching quickly, we either attacked or we would be attacked. Everyone was starting to get antsy. I wished I could ease everyone's mind, but with my own being just as crazy, I didn't think that would be a good idea to try. After a few hours of being gone, Arturo returned. He walked into the dinning room and sat down. "I staked out the complex for an hour and didn't see anything," he said. "Where could they have gone?" I asked, looking around at everyone.

"Into hiding, would be my guess," Misty said. "Okay, but, where?" I asked. "Several of the witches own property in and around Moon Springs," Hale said. "Do we know where?" I asked. Damian pulled out a map and started pointing to different places. The first place he pointed was North of town. "There is a place here, another here" he said pointing west of town. "And another here" he said pointing east of town. "And a couple down here" he said pointing to a spot southwest and a spot southeast of town. "And here" he said, pointing to the middle of town. "The town center?" I asked, confused. "It's underground," Damian replied.

"What do you mean? Are you telling me they have property all around Moon Springs in the form of a pentagram? Could they be more obvious?" I said, a little shocked. "Moon Springs is an ancient place, it's said to be the exact place where the ancient spell was cast that created all of the dimensions" Hale said. "The land has always belonged to the witches," Misty added. "The spot in the town center will hold the most power, that's where I would be if I were them" Damian said. "How do we get there?" I asked. "You have to be a part of the coven for that knowledge" Misty said with a smile. "Does that mean you know how to get in?" I asked with a smirk.

"I do know where the entrance is, but they will be heavily guarded of course," Misty replied. "I wouldn't expect any less," I said. "I think we should just attack, I don't think we should waste anymore time," Hale said. "Maybe we should all relax and get some rest before we charge into battle" I said. "There doesn't need to be any more rest, we should attack at nightfall" Damian said. "Let's take no prisoners, kill them all!" Arturo chimed in. "Hold up! We are not going to kill half of the world's most powerful witches, some of them can and will come to our side" I said.

"Do you really think any of them will convert?" Arturo asked. "Misty did," I replied. Misty smiled at me. "Not everyone is a leader and some people just choose the wrong one" I said. "And their leader?" Arturo asked. "Him you can kill," I replied. "Okay, everyone, go get your battle gear and recharge however you can, we will leave in two hours" I said. Everyone scattered off to their bedrooms to do just that.

James followed me into our bedroom. He sat down on the bed and put his head into his hands. "What's wrong?" I asked. "I know what we have to do, I've known all along. I just don't know how to mentally prepare for this. I don't know how to let you go into a battle that you may not come back from" he said, without lifting his head. "I don't want to lose you either, or anyone else for that matter, but this is what we have been training for, this is our purpose. And hopefully after tonight, it will all be over" I replied, as I sat down on the bed next to him and put my arm around him.

"We didn't choose this, it chose us and it is our duty to end all of this fighting and hate" I said. He nodded his head, "I know," was all he said as he put his head on my shoulder and his arms around me.

"I love you" I said. "I love you too" he replied. I got up and went to the closet to figure out what I could wear. The catsuit was hanging there, I guess Alice had repaired it for me. It was the best thing to wear into battle I suppose, it was dark in color and I could move easily with it on.

I looked back over at James, he was still sitting on the bed pouting. "Do you need me to juju you again?" I asked him. "I'll be fine," he responded. "Okay" I said. I sat down on the bed next to him and put my arms around him. "I love you, more than I can say. I hope, I show you, but I sometimes feel like that would be impossible" I told him. "I love you the same, so yeah, I understand what you are saying" he replied. "Good, neither of us can die tonight," I said, jokingly. The fact that I would joke about it seemed to upset him even more than he already was. "What?" I said in a whiny voice. "Nothing" he replied, shutting down again. "Let's just get ready," he added. I nodded and went to the bathroom to change.

Shortly after we finished getting ready there was a knock on the bedroom door. I opened it, it was Arturo. "Just checking to see if you are ready," he said. "Yeah, coming out now" I replied. It was still hard for me to look at him, I knew what I had to do, I had to make Oscar pay. James and I walked into the kitchen where everyone was waiting. "Here is the plan that we came up with," Arturo began.

"We don't know for certain that they will be in the town center. So, Conan and Levi will go to the North. Hale and Alice will go to the East. Misty, Jason and David will go to the West. Damian and Pearl will go to the Southeast. We will go to the Southwest," he said pointing at James, me and himself. "If any of us find anything at any of the other places, we will contact the others immediately, if not we will all meet at the town center" Arturo said. "Okay, let's do this," I said with a nod.

We all headed out of the house, everyone seemed ready to end this. But I did wonder what would happen when it was all over, would we all just go our separate ways? I hoped not, I had grown to love most of them, if not all, I thought of them as my family. I knew I would protect them all with my life, I wouldn't lose anyone else. Once we were outside, we warped to the vehicles. We paired off just as Arturo had stated in the house and we took off.

James drove and Arturo navigated. I sat quietly in the back. We drove by the diner where I had worked, that seemed like a different lifetime now. I missed my old friends, I was still upset that Jason had been dragged into this because of me. But I suppose this life is better than death. Then I thought of Margo again and the fairy that was never found. I was tired of bringing death and destruction down on all of those that I cared about. I was so ready to end this.

"Turn right here," Arturo said, pointing to what looked like a dirt driveway. It was a dirt country road. "Gabriela, it might be a good idea to do a disguise spell now," Arturo said. So I made us all look different, even the truck would look different to anyone looking our way. "It's up here, on the left," Arturo said, pointing. "Should I pull in, or should we park and walk around?" James asked. "Good idea, pull over here and park, if anyone sees us we will tell them we are just hiking" Arturo said. James nodded and pulled over into a grassy area to the right.

The three of us got out of the truck and started walking toward the driveway that Arturo had pointed out. I couldn't hear anything, and I didn't see anything that indicated anyone was here. We kept walking up the driveway until we could see a building. A house, white, with real wood shutters that were painted black. We squatted down out of view of the windows. "I don't see anything," I whispered. "If Oscar was here, he would have sensed the magic I used to disguise us and come after us already" I whispered, when I didn't get a reply from either James or Arturo.

Arturo stood up, "I think you are right. I don't think they are here," he said. "So, what now? Do we contact the others, or go straight to the town center?" James asked. "No contact unless someone finds them, we go straight to the town center," Arturo replied. We started walking back towards the truck. It was a clear summer day, hot and muggy. I could feel the sweat beading up under the catsuit, maybe it wasn't such a good idea to wear it. I might die of a heat stroke before we even find Oscar. "You okay?" James asked me. "Yeah, just a little hot, did anyone bring any water?" I replied. James shook his head. "I have some in the truck," Arturo replied. "Great, thank you," I said.

We got back in the truck and Arturo shared his water and we took off, going toward town. "How is it that we are just going to walk up to this place again? If we use magic, he will sense it" I said. "Misty said she knows how to get in, this one is on her," Arturo said. "Okay" I said and sat back and let the wind hit my face as we accelerated.

Twenty-Nine

Putting an end to it all

We parked the truck in a parking garage near the courthouse and we started walking toward the park. I spotted Misty sitting on a park bench, pretending to read a paper. Jason was playing with a dog that was being walked by a pretty girl. David was just walking around with his hands in his pockets looking lost. I didn't see anyone else yet.

I looked to Arturo for instruction. "Follow their leads, just try to blend in," Arturo said, as if he could read my mind. James and I both nodded that we understood. I walked over to the bench and sat down, I pulled out my phone and pretended to talk. But really, I was talking to Misty. "Yeah, we went for a nice hike, we didn't see anything interesting" I said. Misty pulled the paper up over her face like she was annoyed with the girl that just sat down next to her while talking on her phone. "Okay, well I guess I will talk to you later" I said, then put my phone down.

Conan and Levi arrived next, they followed everyone's lead and just started wandering around the park, trying to look like they were there just to enjoy the day. I had to look strange to everyone who didn't know me there. I was dressed like a superhero after all. Soon, Damian and Pearl joined and not long after, Hale and Alice. Once everyone was there, Misty stood up and said, "follow me" without looking at anyone. We all followed, even the people that weren't so close, she must have used some sort of communication magic.

My blood boiled. "Are you trying to get everyone killed?!" I said quietly, but with enough anger that she knew I was pissed. "Relax, I wouldn't do that" she replied calmly. My mind was racing, was she secretly still on *their* side? She couldn't be, she couldn't have tricked *all* of us this *whole* time. Or could she? I didn't know what to think or what to do, she could be leading us all into a trap. I grabbed her arm and turned her toward me. "Please don't make a scene, I didn't endanger anyone. If he is down there, he couldn't sense that small speck, trust me" she said, pleadingly. I let her arm go, "if you are lying to me, you will pay" I said as I continued to let her lead us to the entry.

She walked into a flower shop at the corner of the square, we all followed. "Misty darling, it's been such a long time! I didn't know what happened to you!" A woman behind the counter said. She looked confused about the rest of us walking in. "Harmony! It's wonderful to see you, I need to speak with you in private for a moment, if you don't mind?" Misty said to the woman. "Of course, come this way," Harmony said, pointing to a room on the other side of the counter.

I'm not going to lie, I was starting to doubt Misty. I looked over to Arturo, he looked calm and collected, he gave me a slight nod. I gave him a half smile to let him know that I trusted him, even if I didn't fully trust Misty at the moment. After a few minutes Misty and Harmony came back out. "Would you be a dear and turn around and lock that door behind you?" Harmony said, looking at

Jason. "Yeah, sure," Jason replied as he did what she asked. "Okay everyone, right this way then" Harmony said, as she started to walk back into the back room behind the counter. I looked at Misty, she avoided eye contact with me. I looked back at Arturo, "after you" he said with his hand out in front of him.

Something about this just wasn't setting right with me. Maybe it was just deep rooted trust issues, at least I hoped that's what it was. Once we were all in the huge room that housed hardly any flowers, Misty walked over to the corner and lifted a trap door open from the floor. "This way everyone," Misty said. Everyone started going down, when I got over I looked down, there was a ladder leading down into darkness, I couldn't see the bottom. I looked at Misty one more time, this time she looked into my eyes. I couldn't tell what was going on for sure in those eyes, except one thing, I could tell there was no betrayal in them. I felt better, my tension started to ease. I went down the ladder.

After we were all down, I noticed that Harmony wasn't with us. "Is she not coming?" I asked Misty. "No, I just had to convince her to let us down," Misty replied. "And how did you do that?" I asked her. "I told her that I was bringing you all as prisoners for Oscar" Misty replied. At least she wasn't lying to me. "I can't see anything," Levi said. "There are some lanterns along the wall on the right," Misty said. "Does anyone have a lighter for those lanterns?" Alice asked. "Yes, I brought one," Misty replied. Levi grabbed a lantern and Misty lit it up for him. We could see well enough to find the others, every other person carried one as we walked in a line along the tunnel.

"I smell sulfur," Arturo said. I noticed the smell too, it reminded me of when I was held hostage and beaten every day. "Yes, I do as well, demons are here, or have been here recently" Misty said. "How did the demons get here? I thought they couldn't be in our dimension" I said. "Only if they possess someone, and they have to have permission to do so," Arturo said. I should have known that since

I had witnessed it firsthand. "Just keep your eyes and ears sharp, any movement, any sound could be trouble" Misty said. Everyone stopped talking as we kept walking down the tunnel, which seemed to be going further down into the earth.

We finally reached a door. It was a circular metal door. It was huge, definitely big enough for the giants to get through without having to duck hardly at all. "This is odd," Misty said. "What is? The door?" I asked, confused. "No, the fact that there is no one guarding the door" she replied. "Oh, is that good, or bad?" I asked. "It's just odd, there is always someone guarding the door if they are here" Misty said. "Maybe they aren't here," James said. "And that would be more odd, where else could they be?" Misty replied. "Do you know how to open the door?" Arturo asked. Misty nodded. "Then let's keep going," Arturo said.

Misty opened the door by doing a couple of spells silently. "Is it safe to use magic?" I asked. "It's the only way to open it" she replied as the door opened. We listened for a moment before anyone moved, we heard nothing. We walked through the door, single file as we had walked down the tunnel. There was just more tunnel. "Oh come on, does this ever end?" I said. "You don't think a witches' den would be easy to access do you?" Misty replied. "She's right, think about our place" David said. I nodded and we continued down the tunnel.

I noticed that I no longer smelled sulfur, hopefully that was a good sign. After walking for about thirty more minutes, we came to another door that looked the same as the last one. No one was guarding this door either. No need to have the same conversation, Misty went right to opening it. Again, no sounds came from inside. We continued, this time we entered a room. A gorgeous room, it was huge with super high ceilings. The ceilings had beautiful paintings of all kinds of magical creatures. The room was round and the high ceilings formed a dome above our heads. On the far right side of the painted ceiling I saw someone I recognized. It was my mother!

"Why is she painted on the ceiling here?" I asked, surprised. "This is a sacred magical space, not just for who took it over, it was created for all of us," Misty said. "How did they just take it?" I asked. "Brute force," Misty replied. "These people are terrible" I whispered so low that I didn't think anyone heard me. "They aren't here are they?" I asked. "It doesn't look like it, but there is more, we should probably continue until we are certain that they aren't here. We did come all this way" Misty said.

There were several doors around the huge room. "Should we split up?" David asked. "I don't think that is a good idea," Arturo said. "I don't either, we are stronger together" I said. "Okay, which one do we go through first?" David asked, pointing around at all of the doors. I looked around, and counted them, there were seven doors. "It doesn't matter," Misty said. "This one" I said, pointing to the door in front of us.

I walked over and turned the knob, it opened, we all started going through, with me in the lead this time. It was a kitchen, not just an ordinary kitchen, you could tell it was a witch's kitchen. There were cauldrons, potion bottles, herbs and liquids that I didn't recognize. I was half expecting Arturo to give me a pop quiz on everything that was here. He didn't, maybe the old him would have, the him before I convinced him to let go, follow love, then cause that love to die. I would hate me, if I were him. "No one here, let's keep looking," Misty said.

We walked back into the main room and went into another door. It was a library, not just any library, probably the biggest library I have ever seen in my life, public or private. "Who needs this many books?!" I said. "It's every book ever written by a magical creature, and a few humans as well," Misty said. We did split up inside the library, but we found nothing. We went back to the main room to choose another door. The next door was just a den, rather small although it was still big, it just seemed small in comparison to the library.

The next door we tried was locked. Misty tried to use the same spells to open it as she had the doors to get in, but it didn't work. "You guys move on to the other rooms, I will figure out how to open this one" she said. So we did, no sense in wasting even more time. I didn't know why we even kept looking. It was obvious that no one was here, but we did. The next door was a second kitchen, this one looked like it was purely for cooking food. The next door was a meeting room, tables set up like a conference room. There was a TV on the wall, I found the remote lying on one of the tables and turned it on. Just a blue screen.

I was getting bored with all of the dead ends. The next door was just a closet for jackets, there were a couple hanging in there, I checked the pockets, nothing. The next door was another big room, full of crates and boxes, storage. No telling what we might find there if we had time to look. We all went back out to the main room. Misty was still trying to get the last door opened. "Let me give it a try," Levi said. "Okay" Misty said, stepping away from it. Levi raised his leg and kicked as hard as he could, the door didn't budge. "Ouch!" Levi yelled. "You okay?" I asked. "No!" he yelled, falling to the ground. "Arturo, can you heal him? We can't carry him all the way out of here" I said. Arturo nodded and bent down to heal Levi's leg.

"What should we do?" I asked. "Well, we can't open it by force and I've tried every spell I could think of," Misty said. "What if it's an anti spell?" I said. I honestly didn't even know where the idea came from or if it was even a thing. "Okay, let me give it a try," Misty said. "What does that even mean?" James whispered in my ear. I just looked at him and shrugged my shoulders. Misty mumbled something and turned the doorknob, it opened. "How did you know?"

she looked at me and asked, looking half scared. "I don't know," I replied.

This door opened into a hallway with more doors on each side. "Bedrooms," Hale said. It was a long hallway, there had to be at least thirty rooms here. Of course most of them were locked, the ones that weren't didn't appear to be in use. We couldn't get into most of them, a couple we were able to open with magic, and one even with force. But still we didn't find anyone, or anything that would help us. "So what now?" I asked. "We go back to the farm and discuss what is next," Arturo said. I nodded and we all started heading back out the way we came in.

We made our way back to the vehicles and headed back to the farm. We didn't know what else to do. "Can we send him a message on the video service he used before?" I asked. "No, we tried to contact him to make a deal to get you back when he took you," Arturo replied. "How can they just be gone? Where could they go?" I asked. "Well, they could be anywhere in the world in this dimension or any of the other twelve dimensions," Arturo replied. Not what I wanted to hear. "The fact that they are running means they are scared," Arturo said. "Good, they should be," I replied.

We arrived back in time for Cori to serve dinner. We ate in silence mostly. I could tell everyone felt a little defeated, even though there had been no fight. After dinner we all retired to our rooms except for a few who went into the den for wine. James and I went to our room. I lay down on the bed with my catsuit still on. "You look so sexy in that," James said with a smile. I smiled back at him. "You don't look bad yourself" I replied. He lay down next to me and kissed me.

I heard a noise that sent a chill down my spine. It was Phillip neighing very loudly. James and I both sat straight up. We heard the others scrabbling around the house. "I don't like the way that sounded," I said, looking at James. "Let's go check it out," James said. We got up and walked out of the bedroom door. We were met by everyone, Arturo put his finger over his mouth to signal for us to be quiet. "They are here" he mouthed. "How?" I replied in the same way. "Is Phillip okay?" I whispered as quietly as possible. Arturo just shrugged his shoulders, to let me know that he didn't know.

"Are you sure they are here?" I whispered very lightly. "Pretty sure," Hale replied. "Is Cori safe?" I asked. "I'll take care of her," Damian said. He slipped away quietly, he was gone about five minutes before he returned. We were trying to get visual on the grounds without being seen. So far, we couldn't see anyone, including Phillip. The grounds were very dark, we were in the middle of a forest after all, and no outside lights. I couldn't even see the barn.

"I don't think they can get inside, or they would have already," Misty whispered. "The magic on the house is stronger than the magic on the property in general," Hale said. "We should light up the outside, expose them," Damian said. "Illumination spell, let's light it up" Arturo said, with excitement in his voice. The giants watched out of the windows as all of the witches joined hands and started casting a spell to light up the dark. I heard James gasp. "What is it?" I said, concerned. "There's at least fifty of them out there, I don't see Phillip" he replied.

We heard clapping, followed by the most horrible voice I've ever heard saying "good job, now come out and face your fate before we burn down your house." I will never forget that voice, it was Oscar. "Can they hear us?" I whispered to Arturo. "Probably, if we speak loud enough," he replied. I looked around at everyone and said, "are you all still ready to fight?" They all nodded. "They have triple the amount of people, probably all witches" James said. "What choice do we have? They are at our home." I said. I knew there was another option, we could run, go to another dimension, but for what? We could finish this here and now and be free.

"We fight," I said. "We won't run, we won't live our lives in fear, we will fight and win or lose, we will be free" I said. Everyone nodded and waited for my cue. Everyone grabbed their weapons, some with swords and some with clubs with spikes. "We'll charge all at once, we will cast a spell to knock them on their asses, get as many as you can while they are down" I said, looking around at everyone. Everyone nodded, I opened the door.

We hit them with the spell first thing, it worked. Everyone was fast and got a good lot of them while they were down. The illumination spell was starting to fade. Phillip came running up to me, I climbed onto his back. He started running toward the attackers. My weapon was my magic, after all, I was the most powerful witch in existence, right? Every time I saw one of them try to get up, I hit them with a spell to knock them back down. "Enough!" Oscar yelled. I felt my spin snap, I fell from Phillip's back with a scream. "Gabriela!" I heard James yell, followed by a painful scream from him.

"No!" I yelled, I couldn't see much, I was in so much pain and I couldn't feel my legs. The night started lighting up around me, I wasn't sure what it was at first. It was lightning bugs, thousands of them! One of them landed on my nose, it was her! It was the fairy! She had found her own army. I felt my back snap back into place, I didn't know if it was the fairies healing me, or one of my ally witches. I could feel my legs again, I stood up. I looked around trying to get my bearings. I saw James lying on the ground. All I could think was, please don't let him be dead.

I couldn't get to him before I started being attacked again. I felt a searing pain in my arm, I looked at it, there was a huge gash, blood was pouring from it. "YOU WILL DIE TONIGHT! AND ANYONE THAT TRIES TO STOP IT WILL DIE WITH YOU!" Oscar yelled. "FUCK YOU!" I yelled back, because I am classy like that. Looking around I could see a lot of bodies lying on the ground, but it was too dark to tell who they were. The fairies started swarming around Oscar. I didn't know what they could do to him, he was swatting at them, possibly they were just distracting him.

All of a sudden I felt a surge, I knew what it was, my ally witches were casting their magic into me. I started casting spells directly at Oscar. Somehow he was still combating me. They weren't stopping, more magic poured into me each second that passed. It was becoming too much, I couldn't handle it. My body started rising above the battle. I could see light coming from inside me, coming out of my mouth, eyes, ears, and nose. I knew this was what Hale meant when he said 'you will know when it's too much.' "You're going to kill her!" I heard a voice say, I couldn't place the voice. Oscar was trying to use magic against me, but it couldn't get through to me at all. I was about to explode, why were they doing this? Then I heard a voice inside my head, the voice of my mentor, Arturo, *you know what to do.*

But I didn't know what to do. Did he just want me to die? Was I a sacrifice? I guess the war would end after all, if there was nothing left to fight for. *Cast it into him!* Arturo's voice said in my head. Then I knew we would kill him with the magic instead of me. It took everything I had in me to even begin, but once I did it became easier. My body was slowly lowering back down toward the ground. Once my toes touched the ground, I threw every bit of magic that was inside me into Oscar. He used the magic against me of course, he managed to knock me to the ground before he realized what was happening.

His body shot up in the air so fast, it was like someone letting the air out of a balloon, it was almost comical. He kept going and going, finally he exploded with a neat light show. Pieces of his body started hitting the ground around me. Arturo made a bubble around us to protect us from being hit. "He's gone," I said. "Yes, and it doesn't look like he will be coming back," Arturo replied. I smiled.

The reality of the situation started coming down on me hard. "Where is James?!" I said. "Urrg, I'm here" I heard him grunt. Hearing the sound of his voice made me feel so light, I was halfway scared I would start flying again. "Babe!" I yelled as I ran toward his voice, I couldn't see anything still. "Arturo! Can we get some light?" I yelled. He was able to light up the yard a little, it looked like early dawn. I found James, lying on the ground. I sat down next to him and lifted his head and put it in my lap. "Where are you hurt?" I asked him. "Everywhere" he replied. He started coughing up blood. I started a healing spell right away. I couldn't lose him, I wouldn't lose him.

"Arturo! Will you please find everyone and start healing?" I yelled. "Already on it!" He yelled back. "I'm healing the witches first so they can help us heal the others. We need to gather any survivors of Oscar's coven, make sure they don't get away" Arturo said. James started to get up. "Wait!" I said. "I'm fine, I feel good as new," he said. I let him finish standing, he looked sturdy. "You sure?" I asked him. "Healed by the best, of course I'm good," he replied.

"Gabriela!" Levi shouted. I ran over to him. "She won't wake up!" He said, sobbing. He was talking about Alice, who was lying on the ground in front of him. I felt for a pulse, I didn't find one. "Arturo!" I yelled, so he could give a second opinion. James came over and hugged Levi. Arturo walked over, he kneeled down and put his fingers on her neck. "She's gone. We can heal the wounded but we can't bring back the dead. We need to hurry and find the others," Arturo said.

I started crying, "I didn't want this for you," I said as I brushed the hair out of her face. "I'm so sorry." "Did you see how it happened? Who did it?" I asked, looking at Levi. "No" he said, shaking his head, tears running down his face. Yet another lost life, because of me, another lost love. How can this be my life? Do I have to continue to watch friends die? People that I care about lose love? Why did I deserve to have love, when everyone else kept losing theirs because of me?

Everything started becoming too much, it was all starting to catch up to me, I felt light headed. I stood up and everything went black. The next thing I knew I was waking up in the bed. James was sitting next to me. "Welcome back" he said with a smile. I started to smile, but then I remembered that Alice was dead. "Did I pass out again?" I asked. "Just for a little while. Arturo said that all the magic you used plus the heartbreak, your body just couldn't take anymore. You needed a break," James replied. I realized that I hadn't seen everyone else. "Is anyone else dead?" I asked, afraid to hear the answer. "No, none of ours at least. Everyone was pretty banged up, but the witches did their magic and healed them" James replied. I nodded.

"There are several prisoners. Some of them have already broken and sworn allegiance to the new high priestess" James said. "Huh?" I said. "You are the new high priestess, you are the leader of all witches. It was the goal after all, to unite everyone. They will now unite under you as their leader" James said, looking a bit confused that I seemed confused. "And how can we trust them?" I asked. "They will either do as you say or die as Oscar did, as Xavier did. You have more than proved your strength, they have seen first hand what you are capable of doing" James said.

"When you say it like that, you make me feel like I am like *them* like I am just a murderer" I said. "Well, you are. And I'm not saying that to be mean, or to make you feel bad about it. Every army has a leader, and the leader does whatever they can to win the war. We won with you as our leader. Now is the turning point, now you are in charge of the witches. You can teach them that hating was wrong, teach them to learn about things instead of hating them because they were told to. Teach them they can have it all, peace, love and power." James said.

"How is Levi?" I asked. "Devastated," James replied. I started crying again. "She didn't deserve this, he doesn't deserve this" I said through my tears. "I know," James said, putting his arms around me. "Is this always going to be our lives? Losing friends left and right?" I asked him. "I don't know, I hope not," he replied. He held me as I cried myself to sleep.

I had a dream about Alice that night, she was teasing me about the catsuit. "I should have made myself one, maybe I would still be with you guys too" she said, right before I woke up. That was the first time I could remember dreaming anything in a long time. I'm sure it was just my subconscious trying to help me deal with her death. I didn't tell anyone about the dream, I didn't see any point in doing so.

Someone knocked on the bedroom door. I walked over to open it because James was still sleeping. It was Arturo. I opened the door wider and hugged him before he could say anything. "Good morning Gabriela. I thought you might want to come meet our new allies. I'm not releasing them as such until you approve" he said. I looked up at him and nodded my head in agreement. We walked toward the hall where we had kept Misty when she first got here.

He opened one of the bedroom doors. "Gabriela, this is Finn," Arturo said. "Merry meet," Finn said with a bow. I smiled and did a half curtsey bow. Finn was tall, and thin. He had fair skin with brown hair and sported a mustache. "Finn, why were you fighting alongside Oscar?" I asked, getting straight to the point. "He had me convinced that you would be the end of the witches" Finn replied honestly. "And how is that?" I asked. "He said you would take over, allow the witches to reproduce with other creatures and eventually we wouldn't even exist anymore" he replied. "Do you still believe that?" I asked. "No, I understand now that his mind was corrupted from working with demons. They are the ones who made him believe it so much that he was able to convince me and others" Finn said.

"And what will you do to help us, Finn?" I asked. "Whatever it takes," he replied. "Has everyone else interviewed him?" I asked Arturo. "Yes," Arturo replied. "If they are okay with him, I am too," I said. "Finn, I would like for you to stay here for a day or so. You don't have to stay in this room, you can come out, meet everyone, and eat with us. Will you do that?" I asked. "Yes, of course. Thank you," Finn replied. I smiled at him. Arturo and I turned and left the room to go on to the next.

Arturo opened the next door. "Gabriela, this is Vance, I believe you two have met before," Arturo said. I froze for a moment when I looked at him. It was clear that he wasn't possessed by a demon. "No, not really, I mostly interacted with the demon that he let possess him" I replied. "I hope that you can forgive me," Vance said. "Where is your partner in crime?" I asked. "If you are talking about Parker, he didn't make it," Vance replied. "Oh" I replied. "Arturo, can I speak with you in the hallway for a moment?" I said. Arturo followed me out, closing the bedroom door where Vance waited. "I don't know about him, he allowed a demon inside his body, so he could torture me day after day" I said. "People change, isn't that part of our whole campaign?" Arturo said. "I want him kept in that room and watched for at least a couple more days," I said. Something inside me just didn't want to trust him. "Okay," Arturo said.

Arturo locked the door and we moved on to the next. "Gabriela, this is Leticia," Arturo said. "Leticia, weren't you supposed to be spying on the enemy for us?" I asked. "Yes, I was, I believed they put a spell on me. After Oscar died, I felt totally different" Leticia replied. Leticia was very pretty, she had straight blonde hair with fair skin, deep blue eyes and high cheekbones. The rest of our conversation went much the same as it had with Finn. After we were finished talking I gave her the same invitation that I had given to

Finn. She accepted as he did. Arturo and I left the room and walked into the library. "When is the funeral?" I asked him. "Tomorrow," he replied. "Is Levi still here?" I asked. "Yes, he doesn't really have anywhere to go, James is his best friend," Arturo replied. I nodded. "Is Philip okay?" I asked, realizing I hadn't seen him since the fight. "Yes, he's fine. He slept a lot after the battle. Vance admitted that they gave him a carrot with tranquilizer in it, not realizing he was a shapeshifter. If he had been a normal horse, he would have been knocked out straight away. But the magic in his body burned it off until he calmed down afterwards, then it took over and he slept very well" Arturo explained. "I'm glad he's okay," I said.

Thirty

Another funeral and a wedding

After another night's sleep, we headed back to 2 so we could say goodbye to Alice. The funeral was much the same as Margo's. It was hard saying goodbye to another friend. James was with Levi along with Theo, Emma and Philip. I sat with the witches, including the ones that had just joined us. I wanted to keep them close so I could keep an eye on them. I wanted to be able to trust them, and I hoped that I could, but at this point I wasn't sure. Levi stood up and screamed out "I love you! You would never let me tell you and I hate you for that!" James stood up and hugged him and Levi cried on his shoulder. Not gonna lie, that made a few tears stream down my face as well.

I noticed that Arturo had gotten up and walked away. I started looking around to see if I could spot him. He was standing near the forest. He was talking to three giants. A chill shot up my spine. They didn't want her to come with us, she had to hide and run away from them. I watched them closely, I couldn't tell what they were saying. Arturo was shaking his head in disagreement. I stood up to walk over to them. Arturo put his hand up immediately and I felt a force pushing me back down into my seat. Now I was really curious as to what was going on, why wouldn't he let me come speak with them, give my condolences? It's not like they knew who I was.

After a few more minutes, the giants turned and walked away, back into the forest. I don't think anyone else even noticed that they were there. Arturo walked back over and sat down next to me like nothing had happened. I felt the magic release from me and I stood up and said, "I need to speak with you Arturo." He followed my cue and stood up, we walked out of earshot of everyone. "What was that about?" I demanded. Arturo put his head down. "Please tell me," I pleaded. "They want me to turn you over to them. They want you to pay for her death with your life" he replied. "Did you tell them that I am The High Priestess?" I asked. Hoping that would make a difference, that they would forgive me to keep from starting a war.

"No, I didn't tell them. They told me that Alice was a descendant of their royalty. I was afraid if I told them that you were basically the queen of the witches that they would start a fight here and no one wanted that to happen" Arturo replied. "So, Alice was a princess?" I asked. "I didn't ask for her official title. I was more concerned about the fact that they want to *kill* you" Arturo replied. "I guess that part hadn't really sunk in yet. What are we going to do? Do they know what I am?" I asked. "I don't think they know that you have giant blood flowing through your veins, but right now we are going to put this on the back burner, now is not the time. Now we are saying goodbye to our friend" Arturo said as he held up his hand toward my seat. I nodded and walked back to my seat and sat down, he followed and sat back down in the chair next to mine.

After we watched her body float out and the mermaids came to take it, everyone started getting up to leave. James walked over to me, "are you okay?" he asked. I just shrugged my shoulders. He put his arms around me and hugged me. I didn't want to be selfish, I knew his best friend needed him. "I want to stay with Levi tonight, I don't want him to be alone, and I want to make sure he's okay" James said as he continued to hug me. "You can come with us, or you can stay at David and Sarah's place," he said. "Where are y'all staying?" I asked. "Probably camp in the woods," he replied. "Okay, I will let you know if I will come with you after I talk to Arturo about something" I replied.

James pulled back to look at me, "is everything okay?" He asked. I didn't know if I should tell him or not and I didn't want to lie to him. "I just need to talk to Arturo about something," I said vaguely. "Okay, I can tell when you are hiding something, but I won't push. Go talk to Arturo, I'll be over there with Levi until we decide to head out. I'll let you know when we are going so you can let me know what's going on, hopefully. And you can let me know where you are staying" James said. I just nodded at him.

James walked away and I started looking around for Arturo. I finally spotted him speaking with Leticia. I walked toward them. They stopped talking when they noticed I was approaching. "What were you two talking about?" I asked. "We were discussing the future, so to speak," Arturo replied. Leticia seemed like she was a little afraid of me. I didn't know how I felt about that, it did give me a sense of power, but I didn't want that kind of power over my subjects. "And what does the future hold?" I asked. "Probably more of this," Arturo replied, gesturing around at the mourners.

He could tell I wasn't happy with that response. "When your mother had you, she decided you would live, no matter the cost. I don't know if she realized the price that would be paid, or the position you would have to carry. Maybe she did know, either way, her actions sealed your fate for a life of fighting, not a life of luxury or happiness" Arturo said, rather coldly. I fought back tears that were trying to come out. I tried to think about something else. "Did you know my mother?" I asked Leticia. "Yes, I did," she replied. "Can you tell me about her?" I asked. "We will discuss her at a more appropriate time," Leticia replied. I nodded my head in agreement.

"You're right, and I can't keep losing people" I said, as the tears broke free. "No ma'am! You have proved that you are worthy! I'm sorry, but you can't show weakness. There will be no feeling sorry for yourself! You are our leader now and that has totally changed everything for all of us. You won't make me regret my decision to join you and help you," Leticia said sternly. I stopped crying, a bit shocked that she would be brave enough to speak to me that way, I was also very impressed. I nodded my head as I wiped away my tears and she hugged me. I smiled at her, "you're right and I won't disappoint you, I promise." I said.

I felt like I could speak freely around her, so I told Arturo about the conversation I had with James and asked him what I should do. "You need to get back to 12 as soon as possible" was his reply. "Some of us can go back with you and some of us can stay behind to bring them back when they are ready," Leticia said. "Should I tell him why, or should I let him enjoy this night with his friends without having to worry?" I asked Arturo. "Do what you feel like you need to do, it's your choice" he replied. "Okay" I said, a little disappointed, hoping he would tell me what to do. But I guess this was his way of pushing me not only to make my own decisions, but to also start making decisions for my people, the witches.

I walked over to where James and his friends were standing. Someone had managed to get a laugh out of Levi, that made my heart feel a little lighter. I walked up with a smile on my face. "Hey babe, I was just about to come find you" James said with a smile. "Hey, so me and some of the witches are going to go ahead and head back to 12 now, some of the witches will stay behind to bring you guys back when you are ready" I said, trying to keep my face looking happy. He gave me a confused look. "What? Why?" Was his response. "I just want to start getting things more organized and figuring out what to do next. I want you to stay with your friends, try to have some fun and don't worry" I said. He hugged me, "I'm gonna miss you" he whispered in my ear. "It won't be that long" I whispered back and smiled at him. "Okay" he said. "Be careful" I said as I started walking away. "You too, I love you" he replied. I smiled and mouthed "I love you" as I walked away.

I joined back up with the witches. Arturo, Hale and Conan said they would stay on 2, the rest of us would go back. I hugged Arturo and said, "thank you for all that you do for me." He smiled, "I don't have a choice," he said with a laugh. I teasingly pushed his shoulder and the rest of us gathered in a circle to start the spell to return to 12. We landed in between the barn and the house. It felt different here now. I couldn't figure out why, I didn't feel like I was in danger, I just had a different feeling being here. Maybe it was my new position as leader, maybe it was the absence of Philip eating hay in the yard, or maybe it was the absence of James at my side. We all walked silently inside to settle in.

I walked into the kitchen, Cori almost looked surprised to see me. "I didn't think you would be back so soon. I will start preparing dinner" she said. "That would be nice, but if you had other plans, we can fix ourselves something to eat" I said. "No ma'am, I wouldn't think of it!" Cori said. "Okay" I said, throwing my arms up in defeat. She cooked us a delicious meal that everyone enjoyed. I noticed a prepared plate setting to the side. "Who is that for?" I asked, pointing to the plate. "The prisoner, I will pop it in to him," Cori replied. I had almost forgotten about Vance. I needed to make a decision about him. "I will take it to him," I said.

I grabbed the plate and walked toward the hall where we were keeping him. I knocked on the door. "Yeah?" I heard him reply. I opened the door. "Sorry, I didn't want to surprise you" I said as I sat the plate down. I untied his restraints and sat down on the bed. "Thank you, that elf sure doesn't mind scaring the shit out of me every chance she gets" he said as he began eating. "And I thought I was the only one she did that to" I replied with a smile. "You seem a little different, have you changed your mind about letting me into your coven?" Vance asked. "I'm not sure yet, I did want to talk to you some more and try to figure that out" I replied. He smiled and put a fork full of food in his mouth.

"Why would you want to help me now?" I asked. "Well, to be honest, I want to help me. I want to live a life without fear of you doing to me what you did to Oscar. And I certainly don't want to be possessed by anything again, that was horrible, I still have flashes in my dreams of the horrible things it did while it was inside me. So, if that means helping you by being on your side, then that's what I will do" he said. "If I trust you, if I let you out and you do anything to betray me, I will make sure that your fate is worse than Oscars" I said in a threatening voice. "Understood," Vance replied. "Then I will leave you with the door open, I will let the others know of my decision. Please feel free to make yourself at home and introduce yourself to the ones you don't know. Everyone isn't here yet, so try not to startle anyone when they come home in a day or so" I said. He nodded, "thank you, you won't regret it and I will never do anything to betray you, and I am sorry about what happened when I was possessed" Vance said. I nodded and walked out of the room.

I went back into the kitchen to tell everyone my decision and asked them to welcome him to our 'family'. I felt really tired, I knew I needed to tell everyone about the giants, but I wanted to wait until everyone was back. So I went to my bedroom and lay down. Rayne and Stitch jumped up on the bed with me. At least I would have someone to snuggle even though it wasn't James. I missed him, but I knew I couldn't be selfish with him and ask him to choose me over his friends. I lay there, feeling lonely even though I had my cats with me, until I fell asleep.

I woke up feeling surprisingly refreshed the next morning. The others still had not returned. I went out to the kitchen for breakfast. Everyone was already sitting at the table, including Vance. "Good morning," I said as I entered. I sat down and Cori brought me a plate of food and some coffee. I wasn't sure what to do, I didn't want to sit around with them all day. Then I had an idea, I was going to pay my old life a little visit. "Jason, would you like to come to town with me today? I want to go by my old apartment and check the mail and stuff" I said. "I thought we had to leave everything behind?" Jason replied. I gave him a look and suddenly he changed his mind, "yeah, sure" he said. I smiled at him.

After I finished eating I stood up, "I'm gonna go get a shower and get ready, Jason" I said. "Okay, I'll be ready when you are," he replied. I smiled again and walked out of the kitchen, and went back to my room to get ready. After I took my very refreshing shower and got dressed, I went out to find Jason. He didn't hide from me like I was half afraid he was going to do, instead he was waiting on the sofa, the one that he almost died on. Then I started realizing my blessings, yes I had lost some very dear friends, but I still had a lot of very dear friends left, not to mention the love of my life. I smiled, Jason stood up and said, "you ready?" "Yeah, let's go" I replied.

We warped to the vehicles, it was a hot and humid day. I thought for a minute about taking the convertible that James had somehow managed to find time to go buy, but I knew my hair would be a mess if I did that, so we took the pickup truck. I drove, it felt really weird pulling up to my old apartment. I guess a lot of nostalgia hit me. I knew it hadn't been *that* long since I had been here, but so much had happened that it made it seem like decades had passed. My key still worked so I assumed that it hadn't been rented out to someone else yet.

I opened the door and Jason and I walked inside. All my stuff was still as I had left it, I was a bit shocked by that. Mail was piled up on the floor where the mailman had just kept shoving it in the mail slot on the door. I picked it up and started looking through it. Most of it was junk mail, credit card companies, insurance companies and loan companies. One piece of mail stuck out, it was a pink envelope with Monica and Andy on the return address. I let out a little giggle as I opened it. "What's that?" Jason asked curiously. "Just something from someone I used to work with," I replied.

"Awwww," I squealed. "What?" Jason replied. I showed him the invitation and he just nodded his head and smiled. I looked at my watch to see the date, "It's this weekend! I didn't miss it!" I said with excitement. "Okay, I hope James is back by then, I don't do weddings. Especially of people I don't know," Jason said. I rolled my eyes at him. "I'm not using you as a fill-in for James. I thought you might want to come with me because you were a part of this life" I said. "Okay, whatever," he replied. I rolled my eyes again. "So, we can't see our friends, but you are going to go to a wedding? You don't make much sense" Jason said. "Maybe we can see them, give them an official good-bye" I said.

"You really think that's a good idea?" Jason asked. "Why not?" I replied. "Won't you get in trouble for that?" He asked. "From who?

I'm the boss now, remember? The only trouble we can get into is if we get them hurt somehow" I replied. "Is that a chance you want to take?" He replied. "The war is over, we won. There may be more enemies in the future, but they don't know of my past life, right?" I said. "I guess. What are we going to tell them?" He asked. "We'll tell them that we got recruited into a super secret organization and we are putting ourselves and them in danger just to tell them good-bye and we'll tell them that's all we can tell them" I said. "Sounds like you have been thinking about this for a while, but I don't think they will buy it" Jason replied. "It's okay, they don't have to, they just have to let us go" I said. "Okay" he replied.

"Is your old cell at your old place?" I asked. "I don't want to go back there. It's probably gone like the rest of my stuff" he said. I could tell that upset him a little. "Okay, we will just go by Rachel's house and get her to text everyone else and we will meet them for dinner tonight" I said. "Alright, boss, let's do this then" Jason replied. We walked out of my old apartment, and I knew I wouldn't be back. I wasn't really sad, I knew nothing here fit into my new life and my old life was gone for good. I just wanted to have a few 'normal' moments with a few old friends. I needed it so I could let go, I needed to say good-bye. Just like I needed to see Monica and Andy get married, so I could wish them a good life together, knowing that I would not be in it.

I had my phone with me and I knew if James were to return before I got back home that he would call me to find out where I was. So we got in the truck and headed to Rachel's house. Her car was parked in the driveway, so we got out and knocked on the door. She opened the door and started freaking out, grabbing us, hugging us, "Oh my god! What happened to you guys!?" She yelled. "Are you going to let us in? Or do we have to stand outside?" I asked in a joking but serious way. "Oh my god! Yes! Come in!" She said as she opened the door wider. We walked inside. "We missed you too!

That's why we came by. Can you text everyone and ask them if they can meet us for dinner tonight?" I asked. "Can you tell me what's going on? Where have you been?" Rachel demanded.

"Of course we will tell you, but I kinda wanted to tell everyone at once" I said. She started to get angry with me, so I used a little magic to get her to calm down and she did as I asked and sent text messages out to our other friends. Everyone agreed to meet us for dinner. I was happy. "You are just creating a distraction for yourself," Jason whispered in my ear. I ignored him. "What do you need a distraction from? Why are you bringing them into this?" He whispered. "I just want to say good-bye to my old life, kinda like a funeral for the old Gabriela" I whispered back. He nodded his head.

"Okay, we are going to meet at the new hot chicken place in east Nashville," Rachel said. Jason and I both just looked at her. She could tell we didn't know where she was talking about. "It's on Main street," she said, expecting us to suddenly know. "It's fine, you guys can ride with me," she said. "Okay" I replied. Jason didn't say anything, he was acting like he was just along for the ride, like he didn't know anyone. "So, are you two together now?" Rachel asked. I should have expected that question, but somehow it still surprised me. I laughed. "No, she has a boyfriend, he's out of town at the moment" Jason replied.

After a lot of small talk and avoiding answering questions, we got in Rachel's car and headed toward Nashville. I sat up front with Rachel and Jason sat quietly in the backseat. When we finally arrived at the restaurant, Anna came out to meet us. "I'm so glad you are here!" She said, hugging me. "I got us a table, come on!" She said. I followed her into the restaurant and to a table that was big enough for everyone. They had a stage with a band set up playing country and classic rock covers.

"I see the cover bands have moved from Broadway," I said. "Everyone is trying to attract business, this is Nashville," Micheal said. "Nothing wrong with live music, I miss it to be honest" I said. "So why did you two just disappear on us?" Anna asked. "We were approached and recruited into a super secret society with a super secret mission. Just know that your life is safer because of what we do" I said. Micheal and Racheal started laughing. "Laugh all you want, she's telling the truth. And we are only here now because we wanted you guys to know that we are okay, but we aren't staying" Jason said.

"So you are leaving again?" Racheal asked. "Yes, we won't be back again. Like Jason said, we just wanted to say good-bye and assure you that we are fine" I said. "Okay, you guys wanna run off and lead some secret, mysterious life, then I guess that's your choice. I won't say 'thank you' for making my life better, because I don't know what it is that you are doing. But by all means, live the life you want" Racheal said. "It's okay that you guys don't understand, but you were a part of my life for a long time and I just wanted to say good-bye" I replied.

After a lot more small talk, we all hugged and said our good-bye's, Jason and I got back into Racheal's car and she drove us back to her house where our truck was parked. I hugged Racheal and told her good-bye one more time and we got into the truck and drove away. Jason and I rode in silence most of the way. When we were almost back, Jason said, "you really think that was a good idea. Maybe we should have just left them with whatever memories they had of us. Now they think we are douchebags that lied to them about why we left." "I don't care, like I said, I needed to say good-bye to my old life. I needed this so I can take on my new life as Grand High Priestess of the witch community" I replied. I parked the truck by the road and we warped back to the house.

The others had still not returned. I knew that time was different there, so I wasn't going to let myself worry. Instead, I started preparing to go to a wedding. The people from the diner were also a part of my past. I didn't need to tell them good-bye, but I would see Monica and Andy get married. I hoped that James would be back in time to go with me, if not I would go by myself. I found a cute blue dress in my closet, I wasn't really sure where all these clothes came from. I used to think it was Alice, but she wasn't here anymore, it always seemed that whatever I needed would just appear. I looked on James' side of the closet, sure enough there was a three-piece suit the same blue color as the dress. I smiled as I tried it on, of course it fit perfectly and I could drive back into town tomorrow and find some shoes to match it.

I felt tired, so I lay down in the bed, without James again. The cats weren't even here tonight to keep me company, I guess they were out hunting. I cried myself to sleep, I missed James, I missed my old life, I was scared of what the future held for me. It was all just overwhelming. I woke up in the middle of the night and cried some more until I fell back to sleep. When I woke in the morning I jumped straight into the shower. I didn't want anyone to see me in the mess I was. I didn't want to appear weak in any way to anyone.

After I showered and looked presentable, I went out to the dining room where Misty, Vance and Leticia were still sitting at the table, having coffee and biscuits. All of these people had been my enemies at one point, some more recent than others. I couldn't help but to smile at them. Misty smiled back and said, "good morning." "Good morning" I replied, as I poured myself some coffee. "How are you this morning?" Vance asked. I immediately assumed that he heard me crying last night. I smiled and said, "a bit sleepy still, but this will take care of that" I said, holding up my cup of coffee. I knew that my eyes were a bit puffy, but that could be passed off as being tired, or a hangover. They didn't know that Jason and I didn't get hammered last night.

"Do you have any plans today?" Leticia asked. "Why do you ask?" I replied suspiciously. "I just thought we could all do something together today, get to know each other better" Leticia replied. "Maybe this evening, I have an errand to run first" I said, trying to be vague. I was suspicious of everyone, they didn't need to know my every move. "You don't have to be afraid of us, we are here to not only help you, but to protect you as well" Misty said. "What makes you think I need your protection?" I asked curiously. "I'm not saying that you do, but there hasn't been ONE leader of the witches since before the dimensions were created, you may have enemies that we don't even know about yet" Misty replied. I just lowered my head, I wanted to tell them, I didn't want to keep them in the dark, but I needed to wait until the others returned.

"I'll be fine, and hopefully it won't take me long. When I return we can do some training together, like we did to prepare to fight together" I said, looking at Misty. "Okay, that sounds great, but if you would like someone to go with you..." Misty said. "No thanks," I said, cutting her off. I stood up and walked out of the dining room. I went out to sit on the front porch to finish my coffee. Looking around the property, it seemed so empty. No Philip grazing, no Margo stalking the edge of the woods. I started feeling sad again, so I decided to put the coffee down and grab the truck keys and head into town.

I went to the town square where I knew a huge witch base was lying below. I went into the first clothing store I could find, I had brought the dress with me so I could get a close match on the shoes. I found some really cute shoes, but they only had them in pink and red. The store clerk walked up and asked if I needed any help. I told her that I was trying to find shoes to match my dress and that I really liked the pink/red ones and asked her if they had any in blue. She went back behind the counter and opened a catalog. "They do have them in blue, do you think this color will match?" the clerk asked while showing me the picture. "Yes! Can you get them quickly?" I asked.

"I can have them here by tomorrow, will that work?" The clerk asked. "Yes, I suppose it will," I replied. "Great, why don't you try on the red or pink ones so I know what size to order," the clerk said. "Yeah, sure" I said as I walked back to the shoes and did just that. My feet were always big, I guess it is because of the fact that I have giant blood in my veins, sometimes I forget about that part of myself because I'm not as tall as the others. After we got the shoes ordered, and the clerk told me they should be at the store by 10 o'clock a.m. tomorrow, I left and headed back to the farm.

I did what I had told Misty I would do that morning and spent the evening training with everyone. It was interesting to learn everyone's magical strengths and weaknesses. And when we were finished and everyone was healed from their injuries, we went inside for dinner. I then realized that I did need distractions, I needed something to occupy my mind from the fact that my boyfriend and my mentor wasn't here and that the giants wanted me dead. So, after dinner I started drinking some bourbon. It went down smooth, a little too smooth. It wasn't long before I was drunk. Jason offered to help me to bed. "No, no, you are not coming near my bed" I slurred. "Okay" he replied, throwing his arms up. And that is all that I remember, pretty sure I passed out right then.

I woke up the next morning in my bed, alone thank goodness. I looked at the clock, it was nine-thirty. Then I remembered I had to go pick up my shoes! I jumped up and got in the shower and headed out without talking to anyone. I was a little embarrassed by my behavior the night before and wasn't ready to face them. I drove to the department store to get my shoes, I suppose it was just more distractions, but it was working. I walked into the store and the clerk recognized me right away. "Good morning! I guess the mail is running late today, they haven't gotten here yet" the clerk said. "Oh, I guess I can go next door and get some..." looking at my watch "brunch, I guess," I said. "That's a great idea! Hopefully they will be here by the time you are done!" The clerk said, with too much enthusiasm.

I walked out of the store and looked around, one of the buildings was advertising 'the greatest coffee in the world' then I realized that I hadn't had any coffee and my head was starting to hurt, either from the lack of caffeine or from the massive amount of bourbon I had drank the night before. So I walked in and ordered some coffee and chicken and waffles. I sat and ate and drank my coffee in peace and I realized that this was one more thing I missed. I noticed a FedEx truck had parked on the square, hopefully he had my shoes! I finished eating and paid for my meal and walked back to the department store, the FedEx driver was walking out as I was walking in. The clerk smiled at me and held up the shoes I paid for the shoes and headed back to the farm, which was starting to feel more like a prison than a home.

When I got back, everyone was apparently looking for me and was upset with me that I had left and not told anyone. "That was a very dangerous thing for you to do," Misty scolded. "Since when do I have to answer to you? Or to anyone for that matter?" I replied. "You are a part of a different world now, you can't return to the life you lived before you found out who you are," Misty said. "I understand that, that's not what I'm doing. I did go say good-bye to some old friends, and I do plan on attending a wedding on Friday but that's it. I went to go get some shoes to wear to that wedding" I said.

"I understand you wanting to have both lives, but that's just not possible. Your human friends have no way to defend themselves against your enemies, and your enemies will go after them to hurt you" Misty said. "I know this! You don't have to tell me this, I'm not stupid! I'm not trying to get anyone hurt!" I yelled. "Okay" Misty replied, throwing her arms in the air in defeat. I hoped that she would leave me alone about it after this.

I went inside and went to my room, I lay down on the bed and the cats jumped up on there with me. I suppose I was still tired from the night before because I fell asleep. When I woke up I turned over to look at the clock, instead I saw James lying next to me, smiling. I grabbed him and pulled him close and started crying. "What's wrong?" He asked. "I just missed you," I managed to get out through the tears. I started undressing him and kissing his neck. He let out a moan and I jumped on top of him, pushing him down.

After we finished, we got in the shower. "Did you have fun?" I asked him. "It was okay, we just camped in the woods and had a bonfire and reminisced about old times" he replied. "What have you been doing?" He asked me. "Kind of the same thing. I went to see some old friends, to say good-bye. Oh! And we are going to a wedding tomorrow" I said with a smile. "What? Who's wedding?" He asked. "A couple I used to work with at the diner" I said as I turned the water off. "Why would we go to their wedding?" He asked, confused. "Because I want to," I said with a smile. "Okay. There's something I need to tell you, Levi decided not to return. He wanted me to tell you that it has nothing to do with you, he just doesn't think he can handle all the memories that took place here" he said. "I understand, you can let him know that I can help him magically if he wants to try," I said. "He is going on a soul search alone," he replied. I nodded my head to let him know that I understood.

We got dressed and headed out to eat dinner. I looked outside and saw Philip grazing and I smiled. "This place feels like home again" I said with a tear forming in my eye. I was starting to feel happy again. James put his arm around me and kissed my forehead, "I won't leave you alone like that again, I promise" he whispered in my ear. I hugged him and wiped away my tear. We joined everyone in the dining room. I walked over to Arturo and hugged him from behind, "I missed you old man" I said. He laughed and said "I missed you too youngling." "I missed all of you!" I said, looking around at everyone. "Sarah and Julie missed seeing you," David said. "I know,

I feel really bad about not being able to see them this time. I will explain that to all of you soon, right now, let's enjoy this meal and each other" I said with a smile.

Vance was sitting quietly. "I almost forgot, I invited Vance to join us. I believe we can trust him and he will be an asset to our family" I said. Everyone greeted him and welcomed him. We ate our meal and had some small talk before everyone scattered about, some went outside to enjoy the humid night air, some went to their rooms and some gathered in the living room to talk more. Arturo, and myself were the only ones who knew of the pending danger we faced. And I decided to keep it that way at least for a little while.

James and I went into our room and lay down on the bed, I cuddled up to him, it was good to be able to do so. "So, you have a suit for tomorrow in the closet, I hope you have dress shoes to wear. I didn't know what size you are, so I couldn't get you any. I got some super cute shoes for myself" I said. He just looked at me and smiled, then he kissed my forehead. I kissed him on the lips, "did I mention how much I missed you?" I asked, teasingly. He squeezed me tight, it felt so nice. The cats seemed to be upset that he was back and had taken over their spot on the bed. I fell asleep content in James' arms.

The next morning I woke up before James and I just lied there and watched him sleep. After a while he woke up to see me smiling at him. He rubbed his hands down his face and stretched. Then he started tickling me, "stop it!" I yelled as I laughed. He pushed me down on my back and kissed me. I smiled at him. "Let's go eat and start getting ready for the wedding," I said. "Ugh, you're really going to make me go to this thing aren't you?" He asked. I pushed his shoulder and made a pouty face. "Just kidding, I would love to be your date to an event that I don't celebrate of people that I don't know," he said sarcastically. I smiled, "it will be fun, and something different" I said. "Okay, okay, I will go, but I'm not promising I will have fun," James said.

We went out to have breakfast with everyone. I told them that James and I would be attending a wedding of an old friend of mine that evening. "And when are we going to discuss the other matter at hand?" Arturo said. "In a few days, there's plenty of time for that," I replied. James looked at me suspiciously. I knew he would be asking questions later, but I wasn't ready to tell him just yet. Leticia just looked down at her plate, she hadn't heard the whole thing, but she did know that something was up. After breakfast, James and I headed to the bedroom to get ready. I missed Alice as I was trying to figure out who would help me do my hair. I used a curling iron to curl it, it didn't look bad, but I knew it wouldn't hold in the humidity.

After we were ready, we came out and showed off our fancy selves. Everyone said that we looked great. I asked Misty if there was a spell we could do on my head to make my hair stay in place. She did some sort of spell, and I just hoped that it would work. James and I headed out so we could eat before the wedding. I hadn't rsvp'd so I didn't expect them to feed us, but I was hoping for an open bar. I decided to take him to a fancy steakhouse in Nashville. "I've never been to Nashville," James said with a smile. "We should have a little time so I can show you the demon that is Broadway," I replied with a giggle. After dinner we strolled down Broadway. "It's so loud," James said. I smiled. "Yes it is," I replied. "And there's so many people, do people actually enjoy this?" James asked. "Music is it's own kind of magic, feel it" I said as I put my hand on his chest. He smiled at me and kissed me. "We should probably get going shouldn't we?" James said. "Yeah" I replied. So we headed back to the parking garage where we had left the car.

We started the hour drive back to Moon Springs. "You look

really handsome in that suit" I said, in a flirty way. "You always look beautiful," James replied. "Do you want to tell me what Arturo was talking about this morning?" James asked. "No," I replied. James gave me a stern look. "Not yet, I just want to enjoy this day with you" I said. "Fine, but I know it's nothing good, I'm just wondering who wants to kill us now," James said. "Well, stop wondering, just forget about it for today, for me, please?" I said as I batted my eyelashes at him. "I'll do my best, that's all I can offer," James replied. I grabbed his hand and put my fingers between his and smiled.

We pulled up to the venue where the wedding was being held. There were a lot of people here. I recognized the people that I used to work with. An older lady that looked a lot like Monica greeted us. "Welcome" she said. "Hello, my name is Gabriela. I used to work at the diner with Monica and Andy" I told her, because I could tell she was curious as to who we were. "And this is my date, James," I added. "Great!" She said as she guided us to our seats. I noticed Dan was looking at me and I waved, he waved back and smiled. Betty was sitting not far from us, "well hello stranger" she said to me. "Hey, it's great to see you," I said with a smile.

Andy was standing at the altar and the wedding march started playing, we all stood up and looked down the aisle. Monica was so beautiful in her wedding gown, she smiled as she walked by me. I was happy that I could be here for her today. Once she reached the altar, and the music stopped the wedding officiant began. Monica and Andy said their vows. "And you may kiss your bride" was spoken and Andy swooped Monica up into his arms and laid one on her. Everyone cheered and applauded and I wiped tears from my eyes. "Why are you crying?" James whispered. "I'm just happy for them," I replied. Although I wasn't quite sure if that was the reason.

The couple walked back down the aisle and to the reception room, the guests followed. A band started playing 'Tennessee Whiskey' and I rolled my eyes. James looked at me confused. "I hate this song" I said with a laugh. After the newly married couple started dancing, everyone else started joining in. James held out his hand, "can I have this dance?" He asked. I did a curtsey bow and said, "of course, sir." He swished me out on the dance floor and I giggled. He held me close as we began to move. I put my head on his chest. For this moment, everything felt right and good in the world. I forgot what I was hiding from James and the others for a moment. When the music stopped we stopped dancing and went to sit at a table.

Monica walked over to me and hugged me. "I didn't know you were coming! I hadn't heard anything from you in a long time" she said. "I know, I wanted it to be a surprise, we ate before we came so don't worry about feeding us" I said with a smile. She hugged me again, "I'm glad you made it, it's good to see you" she said and she returned to her husband. A waiter brought us both a glass of wine. James held his glass up toward me for a toast, I held mine up. "To the newlyweds," he said. "To the newlyweds" I repeated. "I guess this isn't as bad as I thought it would be," James said. I smiled.

James only had one glass of wine because he was driving us home later. I had four. After a few hours of dancing, and laughing, Monica and Andy headed out to their car, off to their honeymoon, off to their new lives as a married couple. The guests threw birdseed at them instead of rice. After I hugged my friends and told them bye, James and I got back in the car, since the day was over and I didn't care if my hair got messed up anymore, I told James to put the convertible top down as we drove home.

Remember, if something seems too magical for this world, that's because it is. As for me, my story isn't over yet. I will die one day, but not to-fucking-night.

Cora Richardson, author of Mystical Mayhem A New Breed. Cora Richardson grew up in a small town in Tennessee called Red Boiling Springs. She left Red Boiling Springs because she did not enjoy small town life. She traveled around The United States for a few years. Las Vegas, Nevada was the first big city she spent time in, and she loved it! She loved the lights and the excited tourists. Eventually Cora settled down and moved back to Tennessee (Nashville) where she lives now with her daughter, Rosalie. Cora enjoys rock music and really loves the local rock scene in Nashville. She also enjoys the lights and excited tourists of Nashville.